DEATH AND THE MAIDEN

ALSO BY SAMANTHA NORMAN

The Siege Winter

DEATH AND THE MAIDEN

A MISTRESS OF THE ART OF DEATH NOVEL

Ariana Franklin

AND

Samantha Norman

wm

WILLIAM MORROW

An Imprint of HarperCollins*Publishers*

DEATH AND THE MAIDEN. Copyright © 2020 by Samantha Norman. All rights reserved. Printed in the United States of America. No part of this book may be used or reproduced in any manner whatsoever without written permission except in the case of brief quotations embodied in critical articles and reviews. For information, address HarperCollins Publishers, 195 Broadway, New York, NY 10007.

HarperCollins books may be purchased for educational, business, or sales promotional use. For information, please email the Special Markets Department at SPsales@harpercollins.com.

FIRST EDITION

Designed by Kyle O'Brien

Library of Congress Cataloging-in-Publication Data has been applied for.

ISBN 978-0-06-256238-8

20 21 22 23 24   LSC   10 9 8 7 6 5 4 3 2 1

This is for my mum.

DEATH AND THE MAIDEN

CHAPTER 1

ELY CATHEDRAL'S ALMONER, BROTHER ANSELM, stood at his gate flapping his arms to ward off both the insidious cold and the crushing boredom. The great freeze had come unexpectedly, bleaching the landscape overnight and choking the reeds and riverbanks in frost.

"Not a soul," he murmured as he looked out unhappily over the infinite frozen waste.

Not a soul; not even the poor, it seemed, were hungry enough to venture out in this weather.

He glanced down at the sack of food on the ground at his feet, surplus from yesterday's table, wondering what on earth he would do with it all. Perhaps feed it to the swans, although it would be a waste. On the other hand, it was better to scatter it over the frozen pond and feed something rather than haul it back to the undercroft, where it would be left to rot. And yet, what else could he do? So far, he hadn't had so much as a glimpse of a single member of the Wadlow family, whose poverty-sharpened features and grubby outstretched hands were as much a feature of his gate as the hinges it hung on. It was too cold even for such as they to be tempted from their cot, where—according to local gossip—they lived off water rats.

"Primitive, Brother, them Wadlows, like animals they are!" their scandalized neighbors hissed. But Brother Anselm couldn't get too worked up about rats; they were nourishment of sorts, after all—not that he'd have eaten one himself unless he were starving, mind you, but, when it came down to it, rats were no worse than squirrels, and were at least in plentiful supply even in the depths of winter. He wouldn't have dared say any of this out loud, of course—to apologize for the Wadlows was to have opprobrium heaped on one—nevertheless he hoped they were eating something today, keeping body and soul together somehow.

Perhaps it was the image of the family in their dilapidated hut with its larder full of rats that made him shiver, but whatever it was, he suddenly felt so bitterly cold that no amount of arm clapping or jumping up and down could warm him up. The only sensation he had left was the unpleasant chafing on his upper thigh from the eel-skin garter one of the abbey fishermen had given him to ward off the rheumatism.

And then, at last, God be praised! The bell rang for terce, releasing him at last from his frozen sojourn.

He bent down, hefted the sack onto his shoulders and was about to return to the almonry when a gaggle of children came running over the meadow toward him . . .

"Wait, Brother, wait!" they called out, their voices shrill and excitable as they jostled one another to be the first in line to greet him.

He smiled at the small bodies swarming around his legs, the dark heads dipping like pigeons' at the sack as a tangle of nimble fingers sifted and grabbed at the offerings it held.

When the last piece of food had been stuffed into the very last mouth, the children nodded gratefully and left as quickly as they had come . . .

"Good-bye, Brother Anselm!" they called back as they scampered across the frosted meadow. "See you tomorrow! . . ."

He smiled and waved until they disappeared into the mist and was about to turn his back on the gate for a second time when he heard a whistle . . . and a voice.

"Nice arse!"

It was a girl's voice—several girls' voices, in fact—coming from somewhere up the lane.

He turned around and froze, a familiar terror thumping in his ears as the pack sauntered down the track toward him.

He knew all of them by sight but only one by name, Martha, the one who always made him catch his breath.

"Walk on, walk on," he pleaded, pulling his cowl down low over his face to hide his blushes. But it was too late; like the she-wolves they were, they had already scented the blood.

They stopped in front of him, just as he had feared they would, standing so close that his nostrils twitched with their scent and his skin burned with the proximity.

"Come skating with us, Brother?" they asked, mocking him with their eyes, bending their wicked bodies toward him. But Brother Anselm shied away, refusing to look at them.

"Go away . . . In God's name, go away!" he cried, screwing

his eyes shut tight, hoping that if he closed them long enough, when he opened them again they would have vanished.

"What was that, Brother? Did you say something?" one of the girls asked, tossing her hair in his face like a spirited pony so that the ends scoured his cheek. "Oh look, bless 'im," she said, turning to the others. "He's blushing, poor love, look . . ."

More giggling, then another voice.

"River's turned hard, too, see!"

The giggling became raucous, and for the first time in his young life Brother Anselm knew how it felt to want to die . . . and to hate.

"Leave him alone!"

God be praised! A merciful voice at last.

He opened his eyes and immediately wished he hadn't . . .

Martha was standing in front of him. His stomach lurched at the sight of her and he blushed again, knowing that tonight his memories would drive him to those unquiet, sleep-defeating thoughts of which he was so deeply ashamed.

"I'm sorry." The merciful voice again, but not Martha's. Instead it belonged to the girl beside her, whose name he didn't know but whom he recognized as the local reeve's daughter.

He looked from one to the other and back again but just when he felt his legs beginning to crumple, the deliverance he had been praying for came in a sudden roar and rush of wings. A skein of geese flying in low from the east landed on the frozen fishpond in a succession of clumsy thuds, which startled the girls and sent them laughing and shrieking toward the river.

"Good-bye, Brother! See you on the ice!" they called, but

Brother Anselm was already scampering up the path toward the sanctuary of the cathedral.

THE GIRLS WERE STILL LAUGHING when, halfway to the river, they saw the riders on the horizon and stopped abruptly.

"Run!" Hawise hissed, even though they already were. Just as they knew not to venture into the marsh at night, or get too close to a bittern's nest, or skate on the river where the ice was thin, they knew to run from the bishop's men.

Since his investiture, their new bishop, William Longchamp, had brought great wickedness to the diocese. Witchcraft was suspected. How else, everybody wondered, could the king have conferred such power upon such misshapen shoulders? How could such a gargoyle of a man, who had risen without trace from the gutters of Argenton, have been awarded three titles: chancellor, chief justiciar and bishop of Ely? It must be witchcraft! But whatever it was, one thing was certain: no good would ever come of such dominion, and from the moment he came howling into the Fens with his retinue of a thousand and all those diabolical creatures, none did.

CHAPTER 2

B Y THE TIME THEY ARRIVED the river was teeming with people and had adopted the appearance of a small market town. Stalls were dotted everywhere and the air hung thick with the smell of chestnuts roasting on braziers and resounded with the shrieks of excitable children whizzing around on sledges. For safe passage the girls linked arms, pushing their way through the crowd to the middle of the river, where they were immediately encircled by a group of boys like foxes around a chicken coop.

"Hey, Martha, have these!" one of the boys called out, sending an object skidding across the ice toward her. When she bent down to pick it up, she saw that it was a pair of leather-bound skates whose bone blades had been lovingly carved into two sharp edges.

She looked up, searching the faces of the boys until she recognized the handsome lad from Manea whom she remembered from one of Lord Peverell's boon days last summer.

"Thank you," she mouthed, sitting down on the ice to put them on, feeling conspicuous as she wrapped the straps around her ankles, under the envious gaze of the other girls.

"Why is it always Martha?" she heard one of them whine to nobody in particular. "It's not fair! Why's it always her?"

It was a question even she couldn't answer. It wasn't fair. It was just the way things were.

Having always been a pretty child, even as a baby, she was used to the attendant compliments and attention her beauty seemed to bring. But lately something had changed; other people mainly, she had begun to realize, particularly the men, looked at her with strange eyes nowadays, making her feel as though she had unwittingly stepped into a foreign land where, although everything looked the same, the customs were very different, and she felt vulnerable, although to what, exactly, she didn't know.

"It's the curse, Martha, love," her mother had told her when she complained to her about it one day. "It'll start soon, see, you'll have to think about that, you know?"

But she didn't want to think about it—not then, and certainly not now. Whatever this "curse" might be—and her mother had offered no further elucidation—its mystery would have to wait. All she wanted to do now was skate.

She shook the thought from her head and stood up, feeling the familiar thrill in her belly as she took a tentative first step, then another and another, until at last she was moving in beautiful, rhythmic sweeps over the surface of the ice.

TWO ELDERLY WOMEN, SISTERS, BUNDLED up against the cold in practically all the clothes they had ever possessed, were sitting on a log on the riverbank watching the impromptu pageant play in front of them.

"A'ternoon, Lady Penda, Gyltha," the skaters greeted them, although largely unnoticed, as they hissed past.

"Oy, Gylth!" The elder of the two pointed at a lone figure who was inscribing perfect circles in the middle of the ice. "Ain't that a lovely sight! D'you remember the old days when we could do that?"

"Who?" Gyltha replied, screwing up her eyes against the lowering sun in an attempt to follow the direction of her sister's finger. When she couldn't, she replied irritably: "Who? What you pointing at? Can't see a damn bloody thing, 'cept that bloody Wadlow boy! Get out of it . . . " She flapped her hand irritably at the young man clowning around in front of them, blocking their view, as he tried but failed to attract the attention of a group of girls.

"Ignore 'im," Penda said, cupping her hand gently around her chin, turning her head in the direction of the girl. "Look! See? That girl! . . . The one over there."

"Still can't see nothing!" Gyltha snapped, but when she tried to stand up to get a better view, she was thwarted by a sharp downward tug on the hem of her mantle.

"Sit down, you silly bugger," Penda chided, bumping her back down onto the log. "You don't want to go slippin' about on that, not at our age. Old bones don't mend so easy, remember?"

"Stop fussing." Gyltha pushed her hand off. "Gettin' on my nerves, you are . . . Ah, now I see!" she said, brightening all of a sudden. "You mean the pretty girl over in the middle there . . . Tha's Martha . . . Hawise's friend . . . Lovely little skater, ain't she?"

———

SOMEONE ELSE WAS WATCHING THE girl, too, and had been since she first set foot on the ice, his eyes drawn to her not just for her incomparable beauty but for the grace and ease with which she made her way through the crowd with her friends, unaware that almost every head turned to stare at her as she passed.

His enchantment with her deepened as he watched her put on the skates and take her first steps, introducing herself to the ice with the temerity of a fawn breaking cover, until gradually, as a physical memory returned to her, she began to find her rhythm and move with ease, losing herself to everything but the sensation of the frozen surface beneath her feet.

He felt his heart flutter with a long-forgotten thrill, longing to be close to her, to take her hand and swirl across the ice beside her . . . But, with so many people around still, he knew he would have to be patient, stay hidden in the rushes for the time being, content himself simply with watching her for now . . .

As the afternoon wore on and the light began to fade, the crowd thinned at last. Even the two old ladies, who looked as though they had taken up permanent residence on it, left their perch eventually and shuffled off home. And then, just as the sun began its final descent into the marsh, a swathe of fog rolled in from the east, making it almost perfect.

He shivered, a frisson of exquisite anticipation setting his teeth on edge, lifting the hair on the back of his neck.

Not much longer now . . .

He was about to stand up at last, make his way through the

rushes onto the ice, when he heard the other girls calling her and his heart sank.

"Martha! Martha!" Bored, impatient voices rent the air. He glared at them through the reeds, despising the frost-pinched, frustration-contorted faces that were summoning her away.

"Martha! Come! Come on! We're leaving, Martha! . . . It's getting dark! . . . We can't wait any longer! . . . It's too cold . . . Martha! Martha, Martha!"

But their entreaties froze with their breath in the frigid air and got lost before they reached her. His spirits lifted when he saw them shrug their shoulders and turn for home.

She was alone at last, gliding toward him as if spellbound, and yet somehow he knew that it was *his* spell, his power, drawing her to him.

"Come," he murmured softly, fingers twitching inside his gloves. "Come."

It was time.

Creeping silently through the rushes to the water's edge, he slipped, sleek as an otter, down the bank and onto the ice.

He put on his skates and, at first, was content simply to follow her, to move in her tracks like a shadow in the moonlight, and it was only when, unable to resist her any longer, he reached and touched her that she noticed him at all . . . but by then, of course, it was too late.

CHAPTER 3

Wolvercote Manor
-Autumn 1191-

LADY EMMA OF WOLVERCOTE'S USUALLY tranquil cherry orchard was anything but that morning.

Two querulous voices rang out from it, disturbing the static chill of the air, sending a clamor of birds into the sky in search of peace elsewhere. Fortunately there was no one else around to hear them other than Ernulf, Lady Emma's swineherd, who was watching over his pigs in the nearby oak wood, but he was used to them.

A passing stranger, had there been one, might quickly have discerned that the voices were female and inferred, from their impassioned bickering, that they belonged to two strong personalities whose mutual affection ran a good deal deeper than their current irritation with one another. That they were also educated—the robust invective aside, the argument was conducted in impeccable Norman French—was also indubitable, as was the conclusion that any intervention would be unwelcome and, for the hypothetical stranger at least, extremely unwise.

A visual inspection, however—if that stranger had dared pop his head over the hedge for a peek at them—would have revealed that neither of the women was particularly well dressed. Their clothes, elegant once—judging by the quality of their cloth—were worn for utility, not vanity, which was probably just as well, because they were both kneeling in a puddle of mud on either side of a dead hare . . .

Ah then! Necromancers? Witches perhaps? That would explain it. And their interest in the corpse was unusual to say the least. They appeared to be studying it in forensic detail! Poring over it, poking at it with an interest bordering on unhealthy, examining with appalling fascination the wounds that had killed it! The only blessing was that at least they had stopped quarreling at last, apparently too distracted by the body of the animal to continue their argument.

The older of the two flicked a lock of hair out of her eyes, stretched her hand out and, with practiced fingers, began manipulating the fur around the animal's neck to reveal two small puncture wounds.

She looked up at her companion defiantly.

"Fox!" she said. "Your turn!"

The younger woman shook her head, put her own fingers into the fur and bent toward it, inhaling deeply.

"Dog!" She sat up, a flash of triumph in her wide green eyes. "Those marks are too far set for a fox; besides, I got a definite whiff of rosewater, so I might even go so far as to suggest that the culprit is, in fact, Emma's greyhound."

The older woman grinned and rocked back on her heels, clapping her hands in delight.

"Very good, Allie darling!" Adelia said, marveling, as she so often had, at the efficiency of her daughter's nose. "Which might also explain why it wasn't eaten, I suppose. But dead for how long, do you think?"

Allie shook her head and stood up, wiping her muddy hands down the front of her cloak. "God's blood, Ma!" she said. "Isn't that enough? Can't we go home now? It's freezing."

Adelia gave an involuntary groan as she rose stiffly to her feet. "No need to look at me like that," she snapped when she saw Allie's look of concern. "I'm just getting old. I can't help it."

"Well don't!" Allie said, threading her arm through her mother's and squeezing it. "You're not to. I won't have it."

They turned their backs on the hare and set off through the orchard to the common land where a herd of cows grazed contentedly on the wheat stubble.

It was late morning, but other than a group of women in the distance hefting sacks of grain to the mill house, the estate was deserted.

"Do you know what we really need?" Adelia asked brightly, and rhetorically, as they started the long climb up the hill to their cottage. "Some more pigs. It's been a while, hasn't it? I think I'll have a word with Ernulf."

More pigs!

Allie's heart sank. It had been some time since the anatomy of the pig had held any mystery for her.

Ever since she could remember, pig carcasses of every shape, size, age and stage of decomposition had been dragged by Ernulf—usually under the cover of darkness, and always without Lady Emma's knowledge—to the small lean-to withy hut behind their cottage for her mother to dissect. Her childhood memories were littered with them: buried pigs, drowned pigs, diseased pigs, pigs savaged by wolves, pigs who had simply dropped dead mysteriously in their sties; sows, piglets and boars of every shape and size, all homogenized in death by the seething maggots and buzzing flies of the process of putrefaction, which so fascinated Adelia.

"But, darling," she would say when she saw Allie's little nose wrinkle in disgust as yet another festering carcass was slapped onto the makeshift catafalque in front of her, "pigs are the nearest approximation to human flesh and bone. How else are you going to learn medicine?"

It was, after all, the way she herself had learned, almost a lifetime ago and more than a thousand miles away, at the medical school in Salerno in her native Italy.

And as soon as she was able, she had weaned her daughter on the stories of the death farms run by her tutor Gordinus and the pigs he kept there for his students to dissect, telling her proudly about how all the students had quailed at the sight of the flesh flies, blowflies and maggots and fallen away entirely at the stench of the rotting flesh—all, that is, except for Adelia herself, who saw not the horror and decay of death but instead the wonder of the process that reduced a cadaver to nothing. This, she told Allie proudly, was how she had trained to be a doctor and to learn the language of the dead in order to reveal their secrets.

In her day she was known as Dr. Trotula, the mistress of the art of death, one whose reputation had once spread so far and wide that one day, many, many years ago now, it had reached the ear of Henry, king of England, who, when he heard it, summoned her to his realm to investigate the murders of four Cambridgeshire children. When she solved them, he rewarded her by refusing to allow her ever to leave.

"That Plantagenet has a lot to answer for," Adelia would often be heard grumbling, and indeed, he had—not least, of course, Allie's existence.

IT WAS DURING THAT CAMBRIDGESHIRE investigation that the young Rachel Adelia Ortese Aguilar met the young Sir Rowley Picot—who was then the king's tax inspector—and fell madly in love with him.

Like most things in Adelia's life, the courtship had been unorthodox—in its early stages she had even suspected him of involvement in the crimes, until, of course, the real culprit was revealed and Rowley's charm and innate goodness won her heart. And yet, when Allie was conceived and he begged her to marry him, she refused, citing the independence she valued above all else as the reason why. Whether or not she would have capitulated eventually was anybody's guess, but Henry made it impossible shortly afterward when he anointed him bishop of St. Albans.

Oh yes, Henry had a lot to answer for all right, but he was dead now. It was more than two years since the messenger came from Chinon with the news, extinguishing the indefinable spark of whatever it was that only Henry could ignite in Adelia forever.

Then as now, Allie wondered about the nature of her mother's relationship with the king, a conundrum not founded on romantic intrigue but rather a mutual admiration for one another's competence and, in Henry's case, an abiding appreciation of Adelia's usefulness to his various purposes.

Allie was watching her now through the cottage window, pottering around in her beloved herb garden, gathering plants for her various infusions, and noticed again the streaks of gray in her hair, the first of which had appeared when she heard the news of his death, as though his passing had somehow leached the color from her.

The long note of a huntsman's horn sounded from somewhere deep within the forest, distracting Allie from her melancholic meditation at the window and, on the other side of the demesne, Lady Emma of Wolvercote from the endless information her reeve was heaping on her like a penance.

In fact she was trying very hard to control her right foot, which was twitching in its elegant calfskin boot—from a desire not to inflict pain, per se, but to administer a disincentive he might remember. She was also trying hard to remember that, when all was said and done, Wat Hardle was a good man, as honest and meticulous as any she could find, who knew his men and the workings of the estate like the back of his hand . . . But oh dear! She took a deep breath, feeling her foot flex again . . . The extraordinary detail of his annual accounting was a torment she dreaded from one year to the next.

It didn't help that, by necessity, it had to be conducted outside in the cold around a post on which the unlettered Wat habitually carved the notches and tallies of his daily business and that, by this point in the proceedings, boredom and incipient hypothermia had combined.

She took another deep, improving breath . . . It couldn't be too much longer now . . . And then, at long last, her prayers were answered and he turned away from the post.

"Think that's about everythin' then, mistress, unless—"

"Thank you, Wat." Emma nodded, gathering up the hem of her skirts to make a hasty retreat when she saw him scratch his head as though to stimulate it for a forgotten detail. "That will do nicely, Wat," she added quickly before he could remember whatever it was. "I think that will be all for the time being. A fulsome account, if I may say so . . . But now, I fear, I must go and see Osbert about supper." And without waiting for a response, she turned on her heel and set off at a trot toward the house.

She was happy in the fact that she wasn't lying about Osbert, either. There was a great deal she needed to discuss with him. This evening's supper was a surprise she was planning for Adelia, and because, from the sound of it, the huntsmen would be back any moment now with fresh meat for the pot—God's teeth! She was already sick to death of salted beef and winter hadn't even begun yet—she wanted to discuss the preparation of it with her chef. Besides, among her many duties, it was the one she enjoyed most, and at least the kitchen was warm.

Wat stood at his post watching the elegant, ermine-clad figure of his mistress recede into the distance and scratched his head again, wondering, although not for the first time, why she always seemed to be in such a hurry.

CHAPTER 4

A LOUD KNOCK SUMMONED ALLIE to the door. When she opened it, a gust of wind thrust both a swirling eddy of leaves and a small figure, wrapped from head to foot in a large winnowing sheet, into the room. Despite the fact that only a pair of sharp brown eyes was visible above the swaddling, Allie nonetheless recognized them as belonging to the tanner's wife.

"That you, Gonilda?" she asked as the figure bustled past her in a determined bid for the fire. "Everything all right, is it?"

"No. It ain't." Gonilda shook her face free of the sheet and blew out her cheeks like a frog. "It's Albin."

"Oh," said Allie. "I see. That tooth playing him up again, is it?"

Gonilda nodded. "Needs to see the mistress," she said.

When Adelia had been summoned from the garden and the necessary infusions collected from her store in the withy hut, they wrapped themselves up in their warmest mantles and set off after Gonilda along the frost-rutted track to the village.

The journey took longer than usual because every few yards or so they had to stop as one or another of them extended a steadying hand to the perambulatory bundle, who seemed in constant danger of tripping over her own feet.

"Remind me to look out for that old mantle of mine, will you?" Adelia whispered when they had righted Gonilda for the umpteenth time. "It might not be the most beautiful thing in the world but the lining's still good and it's a damned sight better than that old thing. At least she won't go breaking her neck in it."

By the time they reached the tall manure heaps that marked the outskirts of the village, the light was beginning to fade and there were rushlights flickering in the windows of the reed-thatched cottages. Halfway down the main street they startled a large kite scavenging for scraps in the foul-smelling gully running beside it. Gonilda shrieked at it and it flapped off languorously into the gloaming.

The tanner's cottage was at the furthest end of a row of timber-framed shacks, distinguishable from its neighbors by the animal hides that were strewn across its roof and, today at least, the low-level groaning sound emitting from it.

The moment she heard it, Gonilda clutched her hand to her breast and stepped up the pace.

"She's coming, Albin," she called out. "Mistress is coming."

When they got to the cottage, Gonilda flung the door open and stood on the threshold to harry them into a dimly lit room, where they found the stricken tanner lying in one corner and a large sow grunting welcome from another.

Ignoring both the sow and a rather mangy-looking lurcher with a forlorn expression that lifted its lip as she passed, Adelia made immediately for Albin and knelt down on the floor beside him.

"Now, now, Albin," she said, taking his hand. "If you can make this much noise I'll have to assume it's not as bad as all that, won't I?"

Albin turned his face to her, revealing a cheek that had swollen to the size of a stuffed pig's bladder.

"Bloody is . . . 'ook!" he said.

"Been praying to that St. Apollonia for days," said Gonilda, hovering anxiously behind her. "But it ain't got no better."

"So I see." Adelia pursed her lips. She had little truck with the curative powers of St. Apollonia, or any of the martyrs, come to that, and a tendency toward impatience with those who did. "I suspect she's rather busy at the moment. There's been a lot of it about."

She stood up; raised her finger to Albin, who had started groaning again; and began to unpack her medicine bag with the solemnity of a priest unpacking the contents of his chrismatory box, except—as she liked to point out—the items carried in her own bag were a damn sight more effective.

Albin watched transfixed while she and Allie arranged the various cloths and bottles that issued from it on the trestle table beneath the window, and only started moaning again in earnest when he saw her pick up a small iron vise.

"What you goin' to do wiv that?" he wailed. "You ain't comin' near me wiv that, you're not!" Then, clamping his hands across his mouth, he rolled facedown onto his palliasse and refused to move.

"Albin!" Adelia stamped her foot. "We don't have time for any fuss, we're losing the light, so unless you want to spend the rest of your miserable life in pain, that tooth has to come out. Now shut up and turn over."

There were few people brave enough to gainsay Adelia when she was in foot-stamping mode and Albin wasn't one of them; realizing that the game was up, he turned over meekly, got to his feet and followed her over to the window.

"Drink this," Adelia said, thrusting a vial of poppy-head tea at him. "Take a good slug, now, and I promise you won't feel a thing."

With a stifled groan and shaking hands, Albin did as he was told and drank it down.

"Now open your mouth," Adelia said, taking his face in her hands and twisting it gently to the light. "I said open! . . . Good . . . Now, close your eyes . . . Albin, I said close them . . . Thank you. Now . . . Oh, Allie, darling, hold those damned hands of his still for me, would you . . . And . . . there we are!" She inserted the clamp and, with one dexterous flick of her wrist, extracted Albin's tooth.

"There," she said, waggling the blackened remnant at him. "Wasn't so bad, was it! Now, I ought to warn you that the cavity might bleed for a while but a salt gargle twice a day for a week ought to see you right as rain."

But Albin wasn't listening. Allie could tell from the vacant expression and uninhibited drool soaking his chin that the poppy-head tea had done its work and that it would be some time before he would be able to hear or feel anything at all.

By the time they left, the Whitcroft Abbey bells were sounding for vespers.

"Come," Allie said, grabbing Adelia's arm. "We must hurry or else we'll be late."

"Late for what?" Adelia asked.

"Emma, remember? Supper?" Allie replied, ignoring the weary sighs.

"Oh, that. Do you think she'd mind terribly if I didn't go? I'm awfully tired and really not remotely hungry."

Allie turned to look at her and saw that she did, indeed, look exhausted. There was no doubt she needed a good rest, but it just couldn't be this evening.

"But you have to go," she said, tightening her grip as she stepped up the pace. "You can't let Emma down, not tonight. She's got a surprise for you."

CHAPTER 5

ADELIA'S SURPRISE WAS HIMSELF ALSO exhausted, running late and increasingly tetchy.

He'd been riding for two days; his arse was sore and his back ached. Two afflictions reminding him, as though he needed reminding, that he wasn't getting any younger.

He grimaced as he stood up in his stirrups to relieve the discomfort in his nether regions and thought how not so very long ago, he could have completed this journey in half the time *and* without the physical punishment. The fact that this was no longer the case depressed him. On the other hand, he doubted if there was a rider in the land who could get anywhere in a hurry on a nag like this! His own horse, a more biddable, forward-going creature, had let him down badly that morning when it trotted up lame.

"Built for stamina, not speed, my lord," the groom told him when he saw Rowley's face fall as he led the replacement out of the abbey stables.

Too right! Rowley thought bitterly. The bloody thing had

sides like steel; even before they reached the abbey gates his heels had been aching from nagging at them!

He leaned out of his saddle to pluck an encouraging twig from the hedgerow they were ambling beside.

"Move!" he growled, striking the makeshift whip across the horse's rump, but apart from an irritable flick of its ears and a languid rise in its back end, there was no discernible quickening of its pace.

"Bugger!"

He dropped the twig with a weary sigh and slumped back into his saddle, the discomfort and accidie he felt now tinged with shame.

After all, he really shouldn't lose his temper with the horse; it wasn't responsible for the way he felt. A whole constellation of events had conspired toward this particular episode of misery. It was just that, thanks to this animal's obduracy, he had been given time to dwell on them.

It didn't help, of course, that, when he had arrived at Aynsham Abbey last night, hungry, exhausted and salivating at the prospect of the seven-course supper for which that establishment was famed, he had found, to his horror, that the abbot's newly embraced asceticism had reduced the menu to a mere three. This disappointment was only compounded when, as he retired for the evening, looking forward to the plump pillows and sumptuous mattresses he remembered so fondly from previous visits, he discovered they, too, had fallen afoul of the wretched man's austerity measures, which had ruined what ought to have been decent night's sleep.

And last night, of all nights, Rowley had badly needed to sleep.

He had spent the previous day freezing to death on a rain-sodden bridge in the godforsaken hamlet of Loddon, near Reading, with a host of other bishops and barons, all summoned there by John, the Count of Mortain, younger brother of the king, to decide once and for all the fate of the troublesome William Longchamp, bishop of Ely.

The standoff between the two—which was already well established and included at least two sieges—would, Rowley hoped, culminate in the count's favor on the bridge that day.

Only it hadn't. At the very last minute, Longchamp had refused to turn up, barricading himself inside Windsor Castle instead.

Rowley's relief that a battle had been averted—after all, he was much too old and too weary for fighting these days—had been tempered by the fact that, since nothing had been resolved, there would have to be another assembly. And it was this that occasioned such deep melancholy, as he envisaged his future, or what little remained to him, playing out in a series of interminable meetings.

Oh well, he thought, shifting in his saddle again. It would all be resolved eventually, things usually were—at least he had lived long enough to know that much—but in the meantime he had other worries, chief among them his daughter. His beautiful, clever, capricious, *unmarried* daughter.

That he loved her, always had and always would, was indubitable, but her refusal to marry was a torment that, he was beginning to suspect, he would have to carry to his grave.

It was his fault; he accepted that: first for having fallen in love with a woman as unconventional as Adelia, second for failing to persuade her to marry him, and last for having had a child with her at all!

The only thing he couldn't be blamed for was Allie's sex. A boy would have been so much easier, as everybody was always at such pains to point out, but—and this he had known from the moment he clapped eyes on her—a boy would have been so much less fun, less beautiful, less bright, less lovable and less like Adelia.

Oh, she had his eyes, everybody agreed on that, and his humor, but the rest, thank God, was Adelia, and yet now that she had reached the age of twenty-two, or twenty-three?—God's teeth! He was getting so old he was losing track of the passing years—one thing was certain: she was too old not to be married.

And it worried him, terribly. Not for the opprobrium that would inevitably be heaped on her—on them all, in fact—God's eyes! They could and had survived worse, but because for a woman to be unconnected meant that she was also unprotected and therefore vulnerable to all manner of atrocities when her father and protector eventually died.

In the old days, under Henry, he had been secure in the knowledge that, in the event of his own death, a decent match would be procured for her, but Richard was a very different creature from his father, his wards merely pawns in a ruthless pursuit to fund his Crusades, and yet, when Rowley had tried explaining this to Allie, she had rounded on him.

"What about Ma?" she had asked, hands on her hips, eyes

flashing defiantly. "She survived without being married, didn't she!" A riposte that rather took the wind out of his sails, largely because it was true. Adelia had survived—if only by the skin of her teeth at times—but then she was a foreigner in a country arrogant enough to assume that all foreigners were peculiar simply by dint of the misfortune of their place of birth and, therefore, exempt from the mores and expectations of ordinary society. Not only that, but she had enjoyed the protection of the king and the complex subterfuge they had all employed to keep her safe. She also had Mansur, her devoted Arab stepbrother, who had followed her to England from Salerno with the express intention of keeping her safe. How she would have fared without having him to deflect the inevitable accusations of witchcraft, by pretending that he was a real doctor and not her, Rowley dreaded to think. But Mansur was dead, God rest his soul, and Henry, too, God rest his, leaving Rowley as her sole protector. The fact that he was failing in this duty was a burgeoning agony.

Yet what more could he do? He had the will and the means to secure the best of matches, to bestow the dowry to end all dowries on any suitor she would accept, but she thwarted him at every turn by refusing every last damned one of them.

"If I ever marry," she had told him, in no uncertain terms, "it will be for love. Not because you want me to."

In despair he had turned to Adelia.

"Where does she get these ideas?" he pleaded.

Adelia responded with an insouciant shrug. "Us, I suppose," she said.

"But we're not married!"

"No," she said. "We're not. But we've always had love."

It felt like a conspiracy, and there were times when he thought it might drive him mad.

A S THE LATE AFTERNOON SUN slid into the hills at his back, a breeze and a wave of self-pity brushed over him simultaneously. He dropped the reins to wipe his eyes, surprised at himself.

It was exhaustion, that was what it was, sheer bloody exhaustion, but for the time being, for tonight at least, he was going to put his worries behind him, because tonight—just as long as he could get this bloody horse to walk on a bit—he would be at Wolvercote, fed and fêted by the incomparable Osbert, arguably the finest chef in the kingdom. And after such gastronomic indulgence he would lie in the arms of the woman he loved, all his anxiety about the only other woman he loved banished for the time being.

With those happier thoughts, he plucked another twig from the hedgerow, thwacked the implacable horse on its rump and smiled for the first time that day as it broke into a trot.

CHAPTER 6

Wolvercote

N OT THAT ONE!" ALLIE SCREECHED when she saw Adelia stepping blithely into the dowdy moth-eaten bliaut Lena, her maid—one of the doziest girls in Christendom—had idly plucked from the bottom of the clothes chest. "That one's older than God!" she said, snatching it out of Adelia's hands and rummaging furiously for the less tatty blue-and-gold one she knew lurked in the bottom somewhere.

"What about this?" she said when she found it.

"Oh for goodness' sake!" Adelia snapped. "We're having supper with Emma! What on earth are you making such a fuss for?"

Allie tried hard to suppress a smile. "I don't know, Ma," she replied. "I just thought you might feel better, that's all, a little less tired perhaps, if you wore something pretty."

It was clutching at straws and she knew it. Adelia had never been interested in clothes or frippery—she was almost famous for it—but Allie was determined that this evening of all evenings, in honor of her "surprise," she should look her very best.

They finished dressing in silence, Allie somehow ignoring the groans and exaggerated yawns emanating from the other side of the room, knowing that one more false move, one more unwelcome suggestion, and Adelia would simply refuse to budge.

By the time they were ready to leave, the sun was as low as it could be without actually setting and the lone horseman slumped wearily in his saddle on the horizon was little more than a silhouette; nevertheless, the moment she saw him, Adelia gave a gasp of recognition, picked up the hem of her skirts and started scampering over the stubble toward him like an excited child.

Allie stood at a distance watching her father lean down and take Adelia in his arms, then turned away, overwhelmed by that peculiar feeling she so often had when she saw them together, a strange mix of admiration, love and loneliness.

She had no doubt that they adored her—it was a comfort she felt deep in her bones—it was just that, sometimes, their union was so complete, so all-consuming, that there was no room for anyone else, not even her.

UNFORTUNATELY THE EVENING EMMA HAD so meticulously organized didn't turn out as planned.

On their way to the house through the rose garden, Adelia, who was chatting away, oblivious to everyone and everything but Rowley, tripped on a wind-fallen branch and fell heavily.

For a moment she sat where she was, giggling helplessly at her own clumsiness, but when she tried to stand up her ankle gave way and she collapsed onto the grass again.

"Bugger!" she said, holding her arms out to Rowley, whimpering with pain when he tried pulling her to her feet.

"What have you done, woman?" he asked, his amusement giving way suddenly to concern.

"I don't know," she replied, hopping toward a stone bench in the middle of the lawn. "Sprained the bugger, I think . . . But ooh, it hurts!"

Pushing her father out of the way, Allie knelt down in front of the bench.

"Let's get that boot off, shall we?" she said, thrusting the hem of Adelia's chainse at him, revealing her ankle, which was already bruised and swollen.

"What a beautiful shade of blue! Look at that! . . . But . . . ," she said, gently palpating the flesh, "not broken, I don't think . . . Nope . . . But it's a nasty sprain nevertheless, which means you'll have to rest up. No more running about after other people for a change."

Adelia grimaced. "Thank you, darling," she said. "But oh, what a nuisance! And just as I've got you back, too, Rowley! I'm so sorry."

She raised her arms to him again and he lifted her off the bench with a groan.

"God's teeth, but you've gained weight since I last held you!" he said, earning himself a slap.

As he pretended to stagger over the lawn with Adelia giggling helplessly in his arms, they discussed whether or not to send their apologies to Emma and go back to the cottage, or to carry on as planned. Rowley was in favor of going back, but Adelia—who was all too familiar with the tyranny of his stomach—insisted they carry on; besides, as long as she didn't have to put any weight on it, her ankle was comparatively painless and she was rather enjoying being carried.

D ELIA!"
Emma leapt to her feet, her hand to her mouth, when they appeared in the hall.

"I knew there'd be a good reason you were late! What in God's name have you done?" she asked, whipping around to the young page standing behind her and snapping her fingers impatiently. "Don't just stand there, Matthew. What are you thinking of? Go and help my lord bishop!" At which point the tremulous young man launched himself off the dais and went rushing across the floor toward them.

"My lord," he said as he skidded to a halt just in time to avoid knocking Adelia out of Rowley's arms. "May I be of assistance?"

"That's very kind." Ever sensitive to the plight of the newly initiated Wolvercote squire, Rowley smiled at him. "But I think I can manage . . . unless, of course, you'd be so kind as to get that bloody dog out of my way."

Emma's greyhound, the spoiled hare slayer, had become so excited by the latecomers that it was making a spectacle of itself, running figures of eight round Rowley's legs, threatening to knock him over any moment.

"Any closer and I'll drop her on your head," Rowley hissed as it sped past once more. "Then you'll be sorry." And he wasn't entirely surprised when Adelia slapped him again.

As soon as they were settled and seated at the table, laden, to Rowley's delight, with all the dishes he had been fantasizing about on the journey—Osbert's famous miniature pastries filled with marrow, a meat tile of chicken served in a delicately spiced sauce of pounded crayfish tails, almonds and toasted bread and a delightful little suckling pig with an apple in its mouth—a team of servants bearing ewers, basins and towels began orbiting the table. When all the hands had been washed and dried, Father Michael, Emma's confessor, said grace.

They were only seven for supper: Rowley, Adelia, Allie, Emma, Master Roetger—Emma's husband—Father Michael and the abbot of Whitcroft, a charming old man who, though a little too fond of ale for his own good, was forgiven his various indiscretions by dint of the fact that he was such a kindly soul and, of course, his unabashed adoration of Adelia, of whom he was, as usual, making a great fuss.

"Poor Adelia," he said, his chubby fingers idly stroking the back of her hand. "Perhaps you should rest awhile in the solar. Injuries like that ought to be taken seriously, you know, lest the damage be compounded . . . Had a fall myself the other day . . . off a horse though, not a log . . . Nasty sprain, too, very . . . Devil of a time healing."

When they had finished eating, and Allie had bound Adelia's ankle with the strips of muslin Emma had sent for, Allie sat quietly looking out on a room whose beauty, however familiar it became, could still take her breath away. In fact she was thinking that it was probably a little bit like looking out onto heaven, or certainly the way she imagined heaven to be, when an almost equally celestial voice interrupted her.

"I'm sorry, my dear." Master Roetger's warm, deep baritone

always came as a shock, belying, as it did, his physical frailty. "I didn't mean to startle you. I was just saying how good it is to see your father again and how much I've missed him."

Allie turned to him and smiled. She was fond of Roetger; everybody was.

"So am I," she said, although it wasn't entirely true. She had missed him and she was pleased to see him; it was just that this time, her pleasure was tempered by trepidation, knowing that he was here for a reason and that before he left again the dreaded negotiation about her future would have to take place and a decision would have to be made whether she liked it or not . . .

She was looking at him now across the table, deep in conversation with Emma. From their grave expressions and low voices she realized that they were discussing Pip, Emma's son and heir, who had recently brought his otherwise indomitable mother to her knees by announcing that he was going to take the cross and travel to the Holy Land with the king.

When the dreaded day came, the send-off Emma had given him—her precious only child—had been a lesson in courage, and no one, least of all Allie, would ever forget the grace with which she watched him leave, and with such apparently genuine delight that she might have been waving him off on a stag hunt rather than halfway across the world to war. It was only when he was safely out of sight, his cavalcade a dusty memory in the road, that she crumpled, retreating to her solar, refusing to eat or to speak or to see anybody—other than Adelia, of course—for days.

Allie was about to resume her conversation with Roetger when she noticed that Rowley was looking at her and realized, with an awful sinking feeling, that his conversation with Emma had taken a different turn and was now a mutual lament, no longer simply about the perils of poor Pip but about anxiety-inducing offspring in general, one of whom was risking life and limb among the infidels, the other the wrath of God by refusing to marry.

"Oh, Mary, Mother of God! He is! He's going to marry me off, and soon!"

She hadn't meant to say it out loud but the shock of the revelation forced the thought from her lips before she'd had a chance to censor it.

"Oh, my dear!" Roetger turned to her, his expression of concern only adding to her mortification. "Come now. It needn't be as bad as all that, you know? I think we might trust your father to make a good match for you." When he put his hand over hers she had to bite her lip to stop the tears of self-pity.

"But I don't want to be married off," she said, wiping roughly at her eyes with the back of her hand. "I don't want to, Roetger. Not ever!"

"Allie!"

Rowley was kneeling beside her.

"Allie," he repeated when she refused to look at him, reaching for her hand, which she snatched away abruptly.

"Darling," he continued, dropping his voice to a taut whisper. "Have we not discussed this endlessly, you and I? . . . You know as well as I do that you have to marry. You can't continue like this!"

Allie glared at him, her fists so tightly clenched that she could feel the nails biting into her palms. Around them the conversation came to a stuttering halt as all the heads in the room swiveled in their direction. For a moment even the falcons on their perches stopped their baiting and gave the impression that they, too, were holding their breath.

This time the mortification was Rowley's, not hers, but just as she was about to release the maelstrom of fury churning in her belly, there was a loud knock on the door and all the heads that had so recently turned to them turned to that instead.

"Come in!"

Grateful for any reprieve from the horror on the other side of the table, Emma leapt to her feet, prepared, at that moment, to admit even the devil.

The door opened and Sir Jocelyn, her steward, came in.

"Lady Emma," he said with a weary bow, "a visitor has come for Mistress Adelia. I tried to explain that it is very late and that you are dining and therefore not to be disturbed, but, I fear, she is a most insistent person and says that it is a matter of some urgency . . ."

"Oh!" Emma frowned and turned to Adelia, who was looking equally confused. "Urgent, Sir Jocelyn?" she asked with another quizzical glance at Adelia.

Sir Jocelyn nodded.

"Oh . . . well, in that case . . . you had better show her in."

Sir Jocelyn bowed again and disappeared, only to return a moment later with one of the most peculiar-looking women Allie had ever seen.

She was quite jaw-droppingly odd and, in fact, wasn't immediately obviously female, swaddled, as she was, from head to toe in an outlandish ensemble of wolf pelts, exuding a mannish confidence as she strode purposefully over the rushes toward them. It was only as she got closer that Allie could see that she was considerably older than her youthful gait implied and that, beneath all the wrapping—once she had divested herself of it, flinging her mantle at a bemused Sir Jocelyn—she was a good deal slimmer, too.

She came to a stop at the foot of the dais, planting her feet in the manner of a soldier, and lifted her chin, revealing a pair of sharp blue eyes that looked up at them from a fierce little face that was as brown and crinkled as a walnut.

Allie couldn't take her eyes off her and noted, with increasing admiration, that, instead of a wimple, she was wearing a cap, and judging by the spiky fronds escaping from underneath it, her hair was brutally cropped.

Emma left the table and walked to the edge of the dais.

"Welcome, madam," she said warily. "I am Lady Emma of Wolvercote. And you are . . . ?"

"Lady Penda of Elsford," the woman replied, the sharp eyes flicking beyond Emma to scour the other faces on the dais. "My apologies for disturbin' you an' all but I'm here to see Mistress Adelia on an urgent matter."

All eyes turned to Adelia, whose own were fixed on the woman.

There was something disconcertingly familiar about her, but, for the life of her, she couldn't think what.

"I'm Adelia," she said, waving her hand above her head to draw her attention. "Forgive me if I don't get up, but I've sprained my ankle, you see, and I can't stand . . . But . . . well . . . what can I do for you?"

When she saw her a wide, delighted grin spread across the

woman's face. "Should've guessed," she cried as she leapt onto the dais with alarming agility. "She's described you to me more times 'an you could imagine. Talks about you all the time!"

Unable to match her enthusiasm, and disconcerted by the speed and gusto of her approach, Adelia recoiled. "Forgive me," she said. "But I don't understand. Who talks about me? Do we know one another, you and I? . . . I must admit you do seem familiar somehow, Lady . . . erm . . . Lady . . . ?" She clapped her hand to her head. "I'm so sorry but I'm afraid I've forgotten your name."

The woman gave a warm chuckle; almost everything Adelia said or did appeared to delight her.

"Course you 'ave," she said, grinning broadly. "Course you 'ave, and will be excused for 'avin' done so! Only just acquainted with it, ain't you? . . . No, we ain't met, but you'll know me when I tell you I'm Gyltha's sister!"

Allie saw her mother's mouth open and close like that of a newly landed fish, until she absorbed the information, at which point a correspondingly broad smile spread across her face, too.

"Allie, Rowley," she cried, throwing her arms wide. "Look. It's Penda, Gyltha's sister!"

Their spat temporarily forgotten, Rowley and Allie exchanged glances.

"I didn't know she had a sister," Rowley mouthed as he got up. Allie shrugged. Neither did she.

"So you're Rowley!"

The woman extricated herself—and with some difficulty—from Adelia's grasp and bounded toward him. "Heard all about you an' all," she said, taking his hands and shaking them vigorously. "And you!" she said, dropping them unceremoniously and pushing him aside as soon as she saw Allie standing behind him. "You must be little Allie! Well, well, well! And not so little neither. A beauty! Just like Gylth said! Well, I never!"

She stood beaming at Allie, holding her gaze for what felt like an age, until, all of a sudden, her expression clouded and she turned back to Adelia.

"But I'm forgetting myself and the reason I've come," she said. "It's Gylth. She needs you, mistress, needs you badly. She's sick and I'm afraid that 'less there's something you can do for her, she'll die."

Adelia saw the gimlet eyes compress against the burgeoning tears and a lump rose in her throat. The idea of anything happening to Gyltha, the woman on whom she had depended for as long as she could remember, was unconscionable.

"Then I must go to her immediately," she said, trying to stand up, only to be forced back onto her stool by the swingeing pain in her ankle. "God rot it!" she cried, thumping the table with the side of her fist. "For God's sake! Don't just sit there! Help me up, somebody, please!"

A palpable hush descended on the room as Rowley knelt down beside her.

"Adelia, darling," he murmured softly, "you're in no condition to go anywhere or do anything. Even you must realize that, and for once, I'm afraid, you can't help." He reached out to take her hand but she pushed him away, shaking her head as a bitter irony dawned on her.

In the past it had been Rowley, as the king's harbinger, who would turn up, mostly when she least expected, with a summons from Henry, which would invariably involve a perilous journey of some sort and almost always separation from Allie and Gyltha.

Then, as now, she resented him for it, only this time for enforcing the separation by insisting that, for once, she stay put.

She stared at him uncomprehendingly for a moment, wondering how he could possibly not see it, too, then turned away. It was almost too painful to look at him.

"Adelia," he persisted, "listen to me, darling, please! There is nothing you can do, not now, and certainly not with that ankle . . . But if it makes you happy I will send—and tonight, if you insist—to the infirmarian at Ely and ask him to attend Gyltha himself. He's a good chap, certainly knows his medicine. She'll be in good hands!"

He reached for her again, taking her face in his hands and turning it gently toward him, but she twisted free.

"How could you?" she hissed. "How could you? This is Gyltha we're talking about! Not some scrofulous novice with a head cold! It's Gyltha! And she needs me! Do you hear . . . Me!" She broke off for a moment, her voice cracking with emotion. "Not some oaf of an infirmarian who doesn't know his arse from his elbow. Now help me up! Rowley, please. I beg you!"

"Adelia!"

An imperious voice sounded, silencing them both.

Lady Emma had had enough. Now that she had come to terms with the fact that the evening she had so lovingly planned was unsalvageable, she had regained her composure and was determined to employ it to the greater good.

"Adelia, my dear," she said, fixing her with an implacable stare. "For once in your life you are going to have to listen to poor Rowley and do exactly as he says. Why, with that ankle of yours, you're no use to anybody and you certainly can't go charging about the country to . . . Oh my goodness! . . . Where is it they come from, these people? . . . The Fens, is it? . . . Well, good Lord! It's at least four days' ride from here. You simply cannot go and there's an end to the matter!"

Adelia opened her mouth to remonstrate with her but Emma wagged her finger and shook her head. "No, I'm sorry, 'Delia. Really I am, but, for the time being, you will have to stay here."

When she had dealt with Adelia she turned to Penda, the intransigent gaze this time directed at a point fractionally above her eyebrows—a ploy she normally reserved to intimidate the servants.

"Lady Penda," she said coldly. "I'm sorry to have to tell you—but since nobody else seems prepared to do so, I fear it's left to me—that your journey here has been wasted. As you must know, we are all terribly fond of Gyltha, and wish her a speedy recovery, but Mistress Adelia is quite unable to help." When Penda opened her mouth to protest, she scowled and the forbidding finger wagged again.

"However," she continued, closing her eyes to deflect any further dissent, "you are welcome to spend the night here. Sir Jocelyn will see to it that you and your retinue . . ." She paused for a moment as it struck her that a woman as outlandish as this one might equally be reckless enough to travel alone. "You do have one, I presume?"

When, to her surprise, Penda nodded, she carried on.

"Very good . . . Well, in that case, you will be given every comfort, and tomorrow—" And like the exemplary host she was, she was about to promise ample provision for the journey home, when Allie interrupted her.

"Wait!" she said, her face flushed with excitement. "I could go! I could go instead. After all, I know as much medicine as Ma and we can't abandon Gyltha! We simply can't!" She turned to Rowley, dropping to her knees in supplication.

"Get up, Allie! Get up at once!" he hissed, mortified. "You will not go and that's an end to the matter."

Once again silence fell. At one end of the hall the abbot and Father Michael were offering up silent prayers of gratitude for their vows of celibacy; at the other, the servants desperately tried to busy themselves elsewhere.

But Allie was unabashed.

"Do you mean to tell me that you won't lift a finger to help?" She blinked back the tears pricking her eyes, then decided to let them fall. It would serve him right. How could he forget what he owed to Gyltha? His life for a start! If it hadn't been for her tireless nursing of him when he returned from Italy so terribly wounded all those years ago, he would have died. And that apart, how could he forget the support she had given, standing by them all so resolutely through the topsy-turvying of their peripatetic lives, to provide the only constant in hers?

"I tell you," she continued, breathless with emotion, "that I would rather die than let anything happen to Gyltha. But then

I doubt you can see that—in fact I doubt you can see very much at all beyond your miserable obsession with marrying me off!" Before he could respond, she ran out of the hall. While waves of shock swept around the hall like an ill wind, rendering everybody else speechless, Penda had an epiphany: a native cunning—some long-forgotten opportunism—sparked to life like an invisible conspirator handing her a weapon.

"My lord bishop," she said, suppressing a stab of pity when she saw the anxiety etched in Rowley's face, "I'm sorry for everything. But I know what it is to worry about the ones you love and to fear that 'less you do right by 'em you'll lose 'em—we got that between us, you 'n' me." She paused for a moment, trying to gauge his reaction thus far, and, relieved by something that might be construed as a flicker of recognition, continued.

"Now, I know, because Gyltha told me, that you love your daughter like nothin' else and that her safety and future happiness is all that matters to you . . . Well then, I'll offer this: Let her come to the Fens—oh, I'll keep her safe, you have my word on that, and believe me, I can protect her. So let 'er come and help Gyltha like she wants to, and in return, I will help you."

She paused again when he glanced at Adelia, who was still staring at the door in mute misery, as though by sheer force of will she could drag Allie back through it. For a moment Rowley, too, looked as though he was teetering on the brink of chasing after her through it, until, to her enormous relief, he turned his attention back to her.

"How?" he asked, eyes narrowed suspiciously. "How can you help?"

"Well." Penda swallowed, steeling herself to stay calm for

what was to be the crucial stage of the negotiation. It had been a very long time since she had had to think on her feet quite so quickly and with so much at stake. "You want her married off, don't you? Ain't that what your argument was about?"

Rowley nodded slowly, warily.

"Well, back in the Fens there's a young lord, name of Peverell, whose estate marches with mine. He's good-lookin', wealthy 'n' all, got land over more'n fourteen counties and, what's more, is looking for a wife."

While she spilled these facts, she dared not look at him; when at last she did, and saw his expression of implacable suspicion unchanged, her heart sank, until an unexpected champion in the form of Lady Emma piped up.

"Peverell?" she said, her face lighting up. "Peverell, did you say? But what a coincidence! I know the family well!" She turned to Rowley. "The younger boy was a squire here a while back. You remember him, don't you, Rowley, dear? Such a pleasant young man. Took the cross, like his older brother, if I remember correctly, but his brother was killed, poor soul. Oh, Rowley." She clapped her hands in delight. "I think this puts a whole new complexion on things, don't you! They're an extremely good family, they really are! My goodness! If you can arrange it, it would be a most wonderful match for Allie."

Rowley bit his cheek to suppress a nascent smile: it wouldn't do to capitulate quite yet, but, as Emma said, things were beginning to look up. With this renewed optimism he turned to Adelia again, hoping for a sign of encouragement, but she was still staring forlornly at the door.

Actually she had long since given up hope of Allie's reappearing and was instead quietly wrestling a temptation to throw something at Emma's head.

She loved her dearly, but there were times—and this was one—when the differences in their attitudes, especially when it came to Allie, were unbridgeable.

Unlike Adelia, Emma saw no virtue in Allie's idiosyncrasies nor enchantment in what Adelia called her daughter's "freedom of spirit" and Emma termed her "faroucheness." And there had been several occasions when Emma had indulged her irritation with her woundingly, riding roughshod over the unspoken rules of motherhood by haranguing Adelia about her daughter's lack of conformity with many a cautionary tale about where it would lead. So the fact that she had leapt on the mention of this Lord Peverell person with such enthusiasm automatically made Adelia suspicious. A "good match" for Allie, as far as Emma was concerned, was simply a ruse to tidy her up like a frayed end irrespective of Allie's own wishes or future happiness. At times like these she had to dig very deep indeed to stop herself from biting Emma's head off and remember that beneath it all lurked a good and loving soul whose unrivaled generosity had fed, housed and watered them both for longer than she could remember.

She looked up to a row of expectant faces staring at her.

"I don't give a bugger about the match," she said, occasioning a sharp, collective intake of breath. But she didn't care. She was tired, it had been the most dreadful evening, her ankle was hurting and all she wanted to do was find Allie and comfort her.

"Quite frankly," she continued, "I don't care about this Lord Peverell—whoever he may be—or any of that business, in fact." She broke off to glare at Rowley. "I just want Allie to be happy and for Gyltha to be well. And as soon as this bloody ankle of mine is better I will go to the Fens myself . . . But until then I insist that you send Allie in my place, because if anything should happen to Gyltha"—she stopped for a moment, this time fixing Rowley with a stare worthy of the Gorgon—"I will never forgive you."

And so it was decided; at first light the next morning, Allie would leave Wolvercote with Penda for that strange half land in the east known as the Fens.

CHAPTER 7

The Fens

H AWISE, PINIONED ON THE THRESHOLD of her aunt's cottage by the three small whirling bodies excitedly chanting
her name, breathed in the familiar scent of the place: tallow from
the newly lit candles, aromatic spices that hung in gourds from
the ceiling rafters and that tantalizing, hunger-making waft of
something delicious that seemed to bubble in perpetuity on the
trivet over the fire.

"Hush now!" Ediva, the children's mother and her aunt,
scolded the children as she took her mantle from the perch beside
the door and prepared to leave. "Finish your supper, now, and,
for goodness' sake, pipe down! Let Hawise settle afore you start
annoying her, else she'll 'ave to go home and you'll be stuck with
me for the night."

She winked in sly triumph when the children scampered
back to the table and sat down quietly.

"Father's waiting," Hawise said, reaching up to hang her

mantle on the vacant peg. "Mind how you go, though, it's bitter out, so best wrap up warm."

Ediva peered through the window at the forlorn figure who was waiting for her in the cart and shivered.

"Poor bugger!" she said. "It's perishing. Never known the like . . . Lovely 'n' warm in here though, bor, so get yourself over by the fire and tell me the news quickly when you've warmed a bit."

Hawise shuffled to the middle of the room, where a turf fire, which was almost as old as the cottage itself, smoldered, and held out her hands to it, grimacing at the prickling sensation in her fingertips as they began to thaw.

"There isn't any news really," she said with a sigh. "Gyltha's much the same. Father went up this morning as usual but says as how she's sleeping most of the time now . . ."

"No sign of Penda and the mistress, then?"

Hawise shook her head. "Not yet. Day or two more mebbe . . . That's what Father reckons anyway."

Ediva shook her head, put on her gloves and pulled up her hood.

"Well, it's a long way for 'em to come, I suppose. God speed 'em though, bless their hearts . . . And you lot," she said with one last menacing glower at the children. "You be good for Hawise, now. I shan't be long but I don't want to hear no tales about you when I get back. D'you hear?"

When she opened the door an icy blast gusted into the room, sending the children running to Hawise for comfort.

"Hush now, silly old things," she said, gathering them into her arms. "You heard what your mother said: you're to be good for me this evening."

The children gazed up at her, nodding emphatically.

"Good. Well then, first things first. Have you done all your carding?" This was addressed to ten-year-old Cecelia, the eldest of the three, who pointed proudly to the corner of the room where several yarn-laden distaffs were neatly propped.

"There's a good girl," Hawise said, rewarding her with a kiss on the top of her head. "And Arthur?" she asked, turning to the middle child, the only boy. "Have you fed the chickens?" Arthur nodded, blushing to the roots of his hair when she kissed him, too.

"Good," she said, and was just about to marshal them over to the fire when a loud squawk announced the presence of a hen as it dropped clumsily from the rafters in search of leftovers. Arthur yelped and ran toward it, flapping his arms to send it back to its perch in the smoke-blackened timbers.

When both the hen and the boy had settled again, Hawise drew up a stool, pulling baby Eva onto her lap.

"So, what shall we do now, then?" she asked.

The children grinned.

It was part of the ritual, the tireless joke between them, that, whenever she came, Cousin Hawise would pretend to have forgotten that the reason they were so fond of her and craved her company was because she was, by some distance, the finest storyteller in the family.

It was a gift apparently bestowed on her at birth and—as far as anyone knew—without provenance. Neither parent had it, and both were often heard to wonder about its origin and, indeed, why such a blessing—if a blessing it actually was—had been conferred on their only child.

"We want a story! A story!" the children clamored excitedly.

"Oh, a story?" Hawise affected the surprise of the time-honored tradition. "A story? But aren't you a bit old for stories nowadays? Won't you be bored?"

The children scowled. Sometimes she had a tendency to take the teasing a little too far . . .

"No we're not, Hawise! . . . We're not too old! We want a story! You know we do! A story! Please! Please! Please!"

Amused by the indignation on their faces, Hawise smiled and put her finger to her lips, appealing for the silence they knew must be granted before she began.

"Hush," she said.

The children closed their eyes and held their breath in exquisite anticipation of the great moment.

Outside, in the cottage garth, an owl screeched as another wintry gust bowled in over the marsh, rattling the window shutters. The children shivered and shuffled closer to Hawise, darting nervous glances into the darkness of the room behind them.

"It's only the wind, darlings . . . ," Hawise said, hugging baby Eva closer while Arthur and Cecelia nestled into the pooling hem of her skirt like puppies. "Now, if you're comfortable . . . we must decide what sort of story I should tell you this evening."

The children exchanged glances and began whispering among themselves. This was not a decision to make lightly—and when, a moment or two later, they reached their consensus, Arthur announced it:

"A scary one," he said solemnly.

Hawise laughed and ruffled his hair. "A good choice," she told him.

It was. Nights like these were perfect for the sort of harmless fearmongering she was so very good at. Besides, her imagination had been piqued earlier on the short walk through the garth to the cottage door, when she caught a whiff of something indefinably treacherous in the air. A scent of something wicked . . .

She shivered pleasurably at the memory and took a deep breath, ready to begin.

"Hmm. Let me think . . ." She closed her eyes for a moment. "Oh, I know!" she said, opening them wide again. "I think I'll tell you the story about the curse of the Plantagenets . . ." She broke off, looking quizzically at Arthur and Cecelia. "You know who they are, don't you?" she asked. "The Plantagenets, I mean?"

But they stared blankly at her, shaking their heads.

"Oh," said Hawise. "Well, never mind . . . Plantagenet is the family nickname of the king of England. And you know who he is, don't you?"

This time they nodded. Everybody knew about King Richard.

"Good," said Hawise. "Well, this story goes back to the very early days of that family, almost into the mists of time before they ever became kings, or thought they might . . ."

"Even older than King Arthur?" interrupted Cecelia.

"Even older than him," said Hawise. "You see, this story happened a very, very long, long time ago when the rich and handsome Count of Anjou met a beautiful young woman and fell madly in love."

"Eeeugh!" This time the interruption was Arthur's. He stuck out his tongue and clapped his hands over his eyes. "I hate love, it's disgusting."

Cecelia rounded on him. "Shut up, you pillard!" she hissed.

"You're going to spoil it and then Hawise will have to go home and Mama will come back and we won't hear the story." And before Hawise could do anything to prevent it, Cecelia punched him hard on the arm.

Hawise saw the boy's bottom lip quivering, his small hand balling into a fist, ready to hit back.

"Now, now!" she said, aware that unless she was suitably stern with them the skirmish might escalate and the evening would end in chaos. "Do you want to hear the story or not? Because the truth is I know it off by heart and I don't need to hear it . . . or tell it, come to that."

"But I want to hear it," Eva piped up, turning in her lap to admonish her siblings with a chubby finger. "So shhhh."

"Sorry, Hawise," said Cecelia.

"Sorry, Hawise," muttered Arthur.

"I'll forgive you, but just this once," said Hawise. "Now, where was I? . . . Oh yes, the handsome Count of Anjou and the beautiful, mysterious woman . . . I did tell you that she was mysterious as well as beautiful, didn't I? . . . No? . . . Oh, well that's probably because you were being so naughty . . . But anyway, she was, very, very mysterious. Otherworldly, some said. Peculiar, according to the women who were jealous of her, but magical to the men whose hearts she captured—and she was so beautiful and so mysterious that she captured them all, even the hardest, the moment they saw her.

"And yet, no matter how many suitors she had, it was the Count of Anjou she had eyes for, and since he only had eyes for her, they were soon married and had children and for quite some time lived happily." She broke off, raising her finger portentously. The children caught their breath: the raising of the finger invariably heralded an exciting twist in the tale.

"Happily, that is . . . ," she continued, pleased that the gesture had lost none of its potency, "until the fateful day when the count—who was so in love with his wife that he was nearly blinded by it—discovered a strange thing, which was that whenever they went to church, the countess left before the consecration, and whenever he asked her why, she would make up some excuse or another, which, try as he might, he could never quite believe.

"And so, eventually, he started to worry, and the worry built and built and built, the way worry does, until one day he decided that enough was enough and he must get to the bottom of this strange behavior for once and for all.

"So, the very next day, before the family left for church as usual, he took two of his trusted knights to one side and, when the countess wasn't looking, whispered to them.

"And then, that morning, just before communion, when the countess, as was her habit, started backing toward the door, the count gave a signal to the knights to follow her and, this time, when she tried to open the door and escape, they trod on the train of her dress with their great heavy boots so that she couldn't get away.

"Well, at first the countess simply smiled, thinking, perhaps, that they had done it by mistake, but when she saw the look in their eyes she began to panic and struggle to free herself until . . .

"Well, a very strange thing happened . . ."

Hawise paused, looking down at Arthur and Cecelia.

"Can you think what it was?" she asked, lowering her voice

to a whisper. The children swallowed nervously, shaking their heads.

"Well then, I shall tell you . . . Outside the sky grew as black as hell and the walls and roof of the church began to shake as if God's own wrathful hands were upon it and it was filled with the sound of demons shrieking—terrible, terrible screams they were, too, wicked enough and loud enough to wake the dead. And the countess started screaming, too—a sound no mortal soul had ever been heard to make—tearing at her clothes until there she stood, naked as the day that she was born! And when the congregation dared look at her, they recoiled in horror, because beneath her clothes, she had sprouted wings, great, black, fingered wings like a fallen angel's, and as they watched, those wings began to beat, lifting her high above the ground, until with one last dreadful shriek, she flew out of the window, never to be seen again!"

The children gasped and Hawise took a deep, satisfied breath. It was quite the best rendition of the story she had ever given.

"That fritchoo me!" said Eva, twisting in her lap, flinging her arms around her neck and burying her face in her chest.

Arthur's eyes had grown even larger than usual. "And was she really never seen again!?" he asked. "Vanished into thin air? Did she really!?"

"Oh yes." Hawise nodded gravely. "She vanished into thin air all right."

"Vanished!" Cecelia murmured quietly. "Like Martha!"

At the mention of the missing girl the room fell silent, and for a moment, the only sound to be heard was the rattling of the window shutters in the stiffening breeze.

"Yes." Hawise nodded sadly. "Just like Martha."

It was months now since Martha's disappearance. She had vanished like the Plantagenet countess, as far as anyone could tell, into thin air, yet Hawise's memory of that night was still vivid.

She remembered waiting for her with the others on the riverbank for what felt like an age, grumbling about her thoughtlessness, until it got dark and the cathedral bells sounded for vespers, and they turned for home, assuming that, at some point, she would come to her senses and follow them.

But she hadn't.

And later that evening, unable to sleep for worry, they had each stood vigil at their cottage windows watching the torch-lit procession snake through the labyrinthine pathways of the marsh, looking for her.

Hawise remembered standing there long enough to see the rosy glow of the dawn breaking, and the summons, with the others, to take Martha's parents to the place where she had last been seen, and the sense of futility as they all stood staring out over the frozen waste.

When more than a week had passed and there was still no sign of her, no one dared say so, of course, but hope began to fade for her safe return and everyone assumed that somewhere downriver that night the ice had cracked under her and she had drowned. It was, after all, the most likely explanation. Fenland water was treacherous in all its forms; even the creatures that issued from it weren't all they might seem. Even the eels, on whom so many livelihoods depended, were really, as everyone knew, the multiplied mutations of the once-sinful monks and priests whom St. Dunstan, in a holy and miraculous rage one day, had consigned to eternal penance. Perhaps, the rumor went, one of those had taken her in bitter revenge for its own miserable, slithering fate.

Hawise shivered as the unbidden image of Martha's Medusa-like corpse, writhing with eels, came into her mind.

"You fritchood, too, Hawise?" asked Eva, wide eyed.

"No, darlin'," Hawise said, clutching her tightly. "Not frightened. Just sad is all."

Silence fell again and they sat gazing into the fire until a loud knock at the door made them jump.

"We're being silly," Hawise said, lifting Eva off her lap to open it. "It's only your mother, I expect! And you know what that means, don't you? . . . Time for bed."

The children groaned and began the early murmurs of dissent as Ediva came in.

She looked exhausted, too weary even to stamp the frost off her boots, and any hope Hawise may have had that she would return with good news was dashed.

"It ain't good," she said as Hawise helped her off with her cloak. "They've started that business of tying things to her . . . The infirmarian come this afternoon with 'is bag of relics, St. Etheldreda's fingers or summat, who knows; but whatever it was it was no bloody use. The poor old girl's just lying there, burning up and struggling for breath like she's been the past few days." She shook her head. "I tell you, 'less the mistress comes soon, I don't think there's much hope, I really don't." Then, seeing the look of despair on Hawise's face, she mustered a smile and patted her cheek tenderly.

"Thank you for sittin'," she said. "But best run along now, your father's waitin' and it's not just the cold he's sufferin' with tonight, bless 'im."

When Hawise climbed into the cart, Ulf barely acknowledged her, and as she settled herself in beside him, she cursed herself for having dared hope that either he or Ediva would come back announcing a miracle, that by God's grace their beloved Gyltha had been cured and the happy equilibrium of their lives restored.

But it was stupid. She realized that now. Strong as Gyltha was—and she knew none stronger—she was too old, too frail for those fierce adversaries, the Fenland agues and fevers, and very soon they would have to come to terms with life without her.

She glanced at her father, his head still bowed, and cursed herself anew for being so selfish.

If the prospect of a life without Gyltha was unconscionable for her, she couldn't imagine how dreadful it must have been for him, for whom she was all the family he had ever known.

Closer than close, the two of them, always were . . .

"Don't you worry," she said brightly. "Mistress'll be here soon. She'll make her right, you'll see." And she hoped to God that, as he flicked the reins across the oxen's rump, he hadn't noticed her make the armor of Christ as she said it.

CHAPTER 8

Wolvercote

WHEN SHE AWOKE THE NEXT morning Adelia was bad tempered—but couldn't remember why.

Though still half-asleep, she was conscious enough to realize that her surroundings weren't familiar, that she didn't recognize the heavy curtains pulled around a bed that was obviously not her own and that, for a reason she couldn't fathom, her ankle hurt. Not only that, but beside her, enveloped in a hummock of sheets and blankets, a body was snoring loudly.

She sat up, squinting curiously at the cocoon until she remembered . . .

"Oh, Rowley!" she said, clapping her hand over her eyes, groaning at the memory of the previous evening. She flopped back onto her pillows, remembering the fall, the supper, the argument and finally her protest—futile, as it turned out—at being put to bed in Emma's guest chamber . . . And, last but not least, Gyltha.

She lay, for a moment, staring miserably at the ceiling, listening to Rowley's snores and the distant murmur of the servants in the hall below as they roused themselves for the infinite business of preparing Wolvercote Manor for another day.

Gyltha!

She sat upright. This was no time for lying around, there were things to do and plans to make, but as she swung her legs over the side of the bed to get up, a swingeing pain in her ankle reminded her that she couldn't. Cursing loudly, she turned to Rowley in frustration.

"Get up!" she hissed, pummeling his shoulder with her fists. "You have to get up. Now! You have to leave! You promised. You promised me! Remember?"

"God's teeth!" Rowley groaned, stirring reluctantly from a deep and pleasant sleep and wondering why it was with women that, however much you did their bidding and acquiesced to their every whim and command, you somehow always ended up wrong-footed and on the sharp end of their tongues? If he remembered correctly, and he thought he did, Adelia had been fine when he put her to bed last night; more than fine, in fact, once he'd soothed and wooed her—which, admittedly, had taken some doing; she was furious with him, after all—but he had won her round eventually and been rewarded with an act of love both tender and passionate; he certainly remembered that! And yet now, inexplicably, here they were again—the dawn not yet even broken properly—and her mood had turned full circle.

He sighed and stretched out a placatory hand.

"No time for that, Rowley!" she snapped, pushing it away. "Where's Allie?"

He groaned and turned over, and as he did so, the sheet

slipped off him, exposing the livid scar on his back that was both a symbol of his undying love for her and an eternal reproach.

"Oh, Rowley," she whispered softly, chastened by the sight, pulling him closer and pressing her lips into the puckered flesh. "I'm so sorry."

He opened an eye and, for a moment, considered exploiting her contrition; indeed, he might well have done so if, at that very moment, Allie's face hadn't appeared through the curtains.

"I'm ready," she said, glancing disapprovingly at her father, who obviously wasn't.

God's eyes! They were both against him this morning! He thought he'd resolved his differences with Allie last night, too, and had gone to great lengths to reconcile with her when she returned from her sulk. Indeed, if he remembered correctly, he had even agreed to let her go to the bloody Fens if she so pleased, and with his blessing. If he'd neglected to mention Lord Peverell—the discovery of whose existence had been the deciding factor—he refused to feel guilty about it . . . A little disingenuity—particularly when it came to matchmaking for obdurate daughters—was, he felt, forgivable under the circumstances.

Beside him Adelia's taut little body started bristling with efficiency as she reeled off a terrifying list of instructions punctuated every so often by either a lament about not being able to attend to Gyltha herself, or her increasing frustration with her "bloody" ankle . . .

"Now go back to the cottage," she told Allie, "and fetch my medicine bag . . . Make sure you pack at least one of those bottles of the marsh cudweed—it's on the right-hand shelf at the back, I think—oh, and, while you're at it, some of the comfrey concoction; knowing Gyltha it's probably her lungs that are bad and that'll help her breathe."

She paused for a moment, biting her lip.

"Oh! And when you get to Elsford, make sure nobody bleeds her! Her poor old blood's thin enough at the best of times, she can ill afford to lose any, especially in the winter . . . And, as soon as you can, get some watercress down her, and plenty of it."

When Allie left she turned once more to Rowley, her earlier contrition apparently forgotten.

"Now help me up," she said brusquely. "You ought to be going and I want to see you off."

T HE COURTYARD WAS ALREADY BUSY when they got there. Under Emma's direction, an army of grooms was hard at work saddling horses and loading large packs onto the sumpter ponies while various scullions, laden with provisions, dashed to and from the pantry. In the middle of it all Emma and Penda were arguing.

"We ain't going to need all this!" Penda had her hands clamped to the sides of her head in despair. "It'll slow us up. I can't be doing with it . . . I've told you . . ."

But it was clear to all the onlookers that in this encounter, Greek had met Greek. Emma refused to listen to her.

"'Delia! Thank God!" she cried, dashing over the cobbles toward her. "You have to do something! Please! . . . I simply don't understand how that woman can even think about traveling with so little. Look at the food she's refusing to take, and apart from that she has almost no retinue! Only two men-at-arms, as far as I can see . . . Not even a confessor!"

"Oh, Emma!" Adelia put a soothing hand on her arm. "They've got Rowley, darling! They won't need one." But she thought it best not to mention—for the sake of Emma's already ragged nerves—that he would probably only be accompanying them as far as London because he was expecting a summons, at any moment, to attend another assembly about the Longchamp business . . .

"But what about a lady's maid!" Emma wasn't assuaged. "Where's that Lena?"

Adelia shrugged. "It's no use," she said. "Allie won't take her. Besides, she doesn't travel well, and, actually, she'll be far more use here with me until my ankle improves . . . Don't worry so, darling . . . They'll be fine."

"Well, I hope you're right," Emma sniffed. "I really do! But I don't share your confidence."

EVEN ADELIA'S CONFIDENCE FALTERED WHEN they were mounted and she saw them through Emma's eyes. It would be hard to find a more ragged-looking bunch of tatterdemalions: Penda in her wolf pelts, a battered crossbow, of all things, slung across her back; Rowley in his shabby hunting garb—his ecclesiastical robes packed away; and Allie in a most unfortunate assembly of homespun. Her only consolation was that, looking the way they did, they were unlikely to attract the attention of any highway robbers who might be at large.

"God send you safe," she muttered under her breath as she limped over the cobbles to say her good-byes.

"Now, don't forget," she whispered when Rowley leaned down from his horse to kiss her, "that in spite of everything, and all your funny little ways, I love you dearly."

Then she turned to Allie.

"And don't you forget to send a messenger when you've arrived safely. And as soon as this damn ankle's better I'll join you."

Allie grinned. "I will," she said. "But don't worry. All will be well."

A moment later Penda picked up the reins and raised her arm, and they set off.

Adelia stood in the middle of the now-deserted courtyard watching them go, trying to remember when she had last felt quite so lonely.

"Indulgent nonsense," she muttered to herself, wiping her eyes with the back of her hand. She was about to head back into the house when Emma grabbed her arm and pointed tremulously at the large black crow following the riders into the forest.

"Look, 'Delia," she gasped. "It's a harbinger."

Adelia froze and, for a moment, felt her blood run cold.

"I don't believe in harbingers, Emma," she snapped, brushing her hand away. "I refuse to!" But as she limped back to the house chuntering irritably under her breath, she couldn't quite dispel an unaccustomed sense of foreboding.

CHAPTER 9

PENDA RODE LIKE A WOMAN possessed. The merciless pace reminded Rowley—and not pleasantly—of his days charging across England with Henry Plantagenet, who had been equally ruthless with his retinue, except that he had charm, whereas this woman did not, or certainly not as far as he could tell.

She was a very different creature this morning, he thought, studying her irritably from his place at the back of the caval-cade. All the charm and conciliation of yesterday were a distant memory now that she had gotten what she wanted. And that determined little mouth, which had been all smiles and moues until she had gotten her own way, was set firm now, like a small gash across her face.

With little else to think about, and to distract him from his buttocks—still aching from the day before—he had plenty of time to consider the person to whom he was about to entrust his daughter and was beginning to wonder whether he might have been a little rash.

That she was peculiar was obvious from the moment he clapped eyes on her, but it wasn't only her appearance he found outlandish. There was something disconcertingly unfeminine about both her deportment and her demeanor, and there were times when she was so unapologetically, almost deliberately masculine that he was shocked.

And yet, he had to admit, though grudgingly, that there was a good deal more to her than met the eye. She had surprised him more than once this morning, first by revealing—and most unusually for a woman of the Fens—that she understood and spoke perfect Norman French.

He had been having a discussion with Allie in French about the unusual route they were taking when Penda—who had spent most of the journey gabbling away to her men-at-arms in English, or at least the thick, impenetrable dialect that passed for English in the Fens—surprised him by interrupting.

"We're going this way!" she barked at them over her shoulder. "Because the bridge's down at Emm Brook. We got caught up there on the way over."

And there was something else:

When he had seen her climbing into her saddle with a crossbow, of all things, he assumed it was another of her sartorial eccentricities, a bit like those dreadful wolf pelts she wore, but as the day went on, and he saw how she handled the weapon, slipping it with the instinct and dexterity of a battle-hardened mercenary from her shoulder to the pommel of her saddle whenever they passed through outlaw terrain, he realized that, on the contrary, she was an arbalist of some skill. And since he had spent considerable time in the company of the breed, he knew one when he saw one.

So by the end of the morning, he had to concede that although not terribly likeable, she was intriguing, and at least she would indeed be able to protect Allie as she had promised. That was something in her favor at least.

Allie, on the other hand, seemed quite taken with her. He watched her heels nag at her palfrey's sides all morning, coaxing it to keep up with Penda's, chattering away like an old friend when it did . . . And yet, despite knowing it was churlish and feeling a little ashamed of himself, he found her affection for this peculiar stranger had the effect of putting him off the woman even more.

THEY STOPPED ONLY ONCE, AROUND noon, to rest their horses and help themselves to the provisions Emma had managed to smuggle past Penda. One of the men-at-arms lifted a large saddlebag off one of the sumpter ponies, from which he produced several flasks of ale, a large cheese, a ham, some smoked trout and four loaves of bread. As soon as it had been gratefully and greedily devoured, Penda—who appeared to have even less respect for the digestive process than Henry Plantagenet—gave the signal and they set off again!

She pushed them even harder after lunch, so that the discomfort of the morning bled, quite literally in Rowley's case, into an equally uncomfortable afternoon cantering down a succession of boggy tracks. His only solace was his earlier insistence that they spend that night with his old friends Lord and Lady Da Port at Chewton Manor, where they were certain to find good food and comfortable mattresses.

CHAPTER 10

"My LORD BISHOP!" THE GATEKEEPER at Chewton was delighted to see Rowley. "A pleasure to see you again, my lord! Welcome, welcome."

He doffed his cap and turned to a young man waiting in the shadows. "Quick as you please, Enulf, lad. Mustn't keep our lord bishop waiting!"

Moments later, the young man's shoulder hefted to the winch and the heavy apparatus of the portcullis lifted, admitting them to a vast outer bailey where several grooms were waiting to take their horses.

Just as Rowley had hoped, the Da Ports' hospitality was as prompt as it was lavish, and soon they were seated at a table in the hall, where a trout of biblical proportions, festooned with almonds, was laid out on a plate in front of him.

"Fresh from the pond this afternoon, Rowley, dear," Lady Alice told him, amused by his ill-concealed admiration of it. "It was a devil of a job crowning it by all accounts, but I knew you, of all people, would appreciate it."

It turned out to be such a convivial evening that Rowley

even began to thaw toward Penda. Now that he was no longer in any discomfort and his belly was full, she didn't seem quite so bad—and, during the musical interlude, he even felt generous enough to initiate a conversation.

"Lady Penda," he said, leaning across the table to her, "it seems to me that it is a rather strange business, and, I should add, a matter of some regret, that our paths have never crossed before. After all, Adelia and I—Allie, too, of course—have spent a great deal of time in the Fens with Gyltha over the years and yet we've never met."

If he'd expected gratitude for the overture, he didn't get it. Instead Penda looked at him long and hard above the rim of her cup, took a large swig of whatever it held and wiped her mouth indecorously with the back of her hand. Just as he was about to give up hope, she replied.

"Not so strange as you might think in actual fact, my lord. Gylth and I spent most of our lives apart from one another. We was separated when we was little an' it took a long time for me to find 'er again."

"Oh," said Rowley, disconcerted by the response and wondering how best to proceed, and, indeed, whether or not he wanted to, when a distant memory sputtered to life and the fragments of a story he had once heard returned . . .

"Oh," he said again.

For the life of him he couldn't remember the details, nor, indeed, whether he had heard it from Adelia or Gyltha herself, but he knew that it was an intrinsically sad tale, something to do with the Anarchy—that vicious war of accession between the empress Matilda and King Stephen, during which, according to those who had been unfortunate enough to have lived through it, God and his saints had slept.

"I see," he said, shifting uncomfortably, anxious to change the subject, when it suddenly occurred to him that he didn't have to, that Penda's attention had drifted through and beyond him as though into a distant nightmare from which she wouldn't return for a while.

CHAPTER 11

THE NEXT MORNING, WHEN THEY had assembled in the bailey, ready to leave, a messenger arrived with a letter for Rowley bearing the Count of Mortain's seal.

"What does it say?" Allie asked, alarmed by his expression of trepidation when he received it.

"How should I know? I haven't had a chance to read it yet," Rowley replied, spinning away from her for privacy, his eyes rapidly scanning the parchment: "Bugger! Just as I thought."

"Well?" she asked impatiently, standing on tiptoe, trying to read it over his shoulder.

Rowley sighed and turned around reluctantly to read it out. "It says: 'Our best-beloved Rowley, Bishop of St. Albans, greetings from John, Count of Mortain, Lord of Ireland—'"

"Yes, yes," she snapped. "I got that bit, I think I know who it's from! I want to know what it says!"

He took a deep breath and returned to the parchment. "Well . . . ," he continued. "It says: 'Tell your impertinent, infernally impatient daughter to keep her pretty nose out of other people's business . . .'"

"That's not funny." Allie scowled.

"I thought it was," said Rowley. "But, very well, if you insist . . . What it actually says is . . . Oh, God's teeth! I haven't got time to read the bloody thing again . . . It's the summons I've been expecting . . . to go to St. Paul's—the council I told you about for the wretched Longchamp business—and it means that I can't come to the Fens . . . or, not immediately, anyway."

Although Allie didn't say anything, he was pleased to see that she looked disappointed. Perhaps she was going to miss him after all.

"Come along!"

Penda had already mounted and was impatient to leave, and as soon as they were aboard their horses, she set off at a trot toward the gatehouse, only this time Rowley made sure that he rode beside her. Now that he was leaving, there were certain things he wanted to establish.

"Not to put too fine a point on it, Lady Penda," he said, "but you will promise to guard my daughter with your life, won't you?"

She nodded. "I will indeed," she said. "No need to worry on that count, my lord; ain't nothing going to happen to her while she's in my care."

"Thank you," he said, and they rode in silence for a while until he remembered something else.

"And that other business," he said, glancing nervously over his shoulder to make sure Allie wasn't in earshot; he still felt guilty about the subterfuge. "This, erm, this introduction to Lord . . . er . . . whatshisname . . . the fellow you mentioned at Wolvercote. You will endeavor to make it as you promised, won't you?"

Penda glanced sideways at him with, he thought, a rather sardonic look in her eye. "If that's what you want," she said. "After all, what is it they say? 'Better to marry than to burn.' Ain't that right?"

She was smiling as she said it and perhaps hadn't intended the barb, but it struck him nonetheless, stinging him into silence for a while.

Of course, he wanted Allie married off—as any father would—and although the alternative terrified him and he didn't want to countenance it, he refused to believe it extended to the fires of hell and bitterly resented her implication that he might.

"And you, madam?" he asked when he recovered. "You are married, I presume?" After all, she must have been. She was in possession of a title that could only have been conferred by marriage.

To his surprise, though, she shook her head. "Nope," she said.

"Widowed then?"

Again she shook her head, and to his even greater surprise, she started laughing. "Nope," she repeated, shoulders shaking with mirth. "Never married. Never wanted to and . . . now, you'd best hold tight to them reins of yours, my lord, 'cause this'll come as a terrible shock . . ." She was so convulsed at this point that she almost fell off her horse. "Ain't never been asked neither!"

Clutching her sides, bent double over her horse's neck, she was laughing so infectiously that, despite himself, Rowley started laughing, too.

"Well, well, madam," he said, thrusting his arm out to grab the reins she had dropped. "That is indeed a shock, and, if I may say so, enough to make one weep for whatever it is that ails the eyesight of the men of England!"

From the back of the cavalcade Allie looked on, bemused. She was pleased to see them enjoying one another's company at last but couldn't imagine what on earth had caused them such amusement.

CHAPTER 12

The Fens

WE'LL CROWN A FEW JACKS today, won't we, Arthur?" Tom looked up reverently at the boy beside him, who, a few months older and substantially taller than his peers, commanded a certain respect in the hierarchy of boys, especially on fishing expeditions like these, because he also possessed the water wisdom of an otter.

"Shh!" Arthur cowed him with a look, his finger pressed to his lips.

He had taken them on a shortcut through the abbey gardens and was anxious not to attract the attention of the monks, who disapproved of trespassers.

"Hurry," he hissed at Will, the third member of the party, who, as usual, was lagging behind, making heavy weather of the dead heron he was dragging, complaining bitterly about it under his breath:

It wasn't fair! He hadn't wanted to bring the bloody thing

and didn't see why it was he who had to carry it, but Arthur had insisted, thanks to some stupid idea about heron fat being magic and rubbing some on your line meant you'd catch more fish. Well, they'd have to catch a lot of bloody fish to make up for this! Bloody herons!

"Come on!" Ignoring Will's chuntering, Arthur grabbed Tom's puny wrist, pulling him past the dreaded kitchen garden latrines that the monks had dug to enrich their vegetables. The *odeur de merde* emanating from them was almost overwhelming, and because it haunted the boys' olfactory memories from previous visits, they had all been holding their noses for longer than was good for them . . .

"Is it safe yet, Arthur?" Tom asked, pinching his nostrils so tightly that his voice sounded stuffy and peculiar.

Arthur let go of his and gave a cautious sniff, then immediately clapped his hand over his face again.

"Bit longer yet," he said.

They scurried on, holding their breath and noses as though their lives depended on it until they were safely through the gardens and out into the meadow.

"Phew!" Tom gasped, bent double, small hands clutching his knees, as he greedily gulped down the fresh air.

Arthur did the same. "Tha's better," he said, standing upright again.

"'S'all right for you." Will had caught up by now and was glaring morosely at the dead bird at his feet. "This thing stinks worse than them latrines."

"Give it here." Arthur snatched the string out of his hand.

"I'll take it. And I won't make such a fuss neither. Here . . . ," he said, shoving the eel glaive he'd been carrying at him instead. "You can carry this. Can't 'spect me to do everythin'." Then he spat contemptuously into the grass and set off again, complaining bitterly to himself about ingratitude, the nature of responsibility and the burden of leadership, and wondering where they would be without him: lost, most likely, in the great forests of rush and sedge, and even if, by some miracle, they were able to find their way on their own—which he very much doubted—without his superior knowledge to guide them through the secret pathways of the marsh they'd drown in the bogs that lurked there, deep enough to suck in a horse and rider, let alone two stupid little boys.

All that and they expected him to carry the equipment, too!

"Come on, you lazy pillards," he called back over his shoulder. "I ain't telling you again!"

He wouldn't, either. He was too tired for patience this morning. Last night he had slept badly, plagued by the nightmares Cousin Hawise's story had inspired, so if they didn't hurry up he would leave 'em where they stood, and sure as eggs were eggs, they'd probably never get found again. Besides, it was a long time since they had come this way, and in their absence, the cold had crept in like a thief, stripping the place of its foliage and altering the landscape entirely so that the naked willow and alder branches stuck out at harsh, unfamiliar angles and made it look like a foreign land.

For a moment even he was confused. He stopped briefly to get his bearings just as a wavering, soughing bank of birds half a mile long swept in from the North Sea.

He looked up at the sky and saw the rheumy outline of the moon, pale and milky like an old man's eye . . . Like God's eye!

The idea that God himself might even now be fixing on him like a hawk on a mouse made him shiver beneath his heavy sheepskin mantle and hurry on toward the river.

CHAPTER 13

BROTHER GILBERT, RAMSEY ABBEY'S INFIRMARIAN, was equally suspicious of the moon that morning and was staring at it ruefully through the solar window at Elsford Manor.

He wished it weren't there, or, more precisely, that it weren't, in fact, a fourth-day moon and that he could obey his usually impeccable instincts and bleed the patient lying close to death in the bed behind him.

It was his third visit to Elsford Manor in as many days, but the old woman's condition defied him; nothing he had administered so far had reduced her fever or alleviated her symptoms, which meant that bleeding was the only option left. The trouble was that on a day as inauspicious as a fourth moon, it was deemed too dangerous.

He put away the lancet he had been sharpening before he saw the moon and turned back to the room.

He looked out onto a large chamber. Its newly whitewashed walls, ornate tapestries and elegantly carved ceiling spoke of prosperity and announced to all who entered that the lady Penda had done well for herself: sheep farming, someone had told him—and judging by the number of long-legged, black-faced beasts chomping in the numerous wattle pens he had passed on his way in, they were probably right.

His patient was lying in a large wooden bed whose heavy linen curtains were tied back to their posts to allow her exposure to the efficacious fresh air. Not that she seemed to be benefiting from it, mind; she was so deathly pale, almost the color of the sheets she was lying in, and so terribly still. In fact the only sign of life in her this morning was the slight movement of her parched lips, mouthing, every now and then, some silent incantation, or death agony perhaps.

Brother Gilbert shook his head sadly; it wouldn't be too much longer now . . .

Speaking in a low voice, reciting soothing passages from the Gospel of St. John, he picked up his chrismatory box and approached the bed, ready to perform the viaticum when the time came. But when he knelt down beside the bed she murmured something he couldn't quite catch . . .

He stood up, motioning to her family, who were huddled anxiously in the middle of the room and whose unstinting care had, more than once, brought a lump to his throat. She might have been dying, he thought, but she wouldn't die unloved, and certainly not alone, which must have been some comfort at least.

"She speaks," he mouthed as they hurried over.

Ulf knelt beside his grandmother while the others formed a semicircle around him.

"You say something, Gylth?" he asked her softly. "You need summat? Only got to ask. Anything . . . You know that."

Gyltha opened her mouth to speak but her voice was so

faint that he was forced to press his ear almost to her lips to hear it.

The others exchanged anxious glances, bending like saplings in a breeze toward the bed, silent tears dripping onto the top of their boots as they waited to hear her dying words.

They saw her open her eyes and held their breath.

"I said . . ." The faint whisper was audible only to Ulf. "That lad . . ." She gasped, struggling to raise her arm to point toward Brother Gilbert. "Nice boy . . . I'm sure . . . but, oh, Ulf, the bugger's got breath like a basilisk, so 'less you want to finish me off . . ."

Partly out of sympathy for Brother Gilbert and partly because he was laughing so much, it was some time before Ulf could impart the words—which, fortunately, turned out not to be his grandmother's last—to the others.

CHAPTER 14

SITTING ON A WIND-FALLEN ALDER branch gazing out over the river, waiting for the fish to bite, Arthur felt his thoughts drifting to his great-grandmother.

He knew that today might very well be "the day"—as everyone referred to it—and although he fervently hoped it wasn't, he was equally adamant that he didn't want to be at the bedside if it was. But, this morning, when he had put his foot down and refused to go to the manor with the rest of them, his mother had taken it very badly.

"Oh, let 'im be, Ed!" His father's intervention, when she started shouting at him, came as a welcome surprise. "Let 'im go fishin' if tha's what 'e wants. It'll be good for 'im . . . Besides, Gylth won't know the difference and we'll need summat for supper when we get back." It was a rare day that Robert Atewod plucked up the courage to gainsay his wife, and Arthur was extremely grateful that it was this one.

Besides, he had seen Gyltha recently and had stood dutifully at the foot of her bed with the others, for what felt like an age, gazing at her insentient form.

But he hadn't liked it. The body in the bed hadn't looked like her, all desiccated and pathetic, and the experience had reminded him, most unpleasantly, of the time he was taken to St. Etheldreda's shrine at Ely.

Everybody went to see St. Etheldreda at some point in their life, apparently—although he couldn't understand why—and her jeweled shrine in the eastern arm of the cathedral was an object of veneration and a source of great income for the priory. In the spring and summer Ely was awash with pilgrims, who descended like starlings, cartfuls of them clattering noisily over the causeway and splashing through the swamps in their overloaded boats to pay homage to her. So she must have had something. But standing in the cathedral that day, staring at a collection of old bones in a casket, Arthur had been overwhelmed by the cloying atmosphere of death: the incense and the damp stone and the disembodied incantations of the monks had flooded his senses in a suffocating wave, and he had felt the same sensation gazing at the living corpse of his great-grandmother.

Besides, as with St. Etheldreda, he doubted very much that Gyltha was even aware of his presence, nor, for the life of him, could he see what good staring at her was going to do. Nevertheless he had done it, even as he resolved never to repeat the experience, and besides, if she was going to die, he wanted to remember her the way she had been, corpulent, vibrant, funny and alive, not a sapless old stick in a bed.

He glanced up at the sky again, wondering whether God was still watching, relieved to see that the outline of the moon had vanished for the day.

A little while later, he got up from his log, tied his fishing line to a nearby fallen alder branch and went to join Will at the water's edge.

"Pass us that glaive, would you?" he asked him. "Gonna see if'n I can crown us a jack or two."

On the other side of the river he watched a group of men and women wade across the marsh on stilts, dipping like herons every so often as they scoured the lodes and drains of the reeds and rushes that would otherwise choke them. During the autumn and winter water poured in ceaselessly from the uplands, so that without drainage and the rapt attention of every Fenlander, the marsh would revert to a quagmire, the meadow to a marsh, and the world would sink under its weight. So there was barely a section of stream, lode, or riverbank for whose repair somebody wasn't personally responsible, and often on pain of death.

Indeed, Arthur was still having nightmares about another of Hawise's stories, the one about the former abbot of Ramsey, an ill-tempered old boy by all accounts, who, when he discovered a hole in an earthen dam one day, hanged the tenant he deemed responsible and used the poor fellow's corpse to make the repair.

"And sometimes at night," Hawise had told them, her voice dropping to a whisper, the way it did when she was trying to frighten them, "when the wind's in the right direction you can still hear the dead man's moans."

Arthur shivered—he couldn't help it—and put his fingers in his ears, just in case.

———

THE HOURS PASSED SWIFTLY, AS they always did by the river, and before they knew it the abbey bells were sounding for nones.

"Ought to be getting back then, I s'pose," Will said, looking up with a satisfied grin from his bucket brimming with fish. Arthur nodded and began to pack up his things. Only Tom was reluctant to leave.

"Can't we stay a bit longer?" he pleaded. "Just a bit."

Poor Tom. His was the poorest catch, and yet he had promised his mother a pike or two for supper, and because Arthur was acutely sensitive to the effects of maternal disappointment, especially today, he took pity on him.

"All right then," he said, ignoring Will's groan of dissent. "We'll stay a bit longer . . . but you'd best get on with it, we ain't waitin' forever . . ."

It was a bitter irony, the first in his short life, that a decision born from kindness was one he would regret for the rest of it. Because, as it turned out, if he hadn't agreed to wait for Tom, they would have been long gone by the time the wind blew in from the North Sea, disturbing Martha's watery grave and sending her body bobbing over the choppy waters toward them.

CHAPTER 15

ALLIE FOUND IT HARDER TO part from Rowley than she had expected but, because she was still angry with him, refused to show it. Nevertheless, when they reached the outskirts of London and she watched him ride off, she was surprised at how sad she felt. It wasn't as though she wasn't used to long separations from him, from both parents, in fact—her childhood had been littered with them—but in the past there had always been Gyltha to comfort and protect her. Now, all of a sudden, she was completely alone.

They spent that night at Rowley's manor in St. Albans and at the crack of dawn the next morning set off on the final leg of their journey, moving briskly through the gently undulating Hertfordshire countryside and flat monotony of the Cambridgeshire plains until, eventually, they came to the point where the land surrendered to the vast sea of horizons and endless sky of the Fens.

They left the horses on the uplands and waded through the marsh on foot, arriving, eventually, at a small landing stage on the river, where a boat was waiting for them. Through the rushes Allie could just make out the figure of a man hunched in the middle of it, puffed up against the cold like a pigeon, his coif pulled low over his face, the fingers of a heavily gloved hand tapping his knee. At the same time Penda spotted him, too, and, motioning for her to keep quiet, crept over the wooden boards of the quay to the water's edge. When she was directly above him, she put the thumb and forefinger of her left hand into the corners of her mouth and gave a loud, shrill whistle.

The man spun around in alarm, his twisting bulk rocking the boat dangerously, and Allie gave a squeal of delight.

"Ulf!"

As soon as he saw her Ulf leapt out of the boat, took her in his arms and spun her around.

"What a surprise! What a lovely surprise!" he said when he put her down at last. "And the mistress?" he asked, peering over her shoulder as though Adelia might be hiding in the reeds somewhere.

Allie's heart sank. She should have expected this, should have known he would be disappointed that it was her and not Adelia who had come to their aid; after all, the last time he'd clapped eyes on her she was only a child, hardly a fitting substitute for his beloved mistress.

She blushed, a combination of guilt and shame at her hubris.

"Oh, Ulf, she is coming," she said. "It's just that she hurt her ankle badly, you see, and can't travel, but she'll be here as soon as she can. I promise."

But if Ulf was disappointed he had the grace not to show

it—another reason in a long litany of them why she loved him. Instead, and perhaps sensing her mortification, he crooked his finger under her chin and lifted it.

"Never you mind," he said as he picked her up and put her into the boat beside Penda. "You'll do. Chip off the old block, you are, if I remember right." Then he climbed in, took his place at the oars and set off along the King's Delph, to Elsford.

A COMBINATION OF THE EARLY start and the boat's rhythm had a soporific effect, and before long, despite the cold, Allie was curled up on the bench beside Penda, fast asleep.

"She up to it then, d'you think?" Penda asked Ulf when she was sure Allie couldn't overhear.

"Aye." Ulf nodded. "She'll do right enough. Got her mother's blood in her veins, that one, same instinct for healing, allus did, even as a baby."

Penda looked down at the recumbent Allie, took off her mantle and draped it over her.

"And Gylth?" she asked, tucking her pelt neatly around her. "Still with us, I trust? I ain't dragged this poor girl all the way here for nothing, then?"

"No." Ulf rested the oars for a moment and crossed himself. "No you ain't. Still 'ere, thank God, but . . ." He shook his head. "I tell you, Pen, these is strange times right enough, and Gyltha or no Gyltha, it makes me worry if we've done the right thing bringing her here . . ."

Penda looked up. Something in his tone disturbed her, and

when he was reluctant to elaborate, she left her place beside Allie and climbed onto the bench beside him.

"What?" she asked, searching his face. "What d'you mean?"

He turned to her.

"We found Martha," he said.

A S VILLAGE REEVE, AND ARTHUR'S uncle, Ulf was who the boys ran to when they found the body.

"It were dreadful, Pen," Ulf said, shaking his head as though that could expel the memory. "I've seen plenty o' death in my time, natural and unnatural, taken more corpses off gibbets and pulled more bodies outta bogs than I care to remember, but I ain't seen nothin' like that, not even in the old days with the mistress . . . It weren't—" He broke off, his voice cracking with emotion. "It weren't natural, Pen." And he turned to her with an expression of such torment that it made her blood run cold.

For a moment neither of them spoke, the only sounds the cloop of the moorhens as they headed to their nests for the evening and the gentle splash of his oars dipping in the water.

"What d'you mean not 'natural'?" Penda asked. "Drownin', weren't it? Not the first, poor little bugger."

But he shook his head. "That's just it, Pen," he said. "It didn't look like any drownin' I ever seen . . . Didn't look like she'd been in that water very long, for one, certainly not as long as she'd been missin', and . . ." He turned to her again, and again she saw that haunted look. "There was somethin' else . . ." He broke off, glancing at Allie over his shoulder. "There's another girl gone missin', too. An' reports of another one washed up dead at Manea . . . I tell you, Pen, it's the devil at work again."

Again . . .

Penda froze, the embers of an ancient memory stirring to life, and closed her eyes, trying to suppress it. But it was no good. No matter how long nor how hard she tried to forget, she had seen the devil's work with her own eyes and never could.

Then she, too, glanced back at Allie and, relieved to see she was still asleep, clenched her fist and raised it to the heavens.

"God keep you safe, girl," she hissed under her breath. "Or 'e'll 'ave me to answer to."

CHAPTER 16

IT WAS DARK BY THE time the boat bumped up against the moorings at Elsford, jolting Allie awake.

Though still sleepy, with Ulf's arm, she was able to stagger up the steep slope of the riverbank onto the towpath without incident.

Penda lit a lantern and led the way down a meandering track through the marsh that led, eventually, into a long avenue of yew trees at the end of which a disembodied flame was darting this way and that like a will-o'-the-wisp. As they got closer Allie could see that it was, in fact, a brand that a small person was carrying, pacing up and down outside the entrance to a manor house . . .

"This is Hawise," Penda said, introducing the peripatetic beacon, who, it turned out, was a girl. "Ulf's daughter." Then, turning to the girl: "And this here's Allie. Mistress's daughter."

The girl grinned and curtsied low, giggling at the loud rustling her straw-stuffed petticoats made as they brushed on the ground.

Allie stared at her blankly, sleepy disorientation rendering her mute for the time being. Only a moment ago, it seemed, she had been fast asleep in a boat, and suddenly here she was, another world away in Elsford. She was midyawn when Penda took her arm and marshaled her up a short flight of stone steps to a heavily carved entrance door.

"Welcome to Elsford," she said, pushing it open and ushering her into a hall where she was confronted with a staircase that appeared to have ambitions for heaven. "Come," Penda said, setting off up it.

It was a long, hard climb on such tired legs, but eventually, they stopped at a landing and another door, which opened, as if by magic, onto a brightly lit room where two women were waiting.

Allie stood on the threshold, overcome by fatigue, blinking into the unexpected light and the gaze of the strangers, until Ulf took her arm from Penda and guided her into the room.

"This is Rosa, my wife," he said, embracing the elder of the two women. "And that's Jodi, Penda's maid . . . Long-suffering, the both of 'em, as you can imagine," he added, grinning.

The women smiled and curtsied but Allie barely noticed them, because she was already looking beyond them, at the tiny figure—little more than a wrinkle in a blanket—lying in the bed behind them.

"Gyltha!" she cried, tears of joy, relief and fatigue spouting from her eyes as she ran to her. "Darling, darling Gyltha!"

She dropped to her knees at the bedside, clasping the frail hand that had crept out from under the covers and pressing it gratefully to her lips as she wept some more.

"There, there," said Gyltha, stroking her hair with her one dry hand. "There, there, me old darlin'. There, there."

They stayed like that for a while, weeping together and murmuring to one another, until, with a loud sniff, Gyltha withdrew her hand and pointed accusingly at Penda.

"And you!" she hissed. "I told you not to go buggerin' about, draggin' 'em all this way! Got better things to do with their time than fussin' round old women. You should be ashamed o' yourself."

Although the rebuke was harsh, Allie felt it augured well and implied that, despite her obvious physical frailty, Gyltha had lost none of her spark; on the other hand, Penda looked so hurt that she felt compelled to intervene on her behalf.

"Gyltha, that's terribly unfair," she said, sitting up and wiping her eyes. "You must know how worried we've all been, Penda especially, and if you thought for one moment that I wouldn't come when you needed me . . . well . . . you've got another think coming. Besides, it's too late anyway, I'm here now, and as soon as she's better, Ma will be, too, so you'll just have to put up with it, I'm afraid."

Gyltha ignored the admonishment but not the mention of Adelia. "What d'you mean 'as soon as she's better'?" she asked, struggling to sit upright. "What's happened to 'er?"

Allie sat on the bed beside her and explained about the accident.

"It's nothing to worry about," she said when Gyltha still looked concerned. "She is coming, I promise."

When, at last, she had managed to convince her that there was nothing seriously wrong with Adelia, Allie started unpacking her medicine bag.

"I'm going to examine you now," she said, arranging the

contents neatly on a table Ulf had dragged to the bedside. "So open your mouth and don't argue."

When she had finished and was satisfied that, for tonight at least, her patient wasn't in any imminent danger—that there was no discernible pestilence of her tonsils or swelling of her throat—she gave her a vial of the comfrey concoction Adelia had prepared to help Gyltha sleep and sat quietly beside her until she did. When at last she saw her eyelids flutter and her breathing become rhythmic, she stood up.

"She'll live then, d'you think?"

Ulf's voice startled her. She had been so absorbed by Gyltha that she had forgotten all about the others waiting so patiently for her prognosis.

"Oh, Ulf, I'm sorry," she said. "Yes, I do, as a matter of fact. There's no sign of any fever now, thank God, but she is weak and her blood is terribly thin, so tomorrow—if someone will show me where I might find some—I'll get her some watercress; it'll build her strength. In the meantime I think we should all get some rest."

Ulf took her hand and raised it to his lips, then put his arms around Rosa and Hawise and ushered them toward the door.

Just before he left she overheard him tell Penda:

"See! Just like I said, chip off the old block, that one."

CHAPTER 17

WHEN ALLIE WOKE THE NEXT morning she lay for a while gazing drowsily around the room, absorbing her new surroundings.

She had been so tired by the time she eventually climbed into the bed that was laid out for her on the floor beside Gyltha's that she could have fallen asleep anywhere—any lumpy old mattress would have done—but instead, she had found herself slipping into a set of freshly laundered, lavender-scented sheets on an amply filled palliasse.

That night she dreamed about Mansur.

Although he was never far from her thoughts, his absence was always thrown into sharp relief whenever she saw Gyltha, who was the great love of his life, just as he was hers.

It was a strange union, he, a eunuch—castrated as a boy by the Latin church to preserve the beauty of his singing voice—and she a Fenland eel seller, but an inspiration nonetheless, and if there was ever any doubt about how complete a union it was, Gyltha gave that short shrift.

"I know what you're thinking," she would say if anyone

were to raise an eyebrow. "But just because some bits is missin' don't mean the rest don't work like a charm."

Allie suspected that, if he hadn't met and fallen in love with Gyltha, in old age he might have been tempted back to the warmer climes of Salerno, but such was his devotion that when she returned to the Fens, he chose to go with her, to eventually die in her arms.

Gyltha!

God's teeth! Just for a moment she had forgotten why she was there.

She sat up abruptly, poked her head above the bed and, satisfied that her patient was still breathing in and out, flopped back onto her pillows again.

A little while later, as she was gazing drowsily at one of the tapestries on the wall, a pretty, richly woven pattern of birds and griffins in roundels, she heard a knock on the door.

"Come in," she said, sitting up, hastily pulling the blankets up to her neck.

The door opened and a face appeared around it.

"Hawise . . . in case you've forgotten," it announced cheerfully. "Come to take you to fetch the watercress like you asked, mistress . . . if you're ready, that is . . ."

"Thank you," Allie replied. "I am . . . or I will be, if you don't mind giving me a moment."

Hawise grinned, curtsied and disappeared.

B Y THE TIME ALLIE WAS washed and dressed, Gyltha was awake.

"Well, well, Almeison," she said, gazing up at her fondly. "So I didn't dream it, then? 'Tis really you, is it, bor?"

Allie sat beside her. "Of course it is!" she said. "You didn't think I wouldn't come when you needed me, did you?"

Gyltha shook her head and smiled. "No. I suppose not. And I 'ave to admit it's done me a power of good just lookin' at you." She put her hand on Allie's knee and squeezed it.

"And you're feeling better?" Allie asked.

"Yes," said Gyltha. "But you shouldn't 'ave come, I can't help wishin' that meddlin' old bugger hadn't sent for you."

Allie was about to leap to Penda's defense once again when she saw, from Gyltha's expression, that her outburst was prompted by more than simple irritation.

"What is it?" she asked, concerned by the sudden change in her mood and the look of fear on her face.

"I'd 'ave stopped her if I'd known," Gyltha hissed, fixing her eyes on her with unnerving intensity as she struggled to sit upright. "It ain't safe for you here no more. I don't want you here . . . Not now."

Allie started to wonder if she had missed something crucial during her examination, if perhaps Gyltha's brain had been corrupted by the fever, but when she reached for the talisman of her medicine bag Gyltha stopped her.

"Listen to me," she said, grabbing her wrist and pulling her close. "You must leave here, for your own sake. Never mind about me . . . Never mind about anyone . . . You tell Penda—"

"Tell Penda what?" said a voice from the doorway. "Mistress Allie isn't going anywhere." Hawise strode across the floor toward them. "Except to come with me now and fetch that watercress for you."

She winked at Allie.

"You rest now," she told Gyltha. "And don't go filling Mistress Allie's head with nonsense."

When Gyltha's eyes flashed and she opened her mouth to protest, Allie braced herself for the impending storm . . . which, to her enormous surprise, didn't come. Instead Gyltha closed her mouth again and looked away sheepishly.

It was extraordinary. She had never seen Gyltha cowed before and started to recalibrate her opinion of Hawise, whom, last night, she had dismissed as a rather silly giggler of a girl. But in the light of the effect she had just had on Gyltha, Allie recognized a steeliness at her core that was deserving of respect.

"Come, mistress," Hawise said cheerfully. "Best be getting along now."

When the door closed behind them, Gyltha sank back on her pillows.

Even in the depths of her delirium, she had heard them, huddled around her bed, talking about the missing girls and fetching the mistress for her in the same breath. They must have thought that the fever had dimmed her wits, that she was half-dead, the way she looked to them, not realizing that while there was still a breath left in her body they would never be dimmed enough not to spark at the mention of Adelia . . . or Allie.

Oh, she would have stopped them if she could, fought them tooth and nail to stop them dragging her beloveds into danger, but it was too late. What was done was done, and for the time being, at least, there was nothing she could do except, of course, worry herself to death.

HAWISE CHATTERED ALL THE WAY to the hall, so that Allie struggled to get a word in edgewise despite the fact that she was dying to ask her about her exchange with Gyltha. At first she put the loquacity down to nerves, but as time and the chattering wore on, she grew suspicious that it was more a tactic of diversion.

Ulf grinned when he saw them come into the room.

"Mornin', Allie," he said, his voice booming cheerfully across the room. "Slept well, I trust."

He and Penda were sitting at a table on the dais, on either side of a rather dour-looking young man who didn't look up from the ledger he was poring over.

"Likely she did," Penda said. "And long, too. Weren't them the terce bells just chimed? Well?" She crooked a finger at them. "Don't just stand there, come up 'ere and Jodi'll fetch your breakfast . . ." Then, turning to the young man—whom she later introduced as Sir Stephen, her steward—she demanded that he draw up a couple of stools for them.

While the girls ate, the meeting continued. From what little Allie could glean of it, it was a fairly dull affair: the weekly manorial tally of who owed what to whom, with Sir Stephen reading out a long roster of names and their associated expenses.

"Bart the dairyman, six pence a week and a seat at the hall table at Michaelmas," he intoned. "Pampi the shepherd, ten pence a week and four ells of cloth at Christmas."

And so on and so on, his ponderous finger working its way down a seemingly endless list. The only interesting part, as far as Allie was concerned, was the opportunity to observe Penda in her role as lady of the manor.

It was an incongruity she had only recently started thinking about. When they were first introduced she had assumed that Penda's title and estate had been conferred on her by marriage—after all, Gyltha was as poor and lowly as a church mouse—but so far, there didn't appear to be a husband, nor indeed any mention of one.

She took advantage of one of Hawise's rare pauses for breath and asked her about it.

"Oh, she didn't marry it," Hawise replied. "She was given it. She saved someone's life during the Anarchy and got given the house and title out of gratitude."

"Who?" Allie asked.

Hawise shrugged. "I'm not entirely sure . . . A little boy I think." Now that the conversation was no longer under her control, her attention had automatically diverted to her breakfast with equal zeal.

"A little boy conferred the house and title?" It seemed unlikely, but Allie persisted . . .

"No." Hawise grinned. "It was the boy whose life she saved. It was his mother, or someone like that, who gave Penda the estate . . . At least I think so . . ."

Unable to understand such a dereliction of curiosity, Allie decided to ask Gyltha when she saw her next and, failing that, decided she might even pluck up the courage to ask Penda herself.

But as though she had read her mind, Hawise added quickly,

"But I wouldn't go asking Penda, or Gyltha for that matter, if I were you, mistress. They don't like talking about the past and they won't thank you for it."

While Hawise returned to her breakfast, Allie turned to Penda, someone else she found herself reviewing this morning. She even looked different today; divested of her usual chaotic bundle of furs and pelts, she was dressed almost elegantly in a robe of scarlet worsted. She was also wearing a wimple, which, Allie realized, was a concession less to femininity than to business, which she took very seriously indeed: observing her conducting the meeting, Allie could tell that she had instant recall of every acre of plow land, the size of every herd and the extent of every grazing she held; knew by heart which of her tenants were free and which villeins; knew who owed what service to whom and how much rent they had to pay; and leapt on any discrepancy ruthlessly.

"What's this?" she snapped when she came across one. "Well?" she prompted when Sir Stephen was slow to respond.

Allie saw him color as he squinted down at his ledger as though his life depended on it.

"It's my eyes, madam," he said. "Ah yes! Now I see . . . It's . . . er . . . Bertha, madam."

"Bertha the laundress. What about 'er?"

"Well . . . erm . . . Well . . . It says here that she is to receive a penny a day, a pair of shoes at Easter and a cottage near the gatehouse, provided that her husband plows the north field."

"Exactly!" Penda stabbed her finger onto the parchment in triumph. "'Provided her husband plows the north field' . . . But 'e didn't, did 'e? Pampi done it this year, saw 'im wi' me own eyes. So, what was that idle bloody husband of 'ers doin', then?"

Sir Stephen shifted uncomfortably on his stool and looked so nervous that Allie, who had taken an instant dislike to him, began to feel sorry for him instead.

"I believe he was injured in the Lammas Day football game, madam," he replied, recoiling when she started making growling noises in the back of her throat.

"And I'm still payin' 'em and housin' 'em, am I? Ought to kick the lazy buggers out on their arses . . ."

"But she's a good laundress and she's pregnant," said Sir Stephen in such a plaintive tone that it made Allie wonder whether he was a good deal more sensitive than she had first assumed or the paternity of the laundress's unborn baby was in question. "And the husband's leg will mend—or so they tell me . . ."

Despite her earlier reservation, Allie was beginning to find the machinations of Elsford fascinating and would happily have stayed to hear more if, at that moment, Hawise hadn't scraped back her stool and announced that they ought to be setting off.

She followed her out of the hall along a covered walkway and past a kitchen—where a vast oven belched out hot air amid the lively invective of some invisible cooks and scullions—and beyond that to a door that opened onto a courtyard.

It was a bright and chilly day, and as soon as she set foot outside, she felt a breeze tugging on her veil like a bully, making her curse—and not for the first time—the inconvenience of having to wear a wimple.

It was an encumbrance foisted on her by her father comparatively recently—being, or so he said, more appropriate to her age and situation nowadays. Allie had resented the imposition from the first and felt pangs of envy for Hawise, whose own chestnut curls were restrained by a simple circlet and two braids on either side of her pretty face.

Muttering irritably, she tucked the flapping ends into the neck of her cloak and looked around.

Now that she could see it properly, she realized that Penda was meticulous about more than just the accounting. From the neatly swept cobbles to the well-maintained outbuildings, there was no sign of the gimcrack shambles of other, less orderly establishments here. If it didn't quite possess the grandeur and elegance of Wolvercote, it was at least equally utilitarian—and neat.

On the left-hand side were a storehouse, a barn and a stable block; on the right, a small wooden barbican, a laundry and a sturdy-looking gatehouse, in front of which Hawise was waiting for her.

"We have to wait here a moment," Hawise said. "We're not supposed to go out alone, not after Martha—" And, to Allie's astonishment, Hawise suddenly clapped her hand over her mouth and spun away from her, muttering furiously under her breath.

Allie stared at her uncomprehendingly; admittedly, she barely knew the girl, but there was no doubt about it, her behavior was distinctly odd, and there was something else . . . She had the disquieting feeling that there was something going on and there were things she wasn't being told, which, for someone who always wanted to know everything, was frustrating, to say the least.

Resisting the urge to take Hawise by her shoulders and insist that she tell her whatever it was she was concealing, she took a deep breath instead.

"Hawise," she said, addressing the back of Hawise's head and trying hard not to sound irritable, "who is Martha?" It seemed to take an age, but at last, Hawise turned around, muttering something inaudible through her hand.

"Well?" Allie prompted sharply.

Hawise took her hand away reluctantly. "Oh, very well," she sighed. "I'll tell you, because I think you should know, but if I do, you must promise not to let on to Father or Penda, or anyone else, that I did . . . I'm not supposed to talk about it."

Allie nodded emphatically. "On my oath," she said.

"Well . . ." She looked around them furtively and lowered her voice even though the courtyard was deserted. "Well, you see . . . Martha was the girl whose body Father pulled out of the river the day before yesterday . . . Everybody thinks she drowned . . . except for Father."

"Oh," Allie said, trying not to sound as excited as she felt. "What does he think happened to her then?"

Hawise leaned forward conspiratorially and said in a whisper, "He thinks she was murdered like the others . . ." She was about to elaborate, Allie could feel it, when a young man carrying a falcon appeared in front of them and she broke off abruptly.

"Peter!" she cried with palpable relief at this timely intervention. "Peter. This is Mistress Allie, the one who's come to look after Gyltha—and, mistress," she said with an extravagant flourish of her hand in the young man's direction, "this is Peter . . . Elsford's falconer, the person we've been waiting for."

"Greetings, mistress." Peter took off his coif and clasped it to his chest, but Allie barely noticed him, because she was gazing at the magnificent bird on his wrist instead.

"What a beautiful creature," she gasped, running the tip of her finger reverently down the bird's breast. "A tiercel, too."

"Indeed," Peter replied with a broad grin. "I take it you're a falconer yourself then, mistress?"

Allie nodded. "Well, I certainly prefer them," she said. "Peregrines especially."

"Then you're a lady after my own heart . . . But . . ." He turned to Hawise. "I gather it's only watercress we're hunting this morning."

"That's right," she said. "And we best be getting on with it."

As they followed him through the gatehouse over the drawbridge, Allie tried to steer the conversation back to the dead girl, but Hawise's obfuscation was masterful, and she continued to wield her loquacity like a weapon.

"Falcons then, mistress?" she asked as though it was the most fascinating thing she had ever heard. "And, if I remember rightly, wasn't it Queen Eleanor who gave you your first one?"

"It was indeed," Allie replied, taken aback to be reminded of the time, all those years ago, when she and Gyltha were garrisoned with the queen at Sarum Castle.

"Only it wasn't a falcon," she said, unable to suppress a natural inclination to pedantry. "It was a sparrow hawk . . . But how did you know that? Even I'd forgotten about it."

Hawise tapped the side of her nose and grinned. "Gyltha told me!" she said. "Who else? She talks about you all the time. I grew up on stories about you . . . I even tell 'em myself sometimes . . . about you, your ma and pa."

"Oh," Allie said, feeling flattered and a little bemused. After all, she knew that, in certain circles, her upbringing was considered unusual, if, indeed, it was considered at all, but had never imagined it would be of interest to anyone but her. Nevertheless, she found that she was rather enjoying this unexpected moment of fame.

A few yards ahead of them Peter stopped suddenly. Allie saw him glance up at the sky as a ragged skein of plovers flapped languidly overhead, then hurriedly strike his falcon's hood and cast the bird from his wrist.

As the falcon flew upward they all stood still, mouths agape, watching it until it became a tiny, malignant speck high up in the clouds.

Allie marveled, as she always did, at the way it maneuvered itself into the blind spot between the sun and the unsuspecting birds below and held her breath for the stoop: the tiny death thrust of folded wings and outstretched talons as it tore down from the sky like the wrath of God to descend on its prey with a passion and a violence that made her gasp.

It was a clean kill, as it always was with peregrines. A mortal blow to the back of the neck sent the ill-fated plover spinning, lifeless, to the ground.

"Over there!" Peter cried, pointing at a grassy hummock in the marsh where the falcon stood mantling its kill. "Be quick now!" he called back to them as he ran toward it. "Mustn't let him eat too much or I won't get him back."

By the time they had caught up with him, he had coaxed the falcon back to his fist and was praising it like an indulgent father.

"Clever boy! And look," he said, pointing to a stream roughly two bow shots from where they were standing. "He's even found your watercress for you!"

CHAPTER 18

ALLIE DIDN'T SAY SO BUT the watercress was disappointing. The leaves had turned an unattractive yellow in the frost and were crimped around the edges, but because it was all there was, she rolled up her sleeves and, encouraging Hawise to do likewise, started picking.

When they had gathered as much as they could and their fingers were too numb to pick any more, she stood up, trying to flex some warmth into her hands and aching back. She had forgotten quite how pernicious the Fenland chill could be, and yet there was nostalgia in the cold this morning, as though a scent of the past had been delivered on the breeze. And, now that she came to think about it, it was a scent more than anything else, more even than the limitless horizons and overarching skies of the place—that unmistakable trace of river water, willow bark and peat that combined and conspired to send her back to her childhood in this strange half land of earth and water.

She closed her eyes, savoring the moment, then turned to Hawise.

"Which way is Waterbeach from here?" she asked.

"That way," Hawise replied, pointing east. "Where you were born, wasn't it, mistress?"

Allie smiled, remembering the humble cottage, not much more than a reed-thatched hut really, that rose out of the marsh on stilts.

When she was very little the stilts had fascinated her and she had convinced herself that really they were legs whose capricious feet, hidden deep in the reeds, might one day walk off by themselves, making her afraid to stray too far in case her home vanished while her back was turned.

She had loved it there, especially during the long, hot summer days when she would sit on the stoop beside Gyltha, counting eels in a bucket and watching the swallows dip in the river.

"How many eels to a stick then, bor?" Gyltha would ask, plucking another wriggling silver streak out of the bucket to tie on the hemp line coiled at their feet.

"Twenty-five!" Allie would reply, and was invariably rewarded with a bosomy hug and a compliment about her clever counting.

M ISTRESS?"
 She looked up, startled to see Peter looking at her expectantly. She had been miles away.

"I'm sorry," she said, blushing. "Did you say something?"

He looked amused to have caught her off guard. "I said . . . if it's all the same to you, mistress, I think we ought to be getting back."

"Yes, of course." Allie nodded.

"I'll be over there, when you're ready," he said, pointing to where the dead plover lay. "Best get that bagged up now."

When he left they knelt down again to gather up the bushels of watercress and she saw a sharp, sudden movement among the rushes on the other side of the stream.

She sat up abruptly, her ears pricked, eyes fixed on the still-trembling patch of reeds, wondering what it was. Something large, judging by the violent swishing of the stalks. She sat up taller, craning her neck, and looked again. On second thought, perhaps it wasn't some*thing* but some*one*—the movement was too clumsy to be an animal, and besides, she also had a peculiar feeling that they were being watched.

She tapped Hawise on the shoulder and, motioning for her to keep quiet, pointed into the rushes. Crouching down and holding their breath, they peered intently into the rushes until the rustling came again, more vigorous this time and a prelude to a tall, thin young man rearing up at them out of the marsh.

Allie gasped, automatically thrusting her hand out to grab Hawise and drag her to safety if necessary, but before she could do so Hawise had gotten to her feet and was shouting at him at the top of her voice.

"You devil, you, Danny Wadlow!" she shrieked, her cheeks red with fury. "You come over here 'stead of sneaking about spying on people and I'll give you what for."

Allie looked anxiously around for Peter, hoping that he had heard all the commotion and was coming to their rescue, but he was nowhere to be seen.

"Gi' me what for, will you?" the man screamed back, his face a rictus of fury. "You an' whose army, eh, Hawise?"

To Allie's increasing horror he made a sudden feint toward them, and for an awful moment, it looked as if he was going to leap across the stream to tear their throats out; he certainly had the teeth for it. And because, at that moment, there was nothing to be gained—other than injury or death—from cowering in the rushes, she stood up and was ready to make a grab for Hawise again when he changed his mind and ran off in the opposite direction instead, stopping only once to shout something at them.

Allie watched openmouthed until he vanished from sight.

"What did he say?"

Hawise shook her head and unclenched her fists at last. "Don't take any notice, mistress," she said. "I didn't catch what he said . . . It was some sort of threat probably, knowing him . . . I think it was something about how I was 'devil's bait' and how I'd 'be sorry' about something or another . . . But I wouldn't take any notice; I don't." She added brightly, "He's a pillard, really, famous for it. Always spying on people . . . But harmless, just . . . well, irritating . . ."

"Hmm." But Allie wasn't convinced. She had seen something dreadful in that face, an incendiary combination of ignorance and brutality that she found terrifying. "I hope you're right," she murmured.

CHAPTER 19

WHEN PETER RETURNED WITH THE bagged plover, apparently unaware of the encounter with Danny Wadlow, neither girl mentioned it—there didn't seem much point—and they set off back to Elsford as though nothing had happened, Hawise chattering away, barely pausing for breath, much as she had on the way there, apparently untrammeled by the incident. Perhaps, Allie thought, she was inured to peculiar encounters with strange men in marshes. Allie, however, was not, and couldn't help feeling that the Fens weren't quite the way she remembered them.

And yet it wasn't only the strange young man in the marsh. There was a combination of things troubling her: Gyltha's aborted conversation in the solar; the drowned girl, who may or may not have been murdered; and the unshakeable feeling she'd had, almost from the moment they'd set foot in the marsh, that they were being watched.

Something was definitely amiss, and as she followed Peter and Hawise down the track to the house, she determined that, come what may, she would get to the bottom of it. After all, she wasn't her mother's daughter for nothing.

W HEN THEY GOT BACK TO the house, Hawise took her to the kitchen to turn the watercress into a nourishing soup for Gyltha; when she had, they took it up to the solar, where Penda was waiting for them.

"Just missed your ma," she told Hawise. "She came and sat for me, bless 'er, while I went chasing after the bloody abbot's dog—that bugger's been at my sheep again, God rot it! And I'll tell you summat, when I catch that thing I'll have it lawed, abbot or no bloody abbot."

"Not with my Allie around you won't," Gyltha said, pushing away the bowl Allie was encouraging her to drink from. "Wouldn't let anyone lift a finger 'gainst an animal, would you, me darlin'?"

Penda gave a derisory snort. "Well, in that case," she said, turning the gimlet eyes on Allie, "I wish there was more like you round 'ere. Another ram's gone missing, and when I find the bugger that's took that, I'll hang 'im and you'll 'ave nothing to say against that, I hope."

Allie was about to reply that she didn't approve of hanging any more than she approved of lawing, and that they were both brutal, unnecessary practices, when Hawise interrupted her.

"How do you know it wasn't a wolf?" she asked.

Penda gave another snort. "Because I do," she said. "Some bugger stole it, I tell you. For witchcraft, most likely."

There had been a recent rise in the incidence of scapulimancy—
the practice of boiling down rams' bones to determine the future from their shoulder blades—but since Allie didn't believe in
magic and didn't want to argue with Penda, she left them to discuss it among themselves and went to the window overlooking
the village instead.

A straggle of plainly built huts, with small pyramids of thatch
at each end and the ubiquitous stippled rounds of reed bundles
stacked in each garden, was settled along a long, thin street that
ended abruptly at the gates of a reassuringly squat little church.
Beyond the church, and stretching as far as the eye could see,
was the causeway, the famously long, cambered strip of land
running from Ely to Stuntney that was her father's favorite road,
or so he claimed. It held its place in his affections not simply
for the admiration it inspired in him for the monks who had
built it, but because it was the fastest, most direct route out of
the Fens.

"Trouble with this place, Allie," he had once told her—his
antipathy for the place was never a secret—"is that, unlike the
sea, which can be traversed by boat if necessary, or obstructions
of the land, like the hills and forests, which can also be overcome, the marsh is neither land nor water and, as such, is a great,
bothersome barrier to movement . . . And that, my darling, is
why you won't find many horses here . . ."

Perhaps in appealing to her love of horses he had hoped to
put her off, but if so it hadn't worked. Besides, there were horses;
in fact, she was looking at one now, a beautiful, sleek creature
galloping along the causeway with its rider crouched low over
its back.

She leaned further out of the window to get a better look but was disappointed when it began to slow down.

"Don't stop! Don't stop!" she urged under her breath, but the rider was already standing upright in his stirrups, one hand tugging the reins, the other patting the animal's neck, and although they were too far away for her to be able to see it, somehow she knew his face was creased with delight.

She turned back to the others. "Who's that?" she asked, pointing through the window.

Penda got up to join her. "Who's what?" she asked, looking out, and when she spotted them, murmured, as if to herself, "Oh, that's him! That's Lord Peverell!"

Allie looked at her and noticed that she was blushing.

Aware of her scrutiny, Penda cleared her throat.

"Yes," she said, sounding more like herself again. "That's Lord Peverell, all right."

Behind them Hawise squealed with excitement and rushed to the window.

"Let me see! Let me see!" she said, thrusting herself into the narrow gap between them, and then: "Bugger!" when she realized she was too late. "It's not fair! I've still never clapped eyes on him."

"Well, you wouldn't have been able to see much from here anyway," Allie said, holding tight to the back of Hawise's bliaut, afraid that if she leaned out any further she would topple to her death. "Besides, it was the horse I was interested in . . ."

CHAPTER 20

A T SUPPER, TO ALLIE'S DISMAY, the conversation was all
about Lord Peverell, with not a single mention of his horse.

"Not married yet, see," Rosa explained, misinterpret-
ing Allie's boredom for confusion. "So all the girls get excited
when they see 'im, which ain't too often because 'e's hardly ever
around. So you was lucky, mistress . . . More'n likely we won't
catch sight of 'im again 'til Lammas." Allie nodded and smiled
but didn't feel at all lucky, and in fact was beginning to rue that
she had clapped eyes on him in the first place.

"He took the cross," said Penda, who seemed unusually
aroused by the subject. Allie noticed that the moment it was
introduced, Penda had barely taken her eyes off her, her gaze
intensifying disconcertingly at every mention of Lord Peverell's
name. "Brave, too, so they say, when he was wounded in the
Holy Land . . . ," she continued. "Now, when was that?" She
turned to Ulf for clarification, flapping her hand at him irritably
when he turned out to be too busy eating to reply.

"Oh, never mind," she said, turning back to Allie. "Roughly

three years ago, if I remember right . . . In fact, I do . . . It were about the same time as the old bishop died and that Longchamp come in 'is stead."

"And ain't we lived to regret that?" added Jodi, hovering over them with a jug of ale. "Been like a curse on us ever since. All them goings-on . . . an' them poor dead girls . . ."

The dead girls!

Allie's ears pricked up. This was more like it! At last, at long last, somebody might be about to say something interesting for a change. She sat up straighter, willing Jodi to continue, but her hopes were dashed as Ulf thumped his hand on the table with such a resounding bang that the candles guttered and Jodi leapt backward in surprise.

"Sorry, Jodi," he said sheepishly, raising his hand to her apologetically. "Didn't mean to alarm you . . . it's just that, well . . . we don't want to go boring Mistress Allie with our stories, now, do we?"

After that, the evening continued interminably; more inconsequential blather about Lord Peverell and his vast estates and his heroism in the Holy Land, and, and, and . . . If it hadn't been for one of Penda's wolfhounds' choosing Allie's lap to rest his vast head on, she might have died of boredom.

When the abbey bells chimed for compline she got up quickly and was heading to the door when Ulf stopped her.

"Wait here, if you wouldn't mind," he told her in a low voice. "I'd like a word if I may." If he hadn't looked so grave she would have been tempted to reply that he could have as many words as he liked as long as they didn't include "Lord" and "Peverell," but she nodded instead and waited patiently beside him until the others had filed out of the hall.

"I'm sorry," he said, drawing up a couple of stools by the fire. "I shoulda said something before, I know I should, but I didn't want to frighten you, and besides . . ." He hesitated. "Well . . . you see, it might be something or . . . nothing. No one knows . . . not really."

He was trying to smile but his hands were twisting nervously in his lap, making her worry that, any moment now, he would repeat the pattern of the day and change his mind about telling her whatever it was.

She took a breath, torn between compassion and insatiable curiosity.

"Is it about Martha?" she asked, hoping the prompt might make it easier for him. She was reluctant to betray Hawise's confidence, but, when all was said and done, she knew more than he thought she did. "You think she was murdered, don't you?" she continued. "And, Ulf, if so, you know I can help you, don't you? I could examine the body . . . See if there's anything . . . well, you know . . ."

Of course he knew. Of all people, he had spent enough time with Adelia to know that in the right hands, the voices of the dead could be unsilenced.

"But tha's just it," he said. "There's nothin' anyone can do . . . She'll be buried tomorrow and her parents, God love 'em, don't want any fuss. They want to believe she drowned . . . Couldn't bear it else, see."

He looked away, haunted by the expression in the eyes of the girl's mother, the light of hope in them extinguished the moment she opened the door to him and saw the bundle in his arms. A strange alchemy had taken place as they dulled and darkened, against their nature, when, after searching his face for a fragment of comfort to shore herself against the ruin of her life, she found none.

When she fell to her knees he would have done almost anything, breathed his last breath into the body in his arms if he could have, but he wouldn't spare her the truth—there was too much at stake, too many other lives at risk, to deny what he knew, and her howls of pain and protest when she heard it still rang in his ears.

He shivered at the memory.

"But, Ulf," Allie said, leaning toward him on her stool, "what makes you think she didn't drown?"

For a while he sat awkwardly, reluctant to continue, running his hands through his hair, dragging them wearily down his face and tugging the skin around his eyes so that the lower lids showed red.

"Because she'd been missing such a long time, but when I pulled that body out of the water, it didn't look like she'd been there more'n a day or two . . . It weren't drowning, Allie. I know it weren't."

Allie broke the silence that followed.

"And you suspect there were others, don't you?" Even in a whisper her voice sounded shocking in the heavy stillness of the room.

He nodded.

"Like Jodi said . . . Ever since Longchamp came, there's been trouble the like of which we've never known before . . . And girls—two we know of, though God knows how many more—have gone missing and turned up dead. Martha was the third that I know of and 'less something's done, she won't be the last."

CHAPTER 21

A T NOON THE NEXT DAY Martha's funeral bells tolled over the marsh.

Allie stood at the solar window watching the procession wind its way through the village, the mourners' heads bowed in deference to both their grief and the inclement weather.

Despite the rain, it looked as though the entire village had turned out, and she tried to make out Rosa or Hawise—both of whom had been summoned early from their beds to help prepare the body that morning—in the crowd, but the distance, the rain and the universal drabness of mourning made the people indistinguishable from one another.

At the head of the procession she could just make out the funeral bier and, in her imagination, saw the dead girl borne aloft, her hands clasped at her chest in eternal prayer, the agony of death—if, indeed, agony there had been—erased from her sweet face by her mother's loving hands . . . And then, because she couldn't help it, she envisioned the flies and maggots that were even now assailing the corpse and beginning the process of decomposition, burrowing into her body to eat her flesh and expose the white flash of her bones to the deep, dark earth of her grave . . .

Allie shivered; sometimes she appalled even herself with her imaginings, but that was the problem with being her . . . She knew too much, had seen too much, to be mystified by the process of death or ignorant of the truth that, beneath the mortal façade of skin and sinew, she and Martha were the same, and one day the process would begin in her.

She shivered again and turned her back on the window to embrace the comfort of the room, only to find further discomfort in the glare Gyltha was directing at her.

"See! Tha's why I don't want you here," she said, thumping the bed with the side of her fist. "Now do you understand? I told 'em, begged 'em not to bring you here, but they wouldn't listen . . . It ain't safe here no more."

"But it's home, Gylth . . . ," Allie said weakly.

"Not anymore it ain't. It's where women get murdered and bugger-all gets done about it."

Just then the church bells stopped ringing and a silence fell on the room as though it, too, were holding its breath . . .

"Please," Gyltha said, so beseechingly that, for a moment, Allie's heart melted, if not her resolve. "You must leave, darlin'."

THE CONVERSATION WAS NEVER REVISITED; both recognized an impasse when they saw one. Nevertheless, behind each other's back, each set about fortifying her position.

For Gyltha this meant hectoring Penda to take Allie home at her first opportunity. When Penda's tentative reluctance turned into downright refusal, Gyltha's entreaties turned into threats, and the atmosphere in the solar soured, to the bemusement of the others.

For Allie it meant spending as much time in the kitchen as she could, where, she reasoned, there was the highest concentration of human traffic in the house and, therefore, the choicest gossip. Whenever she could, she took herself off to a quiet corner of it—ostensibly to seethe her herbs and prepare nourishing soups for Gyltha, but actually to listen to the chatter of the cooks and scullions as they went about their business, hoping to garner more information about the dead girls.

As it turned out, though, there was little to be had. Although the disappearances dominated most of the conversation—fear, it seemed, made people garrulous, especially the women—most of what they spouted was superstitious twaddle. Their suspicion fell in equal parts on the local fairies—covetous creatures in these parts, apparently, who wanted all the pretty girls for themselves—and the wicked Bishop Longchamp, under whose reign the disappearances had begun in the first place.

Because Allie felt ill qualified to dispute the fairy theory, she didn't; with Longchamp she was on safer ground, but when she pointed out—helpfully, as she thought—that the bishop had left the diocese some time ago and was unlikely to return, she was met with cold, suspicious stares.

The trouble was that she had never been welcome in the kitchen. The other women had taken against her almost from the start, jealous of the protection Penda gave her and increasingly suspicious of the spells she was casting over Gyltha, whose health, since she had been ministering to her, had visibly improved. Besides, they were uneasy about the peculiar plants she worked with and therefore assumed that the bowls of steaming liquid she traipsed to the solar with every day weren't actually soups at all but liquids for the purpose of scrying. Although they were never rude to her—they were too afraid of Penda for that—whenever she appeared, a meticulous but chilly courtesy made their feelings abundantly clear.

In fact, the only person who benefited from the sojourns at all was Gyltha, who was soon well enough to make the short walk from her bed to the window, an exercise Allie insisted on to help her blood flow and ease the congestion in her lungs.

When she wasn't ministering to Gyltha or failing to eavesdrop on the kitchen staff, she spent most of her time with Hawise.

A routine had been established: Hawise would arrive at first light to allow Allie to rise in peace and have her breakfast in the hall, after which she would return to the solar, see to Gyltha and then play games with Hawise. In the afternoon, either Rosa, Jodi or Ediva, sometimes all three together, would relieve the girls at Gyltha's bedside, Hawise so she could attend to her various chores—spinning, mole trapping or collecting rushes—and Allie so she could go hunting with Penda.

But on Fridays, a fast day, when they were allowed only fish for supper, Penda, who didn't have the patience for fishing, took Allie off to a deserted corner of the demesne for her weekly archery lessons.

The lessons were an idea she had come back with from Martha's funeral, prompted, Allie suspected, by a conversation with Ulf. But whatever its origin, she was resolute in its pursuit, and because, as far as Allie was concerned, archery sounded much more fun than, for instance, needlepoint, she happily complied.

She never admitted it to Penda, of course, but it struck her as an unusual skill for a woman and wondered how Penda had come by it. Just before their first session, she asked Gyltha.

"Oh, you'll enjoy it. She's a bloody good archer, is Pen," Gyltha told her with obvious pride.

"I'm sure she is," said Allie. "But how and why did she learn?"

Gyltha looked at her askance. "Well, we all had to get through the Anarchy somehow, defend ourselves and the like, and that's 'ow Pen did it." More than that she wouldn't say.

ONE AFTERNOON THE SESSION BEGAN as usual. Penda took Allie to the barbican to select a crossbow and an amply stocked quiver before marching her over the mud and stubble of the demesne to the old oak tree they used for target practice.

"Watch carefully, now," Penda said, bending down to pick up a muddy nub of chalk with which to draw a target on its trunk. "Trouble with you, I've noticed, is you don't always pay attention, which is why you're a bit slow to learn."

Allie had never been accused of being a slow learner before and was tempted to reply that, on the contrary, she did pay attention but that it was more Penda's instruction—which was often snappy and confused—she found wanting. In the end she kept her mouth shut. Besides, she was getting to know Penda now and coming to realize that her irritation stemmed from something other than a desire to impart her skill—that, for some reason, these lessons were vital to Allie's well-being and more than peda-gogic pride was at stake.

"Right then," Penda said, preparing to demonstrate the ar-balist's stance for the umpteenth time. "Remember, now: stand with your body sideways to the target . . . Sideways, got it?"

Allie nodded enthusiastically.

"Good, now watch closely! . . . Place your feet the same dis-tance apart as your shoulders." She looked back at her over her shoulder, wriggling her hips to demonstrate the perfect balance afforded by feet planted at the optimum distance from one an-other. "Yes?"

"Yes." Allie nodded again, pleased that, so far anyway, she had remembered everything.

"Oh, so we know it all then, do we?" said Penda, putting the bow down and glaring at her. "So, what comes next then?"

Allie's heart sank.

God's teeth! She hadn't expected a test and racked her brains furiously for the next part of the sequence.

"Erm . . ." She could feel herself blushing, her nerves fogging her memory. It was ridiculous, but it mattered so much to Penda that she was terrified of letting her down.

And then, as if by some miracle, it came flooding back to her.

"Yes!" she said triumphantly. "Then . . . then, you lower the bow and notch it?"

"Good." Penda nodded encouragement. "Then what?"

"Ah . . . and then . . . er . . ." *And then what? And then what?* Her mind was blank again. She offered up a silent prayer, hoping it would be answered quickly.

It was.

Oh, God be praised! "Then you nock the arrow with your index finger and the two fingers below ... holding it not too tight but not too loose, either." The words came out in a garbled rush, but at least they were coming.

"Very good." Penda gave a rare smile of approval. "So you 'ave been listenin' after all. Well then, now, watch carefully again, mind: raise the bow—smoothly, now, don't rush it, remember? ... Draw the string to your ear—like this—ear, mind, not cheek ... Aim ... breathe ... and ... loose!"

Chwwt-pt. Penda's arrow flew through the air and landed, as hers always did, right in the middle of the target ...

Allie had barely finished applauding when Penda handed her the bow.

"Your turn."

THAT AFTERNOON SHE MISSED MORE often than not, her arrows flying off her bow at strange angles, landing in the wheat stubble several yards wide of the target, but she refused to give up ...

"You're thinking too much," Penda barked. "And you're not breathing! What 'ave I told you? ... Don't think, let it come natural. Breathe! Now try again!"

So she did, again and again and again, until, at last, one of them made it all the way to the target and stuck there, shuddering an inch or two wide of the center.

Penda sank to her knees.

"At last! God be praised!" she said, clasping her hands to the heavens. "Now go and fetch it. I think we'll finish there for the day."

But Allie was enjoying herself and, buoyed by her success, wanted another go.

"No," Penda said hastily. "Come back fresh another day. We don't want to push our luck now."

They had collected up all the arrows and turned their backs on the oak for the day when Penda saw something and stopped suddenly, pointing in the direction of the causeway.

"Look!" she said.

Allie looked and saw the horse she had seen from the solar that day galloping across the horizon, a streak of burnished gold ripping through the cold gloom like a flame. Once again she thrilled at its grace and speed until, once again, it stopped, only this time so suddenly that it catapulted its rider out of the saddle.

When he didn't get up immediately they exchanged glances, and when, a few moments later, he still hadn't moved, Allie picked up the hem of her skirts and started running toward him. She was more than halfway there when, to her relief, he got to his feet at last.

He managed to hobble a few yards, and by the time Allie got to him he was standing in front of the snorting, skittish horse, trying to coax it back.

"Steady, now, steady," he said, reaching out to grab the reins that were trailing around its hooves, but it shied away, its eyes rolling white in panic. When, out of the corner of his eye, he saw Allie approaching, he flung his arms wide to stop her.

"Stay back," he warned. "I've never seen her like this before, there's no telling what she might do. Stay where you are! Or you may get hurt!"

But Allie ignored him and continued walking slowly toward them. "Don't worry about that," she said, stepping calmly into the space between the man and the horse, confusing both by turning around and walking backward until she was standing by the animal's shoulder.

"Good girl," she said, bending down to pick up the reins. "Now let's see what all this is about, shall we?"

The man watched in astonishment as the horse, calmed by the girl's presence, put her head down to graze and, without any fuss, allowed the inspection of her hooves. He was an accomplished horseman himself but had never seen anything like it, and now that he had recovered from the shock of his fall, he had time to consider the young woman who had come to his aid.

Something about her was familiar, and yet he couldn't remember having seen her before. Perhaps it had been in a dream, but then, perhaps not, because, although she was undoubtedly beautiful, she wasn't particularly dreamlike.

When he had first noticed her, he was still dazed from the fall and so concerned for her safety that he hadn't had the presence of mind to make a physical evaluation of her. Now that he did, he saw that she carried herself well and possessed a length of bone and glossiness of hair that spoke of quality and breeding, but that her natural elegance was belied by her attire. In fact, as he watched her tending his horse, he wondered whether she realized that the hem of her bliaut was ragged or that it had been snagged at the elbow, only to realize, when he saw her casually rip off her veil and wimple and toss them into the grass, that she probably didn't care.

And that was another thing. Watching her work. She had the knowledge and expertise of a farrier and yet didn't look like any farrier's wife or daughter he had ever seen. Besides, when she spoke it was in impeccable Norman French.

"Poor thing's got a thorn in her hoof," she told him, looking up at him at long last. "No wonder she threw you."

For the first time he saw that she had beautiful green eyes and an unflinching gaze; confidence and breeding again, he thought, and made a note of it.

"Can you do anything?" he asked.

She put the hoof down gently and stood up straight, wiping her muddy hands down the sides of her cloak. "Oh, I've already taken it out," she said brightly, opening her fist to reveal the offending thorn. "But, as you can see, it went in very deep, so you'll have to be careful it doesn't get infected. I recommend packing the wound with some sphagnum moss, if you can find any . . ."

"I'd scour the earth if necessary," he replied, disconcertingly misty eyed all of a sudden. "That horse carried me across the Holy Land and back. You could say I owe her my life."

Allie thought he looked as though he was going to cry and started to panic; she wasn't very good with tears, especially not a man's. But at that very moment, and to her enormous relief, Penda appeared, red faced and puffing hard, trudging up the track toward them.

"Lady Penda! Greetings!" the man said, and, with everyone fussing like mother hens, brightened again.

"Lord Peverell." Penda nodded at him. "Glad to see you up-right, young man. Could've broke your neck with a fall like that; you had us worried."

So it's him, Allie thought, wondering why she hadn't real-ized that before. On the other hand she had been so preoccupied with the horse that she hadn't had time to think about anything else.

"I'm grateful for your concern, madam," Lord Peverell said. "But by God's grace, I seem to have escaped serious injury, and, thanks to this lady," he added, smiling at Allie, "so has my horse."

Penda looked from one to the other.

"So you're acquainted now, then, are you?" she asked.

Lord Peverell shook his head. "Not formally," he said.

"Oh, well, in that case, allow me. Lord Peverell, this 'ere's Mistress Almeison Picot . . . And Mistress Almeison Picot, this 'ere's Lord Peverell."

He turned to Allie again. "Almeison." He repeated her name slowly, softly, as though each syllable were a delicacy to be sa-vored. "A beautiful name . . . Unusual, too."

"It's Arabic," Allie replied, surprised to see his face light up as she did so.

"Well! Well!" He pressed his hands together in delight. "What a coincidence! Then it's no wonder that you have such an affinity with my horse! Mistress Almeison, allow me to intro-duce Matilda."

Allie smiled weakly, disappointed not to be able to match his enthusiasm, but the coincidence wasn't obvious to her.

"Also Arabic," he explained, sensing her confusion. "The

horse . . . not the name—I called her after the empress, actually, but . . ." She found it rather endearing to see him blush. "Ah well, no matter . . ."

"It is a lovely name though," she said, hoping to assuage him.

"Indeed." He nodded. "A lovely name for a lovely horse . . ."

Penda cleared her throat. "Never mind about all that," she said, looking up at the sky. "Time you was getting along, my lord, there's still a couple of miles to go to Dunstan and it'll take a while on foot. You don't want to be walkin' in the dark, now . . ."

Lord Peverell nodded. "Very wise, Lady Penda," he said. "I really ought to be getting back, I suppose." He turned to Allie and bowed. "Thank you again, Mistress Almeison . . . And now, I suppose, I ought to wish you both a good day." Then, clucking at his horse, he started limping off down the causeway.

Allie, who was suddenly very tired and hungry, was keen to go home, but Penda was strangely reluctant to move and insisted they watch them for a while.

"Bugger!" she said just before they disappeared from view. "We'll 'ave to go after 'em, you know. Look at 'em, couple of cripples! They won't make it 'less we do."

CHAPTER 22

I T TOOK SOME TIME TO get to Dunstan but Lord Peverell, hobbling along, leaning on Penda, compensated for the arduous journey with his cheerful and lively conversation. And Allie, walking behind them, leading the horse, was frequently amused by the snippets of the conversation that drifted back to her.

"Good Lord, madam! But you're well armed!" he said when he noticed the bow slung across Penda's back. "I hope I'm not around for the invasion you're obviously expecting. Anything I should know about? A siege perhaps?"

Penda laughed. "You never know, bor," she said, tapping the side of her nose. "I've lived through enough o' them to know you can't be too careful, but mebbe not today . . . No, it's them bloody foxes! I was going to bag a few afore you come along and buggered up my plans."

For reasons best known to herself, she preferred to keep their archery lessons secret.

"I can only apologize," Lord Peverell said, "and repeat that although I regret having done so, I am eternally grateful that it was me who 'buggered them up' . . . if you see what I mean."

They were developing an easy rapport, Allie thought, one that was only possible because of the parity in their social standing, the difference in their ages and therefore the lack of any sexual prejudice. She rather envied it.

" 'Ow'd you get that scar then?" she overheard Penda ask him a little later on.

"Oh, that?" he replied, running his finger along the livid mark that ran down his cheek. "Crusade, that one. An assassin's sword. Suits me, don't you think?"

Penda snorted with laughter, nudging him so hard that he almost fell over. "Vain bugger!" she said.

Allie wasn't consulted, of course, and wouldn't have dreamed of offering her opinion, but, actually, she thought it did. In fact, it was one of the first things she had noticed about him, the thin, jagged line running from the corner of his mouth to a point just below his cheekbone, which lent an imperfect charm to a face that might otherwise have been a little too complacent in its beauty.

In fact, now that she came to think about it, she liked the look of him very much and was surprised at how eagerly she was anticipating those moments when he would glance back at her over his shoulder.

At first, she assumed he was doing so out of concern for the horse, but increasingly his gaze came to rest on her, and for longer than was necessary, which caused a peculiar, although by no means unpleasant, sensation around her knees.

B Y THE TIME THEY REACHED Dunstan it was dusk, and their lordship's return was obviously keenly anticipated. The portcullis had been raised, the drawbridge lowered, and the moment he appeared on the horizon a score of anxious men carrying flambeaus rushed out to meet him.

"Well, my lord."

A tall blond-haired man loomed out of the throng, lifted his master's arm unceremoniously off Penda's shoulder and placed it across his own.

"What mischief is it that you return crippled and in the company of women?" he asked.

"No mischief, Will," his lordship replied. "I had an accident, all my own fault, a sprain, but nothing serious."

He turned to Penda.

"Lady Penda, allow me to introduce my steward, Sir William. Sir William, this is Lady Penda. And this lady," he said, with an emphatic flourish of his free arm toward Allie, "is Mistress Almeison Picot . . . I owe them both a huge debt of gratitude."

A pair of cold, pale green eyes slid from Allie to Penda and back again. Sir William gave a perfunctory bow. A little too perfunctory, Allie thought, especially in light of the service they had just performed for his master. On the other hand, since she was tired and hungry and never at her most charitable under these circumstances, she decided to give him the benefit of the doubt and smiled politely.

By now a sizeable crowd had gathered around them, everyone fussing about their master like mother hens. Another young man stepped forward and, equally unceremoniously, snatched the reins out of Allie's hands.

"Come, Matilda," he said, disregarding Allie as though she were a figment of her own imagination. "Let's get you back to the stable." And with a click of his tongue and still no acknowledgment of Allie, he started leading her away. Allie watched them go, feeling an uncomfortable mix of affrontery and dismay.

"Make sure you put plenty of rugs on her," she called out, irritation rising. "She sweated up badly this afternoon so she'll more than likely feel the cold tonight."

He broke stride for a moment but didn't turn around.

"Oh . . . And take a look at that hoof on the left fore before you finish her. You'll find a hole that needs plugging with some sphagnum moss if you want to prevent an abscess."

When she had finished, he shrugged his shoulders and walked on, leaving her standing on the drawbridge staring after him.

"Don't worry."

A voice behind her made her start, and she turned her head to see Lord Peverell limping toward her.

"She's in good hands," he said, amused by her expression of consternation. "Young Henry may not be the most enthusiastic conversationalist but he knows his horses like the back of his hand; besides, I'll be looking in on her myself later on . . ."

"Good," Allie said, although she continued to stare fixedly at the insolent groom until he and the horse disappeared into the shadow of the gatehouse.

L ORD PEVERELL INVITED THEM TO stay for supper.
      "A small thank-you for your kindness," he said.

Allie demurred at first, partly because she assumed that Penda would be anxious to get back to Elsford as soon as possible, but was surprised when, in fact, she accepted with alacrity. On the other hand, she hadn't been privy to the conceit Penda had been nursing all afternoon about the great good fortune—the one that had almost literally fallen into her lap—by which she had fulfilled her promise to Rowley without compromise, contrivance or, indeed, much difficulty.

Ever since she had made it, she had worried about how she might fulfill it, and until now had failed to come up with a single plan. But today God himself had smiled on her, and she was almost euphoric at the felicity. In fact she spent the rest of the evening smiling beatifically at all and sundry, while studiously avoiding eye contact or conversation in case she was distracted from this rare but glorious moment.

"Lovely meal, weren't it?" she said when it was all over and they were nestling into the blankets in the covered cart Lord Peverell had provided to take them home. "Did you have a nice time, Allie? . . . Looked like you was enjoyin' yourself . . . Very chatty, the two of you. Seemed like 'e couldn't take 'is eyes off you . . ."

Allie had to admit that she had, and—although she didn't actually say so—now that she came to think about it, he had been very attentive. They had chatted all night, almost to the exclusion of everyone else, but whether or not he had taken his eyes off her at any point she couldn't say. The only person who she knew hadn't, however, was Sir William, who had spent the evening glowering at her from the other side of the table. It had been unnerving at first, but as the evening wore on, she became inured to it; besides, wherever his antipathy toward her came from, it was entirely mutual; she hadn't liked him much, either.

"Perhaps you'll see 'im again," Penda said, settling back in the cart and closing her eyes.

"Perhaps," Allie said, shifting the curtain slyly to take another peek at him before they set off.

CHAPTER 23

THE NEXT MORNING HAWISE WOKE Allie up as she burst into the solar.

"Well! What's he like?" she shrieked, flinging her cloak onto the foot of the mattress.

"Shhh!" Allie sat up scowling, pressing her finger to her lips. "You'll wake Gyltha!"

"Sorry." Hawise lowered her voice. "But you have to tell me everything!"

Allie yawned—partly because she wanted to appear nonchalant, but also because she was genuinely tired. Last night her dreams—which were all about Lord Peverell—had been spectacularly vivid.

She opened her eyes. Hawise was staring down at her expectantly, jiggling with anticipation.

"He was . . . how should I put it? Well . . . charming, I suppose," she said with another yawn.

"Handsome?"

Allie shrugged. "I suppose so . . . if you like that sort of thing." And she surprised herself by her involuntary squeak of pleasure as she remembered his face. "He's got this scar," she said, absently and dreamily tracing an imaginary line down her cheek with her finger.

Hawise leapt on it. "Ooh, Mistress Allie!" she said. "You're blushing!"

"I most certainly am not," Allie snapped despite all evidence to the contrary.

"So, he was a bit more interesting than his horse this time then, was he?"

Allie gave what she hoped was a derisory sniff. "I wouldn't say that exactly," she said, wrapping her bedsheet around her, hoping Hawise would take the hint and let her rise in peace. "It's a very beautiful horse actually. She's called Matilda . . . after the empress."

But Hawise was undeterred. "Ooh," she squeaked in a way Allie was beginning to find irritating. "On first-name terms with his horse then, are you? Well, you know what that means round here, don't you, mistress? It means—" But she didn't get to finish her sentence because just then Allie launched a pillow at her head and she ran out of the room laughing.

"Don't take any notice, me old lover."

Gyltha's drowsy voice sounded from the bed. "Terrible one for teasing, that girl."

Allie got up and, tightly wrapped in her sheet, shuffled over to the bed. "I'm sorry, Gyltha. Did we wake you?"

"Course you did, all that gigglin's enough to wake the dead . . . But there's worse ways to start the day, I s'pose . . . Well, come on then," she said, folding her arms across her chest. "Did you like 'im, this Lord Peverell?"

Allie felt her cheeks growing hot again. It was impossible to hide anything from Gyltha, who could sniff out the truth like a hound to the spoor of a wolf.

"Yes . . . ," she said. "Or at least, inasmuch as I got to know him, I suppose."

It was a half-truth. Yesterday she had felt a bond between them, developing from more than just their mutual concern for the horse. There were moments when he had revealed aspects of his personality that she liked very much: a tenderness, a sense of humor and a depth of character betrayed in the faraway look in his eyes when he thought no one was watching him, all of which had endeared him to her more than she cared to admit.

"Think you'll see 'im again, then?" Gyltha asked.

She was quiet for a moment, remembering the conversation just before she left, when he had taken her to one side while they waited for the cart to come.

"You will come back?" he had asked. "To see Matilda, that is."

And there had been something so beguiling in the way he said it, a slight faltering of confidence betrayed in his voice, that, for a moment or two, she'd felt unable to trust her own.

"Well?" Gyltha prompted.

"I don't know, Gylth," she said. "We'll have to see."

WHEN HAWISE RETURNED, AND, TO Allie's relief, in a less bullish mood, she went down to the hall for breakfast.

Halfway down the stairs she heard voices, a great many of them, and smelled a waft of damp sheepskin, reminding her that the manorial court was in session that morning. When she got there Sir Stephen was already on the dais calling a large crowd to order.

Jodi saw her hesitating in the doorway and came to her rescue, taking her to a table in the corner of the room.

"Oyez! Oyez! Oyez!" Sir Stephen's voice rang out through the room. "Let the court of Elsford commence and let every soul tell the truth as it stands in the fear of God."

The crowd responded with a collective "Amen" and the business of the day began.

First for consideration that morning was the case of Alice, widow of Albin, who was seeking amends from her neighbor, a certain Bartholomew the smith, who, she said, on the Sabbath before last, had allowed his pigs to enter her garden and root up all her beans and cabbages.

When Bartholomew couldn't offer a reasonable defense, Sir Stephen fined him three pence.

Next was Hereward, son of Bartholomew, who accused Alfred Le Boys of Wisbech of defaming his corn and thereby costing him the sale of it. Alfred offered no defense, either, and was also fined three pence. So was Ducie, widow of Richard, because she had broken the assize of beer, and Albert Merryweather, who refused to join a tithing despite being reminded to do so on numerous occasions.

The largest fine of the day, however, was levied against a Thomas Wayland, who ended the day six pence poorer for not keeping his widowed mother according to their agreement.

Allie suspected that, left to Sir Stephen, he might have got off more lightly, but Penda—who was a stickler for familial duty—made a rare intervention and doubled the original fine, insisting that, in addition to the amercement, all the land he had taken from his mother should revert to her with immediate effect, and that he should have nothing from it until after her death.

"And let that be the doom of the court," she said, fixing him with a glare that could have frozen the fires of hell.

When all the grievances had been dealt with, Sir Stephen moved on, taking up his ledger to read a long litany of rents and debts for collection. When every debtor had shuffled up to the dais and delivered their dues—either livestock or coinage—Sir Stephen sat down, and Ulf took over the proceedings.

As the reeve, he had the duty of reporting on the dilapidations that had accrued since the last court session: which houses had fallen into disrepair, which villein had taken timber from the wood without her ladyship's permission and who was responsible for which hole in which riverbank. All of which he announced with an air of reluctant competence, making no bones about the fact that he took little pleasure from sitting in judgment on his peers, a rare tenderness for which, Allie presumed, they had chosen him in the first place.

When the session ended and before the crowd made its lumbering exodus, Allie, feeling in need of fresh air, got up quickly and made her way to the courtyard.

It was another cold, crisp day, but other than a brief glimpse of Fulke the dairyman before he vanished into the milking shed behind his tail-swishing, sway-bellied herd, and Bertha the laundress, who was struggling to manipulate a mountain of half-frozen sheets into a basket in the drying court, the place was deserted.

The solitude suited Allie. This morning she needed time

alone to think, and she wandered aimlessly for a while until she came to an archway leading to a rose garden. Once inside, she made her way to a lichen-covered bench in the middle of the lawn and sat down on it, feeling the damp of the stone rising through her skirts.

Cold arse, cool head. Gyltha's epithet made her smile. Although whether it was her cold arse or the fresh air, she could feel that something, at least, was doing the job of clearing her head, even if the only thought that was rattling around in it was of Lord Peverell.

Lord Peverell, Lord Peverell, Lord Peverell; his name kept batting around her mind like a trapped moth, and although the sensation wasn't unpleasant, it didn't sound right.

She closed her eyes, trying to remember whether she had heard his Christian name, and then it came to her: James! James, yes, that was it! Much better; a name she could conjure with, or at least murmur wistfully if she had a mind to. "Lord Peverell" sounded too old, too austere. The man she was thinking about was neither of those things.

And yet, she thought gloomily, it was silly to think about him at all; before long she would have to return to Wolvercote. Gyltha was getting better by the day and was adamant that she should leave, and besides, with Christmas approaching Adelia would doubtless want her to go home. Despite Allie's longing to see her, the idea of returning to her old routine was more than she could bear. Besides—and the thought plunged her into even deeper gloom—her father was bound to have come up with a suitor for her by now.

"Good morning, Mistress Allie."

She looked up. Peter the falconer was waving at her through the archway.

"Good morning," she replied without enthusiasm, and immediately tilted her face to the sun, hoping the attitude of repose might encourage him to go away. But instead, through half-closed eyes, she saw him stoop through the arch and make his way over the lawn toward her.

He stopped right in front of the bench, casting a shadow over her.

"Is it not a little cold to be sitting outside, mistress?" he asked.

Allie opened her eyes reluctantly and realized that it was the first time she had really looked at him properly.

When they had first been introduced she had been too distracted, first of all by his falcon and then by the peculiar events in the marsh, to consider him really. Now that she could, she decided that there was something odd about him; nothing she could put her finger on exactly—after all, he was pleasant enough to look at, if you liked that sort of thing—but there was a whiff of arrogance about him, a disconcerting, knowing look in those long, dark eyes that made her uncomfortable. She wished he would go away.

"Well," he said hesitantly, breaking the awkward silence, "perhaps I should leave you in peace, mistress."

Allie nodded, sighing with relief when, after another awkward silence, he turned to leave. She watched him walk away, feeling her heart sink when, halfway across the lawn, he stopped and turned around to her.

"I don't suppose you'd care to go hunting this afternoon, mistress?" he asked. "It's a perfect day for wildfowling."

Allie smiled politely but shook her head. "I'm afraid not."

"Ah well, another time, perhaps," he said, and this time disappeared through the archway.

CHAPTER 24

W HEN SHE GOT BACK TO the solar it was full of several people she recognized from the hall earlier that morning, all of whom had taken advantage of their summons to see how Gyltha was getting on.

Jodi was leaning listlessly in the doorway with a broom in her hand.

"What's the matter?" Allie asked.

"I was going to change them rushes today," she sighed, wiping her brow with the back of her hand. "Don't reckon all the dust is good for Gylth's chest, but what with all these comin's and goin's, I can't get on with it."

"I wouldn't worry," Allie said. "I think she can cope with a bit of dust. Besides, the visitors are doing her a power of good. Look at her!"

Jodi poked her head around the door to see Gyltha holding court with an adoring assembly and smiled, until the sound of footsteps echoing up the stairwell behind them wiped it away again.

"God's eyes!" she said, raising her own to the heavens. "There's bloody more of 'em."

T HAT AFTERNOON ANOTHER VISITOR CAME to Elsford, a messenger, one of the fleet-footed young men employed in the Fens to perform carrier services, thanks to their youthful ability to leap the many bogs and dykes with the aid of long ash poles.

Gyltha, who had indeed been invigorated by her visitors, eschewed her usual afternoon nap and sat at the window instead, elbows resting on the sill, amusing the others with a commentary on the young man's progress through the marsh.

"Oh, look, bless 'im! Oop, there 'e goes . . . Wheeee! Come on, lad, another jump! . . . Go on, bor, you can do it! . . . Aw, that was a big splash! . . . Poor little love's poor little boots is all wet!"

"Is he coming here, do you think?" Hawise asked, leaning over her to see for herself.

"Where else would 'e be going, daft bugger?" Gyltha snapped, pushing her away. "Bringin' a letter for someone, I shouldn't wonder."

Hawise turned to Allie and grinned knowingly. "There you are, mistress," she said. "It's probably a message for you from Lord Peverell declaring his undying love or something."

Allie refused to admit it, least of all to Hawise, but the thought had crossed her mind, too. She tried to banish it but it kept coming back, so that when—after what felt like years of waiting—Jodi came up to the solar with a scroll for her, her heart started jumping like a sack of frogs.

"Thank you," she managed to say, although her mouth felt very dry all of a sudden.

"Well?" said Gyltha. "You just going to stand there, gapin' at it, or you going to open the bloody thing?"

Allie blushed and turned it over to break the seal, then almost collapsed in dismay.

It was from Wolvercote.

"It's from Ma," she said, hoping her disappointment hadn't shown. After all, a dutiful daughter should be pleased to receive a letter from her mother, and she was, really she was, it was just that . . .

Oh dear.

She took a deep breath and went to a quiet corner of the room to read it in private.

My Dearest Allie, it began.

> *I can't tell you how much I've missed you; it feels an age since you were here, and although I know it hasn't really been all that long, I have been so bored without you, my darling, that it's making my teeth itch. (Thank you, by the way, for your message. Such a relief to hear that you arrived safely and that Gyltha is feeling better. I do hope you explained why I haven't come yet. Give her my deepest love, won't you, and tell her that I'm longing to see her.)*
>
> *I must say, though, darling, you're so much better off there than here. It turns out that I'm the most dreadful invalid, impatient and irritable—or so Emma tells me. It also turns out that this wretched ankle wasn't*

sprained after all, but actually broken! I hadn't real-
ized quite how badly I'd injured it until you'd left, and
it started swelling monstrously—by that afternoon my
foot was the size of an inflated pig's bladder. Emma—
whose ministrations, though thorough, are awfully
brusque—consigned me to bed immediately and I've
been at her mercy ever since. Poor me!

I don't mean to sound ungrateful, and of course, I
would only ever say this to you, but all that efficiency
can be rather overwhelming at times. We've had words,
of course, more than once—you, of all people, won't be
surprised to hear that—and I've had to apologize to
her more times than I care to remember when I've lost
my temper with her, but oh, darling, love her as I do,
the woman could try the patience of a saint!

Anyway, today, at long last, she has agreed to re-
view the situation and might even allow me to go back
to the cottage, where at least I'll have some peace—
apart from Lena, of course, but at the moment I prefer
her company to Emma's.

Well, there we are. Enough of me.

In other news, your father came back the other
day—he was exhausted though, poor darling.

I can't remember if I told you—because, I say, it
seems so long since I've seen you—but when he left you
he was on his way to a meeting to sort out that Long-
champ business. Well, it got quite nasty apparently—
armies assembled and the like—but thanks to the great

wisdom and hard work of good men like your father and dear Hugh (bishop of Lincoln) and the ever-faithful William Marshall, of course, a civil war was averted by the skin of its teeth. Anyway, Longchamp was deposed at last and has fled to France, but the manner of his leaving was so funny that your father almost forgave him everything and invited him back.

Apparently Longchamp was waiting on the beach at Dover for his rescue boat, disguised as a woman, when an amorous fisherman approached and turned very nasty indeed when he realized that this damsel in distress wasn't really a damsel at all! Oh, Allie, you should have heard your father telling the story! I thought he was going to die laughing.

Well, my darling, I haven't much more to add. Although you may be interested to know that Richard—who's still on Crusade, of course—has made Walter of Coutances chief justiciar, a much more popular choice than Longchamp, although the Count of Mortain wasn't best pleased. Your father thinks he wanted the title for himself and says that his hunger for power—the throne especially—is becoming troublesome. But you know—and it's such a funny thing—I rather liked him when I knew him as a boy. He was always Henry's favorite, and so bookish and shy, and cut such a lonely little figure at court that I always felt rather sorry for him.

I hope you're well and happy. All that's left for me now is to say that I will be with you as soon as I can.

When she had finished reading, Allie put on a brave face and turned to the others.

"It's good news!" she said. "Longchamp's left the country!"

Everyone in the room gave a jubilant round of applause.

"Well," said Penda, "read it out to us, then."

Allie did so, and, as they insisted, read the Longchamp excerpt twice, to even more cheering and hugging. Jodi, with tears in her eyes, made the sign of the cross and blew a kiss heavenward.

"God be praised!" she said.

"Amen," said Hawise.

"Well that's the end of it, then," said Penda . . . "'Ope the bastard rots in hell."

Allie folded up the letter and took her place on the bed beside Gyltha. "Perhaps you can stop worrying now," she said. "And perhaps you'll let me stay after all . . ."

Gyltha gave her a sideways look. "We'll 'ave to see 'bout that," she said.

A T SUPPER THAT EVENING, ALLIE received so much attention from everyone about Adelia's letter and was persuaded to read it out so often that she barely had time to think about Lord Peverell. It wasn't until the end of the evening that she remembered her disappointment.

"You'll hear from him," Hawise whispered as she left for the night. "You're too kind, too beautiful, to be ignored, mistress. You'll see."

CHAPTER 25

B UT SHE WAS WRONG. SHE was ignored, and as the days
passed and there was still no news from Dunstan, her spirits sank again.

It wasn't just her disappointment that she hadn't heard from
him; she was also increasingly anxious about the horse and was
still wrestling her conscience about not having pursued the insolent groom when she had the chance to make sure he poulticed
her hoof properly. God's teeth! The poor animal might be suffering the torture of an untreated abscess, and when all was said
and done, it would be her fault.

Her listlessness didn't go unnoticed.

Gyltha—who was by now well enough to spend her days in
a chair weaving her beloved bird baskets—noticed how often she
drifted to the window overlooking the causeway, gazing at it for
hours on end.

It reminded her of Adelia and the early days of her courtship
with Rowley, which, because of the unusual circumstances from
which it evolved, had been an equally anxious affair even though
it was a privilege to witness. And now, here it was again, history

repeating itself, the unmistakable signs of early love manifest in the progeny of that unlikely union: the same wistful gazes and longing sighs, the same weight of unbearable expectation hanging over the room whenever Allie was in it—all so reminiscent of her mother and just as exhausting to watch.

She indulged it for a while and kept her mouth shut, but one day her patience ran out and she decided that enough was enough and, apart from the fact that it was getting on her nerves, all this mooching about was doing Allie no good. She put down the basket she was working on, picked up a surplus willow frond and threw it at her.

"Now then, bor," she said when Allie spun around from the window, rubbing the back of her leg where the frond had struck her. "'Stead of moonin' about there all day, why don't you run along to the village with Hawise?"

It was mid-December; a distinct waft of Christmas was in the air, and today a beautiful, clear blue sky hung over the village like a freshly laundered sheet.

"Go on," she insisted when Allie seemed reluctant. "I don' need you here a while. Bit o' fresh air'll do you good, I reckon."

For the first time in a long time, Allie smiled. "And that's your medical opinion, is it?" she asked.

"Yes it bloody is," Gyltha said, taking up her basket again. "Now get on . . . It's wearin' on me nerves, watchin' you in that state."

Affecting reluctance and sighing a good deal as she got herself ready, Allie was secretly pleased for an excuse to get out and do something at last.

It wasn't that she was unhappy at Elsford—far from it—it was just that now that Gyltha was so much better there was little to distract her, and with boredom setting in, she had developed a tendency to think about a certain person rather too much.

Ulf, bless him, had tried his best to keep her busy but was anxious that if the news of her medical skill reached the wrong ears, the inevitable accusations of witchcraft might send her to the village stocks or worse, so he was wary of advertising them beyond the confines of the manor. After all, unlike Adelia, she didn't have a Mansur to deflect suspicion, and also unlike Adelia, who was plain enough to melt into the background when she needed to, Allie stood out like a sore thumb; besides, while she was at Elsford, he was responsible for her.

"I can't have you going about like your ma used to," he told her brusquely when, in desperation one day, she asked him if he knew of any maladies she might treat.

"Nothing too complicated or anything; just an outbreak of the ague, perhaps, or a broken arm or two?"

But he dismissed the idea so resolutely that Allie assumed the matter was closed and was pleasantly surprised when, a few days later, he summoned her to the hall to treat a young swineherd who had dislocated his shoulder trying to wrestle one of his sows out of a bog.

Allie was so delighted to have a patient at last that she set about helping him with alarming enthusiasm.

"Come back in a day or two, won't you? . . . To make sure it's mending properly," she called after the boy when he ran off in a hurry. No one was entirely surprised when he didn't.

After that she was redundant again, bored almost to distraction, so that Gyltha's suggestion that morning was more than welcome.

A little while later, marching along the track to the village with Hawise, she felt content for the first time in ages, and if her gaze flickered to the causeway every now and again—just in case a certain person was riding along it—she was confident Hawise hadn't noticed.

Allie glanced at her fondly and, linking her arm through hers, gave it an affectionate squeeze.

Hawise beamed at her. "You haven't been to our cottage yet, have you, mistress?" she said. "I can't wait to show it to you."

"And I can't wait to see it," said Allie, squeezing her arm again, because this was just the sort of morning for squeezing Hawise's arm and bestowing affection on her.

"Only thing is," Hawise added, "I promised Father I'd check on the mole traps on the way, if you don't mind. I haven't been down there lately and it's not fair to leave 'em there too long, poor things."

Allie said she didn't mind in the least and followed her happily along a narrow, rush-lined path leading to a bend in the river where, like a confused traveler, the current paused, turned back on itself and then, with its sense of direction miraculously restored, rushed off in a hurry toward the forest.

Hawise stopped at the small landing stage and put down the sack she had been carrying. Allie sat down on a nearby hummock of sedge and watched her work for a while until she decided that mole slaying, however expertly performed, was boring and wandered off unnoticed. In fact, by the time Hawise looked up from her digging again she was already some distance away, heading toward the forest, idly swiping at the rushes on either side of the track with an alder twig as she went . . .

Hawise thought about going after her—after all, it wasn't safe to stray too far alone these days—but Allie looked so happy, and since there didn't seem to be anyone else around, she decided to let her enjoy a rare moment of freedom. She had just resumed digging when a cacophony of hunting horns, excited male voices and the deep belling of hounds crashing through the forest undergrowth rent the air.

It stopped Allie dead in her tracks, and a moment later two riders broke the cover of the trees and came galloping toward her.

For an awful moment she thought they wouldn't see her and that she would be trampled to death, but at the very last moment, one of them did and, calling urgently to his companion, stood up in his stirrups, sawing frantically at his horse's mouth, and brought it to an abrupt halt.

When Allie opened her eyes again—a reluctance to witness her own death had made her close them very tightly indeed—two men in hunting leathers were staring down at her from two sweat-lathered horses, the bloodied muzzle of a dead wolf slung over one of their saddles, sneering at her.

"God's teeth!" said a familiar voice. "Mistress Allie! What in God's name are you doing out here alone! You could have been in danger."

Allie let out the breath she had been holding. "Strange as it may seem, the same thought just occurred to me, too," she said, grinning up at Lord Peverell. "But, God be praised, I wasn't . . . And, actually I'm not alone . . ." She turned, pointing at Hawise, now a tiny speck in the distance, and immediately wished she hadn't. When she turned back Lord Peverell was still smiling down at her but Sir William was standing up in his stirrups staring at Hawise. Something in his expression made her uncomfortable . . .

"Come, Will." Perhaps Lord Peverell had sensed it, too. "How do you suggest we recompense this good lady after frightening her half out of her wits?"

Sir William grunted something neither of them could catch but was spared the repetition of it by the sudden appearance of a young man as he was dragged toward them behind four enormous wolfhounds.

"Got 'em back, my lord," he shouted triumphantly, his feet whirling over the ground without seeming to touch it. "Bugger of a job though! They'd got their noses to another spoor but I was quick as lightnin' greased both sides and managed to grab 'em before they took off again!"

As he got closer Allie recognized him as the young man who had reared up out of the marsh at them and felt the hairs on the back of her neck rising.

"Good work, Danny," said Lord Peverell. "That's a relief. Those are good dogs; it'd be a pity to lose them. But hold them hard, now, we don't want to frighten Mistress Allie any more than we have already."

The boy's jubilant expression crumpled to a scowl the moment he saw Allie, but Lord Peverell didn't seem to notice.

"Well, Mistress Allie," he continued, "you must allow me to atone for this somehow. One way or another, it seems, I have put you to a great deal of trouble lately."

Allie smiled and shook her head. "Not at all," she said. "No harm done and no atonement necessary . . . All I ask, though, is that perhaps you would tell me how Matilda is. I often think about her."

"Do you?" He looked delighted. "What a lucky creature she is to have such a place in your thoughts! I shall pass on your good wishes! She is doing very well, thank you. Nearly sound, in fact. Another day or two and I expect to be riding her again."

"That is good news," Allie said, hoping he hadn't noticed that she was blushing. "But if you'll excuse me, I must . . ." She glanced over her shoulder at Hawise. "Well, I ought . . . ought to be getting back, I suppose."

"Indeed," Lord Peverell replied, gathering up his reins and, Allie thought, or perhaps hoped, looking a little crestfallen. "But . . . before you go . . . perhaps you would do me the honor . . . well, you and Lady Penda, of course . . . of attending a feast I shall be hosting soon . . ."

Allie felt an exquisite rippling sensation in her belly and had to steel herself to reply without her voice betraying her excitement.

"I'm sure we would be delighted," she said. "But I will have to ask Lady Penda first, of course."

He nodded. "Of course . . . Well, in that case, the invitation will be with you within the week, but in the meantime, I bid you good day."

WHO WERE THEY, MISTRESS?" HAWISE asked her when she got back. "I was worried when I first saw them but then they seemed friendly enough."

"Well, one was," Allie said, and told her about the encounter.

"Aw," Hawise groaned when she had finished. "I knew I should've come with you! I've still never clapped eyes on him. You're so lucky, mistress."

"Am I?" Allie said, affecting the nonchalance she reserved for discussing Lord Peverell with Hawise for some reason. "Perhaps," she added.

By the time Hawise had packed up her things the Angelus was chiming for terce.

"That boy was with him," Allie told her as they set off to the village.

"What boy?"

Hawise's thoughts, unlike hers, had moved way beyond Lord Peverell some time ago and were now invested in her stomach, which was grumbling audibly for the pottage it knew was waiting for it at the cottage—if they ever got there. Allie, who was usually such a brisk walker, had started to dawdle.

"Oh, you know," Allie said. "That boy . . . The one from the marsh. You remember?"

"Oh, him." Hawise raised her eyebrows. "That pillard! Danny Wadlow, pain in everyone's arse. What about him?"

"Well that's what I was saying," Allie replied, a note of exasperation in her tone. "He was with them!"

"Well, he would be," said Hawise. "They use 'im sometimes when the old boy's off. Good with the dogs, or so they say. That's because he's got a brain like one if you ask me."

They walked along the towpath for some distance and around another sharp bend in the river and saw plumes of smoke rising from the village chimneys, cankering an otherwise pristine sky, and heard the unmistakable hubbub of the village going about its business: smiths hammering in their forges, babies crying, hogs bawling, dogs barking and cart wheels clanking along its rutted streets.

When they got to the main street they were engulfed by a crowd heading for the weekly market outside the gates of Ely Cathedral. Hawise took Allie's hand, leading her expertly through it until she had to stop abruptly to avoid a woman coming toward them.

Allie was surprised that Hawise hadn't noticed her before and that a collision was only narrowly avoided, because even from a distance, the woman stood out—something about the pallor of her skin, the misery in her expression and her apparent obliviousness to her surroundings. Indeed, she was so unaware of anyone or anything that if Hawise hadn't stopped in time, Allie suspected the woman would have tried walking through her like a shadow.

"Who was that?" she asked as she turned to watch her disappear into the crowd.

"Nobody knows," Hawise replied in a low voice. "Or at least, nobody knows her name. She's from another village. The poor soul haunts the place looking for her daughter who went missing."

The rest of the journey was rather somber after that. Allie was so distracted thinking about the woman that as they crossed the village green, she barely noticed the corpse hanging from the gibbet in the middle of it—which is to say that, although she didn't avert her eyes and scuttle past, the way Hawise did, she didn't linger in front of it as she might have done previously, nor, for once, did she envy the crows their early possession of such a valuable resource.

T HEIR ARRIVAL AT THE COTTAGE sent Rosa into a flap.
"Wish you'd warned me you was bringing Mistress Allie," she chided, wagging her finger at Hawise. "I woulda tidied the place a bit. We must look such a mess! I ain't even had the chance to change them rushes this mornin'! What must you think, mistress?"

"It's lovely," Allie said, looking around the neatly, if sparsely, furnished room, where there was barely a mote of dust visible even among the proliferation of rush-woven pots, bottles and baskets that lined the walls. Even the hens in the rafters were sitting tidily, not a dropping in sight, and the cauldron on the trivet was polished to a gleam.

"Stop fussing, Ma," Hawise snapped; hunger was making her irritable. "Mistress Allie doesn't mind how she finds us, do you?"

"No," Allie said quickly. "Really I don't. Besides, it's perfect. It's like the cottage where I grew up in Wisbech . . . only much, much tidier, of course."

The reassurance had a calming effect on Rosa, who stopped flapping and ushered them to the table and the bowls of pottage Hawise had lusted after all morning.

When they had finished eating they stayed at the table discussing the weather, various village affairs, Bishop Longchamp's departure and Penda's Christmas feast, which, according to Rosa, was something to look forward to.

"She makes the place look so beautiful," she said with pride. "And the food! Oh, Mistress Allie, you'll never eat the like again!"

"Mistress's got another feast to look forward to first," Hawise piped up, to Allie's horror. "She'll be sick to the teeth of 'em by Christmas, won't you, mistress?" she continued, ignoring Allie's warning look. "Oh, don't be shy. You will, won't you? You'll be sick to death of 'em by then."

Allie's heart sank further when Rosa turned to her, looking excited.

"Ooh," she said, "what's this then, mistress? Do tell."

Allie took a deep breath and, because she didn't have a choice, told her about her encounter with Lord Peverell.

"So that was them in the forest, was it?" Rosa asked when she had finished. "Thought I heard 'em calling when I was on the way back from the mill. So that was Lord Peverell then, eh?"

Allie nodded.

"He's got that Danny Wadlow workin' for 'im again," Hawise said.

Rosa looked grave all of a sudden. "I don't like 'im," she snapped, her fingers fretting nervously at the threads of her shawl. "Wouldn't trust that boy far as I could throw 'im. Got the hair of the wolf about him if you ask me."

"He's harmless, Ma," Hawise said, taking her hand and stroking it gently. "Don't worry so."

But, refusing to be mollified, Rosa stamped her foot under the table. "Don't you 'He's harmless, Ma' me! He's trouble, and don't forget, he was there that day on the ice when Martha went missing—and don't you shake your head at me, everyone saw 'im foolin' around like 'e does, makin' mischief of hisself as always . . ."

Hawise took her hand again. "But that's all he is, Ma," she said. "A nuisance, not a killer."

Rosa stared at her for a moment, then got up and went to the window. Hawise and Allie exchanged glances.

"I hope you're right," Rosa said with her back to them, staring out over the marsh. "But you'd better be getting along now. It's going to be dark soon and I don't want you wanderin' about in it."

As they got ready to leave, grateful for the mantles she had warmed by the fire for them, Allie congratulated her again on the delicious soup and the tidy conviviality of the cottage and was rewarded with a hug.

I THINK YOUR MOTHER MIGHT benefit from some vervain . . . or maybe lady's slipper," she told Hawise on the walk home. "Remind me to look out for some, will you? She needs something for her nerves."

"She certainly does," said Hawise with feeling.

Perhaps it was having spent too long in Rosa's nervy company, or perhaps it was the eerie shadows cast by the dusk, but all the way home Allie had a peculiar sense of conspicuousness again, as though there were unseen eyes on her.

CHAPTER 26

THERE WAS NO DOUBT ABOUT it, Rosa needed something for her nerves.

For some time now she had been struggling with a growing sense of unease—nothing she could define precisely, but a gnawing feeling in the pit of her stomach that something was amiss . . . or might be.

She had hoped, now that Bishop Longchamp had gone, that it would abate, but it didn't; in fact, it was getting worse, and today she felt almost crippled by it.

That morning she had wanted to get on with her chores but, most unusually, was finding it hard to settle down to anything.

Perhaps it was the weather.

The cloud-bruised sky didn't augur well; there was something ominous coming in from the east.

And it was chilly, too.

She got up to prod the fire and, as the smoke rose and disappeared through the louvered opening in the roof, lit some tallow candles, hoping they might brighten the room and her mood.

They didn't. Perhaps nothing would; she would simply have to resign herself to the fact that the Nameless Dreads were back.

She called them "Nameless," these peculiar feelings of hers, because she didn't know how else to define them, and "Dreads" because of what they were: insuperable fears of and for almost everything, washing over her, when they came, like a wave and an affliction she had endured ever since Hawise's birth almost sixteen years ago.

God, in his infinite wisdom, had granted her only one child, and after that, for reasons best known to himself, had closed her womb forevermore.

She had wanted more children, of course, so had Ulf, but they had learned to accept the divine forfeit they had unwittingly made for this one and didn't question it. And yet even while she knew deep down, when the baby was born, that she would be her first and last child, she had obeyed the tradition of the Fens, tending the child with indifference for the first year of her life, neither naming her nor showing her affection, because, as all sensible Fen women knew, love for a baby that was as likely to die as it was to live was a poor investment.

But on her first birthday a terrifying storm of love had erupted inside Rosa and she had rushed to the baby's cot weeping tears of joy and gratitude, taking the child in her arms and, throwing wide the window shutters, proclaiming her love for her for the world to hear.

"You gone soft, ol' girl," Ulf had told her, fearful of the vulnerability such love would bring her, but Rosa had smiled and waited patiently until, inevitably, he succumbed to it, too.

Poor Ulf! Poor her! she thought as she stared out over the

sullen marsh. Such a curse it was, such a terrible thing to love a child, more terrible even than her fear of poverty, this overwhelming terror that one day something dreadful would happen to Hawise and she would be forced to survive it.

She shuddered, irritable for having succumbed to this latest bout of accidie, or whatever it was, and yet she felt it so acutely this morning that she barely knew what to do with herself.

It was never far away, of course, a reproachful presence in the shadows, but since Martha's death and all the rumors about the missing girls, and what with Gyltha's illness, she felt its presence more keenly, and it was shredding her nerves and opening her eyes to portents she might otherwise have ignored.

Only the other day she had seen a bat fluttering around in broad daylight, and just last week, there had been that strange encounter with the hermit.

She tried to avoid the Elsford hermit as much as she could but because he kept the bridge over the river Nene, levying a toll on all those who tried to cross it, it wasn't always easy. Sometimes, when she had no choice but to go that way, she would try to get across before he spotted her, but she was rarely successful; despite his advanced age, there was something in his constitution, or perhaps the eremitic lifestyle, that endowed him with the speed and agility of youth.

Nobody quite knew when he had come to the Fens, or, indeed, where he had come from, but rumors abounded: one that he was once a fisherman to whom St. Anthony had appeared one night in a vision telling him to forsake society and all his worldly goods and spend the rest of his life performing penance in the service of God, another that he was a wealthy nobleman to whom another saint had appeared—with much the same message as St. Anthony—but nobody knew for certain. He was just there, like the Fenland bogs and mires, the alders and the fog.

As a child she had been terrified of him but as she got older, she wondered if, perhaps, she wasn't a little envious of him, too, unbound as he was from the earthly responsibilities that ground so many into the mire, free to renounce the muddy turbulence of the world and spend his life in the service of a bountiful God. This envy, if that was what it was, had only increased when Hawise was born; after all, she reasoned, at least you knew where you were in the service of God, which wasn't always the case with daughters.

That morning, as she made her way to the market, approaching the bridge with her usual trepidation, she was relieved not to see any smoke rising from the roof of his hut and even more relieved that she couldn't see a deer carcass strewn across it, either. Since the hermit was famously partial to venison, if there wasn't a carcass splayed across the thatch—where he kept them safe from the predation of wolves—it meant that he was probably out hunting for a replacement and would be gone for a while.

"Good," Rosa muttered to herself, about to dash across, when, from nowhere, the hermit suddenly appeared in front of her.

"God's teeth!" she screeched, flapping her hands in alarm. "What'd you do that for? You frightened me half to death!"

The hermit stared at her silently over the top of his staff, his icy blue eyes glinting like distant tarns under wild gray eyebrows.

He's enjoying this, Rosa thought indignantly. *He likes frightening people.*

"Ask for a blessing and beg a prophecy," the hermit said.

Too startled to speak, or run away, although she wanted to, Rosa waited, fear wedged tight in her chest, while he performed his prophesying ritual; stabbing his staff into the ground between them, he tilted his head back and sniffed the air like a dog. When he stopped sniffing, he lowered his head again and fixed her with a strange, mesmeric gaze.

"Pride comes before a fall," he intoned gravely. "Repent now and ye may be saved; for he is coming." When he had finished he pulled his staff out of the mud, turned on his heel and vanished into the hut.

"What about my blessing?" Rosa called after him, but he didn't come back.

THAT EVENING, WHEN ULF GOT home he immediately noticed that something was wrong.

"Them ol' Namelesses back again, are they?" he asked gently.

Rosa nodded, relieved to have them acknowledged at last, and then told him about the hermit.

"Have I been proud, do you think, Ulf?" she asked.

But he shook his head with an expression of such tenderness that it made her want to weep. "You?" he said, reaching across the table to take her hands in his. "Not my Rosa."

Sniffing back her tears, she returned his smile, even though she could derive no comfort from his reassurance.

There was none to be had. It wasn't true. She was proud. Not of herself, perhaps, but of Hawise, who was her life's prize beyond rubies and for whom, she sometimes felt, she might burst with it.

And yet it was a sin nonetheless. The Bible said so: "Everyone that is proud in heart is an abomination to the Lord and shall not be unpunished." Her feelings for Hawise made her an abomination to God, for which, as the hermit had warned her, she was going to be punished.

A WEEK LATER SHE WAS still preoccupied and had stood at the cottage window muttering to herself from the book of Proverbs long enough to see the day change, the soft gray light of the morning darkening as the storm clouds chased across the sky like the Horsemen of the Apocalypse, casting long shadows over the wildfowlers crouched low in their punts in the marsh.

The auditory rebuke of the chapel bells sounding for nones brought her to her senses eventually and sent her scuttling to her clothes chest for her apron to prepare the supper for Ulf and Hawise's return.

CHAPTER 27

ALLIE HAD EVERY INTENTION OF doing something for Rosa's nerves and might well have done, if the arrival of a messenger the very next day hadn't sent her into a spin.

She had spotted him from the solar window, a lone figure on horseback picking his way through the marsh, and had stood transfixed, her heart thumping with anticipation, mouth moving in prayer.

"Please, God, don't let him be from Wolvercote; please don't let him be from Wolvercote," she muttered, fixing on him like a hawk on a mouse, hoping against hope that, as he got closer, the livery he was wearing would reveal his provenance and put her out of her misery.

But it didn't. As it turned out he was in plain clothes, and the agony continued until Jodi came up to the solar and handed her a scroll.

"Another letter for you, mistress," she said. "An' one for Lady Penda," she added, brandishing another.

Allie took hers and, hands trembling, turned it over to inspect the seal.

Thank God!

It wasn't from Wolvercote! She felt like dancing around the room. At last it was the long-awaited invitation to the Dunstan feast.

GYLTHA SET ABOUT PREPARING FOR it as if it were a military campaign.

"Ain't havin' you two turnin' up lookin' like a couple of tatterdemalions," she told Allie and Penda. "I'll get a nice piece of samite . . . or maybe some damask," she said, addressing Jodi this time, whom she was dispatching to Cambridge to buy ells of cloth for the new dresses. "And we'll get a new mantle for you while we're at it," she said sternly to Penda before turning back to Jodi, whose mouth and fingers were moving furiously as she committed Gyltha's growing list to memory.

"Miniver be best, I think . . . and some lye. Plenty of that, mind . . . and some cloves . . . for their baths. We want 'em smellin' nice."

When the initial flurry of excitement had died down, the days dragged so murderously that Allie began to wonder whether death by anticipation was a possibility.

One morning, if only as a distraction, she decided to write to Adelia.

She had been feeling guilty for not sending news of Gyltha's recovery and, with little else to do, thought the business of writing a letter might help pass the time.

Whether she would mention James Peverell or not, she wasn't

sure. Perhaps not quite yet; perhaps it would be better to wait until Christmas, tell her face-to-face. Besides, just at the moment, there wasn't very much to tell.

When she finished the letter, she applied the seal and had just risen with a yawn from the desk when the solar door flew open and Ulf, face ashen and breathless, burst in.

"What is it?" she asked as he pushed past her, his eyes frantically scouring the room for something.

"We'll need this!" he said, confusing her even more by snatching up her medicine bag. "Now put on your warmest mantle and follow me, quick as you can . . . Please."

She barely had time to wrap the cloak around her before he had hold of her wrist and was pulling her through the door behind him.

At the head of the stairs he turned to her briefly.

"I'm sorry, Allie . . . I'll explain later and you'll forgive me then," he said. "But we have to be quick . . ."

They tore down the staircase and out into the courtyard, where heads turned and tongues tutted as they sprinted past. By the time they got to the gatehouse, Allie was breathless and getting increasingly alarmed.

She had never seen Ulf in such a panic, nor, come to that, moving so fast, and she couldn't imagine what could possibly have prompted it. Nevertheless she managed to keep pace with him all the way into the marsh until he made a sudden lurch to the right, taking her down a path so narrow that the bushes on either side snatched at her skirts like wicked fingers and tripped her up.

"Stop, Ulf! In pity's name, stop!" she cried out from her hands and knees. "You have to stop!"

She saw him pull up in the distance and turn back.

"I'm sorry, Allie, love," he said, helping her to her feet. "But, the thing is, there's another body turned up . . . another girl . . . like Martha . . . only this time . . ."

She nodded. He didn't have to say any more. She knew what he was asking of her: he had summoned her to examine the girl's body and determine the cause of her death, which, by necessity, had to be done as quickly and clandestinely as possible. Quickly because, in compliance with common law, he was under pressure to summon the county sheriff to perform his official inquest, and clandestinely to spare Allie the inevitable accusations of witchcraft if she were to be seen defiling a body.

He helped her put on the boot she had lost when she fell and led her along another path down to the river, where the bowed figure of an old man, dressed from head to toe in moleskin, was standing on the shingle beside what looked, at first, like a bundle of old rags.

Allie stared at the scene blankly for a moment, trying to con-jure the part of herself she had almost forgotten, feeling the goose-flesh rising on her arms as that peculiar but familiar sensation—a mixture of fear and excitement—began to stir inside her.

Ulf pointed at the old man.

"Harry the Fish," he whispered. "The one that found her, poor bugger."

Earlier that morning, as he loaded the fishing creels onto his boat, old Harry had heard something bump against the hull, and when he looked over the side saw the sightless white eyes of the dead girl staring back at him from underneath the water.

When he recovered his wits—although it took a while—he recovered the body, pulling it to the shore and, for decency's sake, covering it with his sheepskin mantle, and then ran as fast as his eel-skin boots could carry him to fetch Ulf.

N OBODY ELSE SEEN 'ER, I trust?" Ulf asked when, startled by the sound of their footsteps, Harry spun around.

The old man shook his head.

"Good." Ulf patted his shoulder. "Like I said, fewer that knows about this at the moment, the better."

He looked around them furtively but, seeing no one, turned to Allie.

"You understand why I brought you here . . . in case . . . ?"

She nodded; she did. He was hoping that, by some miracle, she would be able to find some evidence to reveal the cause of the girl's death, even though, as they both knew, a body dumped in water would have been washed clean of any long since.

He turned back to Harry.

"Thank you," he said. "You can be on your way now. Mistress Allie's here to prepare the body."

The fiction was a good one. Preparing the dead for burial was a woman's job. Ulf had explained her presence that morning and preempted further inquiry.

Harry hesitated a moment, staring hard at Allie, as though

deciding whether or not she was fit for the task, and then he made the armor of Christ and set off toward the village.

As soon as he left, Allie started walking toward the body.

"Wait," Ulf said, thrusting an arm out to bar her way until Harry had completely disappeared from view.

He let her go and watched her make her way over to the body, then turned his back.

He refused to watch her work, just as he had refused to watch her mother. Despite keeping vigil for Adelia more times than he cared to remember, he had never once allowed himself so much as a glimpse of her while she did whatever it was that she did.

The very idea of the death investigations made him shiver, not through lack of respect for either them or their expertise—he knew the good that could come of it, had seen that with his own eyes; it was just that he had never been comfortable with the process. Whichever way you looked at it, it was a defilement of sorts, ungodly, unnatural . . . And there had been times, recurrent in his nightmares, when, standing guard over Adelia, he, too, had fancied that he heard the voices of the dead.

He shivered, the cruelty of the cold, or perhaps it was something else, seeping into his bones, and yet knew that however uncomfortable he was, he would stand there until hell froze if he had to, watching over that girl just as he had her mother.

Allie knelt beside the body, feeling the damp of the shingle seeping through her skirt to her knees, adding a physical dimension to the nervous chill she already felt.

She took a deep breath, steadying herself for what she was about to do, then stretched her hand out toward the body . . . and immediately withdrew it.

Her hand was trembling; she was losing her nerve.

In the past there had always been Adelia beside her to guide and prompt her through the process of an investigation. But now, for the first time, she was alone, and the sense of accountability was overwhelming.

She rocked back on her heels, shaking the nerves and cold out of her hands. As she stared out over the river a breeze picked up, shuddering the surface of the water and rocking the boats by the landing stage into a rhythmic percussion, and then, from somewhere, she heard a blackbird sing.

She let out the long, deep breath she had been holding; something about the infinite beauty of this strange, mysterious landscape had restored her courage.

Now just get on with it, woman!

The voice inside her head was her mother's. She sat up straight, preparing to address the body with the formula Adelia had taught her.

"Forgive me for what I am about to do. But permit your flesh and bones to tell me what your voice cannot."

At last she was ready.

CHAPTER 28

THE FIRST THING SHE NOTICED when she lifted the make-shift pall was the small act of tenderness Harry had per-formed by closing the girl's eyes—that and the fact that she was very young. She was probably around Hawise's age, fifteen, six-teen at the most; pretty like her, too, and, judging by the little Allie could see of her complexion—under all the weeds and mud the river had smothered her with—the Fenland air, while she was still able to breathe it, had obviously agreed with her.

Allie opened her bag, took out an oilcloth apron and stood up again to tie its strings around her waist.

"Do we know who she is?" she called out to Ulf.

"No," he replied without turning around, for which she was grateful. Even in death the girl at her feet seemed so vulnerable that she couldn't bear eyes on her, not even ones as kind as his.

Be careful, Allie. It is not our job to pity the dead but to speak for them.

Adelia's voice again, reminding her that if she had taught her anything, it was that pity was an encumbrance to an investigation, the enemy of logic, and, if unchecked, would be an impediment. She had to remember the discipline she had learned.

Never look at a corpse and see the body of a person; see the cadaver of a pig. It takes practice, darling, but you'll learn. Always pigs, remember. Never people. Not until the job is done. Don't allow your feelings to cloud your judgment.

She knelt back down on the shingle, took her slate and a piece of chalk out of her bag and got to work.

Use your eyes, Allie. See the wider picture first in case you miss something important. Details come later, remember. Now look! And tell me what you see.

Allie looked.

The girl was of average height and build and, now that her hair was beginning to dry, looked to be fair in color.

As far as she could see, there weren't any flesh wounds, which implied, at this early stage, that the likely cause of death was drowning. But unless she could defile the body by opening the chest and removing a section of one of her lungs—which she could not—it would be impossible to ascertain whether they contained silt and therefore whether the girl had entered the water before or after her death.

Allie scribbled down a note on her slate, then returned to the body, this time her focus on the girl's stomach.

The abdomen is mildly inflated.

Good! She was beginning to think with the clinical fluency she had learned.

And there are indications, from a discernible, if mild, marbling of the skin, that the bloat stage of decomposition has begun.

She made another note.

However, there is no maceration of the hands or feet and no loosening of the skin, hair or nails, suggesting that the body has been in the water no longer than a day or two at most.

She made another note, then put the slate aside for a moment to blow some warmth into her numbing hands. When the feeling returned, she started peeling back the thick, sticky fronds of hair that were plastered around the girl's neck.

Allie's fingers worked delicately around the girl's skull and face, moving methodically to her throat, feeling the gentle yield of muscle and sinew, the taut skin of her thorax, and then something else . . . something she hadn't expected.

A less diligent hand, a sheriff's perhaps, might have missed it; the fracture was slight but, to Allie, unmistakable.

She leaned closer to the body and saw the faint but unmistakable mark of a thumb-sized bruise on the front of the girl's neck.

The evidence was irrefutable: it wasn't a drowning. A pair of hands had wrapped around her neck, its thumbs pressing hard on her jugular vein, clamping down her trachea without release even as she struggled to take her last breath . . .

Nor was Allie in any doubt that the girl had struggled. Clearly visible above the bruise was a set of crescent-shaped marks: defensive wounds that her own fingernails had gouged in her skin as she fought for her life.

Suddenly she could see the girl alive, her face contorted in terror as an assailant—glimpsed in Allie's vision like a shadow in the fog—throttled her to death.

"Everything all right, Allie?"

She spun around, her heart pounding. She had been so absorbed that, for a moment, she had forgotten that she wasn't alone and that Ulf had been standing guard so patiently all this time.

"Yes . . . Yes . . . Just one more thing," she called back when she had caught her breath.

She finished her examination and made her last note, but as she was lifting the girl's arms to place them across her chest in a last act of respect, she noticed a tiny set of marks on the inside of one of her wrists: scratches, driftwood abrasions from the river probably, which, judging by the lack of blood or bruising around them, were inflicted postmortem.

She rubbed her eyes, which were now misty with fatigue, and looked again, only this time she saw they were deliberately carved, two distinct letters etched into the skin.

"DV."

She took up her slate again and made another note, then covered the body with Harry's mantle and stood up at last.

"I'm ready," she said.

A LTHOUGH ULF WAS SHOCKED, HE wasn't surprised when she told him about her findings.

"It's the devil's work," he said.

Had she not been so tired she might have argued the point. She didn't believe in the devil. Her life experience, her medical training, indeed, her mother, had taught her enough about human nature for her to know that it didn't need supernatural help to perform great wickedness. It was simply that, in certain circumstances and certain people, there was an absence of God, a vacuum of morality.

"Ulf," she said, taking the hand he had offered to help her up the bank. "When you saw Martha's body . . . were there any markings on her wrists?"

He thought for a moment, then shook his head.

"Can't say I noticed any. Like what?"

"Letters, on the inside of one of her wrists. Like a set of initials or something."

"Carved there, d'you mean?"

"Yes," she replied. "Not deep but deliberately inscribed: 'DV' or something like that."

Ulf shook his head again, then, seeing how pale and tired she looked, suddenly took his cloak off and wrapped it around her shoulders.

Just before they set off she turned back for one last look at the body.

"I don't like leaving her there, Ulf," she said. "Supposing . . . ?"

"Don't you worry." He put his arm around her. "Harry'll be back with the priest soon and they'll take her to the church."

"But who's going to bury her?" she asked, reluctant to leave the little heap of rags on the shingle, which seemed to her one of the most pitiful, lonely sights she had ever seen.

Ulf shrugged. "I don't know, Allie. We don't even know who she is," he said. "We'll 'ave to wait until somebody claims her."

She didn't know why, but she thought the girl looked as though she had been loved, and she was tormented by the idea of a family's missing her, then remembered the woman with the haunted face who had nearly crashed into Hawise the other day.

"Aye," he said when she mentioned her. "I know the one you mean. We'll find 'er and hope to God it is her daughter and that she can bury her at last. But, don't forget, there's more than one girl missing."

They walked on in weary silence for a while.

"When do you think the sheriff will come?" Allie asked.

"Oh, don't you worry 'bout that, either," Ulf replied. "He's been sent for and 'e'll turn up in 'is own good time, idle bastard! But don't get your hopes up; likely he'll take a look at the body; find nothing wrong, other than that she's dead—leastways let's 'ope 'e gets that right; and then say she drowned. Easier that way, see."

Allie nodded. For different reasons, she would have found that easier, too. It would have been so much more palatable to believe that there had been no malice, no cruelty, no human hand involved in this girl's death, that it was simply a case of terrible bad luck. But the evidence to the contrary was irrefutable.

CHAPTER 29

WHEN THEY GOT BACK TO the house they found Gyltha and Penda asleep in front of the fire in the hall. A wolf-hound sniffing languidly at their feet, searching for scraps, barked when he saw them, waking Gyltha with a start.

"Noisy bugger!" she grumbled, aiming an idle kick at the animal as it lumbered past. "I've a good mind to turn you into a mantle for 'er," she said, glaring at Penda, who was also beginning to stir. "Ooh," she said, brightening when she saw Allie and Ulf in the doorway. "Back at last. Come on in then, tell!"

Gyltha's omniscience was a source of fascination for Allie. There was almost nothing she didn't know. No snippet of news or secret ever slipped past her unimbibed, and there were times when Allie suspected that she could even interpret the whisper of a breeze.

Penda drew up a couple of stools for them by the fire.

"Sit yourself down, bor," she said, propelling Allie toward one of them. "You're lookin' thrawn, if I may say so."

Allie sat, grateful for the warmth and a chance to sit quietly for a moment, even though it didn't last. Even as she closed her eyes, she could feel the pressure of theirs, ravenous for her information.

"Murdered then," Gyltha said when she had told them about the investigation.

Allie nodded.

"Poor girl," murmured Penda, almost to herself. She had been exceptionally quiet during the telling and more stricken by it than the others, as though it held some sort of personal resonance for her, reminding Allie of her long-held suspicion that a great mystery lay in Penda's past that she had yet to get to the bottom of.

After that they sat silently, staring into the fire, until Ulf sighed wearily and got up from his stool.

"Best be gettin' off, then," he said, resting his hand on Allie's shoulder.

She looked up at him, feeling the tears she had been resisting all day prick the back of her eyes. After everything they had been through recently, she couldn't bear to see him leave.

"I have to go, Allie, love," he said, seeing her distress. "I have to make sure they got her body to the church safely and that the bloody sheriff's turning up. You understand that, don't you?"

She nodded. Of course she did. So much rested on the sheriff's verdict, and it had implications for Ulf himself. In the unlikely event that he returned a murder verdict, it would fall on Ulf to organize a vigil around the village boundary in case the murderer—whoever he might have been—escaped, in which case the village would be heavily fined.

They watched him to the door, and when it closed behind him Gyltha turned to Allie.

"Right then, you . . . Bed!" she said firmly. "Seen your ma in that state more times 'an I care to remember . . . Sleep! That's what you need, and plenty of it."

When she was resolute like that, Allie knew better than to argue with her; besides, before she knew it, Jodi was gently coaxing her off her stool and steering her toward the staircase.

S HE WOKE UP TO A fading light and Hawise in silhouette at the window. Disoriented by sleep, she didn't see her properly at first, but instead saw a living facsimile of the murdered girl. An instinct she had never felt before propelled her out of bed and across the room.

"Be careful," she said, wrapping her arms around her. "Promise me you will be very careful."

T HAT EVENING ULF'S TITHING TOOK up the vigil outside the church, while inside the women tended to the body of the girl and laid her to rest on a bier. When the priest had said an antiphon and a psalm over her and sprinkled her body with holy water, they left.

The next day a mass was held for her, and throughout the diocese, all parish priests—or, at least, those able to read the notices pinned to the church gates—appealed to their congregations to help identify her.

By the Sabbath, when she was still anonymous, Father Edward, in whose crypt she lay, was making his way down the altar steps, preparing to address his congregation, when a peculiar thing happened.

He suddenly felt imbued not with the disaffection usually accompanying this great mimetic rite—most of his congregation, after all, wouldn't have known a word of Latin if it leapt out of the Bible and bit them in the arse—but something else entirely, something quite extraordinary, in fact: an overweening sense of elation that, at last, he was at the very center of a genuine mystery.

He looked out almost affectionately on his worshippers, who were still pouring into the nave in their droves, and noticed how quietly, how respectfully, they were coming in. Perhaps, for once, they had come not from curiosity or boredom but for genuine enlightenment and comfort. Perhaps, at long last, he was the light to which they were turning in these dark, uncertain times and the mysterious dead girl in the crypt wasn't simply a puller of crowds but a symbol of something more meaningful.

The hair on the back of his neck rose with the thrill of this extraordinary revelation and he decided that he would reward them with a sermon in English for a change.

He looked down at the sea of upturned, expectant faces, smiled genially upon them, put his shoulders back and prepared to deliver the sermon to end all sermons . . .

A FTER MASS THE CONGREGATION SPILLED out into the churchyard. Neighbor garrulously greeted neighbor until the cacophony of voices rose to such a pitch that even the rooks in the elm tops were drowned out.

Rosa leaned against a gravestone, wondering whether—if it wasn't for the blacksmith—she would still want to go home.

The man had purloined poor Ulf ruthlessly from the moment they stepped out of church, something to do with his neighbor's dilapidated cottage, which, he said, was bringing his corner of the village into disrepute. In fact, he insisted Ulf go with him that moment to put a stake in the cottage garth as a reminder to the slummocking fumble-fist that the authorities were onto him and that he should make the repairs immediately.

Or something; she was only half listening. The rest of the time she was looking idly around, wondering whether to stay put and risk the blacksmith's boring her to death or try to slip off home unnoticed.

But it wasn't just the blacksmith. The advent of the dead girl and her recent attack of the Nameless Dreads had done nothing to lift her spirits, which meant that she was in no mood for idle chat this morning and increasingly anxious to get back to the sanctuary of the cottage.

While the blacksmith droned on, she looked around, hoping to see Hawise. She had something she wanted to discuss with her, but all of a sudden, the girl was nowhere to be seen.

They had sat together in church as usual but because Father Edward's sermon—which was a surprise, being in English for a change—went on rather, halfway through it Rosa was easily distracted by a falcon when it squawked loudly at the back.

When she turned around to look at it, she saw Peter make a clumsy and belated attempt to hood it, and when he caught her eye, they had exchanged amused glances. She had turned back to Father Edward, thinking about what a refreshingly pleasant young man Peter was and, more important, whether Hawise thought so, and how the day was fast approaching when they would have to start thinking about a match for her . . .

In the meantime, Father Edward, who had the bit between his teeth this morning, droned on and on with his sermon, and before long Rosa got distracted again, this time by a shaft of glorious sunlight shining through one of the belfry windows onto Hawise's hair, giving her voluptuous curls such an astonishing gleam that it made her gasp in admiration. Sometimes she quite forgot how beautiful that hair was, how beautiful, in fact, her daughter was . . .

She turned around again, only this time casting a maternally critical eye over the other girls in the congregation, whom she found wanting in comparison. Ulf would tell her it was a mother's bias, but it was nothing of the sort; she was very fond of those girls, had known most of them all their lives, but it was obvious to anyone with half an eye—even their own mothers— that not one was a patch on her Hawise.

In fact, now she came to think about it, they all looked much of a muchness these days; it was almost impossible to tell them apart . . . And then it dawned on her why that was, and her head whipped around a third time.

Of course! That was why! They all had their hair covered.

She turned back to Hawise, her hubris of a moment ago banished now that she realized as things stood, with a killer of young women on the loose, it probably wasn't such a blessing to stand out from the crowd.

Her heart was pounding with such renewed anxiety that she could barely sit still and decided that, at the earliest opportunity, she would have a word with Hawise and insist that she follow the example of the others and wear a wimple in future.

But, when the time came, Hawise was nowhere to be seen.

She was about to interrupt Ulf and the blacksmith, make her excuses and go home, when she saw Ediva on the other side of the graveyard, beneath the old yew tree, playing with the children, laughing as they tugged on her skirts, spinning her around. The unexpectedly joyful sight changed her mind about going home and she set off toward them instead, dexterously weaving her way through the crowd, nodding politely to anyone she recognized and gathering snippets of conversation as she went— mostly about the weather, people wondering whether the cold snap would last until Christmas and whether or not it would snow. But there was also a great deal of conjecture about the dead girl, as people wondered who she was, where she had come from and how she had turned up dead in their river.

Just as she was trying to squeeze unnoticed past a particular group of women who were holding forth in the middle of the path through the gravestones, one noticed her.

"Rosa!"

She froze.

It was Magge, the thatcher's wife, a garrulous woman who had a voice like a corncrake.

"Oh, Rosa, just the person! We was just talking about that poor girl," Magge said, lowering her voice with such exaggerated reverence that the end of her sentence was more mouthed than spoken.

"Oh . . . Yes . . . the poor girl . . . ," Rosa said, straining to look past her to make sure Ediva and the children were still there, hoping that, if she looked distracted enough, Magge might let her go.

But Magge had other ideas. In fact, she had been looking out for her all morning. She assumed that Rosa, as wife of the village reeve, would be privy to information they were not and was determined to winkle it out of her . . .

"You see, Rosa," Magge continued, lips pursed, arms folded across her ample chest, "we was wondering what Ulf thought about it."

Rosa's eyes narrowed. "I'm not sure there's much for him to think," she replied.

"Well." Magge was undeterred. "Thing is, and not to put too fine a point on it, what we're wonderin' is: does 'e think she drowned or was she murdered? You see, we can't help thinkin' about Martha and all them rumors when they found 'er body, and nobody ever knew for sure what happened to 'er, did they?"

"Shh!" Rosa shocked even herself when her hand suddenly shot out and clamped itself over Magge's mouth. "Don't talk about Martha!" she hissed. "I shouldn't 'ave to remind you, as it was my nephew what found the body and 'ad nightmares ever since, poor little mite . . . Martha drowned! That girl, too, if you want the truth! And tha's all there is to say on the matter!"

She could feel herself turning crimson as her blood seethed with a combination of anger and contrition. It was wrong to get so angry and she shouldn't have put her hand over Magge's mouth like that, but she was so desperate not to be part of all the fear and rumormongering that had descended on the parish like a funeral pall ever since Longchamp's investiture that, now that he was gone, she was damned if she was going to crawl back under it, even if they weren't.

"Well! We don't care what you say, Rosa." The other women were joining in, their circle closing in around her.

The truth was that the others had never really liked her and, since her marriage to Ulf, had thought that she considered herself above them. Therefore her reluctance to contribute to the gossip that morning was all the excuse they needed to turn on her.

"I say she was murdered, and I'll tell you another thing." Buoyed by the support of the others, Magge had recovered from the hand-over-the-mouth incident and was wagging her finger threateningly in Rosa's face. "I reckon if that Father Edward goes and looks at 'er now, 'e'll find that she's bleeding."

A murmur of intrigue rippled around the group, making them huddle even closer together.

"What d'you think, then?" another asked with a furtive glance at the church. "Was he in there then? The murderer? In the church? Do you think so?"

"Oh! He was there all right, bor," said yet another. "Wouldn't doubt that for a moment."

Captivated by the latest intrigue, they ignored Rosa's howl of derision and barely noticed when she wandered off.

"Ridiculous!" she muttered to herself as she stomped off toward the yew tree. "Ridiculous!"

It was true that sometimes, even in her own mind, the boundaries of religion and superstition were a little blurred, but she had sense enough to know—married to Ulf, how could she not?—that a corpse did not spontaneously bleed in the presence of its murderer. Even so, she couldn't help running through the faces of the men she had seen in church that morning, wondering who it might be.

Early the next morning the sheriff came to Elsford. His cavalcade clattered down the main street and, with a shrill blast of horns and unnecessary pomp, came to an abrupt halt at the church gate.

Father Edward—dragged from his bed only moments before by the alewife, who had heard the horses while she was emptying her chamber pots—arrived only just in time to greet him.

Stifling a yawn, he helped him from his horse and led him to the body.

The air in the crypt, already smelling of damp, became even more malodorous when Father Edward lit the fat-dipped tapers and it mingled with the stench of stale cooking.

The sheriff grimaced when it reached his delicate nostrils and vowed that, however poor the light was—and it was—he wouldn't request any more in case it made things worse. When he had made his displeasure at the olfactory conditions clear to the young priest—wafting a pudgy, jewel-encrusted hand in front of his nose—he felt better. Anxious to get on and out as quickly as possible, he hastened over to the bier.

"Dead for how long, did you say?" he asked Father Edward as he pulled back the pall.

"Erm. I didn't?" said Father Edward hesitantly, trying to remember what Ulf had told him.

"Hmm . . . Ah well. No matter," the sheriff said, whipping back the last of the sheet and exposing the body. "Poor girl!" he murmured, looking down on her. So young! So sad! . . . So . . .

Goodness, the light really was awfully poor! He blinked and leaned in closer . . . So terribly . . . Eughhh . . . Mottled around the edges!

He recoiled involuntarily, crossing himself and hoping Father Edward hadn't noticed this moment of frailty, but it couldn't be helped; that skin of hers was definitely on the turn, and he prayed, for all their sakes, that she could be buried soon.

"Name? Occupation?" he barked.

"Unknown," Father Edward replied, stifling another yawn.

"Drowning!" the sheriff pronounced, and hastily whipped the sheet back over the body.

D ROWNING!" ALLIE SCREECHED WHEN ULF told her the verdict. "How could he possibly say it was drowning? Is he blind? . . . But . . . but . . . what about the contusions on her neck? What about the fracture, for goodness' sake? How could he possibly have missed that?"

Watching her pace up and down, spitting vitriol about the sheriff, Ulf was reminded of Adelia, who behaved very similarly when her blood was up.

"The man's a pillard!" Allie spat, stamping her foot in frustration. "Stupid, blind bastard! I bet he hardly looked at her!"

Ulf had been equally frustrated when Father Edward gave him the news, but he wasn't surprised; it was what he had expected, after all, and, when it came down to it, another verdict was unlikely to make any difference.

Allie stopped pacing for a moment.

"What are we going to do?" she asked.

"Not much we can do." He shrugged. "But there is some good news," he added. "She's been identified at least. Turns out she's the tanner's daughter from March; been missing for weeks apparently. Her parents came to fetch her today."

"That's something, I suppose," Allie replied vaguely.

She was standing with her back to him at the window, apparently deep in thought, when the implication of what he had just told her struck her and she spun around.

"But, Ulf. That's it! This girl had also been missing for some time but when I examined her, it was obvious she'd only been dead, what, a day . . . two at the most. I told you, remember? Well, that was the same with Martha! And if, as I think we have to assume, Martha was murdered, too, then it looks increasingly likely that both girls were killed by the same person!"

CHAPTER 30

WHEN HE LEFT THE SOLAR Ulf went to look for Hawise. When he couldn't find her in any of her usual haunts he began to worry and was relieved when he eventually found her in the courtyard sitting between Peter and Bertha, the heavily pregnant laundress, on the fishpond wall.

As he started toward them, a dairy maid in hot pursuit of a goose she was trying to herd into a pen ready for tomorrow's pot darted across his path. The squawk it occasioned when she had to resort to flinging the hem of her skirt over its head to stop it was loud enough to interrupt Hawise midsentence.

She looked up.

"There you are," Ulf said irritably.

"Sorry, Pa. But I had to come out here to help Bertha. Her belly's too big to carry much nowadays, see."

Ulf glanced at Bertha's incapacitating belly and then at Peter, who, for reasons he didn't understand but found irritating none-theless, started blushing as he scrambled to his feet.

"Did you get that bird o' yours back the other day?" Ulf asked.

"Thank you, I did," Peter replied, the blush deepening. "Lucky I did, too. She wouldn't 'ave lasted much longer if Mistress Allie hadn't spotted her when she did."

The day before the girl's body had been found, during one of her archery lessons Allie had spotted a falcon with its jesses snagged on a tree branch. Worried that unless it was rescued it would die of starvation, she rushed back to the mews to tell Peter. When she couldn't find him, she alerted Ulf to it instead.

"Aye, well," Ulf said grudgingly. "Glad it turned out all right, in that case, but don't let it happen again. Mistress Allie was very upset by it."

He turned to Hawise, holding out his hand to help her up.

"Come on. Let's be off. It's getting late."

On the way home he told her about the sheriff.

"Best not mention it to your mother though," he warned. "Not with her nerves the way they are at the moment. She knows, o' course, but she won't want to dwell on it."

I T WAS DUSK WHEN THEY reached the outskirts of the village, quiet at last, the most peaceful time of the day, Ulf had always thought, all the animals safely put away for the night, all the villagers settled around their hearths, the only sound for miles around the occasional hoot of an owl and the faint, low drone of conversation drifting out of the rush-lit cottages.

They walked in companionable silence until they got to the church, which, unusually, still had candles burning in the windows.

Ulf stopped at the gate.

"Mind if I look in for a moment? I've been meaning to have a word with the pastor and by the looks of things he's still there . . ."

He wanted to remind Father Edward, who could be very forgetful at times, to lock the font before he retired for the evening. Someone had been stealing holy water from it, for the purposes of witchcraft, it was presumed.

He left Hawise on the porch and went inside, surprised to find it unusually brightly lit and that the usual godly scent of damp stone and incense was corrupted, this evening, by heavy notes of beeswax from all the candles burning in the wall sconces. Nor, as he expected, was Father Edward alone; rather he was standing on the chancel steps, his back to Ulf, deep in conversation with another young man, who was also in clerical robes.

"Evenin', Father," Ulf called out from the doorway.

Father Edward turned around and smiled when he saw him. "Oh, Ulf! Just the person! Perhaps you could help us." He beckoned him over. "Have you met our friend?" he asked, shuffling sideways to make room for Ulf on the step beside them.

Now that he could see his face, Ulf recognized the young almoner from the cathedral.

"Brother John, ain't it?" he replied.

"Indeed." Father Edward nodded. "And also a very talented artist if I may say so. But I fear I've had to bring him in because we're having such trouble with Our Lady's feet." He sighed sadly, inclining his head toward the painting on the wall, a depiction of the doom and the Virgin Mary sitting at Christ's right hand.

Ulf took off his coif and peered at it, then scratched his head.

He could feel Father Edward's expectant gaze as he awaited his response, but he didn't have one. The problem with the painting, whatever it was, wasn't obvious to him. In fact, to his admittedly untrained eye, everything looked pretty much as it had last Sunday and, now he came to think of it, every Sunday before that. In the end, although he was loath to disappoint the young priest, he had to admit defeat.

"What's wrong with 'em, then?" he asked.

"Well! It's this!" said Father Edward with a pained expression as he wafted his hand in the vicinity of the divine toes. "They're terribly faint, you see . . . It's all the kissing!"

"Kissing?" Ulf turned to Brother John for elucidation. Father Edward wasn't making any sense.

"It's the congregation," the monk explained. "It's quite common, actually. They can't resist kissing the images when they see them and the trouble is, you see, that it takes the paint off eventually. I get an awful lot of this sort of remedial work nowadays."

"Oh," said Ulf. "I see." And now that it had been pointed out to him, he did: when he looked again—and certainly compared with the images that weren't within kissing distance—the bottom half of the Blessed Mother was beginning to look distinctly vague.

They stood in silent contemplation for a while until Ulf had an idea.

"Perhaps it's all the flesh," he said, scratching his chin thoughtfully. "Perhaps that's what provokes 'em. Give 'er a longer skirt?" he suggested.

WAITING FOR ULF ON THE porch, looking out over the moonlit graveyard, Hawise found her thoughts drifting to the dead girl who so recently had lain in the crypt beneath her feet.

"She were about your age," Ulf had told her when he came back after Allie's investigation. He had told her other things, too, the few details that he knew, but it was the comparison of their ages that had resonated with her most.

Ever since that day she had thought about her often, wondering, like everybody else, who she was, where she had come from and whether or not her unshriven soul had been admitted to heaven at last or made to wander the earth a poor lost soul forever. She imagined her rising from her grave in bridal dress, a beautiful blue bliaut, with a jewel-encrusted torque around her neck and golden bracelets on her arms, reaching into the celestial light around the Blessed Virgin.

Hawise very much hoped that it was less an imagining and more of a vision and that the girl, whoever she was, had found her bliss at last.

A BOISTEROUS RUSTLING IN THE yew hedge on the other side of the graveyard distracted her from the dead girl and alerted her to the presence of a fox instead, emerging from the earth beneath the knotted roots.

She watched it saunter through the graveyard, pausing every now and again to either sniff the air or relieve itself against a tombstone, stopping only when it reached the freshly churned earth of Martha's grave, its ears pricked, eyes sweeping the churchyard until they came to rest on her.

They stared at one another in mutual curiosity for a while until the fox lowered its head and darted off across the graveyard into the meadow.

She was still staring after it when the door behind her creaked open and she turned to see Brother John coming through it.

For a moment he didn't seem to recognize her, but then his expression clouded and he stopped suddenly, teetering on the step as if unsure whether he should brave pushing past her or retreat into the sanctuary of the church, while Hawise prayed that the ground might open up and swallow them both.

By rights, of course, she knew it should be her that was swallowed and her alone. After all, her discomfort was the wages of sin for having teased him so mercilessly with the other girls, or, at the very least, not trying harder to stop them; his only crime was to have fallen in love with the beautiful Martha and let it show.

Withering under the hostile gaze, wondering whether it was too late for an apology, she saw his expression change again as, to her enormous relief, he recovered his wits, tugging his cowl low over his face and pushing past her into the night.

Just as she let out the breath she had been holding, she felt a hand on her shoulder and gasped it in again.

"Sorry, little love," Ulf said, amused by her startled expression as she spun around to him. "I didn't mean to frighten you, but we can go home now."

CHAPTER 31

Wolvercote Manor

R OWLEY, ROWLEY."
He woke to Adelia's singing his name, pressing her lips into the nape of his neck with a noisy kiss. She had been lying beside him fully awake for a while now but she was starting to get fidgety. She had things to do and things she wanted to discuss.

She gave him a moment and then, when he didn't respond, kissed him again, softly this time, breathing in the warmth and scent of his skin, feeling the reassuring rise and fall of his chest beneath her arm.

"I love you," she whispered.

He opened a wary eye.

"You mean you want something," he said.

"Well . . ." She rolled onto her back. "That, too, I suppose," she murmured, distracted suddenly by an intricate dusty-looking cobweb in the corner of one of the ceiling rafters, and considered waking that idle Lena next—not with kisses, either—and shoving her nose in it.

When Rowley still showed no sign of stirring, she sat up.

"I have received a letter from our daughter," she said.

Rowley muttered an unintelligible response, his voice croaky with sleep, and pulled the blanket over his head.

He was always so tired these days.

He had arrived late last night, an impromptu visit for some much-needed respite after a series of episcopal meetings prompted by the recent rash of excommunications that had been imposed on almost everybody by Bishop William Longchamp.

He had sent a letter with the mandate of the Pope, addressed to all bishops, demanding that they should assemble with candles burning and bells ringing to excommunicate and publicly denounce Count John and all his advisers, accomplices and partisans.

The roster of the names he wanted denounced included Archbishop Walter of Coutances; the bishops of Winchester and Coventry; and the four justiciars: Gerard of Camville; William Marshall; Count John's chancellor, Stephen Ridel; and Rowley himself.

Soon after the letter's publication, however, Longchamp capitulated, postponing the count's excommunication until Quinquagesima Sunday in February of the following year, hoping that a reprieve might give him time to repent of his wicked ways.

Nobody took much notice and the directive was roundly ignored, but, nevertheless, it was a symptom of trouble brewing, and there was already more than a whiff of anarchy in the air, not least the rumors that Philip of France—who had ignominiously deserted the Crusade that summer—was plotting against Richard.

As soon as he got back to France he had attempted to invade Normandy, an act of aggression that his own barons scuppered when they refused to break the truce of God by plundering a crusading noble's lands. When that failed, he started making overtures to Count John—whose hunger for power, and the English throne in particular, was an ill-kept secret.

It was this matter the bishops had met to discuss, because, while they could disregard the odd excommunication or two, it was considered imprudent to ignore a potential invasion or the threat of civil war.

"Rowley!" Adelia pulled the blanket off his head. "You might show some interest."

"I'm sorry," he said, squinting in the harsh morning light. "I was thinking about other things." He yawned, rubbing his eyes, then added, "You do realize that you have a peculiar tendency toward aggression in the mornings, don't you?"

"It's not aggression, Rowley," she said, picking a lock of hair out of his eyes. "It's called being awake. Now, there are things I need to discuss and your daughter is one of them."

"My daughter, is it now?" he said. "Then am I to presume there's a problem of some sort? After all, she's usually only my daughter when there is."

"I received a letter from her," said Adelia, getting out of the bed. "And I think there is."

She went to the basin, with a blanket wrapped around her like a chrysalis, and struggled to lift a large water-filled aquamanile without exposing too much flesh to the chill of the room, then took a piece of willow bark from a pile beside her on the sill to clean her teeth.

Rowley watched her going about her ablutions with a lustful affection.

"Come back to bed, you succubus," he said. "It's cold in here without you."

His heart sank when she turned to him. He knew that expression only too well: the thin but conciliatory smile, the cold eyes. She wouldn't be coming back to bed; she meant business this morning.

"I want to know," she said, ignoring his groan of disappointment, "whether or not I should read you Almeison's letter."

He didn't know what to say. He wouldn't admit it, of course, but actually, he thought it wasn't necessary. He had heard Allie's news already because Penda had written to him, delighting him with details of the burgeoning relationship between her and this Lord Peverell. He hadn't relayed it to Adelia because he had assumed she would be cross.

"Well, perhaps you don't need to read it all," he said, turning over. "Perhaps just the gist."

Adelia didn't reply at first. She didn't have to; even through the back of his head he could feel the sting of her glare.

"Very well," she said. "Well, the gist of it, Rowley, is that it is my opinion that we must go to Elsford immediately. According to our daughter there have been at least two murders recently and she means to investigate them."

Rowley sat up. All of a sudden she had his undivided attention.

"But she can't!" he said, his voice rising in panic. "What authority does she have? Come to that, what are the authorities doing?"

"None and nothing," Adelia replied. "Which is precisely why we need to go. She needs us, Rowley."

But for a moment, Rowley was lost, engulfed in a dark, familiar shadow, remembering all the blighted years he had spent worrying about Adelia.

They had first met one summer in Cambridge, both sent there on separate assignments for the king: Adelia, in her capacity as a doctor, summoned from her native Salerno to investigate the murders of three children; Rowley, as the king's tax inspector, ostensibly there to protect the Jews who had been falsely accused of the crimes, but really to protect Henry's zealously sought tax revenue.

By sheer misfortune he had been in attendance while Adelia performed the autopsies on the children and had ruthlessly co-opted him to help her, first by keeping the flies off the tiny mutilated corpses and then by recording her findings on a slate she had thrust at him for the purpose.

The abhorrence of what he had witnessed that day still haunted him and there had been times when he had almost hated her for it.

No female voice, he had thought as he watched her pore over the bodies in that cramped, heat-soaked anchorage, should ever articulate a litany of injuries as hers had, nor become the mouthpiece for a murderer's brutal crimes. No eyes, certainly no female eyes, should ever be able to look on such a scene without expelling blood, and yet hers had.

When it was over he had begged her to attend vespers with him, needing the balm of that evening litany like never before.

Would she not pray for the souls of the children? he had asked her. But she had turned on him.

"I'm not here to pray for them," she had hissed savagely. "I am here to speak for them."

And yet, and yet, he had seen her work the oracle that day and, later, bring the children's killers to justice . . .

He wiped his brow, a cold sweat pricking his temples at the idea that history was repeating itself in his daughter.

"God's teeth! Give me that bloody thing," he said, snatching the letter.

Adelia sat beside him, watching fixedly while he read.

"Well?" she said when he had finished.

"Write back to her at once! Tell her to do nothing! Nothing, do you understand? Under no circumstances is she to leave Penda's sight until we get there. She must leave everything to the sheriff or the justices in eyre. She must not interfere!"

"But, Rowley," Adelia said, this time pleading with him, "you read the letter! They were just village girls! You know the limits of justice under those circumstances. No one else will lift a finger for them! Besides, a letter could take days! We don't have time."

She put her head in her hands. When she had first read Allie's letter, delighted to receive one at last, it was with disinterest, her judgment skewed, she realized now, by her hubris at the fact that Allie was following in her footsteps and doing so admirably. Therefore she had assimilated the details only in her capacity as a doctor and not as a mother, which had blinded her temporarily to the risks involved. But now, in the light of Rowley's reaction, she saw it very differently indeed.

She leapt up, her heart pounding.

"No," she said. "There simply isn't time for letters. We have to go to her now."

Rowley looked up at her incredulously. "But we can't," he said. "Not now. In a couple of days' time, perhaps, but I have to go back to London first."

When Adelia opened her mouth to remonstrate, he raised his hand and cut her off.

"Don't, Adelia," he said. "For once don't argue with me, please. Just send that damned letter."

CHAPTER 32

PENDA'S REACTION TO THE NEWS of the murder was to impose new security measures on Elsford; few of them were popular.

"Don't know what she thinks she's doin'," Jodi grumbled. "It's as if she's expectin' a siege or summat."

She had spent the morning having her ear bent by Albert, the gooseherd, who had been railing against the injustice of the extra duty Penda was imposing on him by insisting that, from now on, he let his birds out at night to patrol the perimeter—something to do, so she said, with the alarm calls of geese saving Rome from the Gauls.

But Albert didn't know about Romans or Gauls, and cared even less, and continued complaining bitterly even when she upped his pay by a penny a week.

Geoffrey, the gatekeeper, was also unhappy, but in his case because of the new password she was insisting on using, which, because he had trouble remembering it—remembering much at all these days, to be honest—he found irksome. Besides, he thought it was unnecessary; the cold snap was deterrent enough for most visitors these days, whether welcome or not.

No one, it seemed, was immune, especially not Allie, whose archery lessons were upped, with immediate effect, from once to twice a week. Long, cold, joyless affairs they were, too, during which any moment of inattention or levity was punishable by even more practice. Under such duress, she felt her marksmanship was unlikely to improve, and it didn't, but, unbeknownst to her, it was part of the larger plan to keep an eye on her from now on.

When Penda herself was unavailable for that duty, she sent deputies—in the form of either Jodi, Hawise or Ediva, sometimes even Ulf—who were instructed to follow Allie like shadows.

Despite remaining ignorant of the surveillance, Allie was increasingly aware of a pervading atmosphere of tension, so that when, at last, the day of the long-awaited Dunstan feast dawned, it was a relief in more ways than one.

That morning she woke early, leapt out of bed with an enthusiasm she hadn't felt in a long time and dashed to the window. Outside, a frost-nipped marsh spread out before her like a glorious ermine cloak.

At last, a day to savor!

"Look, Gyltha!" she cried, leaning on the sill, her eyes closed, her face tilted to the sun. "The sun's shining! It's a beautiful day!"

"God's breath!" Gyltha muttered, refusing the invocation to marvel at it and dragging the bedclothes over her face instead. "So it is. Now close them bloody shutters like a good girl afore you give us both the ague and get back to bed. You'll regret it else. Lord knows what time you'll be back from Dunstan."

But Allie was too excited to sleep, and when Gyltha had dozed off again, she quietly got washed and dressed and went outside.

Despite an early sun, the courtyard, when she got there, was still treacherous underfoot, and she had to tread gingerly over the cobbles to get to the ivy-clad door leading to the kitchen garden.

Of all the spaces at Elsford, this was her favorite.

Not long after she'd arrived, Penda had given over a large plot of it to grow her herbs, and she had worked tirelessly cultivating the bare earth and filling it with all the medicinal shrubs Adelia had sent, and others—those that had survived the cold weather—that she had found among the rich plant life in the marsh: juniper and sage, mugwort, lavender, vervain, comfrey and catnip, all neatly marked and sectioned off by an intricate latticework of birch twigs that she had made herself.

She felt an unrivaled sense of pride and peace here, which was why she had come this morning; tending to her plants was the perfect antidote—the only one she could think of—to sitting around in the solar waiting for the hours to pass.

AS USUAL, SHE WAS BEING watched.

"You take her back," Gyltha snapped, standing beside Penda at their vantage point of the guest chamber window.

Penda sighed. It was a conversation they had had many times, and although she had tried to explain about the promise she had made to Rowley and the enormous pressure she felt to grant it, her words fell on deaf ears and Gyltha was as intransigent as ever.

"I don't give a bugger about getting her married off," was her response. "I just want her safe and she ain't safe here."

That morning it had started up again.

"Just give me 'til after the feast, Gylth, I'll have another think then," Penda said.

Unusually, Gyltha was quiet for a moment.

"After the feast then." Her concession was reluctant. "But after that you take 'er back, understand? It's bad for me nerves having 'er 'ere, not to mention me health."

During the exchange, having forgotten about their surveillance temporarily, they had taken their eyes off Allie and were shocked when they turned back to see a figure striding purposefully across the garden toward her.

"Who's that?" Gyltha asked in alarm. Penda leaned out of the window as far as she dared to get a better look, then gave a sigh of relief.

"Well it ain't the murderer, you daft bugger," she said, chuckling. "It's Peter, can't you see?"

"I don't care who it is," said Gyltha. "Fetch her in. It's time she was getting ready besides."

CHAPTER 33

IT HAD BEEN SO LONG since Allie had dressed up—and never
this elaborately since her days with Eleanor—that she had
forgotten what a distressing process it was.

It was more like an ordeal during which she was forcibly
bathed and scrubbed and set upon with brickbats until her skin
burned; her hair was brushed, pulled and plaited until she was
astonished she had any left, and then she was forced to stand for
hours on end, or so it seemed, while Gyltha and Jodi dragged
layer upon layer of shifts and underdresses over her upraised
arms until she thought she was going to suffocate in all the ma-
terial.

"There," Gyltha said, standing back to admire her work,
when, at last, they had finished.

"You look beautiful," sighed Jodi with a tear in her eye.

"Like a princess," said Hawise, holding up the shield they
had borrowed from Sir Stephen so that Allie could admire her
reflection in its polished surface.

Allie stood before it, turning slowly to see her transforma-
tion from every angle, and because even she had to admit that

she did indeed look lovely, she was just about to apologize for the robust invective of earlier on, when the solar door opened.

"Ready?"

Penda stood on the threshold looking, against all expectations, if not pretty, exactly, more than passably elegant and most un-Penda-like. Gone were her moleskin cap and wolf-skin mantle, and in their place were a fine white silk wimple and elegant ermine cloak, pinned at the shoulder over a pristine bliaut in a beautiful crimson damask.

Gyltha's mouth began to move in silent prayer, thanking whichever saint she had invoked for their kind intervention.

"That's enough o' that, thank you," Penda said crisply, blushing to the shade of her bliaut with the unwelcome attention. "You ready, Allie?"

CHAPTER 34

A LARGE CROWD HAD ASSEMBLED by the time they reached Dunstan, some, like them, alighting from carts and palanquins, others from horseback, and others still—the hems of their mantles and cloaks held high above the mud—trudging up the riverbank by torchlight, from the flotilla of barges and boats that had transported them there.

Lord Peverell stood in the great arched doorway of his castle greeting his guests with patient bows and handshakes until he caught sight of the Elsford party and, beaming with delight, came bounding over to them.

"Welcome," he said, taking Allie's hand, his large, soft brown eyes fixing hers with that expression—the one she had almost forgotten about, but not quite—that made her stomach feel as though a small bird had gotten trapped inside it.

"I'm delighted you could come," he whispered. Allie was about to reply that so was she when a page, concerned about the queue forming behind them, chivvied them along to another courtyard, where enormous joints of meat sizzled on vast spits and botilers dressed in smart livery handed them cups of warm spiced wine, before they were encouraged through yet another archway into the great hall.

She had forgotten how glorious a room it was, or perhaps had been too distracted during her last visit to appreciate it properly, but this evening, brightly lit by the myriad flambeaux lining the walls, it had an almost cathedral-like grandeur about it. An intricately carved roof—as fine as any she had ever seen—reached to the heavens, and a series of arched windows of colored glass cast exquisite prisms of light onto freshly painted ashlar.

The Elsford contingent huddled together shyly at first, until Penda and Sir Stephen got their bearings, found people they knew and wandered off into the crowd, leaving Allie to amuse herself.

For a while she did so, watching the people around her; the men—mostly barons, bishops and abbots, judging by their attire—paraded like peacocks, barking one-sided conversations at one another, while ladies in fine dresses fluttered like butterflies around them, apparently oblivious to their attendant pages, who hovered at a distance carrying their ridiculous-looking lapdogs.

It was frivolity at its best. It amused her to think how much her mother would disapprove of the "courtly frivolity," as she referred to it, and yet, there was something undeniably magical about it. Despite Adelia's condemnation, or possibly because of it, Allie had developed a sneaking admiration for it during the time she had spent with Queen Eleanor. Not the banquets per se, perhaps—she had always been too young to attend those—but the courts of love Eleanor organized to entertain her ladies: Allie could still remember the rippling thrill of anticipation in the hall at Sarum before she called the court to order, when the trou-badours sang and the minstrels recounted their tales of King Ar-thur and his knights, and the exquisitely dressed young women took their places on the dais—sometimes as many as sixty of them—ready to preside over the issues of the heart brought for their consideration by the young knights.

Most were too silly to remember, but one case in particular had stayed with her, that of a young knight asking the court to decide on whether or not true love could exist within marriage. She remembered how the ladies took longer than usual to come to their decision but in the end had ruled—rather wistfully, she noticed—that it could not, because marriage was a commercial contract uniting only lands and fortunes and not, alas, people in love.

"Self-indulgent nonsense," Adelia had said when, some years later, Allie told her about it. "But at least they got the right ver-dict, I suppose."

When she closed her eyes she could feel the magic of Sarum this evening and was enjoying it enormously until she opened them again and saw Sir William glaring at her over the heads of the crowd. She looked away quickly, relieved to find Penda by her side.

"You all right, bor?" she asked, sensing Allie's discomfort.

"I think so," Allie replied. "I was just wondering what on earth I could have done to offend Sir William so badly . . . Oh, don't look now," she added when Penda's head swiveled to look for him. "I don't want him to think—"

But Penda flapped her hand. "Don't matter what 'e thinks," she said. "Funny bugger, that one, if you ask me . . . Lord only knows what sets 'is maggots bitin' but it ain't nothin' to do with you, I expect."

Just then a trumpet sounded, summoning the guests to dine.

To their surprise they were shown to the high table—although Allie wished Penda hadn't winked at her quite so blatantly as she was shown to a seat near Lord Peverell's. In fact, she was still blushing with the mortification and trying not to catch her eye again when the stool beside her scraped back.

She looked up, and her heart sank when she saw Sir William and realized that she would have to prepare herself for a blighted evening.

Once the pages had done the rounds of the tables with the bowls and aquamaniles and all hands had been washed and dried, they sat silently for the priest's blessing and another fanfare of trumpets announcing the arrival of the feast.

A succession of enormous platters, each requiring two men to carry it, was paraded through the hall: roasted peacocks displaying their tails still, litters of crispy baby pigs with apples in their mouths, a roasted bittern and a swan in full plumage resting on a bed of pastry painted green to resemble grass. Each was met with raucous cheers from the diners, except for Sir William—who never seemed to get enthusiastic about anything—and Allie, who had lost her appetite the moment he sat beside her. The loudest cheer in the room was the abbot of Aynsham's, sitting opposite her, who was so distracted by the pageant that he didn't notice Allie's scrutiny, which he might otherwise have found distressing: the narrowed eyes, the forensic intensity of her gaze, the inclination of her head as she adopted the attitude necessary for the game she and Adelia had invented for the long, often excruciatingly dull banquets at Wolvercote.

At some point, when the tedium became eye-rollingly unbearable, they had each taken it in turns to point surreptitiously at one of their fellow diners with a challenge to the other to diagnose that person's medical affliction. It was not a particularly useful excuse—and one which would infuriate Emma if she knew—but it amused them and helped to pass the time.

Unfortunately the abbot wasn't an inspiring candidate and Allie came to his diagnosis swiftly. His skin color, too yellow for health, was probably the result of jaundice, and, judging by the way he was knocking back his mead, probably due to a liver affliction of some sort. The only question remaining was whether or not she could tell him without either offending him or exposing herself to accusations of witchcraft.

In the end she decided it was probably best not to, especially when she saw the unbridled delight in his piggy little eyes as the roasted swan on its grassy nest was put onto the table in front of him. After all, she thought, she could tell him and he *might* heed her advice, and might live longer as a result, but for a man with such apparently large appetites, it would certainly feel like it.

No, for people like the abbot, she decided, a shorter, happier, more indulgent life was preferable; besides, her diagnosis might be wrong and Penda loathed him.

She was still thinking about the abbot when the elderly nun beside her introduced herself.

"Sister Margaret," she said, turning to Allie with a warm smile.

"Allie," said Allie, relieved to have somebody to talk to, especially someone like Sister Margaret, whose ample bosom and crab apple cheeks made for a cozy antidote to the chilly proposition on her right.

"Have you been to one of these before?" Sister Margaret asked.

Allie shook her head.

"Oh, well . . . You have a treat in store in that case. He is a very generous host, is our young Lord Peverell." She broke off and looked around furtively, then whispered: "Rather different from his father, who was a rather curmudgeonly old man, I'm afraid."

Allie followed her gaze to the present Lord Peverell, who was talking to a young woman who, she noticed, had been monopolizing his attention since they sat down.

Feeling a sharp pang of disappointment, she turned back to Sister Margaret quickly.

"His hospitality certainly seems very lavish," she said, hoping it didn't show.

"Oh, indeed!" Sister Margaret beamed. "And bestowed with such charm . . . He really is quite, quite . . ." And Allie noticed that her cheeks were becoming ever more flushed as she spoke about him and that there was a rather wistful look in her rheumy eyes.

A S THE EVENING WORE ON the diners became increasingly lively, except, of course, for Sir William. Oh, he was courteous enough—Allie couldn't fault him on that—performing his duties with politesse, passing her things when necessary, refilling her cup when it was empty, even putting her gravy-stained trencher on the wheelbarrow as it was trundled around to take the leftovers.

But he didn't speak to her and showed no inclination to do so, and although she was no more enthusiastic about engaging with him, the ensuing silence made her uncomfortable.

When they finished eating she hoped to resume her conversation with Sister Margaret, only to find, when the time came, that she was talking to someone else.

She looked around, increasingly self-conscious as it dawned on her that the only people in the room who weren't engaged in conversation were Sir William and herself. Apart from the fact that it was a boring state of affairs, she worried that were Lord Peverell to see her in such social isolation, he might assume that it was because she was too dull to be trifled with and would therefore think less of her.

Partly from a refusal to let that happen and partly because she didn't think the evening could get any worse, she snatched up her cup, took a hefty swig of whatever liquid was in it—wine, mead, frankly it was all beginning to taste the same—and turned to Sir William.

"Sir William," she said, addressing him rather more robustly than she had intended, which had the effect of startling them both. "I was wondering if you wouldn't mind telling me how Matilda—erm, Lord Peverell's horse is . . . You might not remember but I treated her some weeks back when she picked up a thorn in her hoof."

Sir William lowered his own cup slowly. The cool gaze he

returned was disconcerting, but Allie managed to hold it and her nerve, and was rewarded for having done so when a rare flicker of uncertainty crossed his face.

"As far as I am aware, she fares very well," he said. "I hear you know a great deal about horses."

Allie nodded and took another swig from her cup. "Yes," she said. "I certainly do." Her immodesty was uncharacteristic, but she didn't care. *After all,* she thought, raising her cup again, *since he abhors me anyway, I might as well give him good cause.*

Sir William turned away peevishly, signaling that, as far as he was concerned, the exchange had come to an end. Allie, however, had other ideas.

"I gather he brought her all the way back from the Holy Land," she continued, surprised to see him turn back to her with a wistful expression and a willingness to continue the conversation.

"And me with them," he said softly.

"You took the cross?" It came as a surprise, but in a strange way, it also made sense.

She had inherited Adelia's contempt for Crusaders—with the obvious exceptions of the rare decent ones, like her father and now, of course, Lord Peverell—having heard too many atrocity stories about them not to be suspicious of the breed; the cold, brutal, arrogant killers . . . like Sir William. Coming from Salerno, one of the direct routes to the Holy Land, Adelia was well versed on Crusaders, witnessing at first hand the wickedness and brutality of the men who came through that city and created havoc in the name of God.

On the way out, she told Allie, they were insufferable pigs

and twice as ignorant, as enthusiastic for God's work as for disrupting the harmony in which the different creeds and races had lived together for centuries. And on the way back, they were embittered—only a few rewarded with the fortune or holy grace they had come for—diseased and impoverished.

"Yes," Sir William said at last.

"I see," said Allie, and was wondering what she was going to say next, when a group of musicians struck up in the gallery, prompting a mass exodus of diners into the garden in search of quiet places to relieve themselves. Sir William's own relief at the interruption was palpable, and with a cursory nod, he rose quickly from his stool, leaving Allie, with no other companion, no ear for music and no inclination to dance, no alternative but to follow the crowd.

As they shuffled to the exit a large tapestry on the wall caught her eye. It was a depiction of the wheel of fortune in which Fortune, richly dressed and blindfolded, was seated on a claw-footed throne, one hand brandishing a sword, the other spinning her wheel—to which four figures in varying degrees of despondency were clinging.

I think you're a pig, Allie muttered at her as she reflected on her own fortune, or, rather, lack of it this evening, wondering why it was that, so often, the things one most looked forward to turned out to be the most crushingly disappointing.

CHAPTER 35

I F SHE HAD EXPECTED TO find peace in the garden, a dark corner in which to hide and recover her equanimity, she was to be disappointed.

When she got there it was awash with micturating people, most of whom were completely unabashed that their modesty was compromised this evening by the light of a very bright moon.

Everywhere she looked there were men relieving themselves against tree trunks or women squatting in bushes like broody hens, all rowdy with too much drink, and when they weren't pissing, or giggling, or shouting at the tops of their voices, they were tripping over their own feet like lumpen idiots.

She felt suddenly homesick, although not for Elsford but, for once, and probably for the first time since she had left it, for her real home . . . with her mother . . . in Wolvercote. She wished to be as far away from this strange land and its peculiar, indecorous people as she possibly could.

Perhaps it was the loftiness of this moral high ground, or perhaps it was all the mead she had drunk at supper, but the unexpected wave of homesickness was followed by an equally unexpected bout of nausea, and before she knew it, she was doubled up, vomiting onto the grass.

When it was over, she stood up and looked around, and when she was satisfied that most of the people in the immediate vicinity were too inebriated to have noticed her indiscretion, she set off back to the hall to find Penda, whom she would beg to take her home. But as she picked her way through the supine bodies on the lawn, the faint, distant whickering of a horse drifted through to her on the crystalline air and she changed her mind.

In times of uncertainty—and Adelia's absence—Allie invariably turned to horses. They were an infallible salve for her soul, and because she was longing to see Matilda again anyway, she felt that even a glimpse of her would be compensation enough for what had otherwise been an unutterably miserable evening.

With that in mind, she followed the sound, stumbling blindly in the dark through an intricate series of archways, courtyards and pathways until she arrived eventually at the stable block.

I N CONTRAST WITH THE GARDEN, the stable was almost biblical in its serenity and as impressive, to Allie's mind, anyway, as the great hall. It had obviously been built by someone with a love of horses: A wide, meticulously swept flagstone path ran between two rows of neatly constructed blocks, each with sufficient stalls for twenty horses or more. At one end was a large forge from whose shingle roof the smell of hot iron still bled into the air, and at the other was a timber-framed two-story hayloft.

She walked slowly between the rows of stalls, soothed by the sound of hooves shifting sleepily on straw, relishing the familiar smell of horseflesh and hay and stopping every so often to pat the nose of one or another of the animals curious enough to have left their trough for a glimpse of their nocturnal visitor.

She found Matilda in the very last block, standing at the back of her stall, her head drooped in sleep until Allie called and it lifted, ears pricked, as if she had been waiting for her.

"There you are, beautiful girl." Allie patted the white blaze of the pretty dished face, grazing her lips against the soft velvety indent of her nose.

"Oh, I'm sorry," she said, amused, when Matilda started nuzzling her arm in search of treats. "But I haven't brought anything for you and I didn't think you'd like roasted swan . . . You see, I wasn't expecting to see you this evening. But what I can do, if you don't mind, is take a look at that hoof."

She lifted the latch and went into the stall, then ran her hand down Matilda's foreleg, gently angling the hoof when it lifted into a pool of moonlight.

"Well!" she said, putting it down again.

It was astonishing, but however hard she looked, there was nothing—neither mark nor blemish—to suggest it had ever been injured, and although she usually hated to be proved wrong, in this instance, she was delighted that the young groom about whom she had had so many misgivings had done such a remarkably good job.

"You are a lucky girl," she said, patting Matilda's neck and fussing over her until, bored with her attention, Matilda turned her back on her and returned to her hay.

Allie watched her munching contentedly for a while, then decided it was time to head back.

Quite what prompted the prickling feeling of unease she had as she turned to leave, she wasn't sure—perhaps a combination of the last effects of the mead wearing off and, just then, a cloud drifting across the face of the moon—but all of a sudden it felt as if the night were closing in around her, isolating her for some wicked purpose, making her feel vulnerable and conspicuously alone.

And then she heard footsteps . . . Instinct dropped her to the floor, and she crouched like a leveret in its form, hoping that whoever they belonged to would pass without noticing her.

In her rational mind—when she could hear it above the deafening rush of blood pounding in her ears—she knew that they probably belonged to the marshal, no doubt making his final rounds for the evening, and that although it would be embarrassing to be found crawling around in a stable at night, no further harm would come to her. But that voice was drowned out by another, a much louder one, as convinced as it was convincing that, in fact, they belonged to the marsh murderer and that, on the contrary, she was in very grave danger indeed.

She held her breath until it felt as if her lungs were going to burst, screwing her eyes shut tight. Whoever he was, whether benign or not, she didn't want to see him.

"Mistress Allie!"

She opened her eyes to a familiar voice and saw Lord Peverell peering curiously at her from the other side of the stable door.

She stood up, brushing the straw off her clothes, wondering what on earth he was thinking as he looked at her and what Gyltha would say if she could see her now.

"Mistress Allie!" he repeated with an expression of amused

astonishment. "I probably should have mentioned this before, but for my esteemed guests, there is a place of easement in the castle; I had it built quite recently, you know. You needed only to ask!"

For a moment Allie thought she might die of embarrassment until she realized he was joking.

"It's not funny." She scowled, picking another piece of hay out of her hair.

"No," he said, struggling to suppress a grin, "I suppose it isn't. But, God strike me, madam! I'm clumsy when I'm worried, and I've been terribly worried, you know. I've been looking everywhere for you . . . although, of course, I should have known to come here first."

He opened the door and she stepped into the yard, feeling as if she were in the middle of a very strange dream.

"She's in fine fettle, wouldn't you say?" he said as though it were the most natural thing in the world to be conversing with a muddy, disheveled woman in his stable yard in the middle of the night.

"Yes," said Allie, relieved by the one small blessing that in all the topsy-turvying of this increasingly peculiar evening she had at least retained the power of speech. "I think she looks magnificent."

They stood side by side gazing at the horse, even though, for an exquisite moment, even she didn't exist for either of them; they were both too intoxicated by their proximity to one another to notice anything or anyone else at all.

The next thing she knew they were standing face-to-face but moving toward one another, slowly, inexorably, as though they were being drawn together by invisible threads, and when they were almost touching, she felt that strange sensation in her stomach again, her heart pounding once more—except not from fear this time—and then . . .

She gasped.

At the far end of the stable block, she saw the figure of a man seep furtively out of the shadows like a stain. Although it was too dark and he was too far away for her to see his face clearly, she knew that he was staring at her.

But by the time Lord Peverell had turned around, it was too late; whoever it was had vanished.

"I . . . I saw someone," Allie stammered, pointing over his shoulder into the darkness. "Standing, watching us, over there."

"A man?"

She nodded. "At least I think so."

It had been a brief glimpse, but she was sure it was a man; after all, what woman in her right mind—other than she herself, of course—would be foolish enough to venture out alone at night?

They stood staring blankly into the night, feeling the space between them expanding.

"I think it was Will," Lord Peverell said at last.

"Sir William?" Allie asked. "Why would he have come here?"

He shook his head, the levity of a moment ago eliding into weary resignation. "I don't know," he said. "But, if it was, then it's nothing to worry about . . . It's just that . . . well, he has a habit of following me . . . And yet I ought to be grateful, I suppose. He saved my life once . . . Likes to keep me out of harm's way."

Allie was quiet, although her mind was anything but as the realization of Sir William's hostility dawned on her.

He was jealous, like a dog protecting his territory, baring his teeth when his master was approached. *Stay away!* he had been warning her all this time. *He's mine!*

She had heard about men like him and had pitied them for the persecution they suffered, but not Sir William. She sensed a malignancy, an arrogance about him that made him too dangerous for pity; besides, she had better things to do with her time than try to fathom the depths of human obsession.

And yet . . . and yet . . . She couldn't help but wonder, especially in the light of recent events, whether his antipathy extended to all women or only those, like her, who became too close to his master, and, more important perhaps, whether it was powerful enough to drive him to kill.

"Allie! Allie!"

A disembodied voice rang out of the darkness and she turned around to see Penda, wearing an expression of uncompromising belligerence, stomping up the yard like a juggernaut toward them.

"God be praised! God be bloody praised!" Penda cried when she saw Allie, shaking her fist at the heavens. "I been goin' mad wonderin' what, in God's name, I was goin' to tell your father when they found your poor strangled little body in the marsh!"

"I'm sorry." Allie blushed like a guilty child. In all the ups and downs of this increasingly peculiar evening she hadn't given a thought to Penda, who must have been worried out of her mind. "Oh, Penda . . . I . . ." She was about to stammer an explanation and further apology when Lord Peverell intervened.

"It's all my fault, Lady Penda," he said. "I knew how worried Mistress Allie has been about my horse, so I brought her here to put her mind at rest . . . And yet, of course, I realize I should have returned her to you much, much earlier and spared you all this worry. My sincere apologies."

He bowed, and to her relief, Allie saw Penda's expression soften enough to allow her to release the breath she had been holding as a hostage against the storm that, until a moment ago, had seemed so inevitable.

"Hmm," Penda grumbled. "Well, no harm done, I s'pose . . . But all the same, it's time we was gettin' back."

Lord Peverell escorted them back to the bailey and the cart waiting for them. When it listed to their weight as they climbed in, Sir Stephen, dozing in a corner, opened a bleary eye.

"Jolly good . . . Found her then, did you?" he murmured.

"Hmm," Penda muttered, tucking the folds of her mantle around Allie's knees to keep her warm. "And no bloody thanks to you neither."

They said their farewells and were about to set off when Lord Peverell popped his head over the side of the cart.

"May I call on you at Elsford, Lady Penda?" he asked. "I . . . I was due to spend Christmas elsewhere, but something tells me my time might be better spent here."

"Don't see why not," Penda replied with a wink that sent Allie into another paroxysm of mortification with an urgent desire to throw herself onto the floor.

She spent the journey home mulling over Lord Peverell's parting request, wondering whether it had come from a genuine desire to call on Penda, for some unfathomable reason, as he had asked, or, as she desperately hoped, a desire to see her again. And yet, she dared not hope too much for fear of the crushing disappointment that might bring. And as the cart bumped along the rutted tracks, she stared gloomily into the darkness, wishing that matters of the heart didn't have to be quite so opaque and that, before they left, she had mustered the courage to demand that he explain himself fully and immediately. At least if she had, all the fruitless hours and days—maybe even weeks—she would now spend worrying about it would have been nipped neatly in the bud.

L ORD PEVERELL WAS EQUALLY DESPONDENT as he stood in the now-deserted courtyard watching the cart rumble off into the snow-flecked night, wondering why Allie had refused to look at him before she left and whether, perhaps, he had revealed a little too much, too soon.

CHAPTER 36

WITH ONLY TWO DAYS TO Christmas, all Elsford was in a state of feverish anticipation for this, the brightest spark in the long dark days of this already hard winter—all except Father Edward, who was dreading it, just as he did every year.

He didn't approve of bright sparks. It had been the dreary desolation of these marshes that had drawn him there in the first place, just as the deserts of the East had lured the pioneer monks, and he didn't relish having to stand by while all the hard work of these last twelve months unraveled and the boundary between religion and superstition became blurred again.

It was already happening. Only the day before yesterday his seasonal misery had been compounded when the mummers returned, setting up in the churchyard to perform their beastly plays, "excerpts" from the Bible and "portraits of the lives of saints"! But it was nothing more than sacrilege really, the way they capered around with their blackened faces and animal masks. And what, in the name of Christ, had stags or hares or wolves to do with the Nativity? It was little wonder then that the village boys were inspired to such mischief, cavorting through the streets in their homespun masks, extorting money from their neighbors, their parents having long since absconded to the alehouse, of course, and with no one around to sanction them.

"WHY'S HE LOOK SO MISERABLE, d'you think?" Hawise asked. She and Allie were among the audience for that afternoon's performance.

"The priest, do you mean?" Allie asked, catching sight of the forlorn figure staring out of the porch.

Hawise nodded.

"Don't ask me." Allie shrugged. "For all I know he always looks like that. Perhaps he isn't enjoying the play." After all, who could blame him? She wasn't, either, and was only there under sufferance to keep Hawise company.

"Who's that supposed to be?" she asked, pointing at one of the mummers dressed in a long robe and wearing such a cumbersome mask that he was rendered inaudible through it. His recent monologue had been met with heckles of: "Speak up, bor!" and "Get some other bugger to do it!" Which had done nothing to help her follow the narrative.

"I think he's supposed to be God," Hawise whispered. She had seen the play before and, being more attuned to the local dialect than Allie, was enjoying it.

"Oh," Allie said, even though she was none the wiser and was amusing herself instead by watching Hawise watch the play, enjoying the expression of bewitched concentration on her lovely face.

But when even that began to pall, and the play showed no sign of ending, she put her head on Hawise's shoulder and went to sleep.

She was awoken sometime later by the sensation that she was being watched, and she opened her eyes to see Danny Wadlow leaning against a tree trunk on the other side of the graveyard, staring at them.

"Don't look now," she gasped, grabbing Hawise's arm. "Danny Wadlow's over there, staring at us."

Despite the entreaty not to, Hawise looked and, when she saw Danny, stuck her tongue out at him.

"Stop it!" Allie rounded on her. "You mustn't provoke him like that. There's no telling what he might do."

"He won't do anything," Hawise said, grinning. "Look, it's worked, see? He's not staring anymore."

When she dared look up again, she saw that Hawise was right, and a little while later, she was relieved to see him leave the churchyard and saunter off toward the village.

WHEN THEY GOT HOME, IT was to a hive of pre-Christmas activity and a drawbridge so crowded with servants carrying armfuls of holly, ivy and mistletoe for the Christmas decorations that they had to wait at the entrance to cross it.

"Leave it all outside, please!"

Penda stood on the front steps, cocooned in wolf skin, orchestrating the proceedings.

"Not a sprig in 'ere 'til tomorrow, remember," she told the

servants. Despite her otherwise anarchic tendencies, she was a stickler for superstition, which decreed it was bad luck if a house was decorated before Christmas Eve.

The girls took their horses to the stables and went looking for Gyltha, whom they found eventually, in the kitchen, presiding over the baking of the great Christmas pie.

The place had been transformed since Allie's last visit, every surface and every person in it looking almost spectral under a thick film of the flour that had been freshly ground in the mill that morning, for a pie large enough to feed five thousand and a good many of their friends besides.

Their mouths watered watching the cooks and scullions ladling layers of the most delicious-looking meats, fruits and spices into an enormous pastry-lined vat. When it could hold no more, an ecclesiastical hush descended on the room while everyone stood back to make way for Gyltha's somber passage carrying the pièce de résistance, a perfect pastry sculpture of the baby Jesus.

"There!" she said to a murmur of approval, setting the marvel on top of the pie.

"It's beautiful!" Allie said, reaching out to wipe a smudge of flour off the end of Gyltha's nose.

"Thankee kindly," said Gyltha, pushing her hand away brusquely. "Now bugger off, I'm busy."

After that they went to the solar, where Jodi was waiting for them with a letter from Adelia.

Allie opened it.

My darling, it began.

I am so, so cross, but it turns out that I won't be able to come to Elsford for Christmas! I'd give anything to be with you all, especially since there's really nothing to stop me—my ankle has mended beautifully, better than expected, actually—and I'm as fit as a flea but your father, blast his eyes, thinks he can smell snow and that there might even be a civil war to avert! Why he can't just leave it to somebody else I simply don't know. He's getting too old for all this . . . but, there we are.

You probably haven't heard them yet, but there are all sorts of rumors about Count John and Philip of France conspiring against the king. Your father expects to be sent to France any day now to see Eleanor. She won't like it, of course, but he's going to have to insist that she come back to England, if only to beat some sense into John.

Which reminds me, while we're on the subject of things your father insists on, the reason for this letter is to tell you that under no circumstances are you to go looking into the murders you wrote to me about. I mean it, Allie!!! Until we come to Elsford—and we will, come hell or high water—you're to stay close to Penda. If young women are being murdered all over the place, your father is strangely adamant that you shouldn't become one of them!

Now, darling, I know how you feel—we have the same instincts, you and I—and I also know that you will be itching to get to the bottom of whatever it is that's going on, but, for once, you must listen to me and do nothing! You don't have the protection I had, you don't have a Mansur, or a Henry, come to that, and it's much too dangerous to act alone. By all means keep your eyes and ears open but don't, under any circumstances, go looking for trouble, because knowing you, you'll find it.

I've promised your father that I'll stay in Wolvercote until Holy Innocents' Day but after that, come what may, come snow, come civil war, come the Four Horsemen of the bloody Apocalypse, I will be leaving for Elsford and there is nothing either your father or anybody else can do to stop me.

When she finished it, she rolled it up, shoved it up her sleeve for safekeeping and then took herself off to a quiet corner of the room to think about it.

After all, there was a lot to think about, a lot she found disturbing. It wasn't so much Adelia's directive that she shouldn't get involved in investigating the murders, although that was irritating enough; it was more the internal conflict it provoked between, on one hand, desperately wanting to see her mother again and, on the other, desperately not.

So much had happened and changed since she came to Elsford that she was a very different person now, enjoying a freedom that she would have to relinquish when Adelia arrived. Apart from anything else, her mother's compulsion to interfere and to know everything about everything meant that she would have to fight for every mote of independence and privacy she had gained there, battles that would prove futile in any case, because once Christmas was over, Adelia would inevitably insist that she return to Wolvercote.

She went to bed that evening feeling miserable.

CHAPTER 37

THE SNOW ROWLEY HAD SO confidently predicted didn't come, at least not in the south, so that, by the time the summons came to attend Eleanor at her Christmas court in Normandy, there was nothing to stop him from obeying it.

Of course he had known it was in the offing, but, as dreaded things will, it came quite suddenly, and on the wrong side of Christmas, forcing him to leave St. Albans in a hurry, dressed in full bishop's regalia, with the smell of incense still clinging to his robes from a mass he'd only just finished celebrating.

Because speed was of the essence, he took only a small retinue with him, arriving in Dover as the bells rang for vespers on the day before Christmas Eve.

It was barely dawn as they rode to the quayside but the air was already shrill with the cries of gulls and the excitable voices of the fishermen and merchants dashing around a boarded dock that groaned under the weight of a veritable Noah's ark of animals in cages, vast crates of vegetables and casks of wine.

Rowley hated Dover—all ports, in fact—because he loathed

being at the mercy of anything as capricious as the weather, be-calmed one moment, for weeks on end sometimes, then tossed around on the high seas with a ship's timbers grinding treacher-ously underfoot the next. Unlike other people he knew, when he looked out over the channel, he saw not the wonder of adventure and the promise of foreign lands, but the morose, undulating back of a liquid monster.

Under Henry, who had spent only sixteen years of his thirty-four-year reign in England, Rowley had gone continually back and forth to the Continent, and despite loathing and dreading every one of those crossings, it was the last that had left him finished with the sea—almost literally—when he had sailed back from Italy with an assassin's knife in his back.

Fortunately he remembered very little of the voyage—he had been half-dead, after all—but when he had recovered, many months later, he had vowed never to set foot in a boat again. And yet here he was again, waiting for the bloody tide, watching mis-erably as Walter, his groom, led their horses up the gangplank onto the clinker-built hulk waiting to take them to France.

FOUR MERCIFULLY UNEVENTFUL DAYS LATER, they arrived at the queen's dower house in Bonneville-sur-Touques, where he was shown immediately into a wood-paneled room decorated like many of the grand rooms of Europe, with lav-ish gold leaf on the ceiling and heavy Flemish tapestries on the walls, but also remarkably unlike them. Its present incumbent had embellished it with touches of her own, introducing an air of exoticism to the otherwise somber grandeur, adding vibrant flashes of color from a multitude of Persian carpets, cushions and artifacts brought back with her from the Crusade.

Indeed, her presence was so palpable here that it took him a while to realize that he hadn't seen her yet and that, apart from the page who had shown him in and a harpist perched on a stool in the corner, the room appeared to be empty.

It was only when he noticed the harpist glance nervously in the direction of a large oak-framed chair that he saw the tiny figure recumbent in the back.

"Eleanor!"

The utterance was quite involuntary, forced from his chest by an emotion that was almost as shocking as the realization that she had grown so old since he had last seen her. Precisely when that was, he couldn't recall, but it was less than three years since he had ridden to Salisbury castle with William Marshall to break the news of Henry's death and to release her from incarceration.

As he took a step toward her chair he saw her stir, and was shocked again to see that the lustrous rose gold of her hair, once the envy of every woman in Christendom, had turned white in his absence and that the taut, fierce beauty of her face, which, in its day, had inspired gossip in every court in the land, had crumpled around its tiny bones.

The other shock, of course, was that she was asleep at all. The Eleanor of old had never slept. She was like Henry in that regard, indefatigable, restless and crackling with an energy that, if misdirected, could be terrifying.

She raised her arms, stretching catlike, but when she turned her head and noticed him at last, a slow, bewitching smile spread across her face, immediately sloughing away the years.

"My lord bishop," she said, rising from her chair and, he could have sworn, getting taller as she came toward him. "Rowley." She extended her hand. "At last."

He knelt in front of her, pressing her delicate beringed fingers to his lips, feeling the strange alchemy of her extraordinary presence, which not even age could diminish.

"Sit down," she said, indicating a chair with a grimace when the confused harpist took it as his cue to start playing again.

"Thank you, Phillipe," she said crisply. "You have delighted us for long enough, I think. You may leave now."

When the young man had hurriedly packed up his things and left the room, she turned to Rowley, who withered under her forensic gaze, wondering whether she had noticed the passing of the years in him, too, and whether or not she thought they had been kind.

They chatted inconsequentially for a while. Like most relationships founded in a shared history, theirs transcended the usual mores of conversation with an implicit understanding that, whenever they met, there would always be too much to say and too little time to say it. And if their fluency foundered occasionally, it was because they were both aware of the strong undercurrent of suspicion running between them.

They were both Henry's creatures, after all, and, at various times, during various crises in his reign, had taken opposing sides. Since they had survived those differences—although Rowley sometimes only by the skin of his teeth—a tacit understanding had developed that they were best not revisited.

So it was that by the time he got around to broaching the purpose of his visit, it was late afternoon and they were interrupted by a servant coming in to light the candles.

Rowley leaned forward on his chair. "I am here to advise you, lady," he said, lowering his voice, "that your presence may be required in England soon."

Her unwavering expression of polite indifference gave nothing away, but Rowley blanched anyway. She might have aged, he thought, but so far there was nothing to suggest that she had also mellowed; besides, she was famously contemptuous of England, not only because it was where she had been kept prisoner by Henry for all those years but because, as she had once told him, English wine tasted of piss.

During the long silence Rowley developed a creeping nostalgia for the harpist, or, indeed, anyone who might divert the inscrutable gaze.

"Well," Eleanor said at last, idly fingering the delicate embroidery at her sleeve. "You won't be surprised to know that the request is not unexpected."

He wasn't. Of course she was aware of the situation and had already commanded her seneschals on the Angevin borders to repair and strengthen their fortifications in case of an invasion and, because she was also regent in Richard's absence, had encouraged their English counterparts to do the same.

"John making a nuisance of himself again, is he?" she asked.

Rowley nodded. "I fear he is, lady," he replied. "And worse, I have heard reports—on good authority, too—that he travels the country these days with an armed retinue, among whom there is no one with influence enough to correct him when he refers to himself, as he does increasingly, I fear, as 'the next king.'"

Again the inscrutable gaze, only this time tempered by the merest suggestion of a smile.

"So he needs his mother's influence, then, you think, Rowley?"

Rowley smiled. "I believe he does."

She stared into her lap, muttering something under her breath, then looked up.

"How soon should I come? Is the threat imminent, do you think?"

He took a deep breath as he considered his response.

It was a difficult question to answer. There had been trouble brewing, as well she knew, ever since Richard left behind him an incendiary combination of a great vacuum of power and the parting gift of an entire principality—all of southwest England and a broad swathe of the Midlands—to his avaricious brother. Not since the conquest had anyone, other than the king himself, controlled such a vast territory, and the reckless generosity gave many cause to wonder whether he ever intended to come back.

And yet, other than John's interminable posturing and his skirmishes with Longchamp, nothing had happened. However, the creeping sense that it might was dangerous to the fabric of a country over which the shadow of the Anarchy still loomed large.

"On reflection," he said at last, "although the threat is imminent, I don't think it is yet immediate, so my advice, lady, would be to monitor the situation for now and be ready to sail when the time comes."

Eleanor nodded. "Very well. Then I presume that you and I will have to reconvene at a later stage?"

When Rowley nodded, she inclined her head with a smile of benign detachment, the signal that their audience was at an end and that, like the harpist before him, he had delighted her for quite long enough.

He rose stiffly from his chair, bade her farewell and was almost at the door when she called him back.

"I almost forgot," she said, rising with, he noted bitterly, greater ease than he had. "Before you go you must tell me how Almeison is. I presume that you have married her off by now and that you made a good match for her?"

His heart sank to his boots. For a few blissful days he had forgotten about Allie, but to be reminded of her now, by Eleanor of all people, was a humiliation too far, and he didn't know how to respond. How could he admit his failure to his queen? He stood at the door racking his brains for some sort of credible obfuscation.

"She is . . ." God's eyes! What on earth was he going to say? He could hardly admit the truth—that she was obstinately refusing to marry and driving him to an early grave—and yet he had to say something . . . Eleanor was looking at him with that expectant look of hers.

"I've sent her to the Fens," he managed to say eventually, and boldly, as if it were a universally acknowledged fact that sending one's daughter to the Fens gave her an automatic, unrivaled passage to future wedded bliss. For a moment he even felt quite pleased with himself, until he saw that Eleanor was frowning.

"Did you say the Fens, Rowley?" she asked, the frown deepening.

He nodded.

"But isn't Ely in the Fens?"

He nodded again.

"Then you must get her out of there immediately," she snapped. "I've just received news that Longchamp went squealing to the Pope when you bishops confiscated his estates. He's about to impose an interdict on the diocese. Things are about to become very unpleasant there, and very quickly!"

She said it with such uncharacteristic urgency that in his confusion he couldn't remember leaving the room, only that he had done so in a fumbling great hurry with her warning echoing in his mind.

He slept fitfully that night, cursing Allie, who, even at a distance, was managing to heap worry on him.

Left to himself, he would have made for the coast there and then, but having driven his men so hard to get there in the first place, he was reluctant to drag them from their beds on a whim. Besides, now he came to think about it, perhaps it wouldn't be all that bad. Interdicts were passed as frequently as they were ignored, and from what he knew of the Fens, by the time news of any sort reached there, it was often altered beyond recognition, blunted and mutated by the remoteness of myth and nothing to do with real life. Perhaps, by the time it came, Longchamp's interdict would have undergone the same process and might, with any luck, have lost its teeth.

On that more optimistic note he turned over and closed his eyes, hoping for the oblivion of sleep.

But it didn't come.

He sat up again.

But suppose he was wrong? Suppose it was imposed just the way Longchamp had intended? The effects would be devastating: no sacrament given, no sepulture for the dead, no masses celebrated, the dying denied the viaticum. He had seen the devastation wrought by an interdict before and had never forgotten the countless dead bodies hummocking the ground, their grieving relatives helpless to do anything but stand over them and weep.

After that he gave up hope of trying to sleep, and at first light the next morning, he roused his men and set off for the coast at speed.

CHAPTER 38

HOLY INNOCENTS' DAY HAD DAWNED dull after the excess of Christmas and, because it was also a fast day, engendered a certain tetchiness in those whose bellies had become accustomed to being full: from Elsford to Wolvercote, the joyful atmosphere pervading the country over the last few days was swept away by an air of melancholic ennui and increasingly bad temper.

Which was probably why it was also the day that Hawise and Allie had their first argument; an inconsequential matter, as these things so often are, engendered by hunger and boredom more than anything else—but bad enough for Hawise to stomp out of the solar in a huff.

Allie had been teaching her to play chess, and in the middle of a game, Hawise had said something about Lord Peverell—an innocuous remark; afterward she couldn't even remember what it was—but Allie had rounded on her venomously and hurt her feelings, and she had trudged home, muttering indignantly under her breath. Even as she did so she was planning to return as usual the next day to make her peace, but when she woke up the following morning, still full of resentment, she decided it might be better if she didn't.

By midmorning, however, she was beginning to regret her decision.

Rosa had left early to go to the mill, and Ulf was, as usual, on business somewhere for Penda, and so, by lunchtime, bored and lonely, she decided it was probably time to swallow her pride and go up to the manor after all. And, just in case Ulf found out that she had gone alone and got cross about it, she thought it would be a good idea to take the sting out of his anger by checking on her mole traps on the way.

B Y THE TIME SHE TURNED off the lane and took the track to the river, a thick haar was settling on the water and the light was getting dimpsy; nevertheless she found her first trap easily enough and, in no time, had unearthed the small clay pot, lifted it clear of the mud and felt the satisfying judder of the animal inside. She flipped down the tailgate and inserted her hand cautiously—she bore too many scars not to be wary of the sharp little teeth inside—removed the tiny velvet body between her thumb and forefinger and, in one deft movement, struck its nose on the spade, killing it instantly. Then she stuffed the little corpse into her sack, reburied the trap and moved on to the next one.

She repeated the process several times, moving steadily along the riverbank until she came to the section of the river where Harry the Fish hung his nets out to dry. More often than not he would be there waiting for her, a fulsome account of the morning's catch rehearsed and ready on his lips, but today he was long gone, his nets almost dry beside his upturned fishing creel.

She missed seeing him but there were other presences by the river. Somewhere in the rushes she could hear the thin high whistle of an otter, and in the distance, flying above the mist, she saw the ghostly outline of a barn owl flash white against the gray sky.

She came to her last trap and dug quickly. Her stomach was rumbling furiously, reminding her that if she didn't hurry up she would miss lunch; besides, a cold, nagging breeze at her back alerted her to the fact that something nasty was coming in from the North Sea.

She dispatched her last mole, reburied her last trap and was gathering up her things when she felt a sharp blow on the back of her head and the world turned black.

CHAPTER 39

WHEN SHE OPENED HER EYES again she was met with such suffocating blackness that she closed them again immediately, preferring a blindness of her own making.

At first she assumed she was dead, but as time passed and her senses returned, she realized that she couldn't be because she was in such pain—not, thank God, the searing heat of the cauldrons of hell, but a dull, secular throbbing in the back of her head and a peculiar soreness under her arms, the physical memories from the hands that had inflicted this darkness and dragged her from wherever she had been to wherever she was now.

Gulping down a wave of panic that threatened to suffocate her, she forced herself upright and without opening her eyes— she didn't have the courage to face the entombing darkness again quite yet—stretched out her hand to explore the ground around her, feeling neither mud nor stone beneath her fingertips but the dusty crumble of compressed dry earth.

She was in a cave perhaps? Some sort of undercroft? Her instinct told her that she was almost certainly underground; the lack of any breeze; the dank, stale air; and the cloying absence of light confirmed it.

She tried to stand up but a swingeing pain in the back of her head jammed her teeth together and forced her back onto the ground. She clenched her fists against the pain and tried again, forcing herself off the ground, but when she tried to move her feet, she felt the pull of a rope tied fast around her ankle.

In the end it was neither fear nor pain but futility that broke her and made her weep, until, too exhausted to weep anymore, she curled up on the dusty floor and slept . . . and dreamed.

In her dream she was a figure in the painting of the Last Judgment, the one hanging above the chancel in the parish church, where she was standing before an enthroned Christ as he meted out his doom.

On the right-hand side of the throne of grace she could see the souls of the saved, ecstasy on their faces as they were wrapped in the arms of the angels, but to the left, grotesque in their pleading and fear, the damned stood waiting to be seized on the pendulum of the devil's flesh hook and flung into the cauldrons of everlasting fire.

Hawise watched in mute horror as each one met their fate, feeling the searing heat of the flames of hell on her skin and then something even more terrible, Christ's own gaze upon her.

"And you, Hawise," Christ said in a voice even more terrible than his gaze. "To which side do you belong?"

"With you! With you! I belong with you, my Lord!" she cried out, but her plea was drowned out by the clanking of the chain as it swung the hook toward her.

S HE WOKE WITH A START to the sound of footsteps and a figure emerging out of the darkness like vapor solidifying into
form.

"Who are you?" she asked, peering up at the seemingly endless column of darkness that had risen in front of her.

"This is a m-mistake," she stammered, her voice sounding tremulous, contemptible even to her own ears. "I'm . . . I'm
Hawise . . . from Elsford . . . Perhaps you know the place . . . I'm
the reeve's daughter."

She cowered when the figure silently bent toward her, haul-
ing her to her feet, but when he clamped his hands around her
throat, instead of feeling fear, she felt guilt. This was her fault.
She was responsible for this; her own willful disobedience had
conjured the devil and brought her to her moment of death. For
a moment she almost accepted it . . .

Almost, but not quite . . . Something deep inside her wanted
to live.

"Wait!" By some miracle she recovered her voice and felt his
grip loosen slightly. "You mustn't kill me today!" The words
came out in an incontinent rush and, for one glorious moment,
filled the deathly quiet of the cave before it elapsed into silence
and his hands tightened again, squeezing the air from her lungs
and the hope from her heart. In a last act of serenity, she had
closed her eyes only to open them again at an incongruous
sound: an involuntary snort of laughter.

She looked up into the dark nothingness of a face concealed

beneath a cowl and saw the silhouette of his head tilted as if he were listening. At last he spoke.

"Why not?" he asked, his tone unexpectedly curious and amused.

Why not?

Think, Hawise! Think, think! Why not? Why shouldn't he kill you? Sweet Mary, Mother of God! For all she knew her life depended on the answer to this question and she didn't have the wit to answer it! For a moment it even crossed her mind that it might be simpler just to give in and die than to wade through the impenetrable fog of her own mind. And yet, she didn't want to die, she really, really didn't. She had to think. She must come up with something! But whatever it was, it had to be now.

"Because . . ." No! No! She could hear the treachery in her voice again, making her sound pathetic. For one fleeting moment self-preservation had given her fluency, which fear was taking away.

Try harder!

And then, by some miracle, despite the constriction of his hands, she was able to swallow and begin again.

"Because . . ." At last her voice had some strength in it, but this time her mind was failing her . . . She couldn't think of anything to say . . .

Because what? Why? How could she plead for her life? What distinguished hers that it should be spared? But as terror churned her blood it stimulated her senses, and all at once, it occurred to her that, in fact, what she said didn't matter; she had learned something from the pressure of those hands: that whenever she spoke, whatever she said, he listened to her, and while he was listening he wasn't killing her. She would simply talk and talk and keep on talking, perhaps even bore him to death if she could.

"Because on this very night a spirit roams the earth." The words spewed out of her. "An evil, vengeful spirit. A local woman who was once a witch walks abroad on the anniversary of her terrible, terrible death looking for a body to replace the one so brutally taken from her . . ." Taking advantage of his slackening hold on her throat, she took a much-needed breath and plowed on. "So you see, if you kill me now, on this day, she will take mine and bedevil you for eternity."

She dared not look up but somehow sensed that she had his attention and that although his hands were still locked around her throat, crucially, they hadn't tightened again quite yet. He was still listening. By some miracle she had bought herself time, and if she could keep her wits about her, she might be able to barter for some more.

She had just drawn breath, ready to start babbling again, when at last he spoke.

"Well, Hawise," he said. "For clarity then: I should spare your life to save my own, is that it?"

Hawise nodded as emphatically as his hands allowed.

"Just for tonight then?"

She nodded again.

"You, you could always kill me tomorrow . . . if you had a mind to, of course," she said. "But for the sake of your soul, sir, I beg you, not tonight."

And then an extraordinary thing happened. She heard him laugh, full-bodied and helpless.

"Sit down, reeve's daughter," he said, taking his hands off her throat for a moment to wipe his own eyes. "And tell me more about this witch of yours."

CHAPTER 40

WHEN ROSA GOT HOME TO find the cottage empty she assumed that Ulf had persuaded Hawise to go up to the manor after all. Although she was disappointed not to see her, there was consolation in her absence; without the girl's incessant chatter she would get on with her chores more efficiently.

By midafternoon she had achieved a great deal—the bread was made, a delicious pottage bubbling on the trivet—and so, with time on her hands, she went over to the window to watch the comings and goings in the marsh, and stood long enough to see the weather change, the soft gray light bruise and darken as storm clouds gathered, casting long shadows over the wildfowlers crouching low in their punts as they waited for the birds.

Time passed almost unnoticed and the afternoon came and went; it was only the auditory rebuke of the chapel bells ringing for nones that jolted her out of her reverie at last and sent her scuttling to her clothes chest to fetch her apron.

"Sweet Mary, Mother of God!" she muttered to herself, fumbling to tie the strings around her waist. Any moment now

Ulf and Hawise would be home and hungry, and the table wasn't even set!

But when Ulf came back alone, she knew something was wrong.

Today is the day I warned you about, Rosa, the Nameless Dreads told her. *The day of judgment. She won't be coming back. Not now. Not ever.*

"Where's Hawise?" she asked, struggling to steady her voice and her irritation as she watched him busy himself with his homecoming ritual, putting his cap on the stool, stowing his boots neatly by the door, hanging his mantle on its perch, as if such things mattered anymore.

"Ulf!" she said, no longer able to suppress the rising note of panic now. "Did you hear me? I asked you where Hawise was."

He looked up at last, but when he saw her face, he felt the color drain from his.

"I . . . thought she was here, with you," he stammered. "I—"

But Rosa had already torn her mantle from its hook and before he could stop her, she barged past him out the door.

CHAPTER 41

THAT NIGHT THE WIND SHUDDERED through the marsh, carrying Ulf's and Rosa's cries, and with them, of course, the news of Hawise's disappearance.

By the time it reached Elsford Manor the hue and cry had been raised and every able-bodied man and woman had left their cozy bed to join the search. Even the alehouse stood empty, divested of its clientele by the sobering news that another girl was missing.

JODI BURST INTO THE SOLAR ashen faced and tearful. She had been woken by the sound of voices and, seeing the torch-lit procession from her window, rushed downstairs and opened the door to an Ulf and Rosa she barely recognized.

"Like ghosts they were," she said, wiping her eyes. "Never seen such a change in anyone afore. I begged 'em to come inside even for a moment, soaked to the skin, the pair of 'em, but they said that if she weren't here they had to press on. Find 'er wherever she was."

Allie had to react quickly to stop Gyltha from getting out of bed to join the search, almost pinning her to it.

"Oh no you don't," she said, holding her tight. "There is nothing you can do. You're to stay here with Jodi. Penda and I will go, and God willing, we'll find her and bring her back, I promise."

Her words sounded as hollow as they tasted but they were all she had.

"Is it him, do you think?" Gyltha asked, turning her face to the wall. "The one that took Martha and the other girls?"

It was the question that they were secretly all asking but nobody dared answer.

"I don't know." Allie took her hand. "All I know is that I will do everything I can to find her. Everything . . . Oh no! Please don't!" Gyltha had started to cry. "We don't know anything yet. She might have—"

Just then the door flew open.

"Come on, then!"

Penda was standing in the doorway with her crossbow. "Be quick now," she barked at Allie. "No time for fartin' about."

Allie leapt up, grabbed her cloak and followed her out. When they reached the head of the stairs Penda turned to her.

"Might need this," she said, thrusting a small, sheathed object into her hand. "It's a poignard," she explained when Allie looked at it quizzically. "Tuck it up your sleeve but watch you don' cut yourself. That's sharp enough to kill a man, that is, and did once."

Allie did as she was told and followed her down the staircase and out into the night.

When they got to the drawbridge they saw the search party

in the distance, heading into the marsh, the wind blowing the husks of the reeds and the flares of their torches in the same shearing direction.

They caught up quickly, pushing their way through the crowd until they reached Ulf and Rosa at the head. As they drew alongside them, Allie put her hand on Rosa's forearm in the dumb eloquence of touch, but although she turned to look at her, her eyes were blank, unreachable through the impenetrable fog of her suffering.

CHAPTER 42

B Y THE NEXT MORNING THE news of the latest disappearance hadn't yet reached Dunstan, where, in the great hall
of the castle, a pervading air of tetchiness was manifest in the
low-level grumbling and feet-shuffling of the villagers who, summoned early from their beds for the monthly court session, had
been kept waiting.

Sir William, who was due to be presiding over the proceedings and without whom they couldn't begin, had turned up late,
and in an extremely bad mood by the look of him.

"Bad night, Will?" Lord Peverell whispered as he took the
seat beside him on the dais.

Sir William didn't reply but gave him a sidelong look as he
unrolled his ledger onto the table.

"Oh dear. Be kind," Lord Peverell whispered, looking out
on all the anxious faces awaiting his steward's judgment that
morning. "Whatever ails you, Will, it isn't their fault, remember."

Sir William mumbled something and stood up.

"Oyez, oyez," he intoned wearily. "Let the court of Dunstan commence and let every soul tell the truth as it stands in the fear of God."

He conducted the business efficiently but without enthusiasm, and when all the rents and debts had been collected, he moved on swiftly to the appeals, which were surprisingly few: nobody, it seemed, had offended anybody recently or allowed their animals to break a hedge or trample a neighbor's crops. Only the tiny hamlet of Ditchling was fined—a total of three shillings—for neglecting to put its sheep on the manor fallow to manure it.

He was about to bring the session to a close, relieved at how little fuss there had been, when a woman rushed into the hall.

"Hold up!" she cried, turning heads as she fought her way through the crowd, waving her arms frantically at Sir William. "Some bugger's stole my ram!"

The news was greeted with a sharp intake of breath from the crowd, and the atmosphere changed. Things had suddenly become interesting.

Sir William fixed her with a stare, loathing her presence and the delay she was causing.

"Are you accusing somebody in this room?" he asked, very much hoping she wasn't. Livestock theft was a hanging offense and, therefore, enormously time-consuming.

"Bloody right," the woman replied, her hands thrust onto her hips.

Sir William wiped his brow wearily with the back of his hand. "Then, may I inquire, madam, as to whom?"

The woman turned and raised her arm, pointing into a corner of the room.

"Him!" she said.

Every head in the hall swiveled with her accusing finger to see an ashen-faced Danny Wadlow sidle surreptitiously toward the exit before he was stopped by two burly men in sheepskin.

Sir William looked from the struggling boy—who was now loudly protesting his innocence—back to the woman.

"Do you mean that person?" he asked. "By the name of Daniel Wadlow?"

The woman nodded.

"And you saw him take the animal, did you?"

The woman hesitated for a moment. "Well, I didn't actually see 'im take it," she said, flushing under the interrogation. "Not actually take it. Can't say as I did, but I know, sure as eggs is eggs, that it were 'im. Ask anybody." She broke off, her eyes sweeping the crowd for support. "It's that scap . . . scapu . . . scapuli . . . whatsit . . . all that witchcraft and scrying malarkey. Tha's what 'e takes 'em for."

"Them?" Sir William asked sharply. "Are you suggesting that he's responsible for the theft of more than one ram?"

"Bloody right," the woman said, glaring at Danny, who was shouting so loudly by this time that one of his burly captors had to clap his hand over his mouth to shut him up.

"But have you seen any of these rams in this person's possession?" Sir William asked.

"No, course I ain't," the woman snapped irritably. "'E's too clever for that; besides, 'e kills 'em right off and boils 'em down for their bones for that . . . well, that . . . thing 'e does."

Stimulated by the prospect of a hanging, and a Wadlow hanging at that, the crowd had begun debating the case among themselves.

"Silence!" Sir William shouted, glaring ferociously. "I am sorry for the loss of your ram," he told the woman when he could be heard again and order was restored. "But without proof it is, I fear, your word against his, and therefore I cannot, in all conscience, pass judgment."

Murmurs of shock and outrage rumbled around the hall like distant thunder.

"Who cares about proof!" somebody shouted. "Hang the bastard and be done with it. Do us all a favor!"

As the crowd became increasingly restive, baying for Danny Wadlow's blood, Lord Peverell, who had been sitting quietly throughout, decided to intervene, raising his hand in an appeal for silence.

"And that is the doom of the court, Sir William, is it?" he asked when it had been granted.

Sir William nodded. "Indeed, my lord."

After a signal from his lordship, the burly men reluctantly let Danny go and watched him scamper out of the hall.

WHEN HE DEEMED THAT DANNY was far enough away for his own safety, Sir William dismissed the court and the crowd dispersed. When they were alone at last, Lord Peverell put his hand on his shoulder.

"I wasn't expecting such leniency from you today, Will," he said. "You seemed so out of sorts this morning that I—"

"I didn't think he was guilty," Sir William said, interrupting him. "And, strange though it may seem, I had no appetite for a hanging today . . ." Then, muttering something about a lack of sleep, he rolled up his ledger and left the hall.

CHAPTER 43

ADELIA COULDN'T WAIT TO GET to Elsford, not only because she was impatient to see Allie and Gyltha again but
because—after two days and nights with only Lena and the taci-
turn men-at-arms Emma had sent to accompany them—she was
desperate for more stimulating company.

When they reached the river Delph, swapping their horses
for a boat, she left hers without a backward glance. That was
another reason she was keen to get the journey over with: she
hated riding horses generally but had eschewed Emma's offer of
a cart to save time.

"Why are you always in such a hurry!" Emma had asked
testily. "Just think about your poor bottom, 'Delia."

Well, she wouldn't admit it, certainly not to Emma, but she
was thinking about it now. Three days' riding and it was raw to
the bone, so that when the boatmen took her arm and helped
her into the hull of the boat at last, she vowed that, all things being equal, she would never ride again. Unlike Rowley, she liked
boats; something about the enforced confinement suited her. The

luxury of time alone with her own thoughts, with no pressure to do anything, was her idea of bliss.

She took a seat at the back, enjoying the rhythmic push and pull of the boat's passage through the water, and as she looked out at the willows that dotted the banks was reminded of her very first sight of the Fens.

It was thirty years since she and Mansur had been unceremoniously jolted into the marsh on the back of a mule cart. Having lived among the hills of Salerno all their lives, they had expected to find the flatness of the land repellent, and at first they had. But something strange happened and soon she began to appreciate the wonder of its enormous skies and horizons, the lushness and the herbal treasures that grew there, feeling as if she had landed in an apothecary's Eden. Most precious among her discoveries was the abundance and variety of its willows: golden willows, white willows, gray willows, goat willows, willows for making bats or growing osiers, bay willows, almond willows, all of them beautiful in the way the sun dappled their branches and more beautiful still because, with a concoction of willow bark, you could relieve pain.

Which was exactly what she had done almost the moment she arrived, employing the anesthetic property of the willow to ease the passage of a reed up Prior Geoffrey's penis to relieve an enlarged prostate.

She smiled to herself, partly at the memory of a job well done but also remembering the dear old prior, who would always hold a special place in her heart, not only for introducing her to her beloved Gyltha but also because he was probably Ulf's grandfather.

Probably; she couldn't say for certain because Ulf's paternal line was never openly discussed. She simply presumed, as everyone else did, that the young Norman priest—as Prior Geoffrey had been then—and the well-set-up young Fenland woman who kept house for him were more than just employer and employee. Whether they were or not, nobody cared; in those days England's attitude toward clerical celibacy was tolerant—or slack, depending on your point of view—and Rome hadn't yet begun to shake its fist at "priests' wives," as it did now. But for Adelia, at least, it was enough to know that Ulf came in to existence around that time, before the prior died and Gyltha met Mansur.

The willows, the memories, the motion of the boat, gradually sent her off to sleep, and the next thing she knew they were mooring at Elsford and Lena was shaking her awake.

She climbed out of the boat, surprised not to see anyone there to greet them. Emma had sent outriders ahead to organize their accommodation along the route and to alert Elsford to their arrival, so she had half expected to find Ulf waiting for them at the quay on the Delph. When he wasn't, she automatically assumed he would pop up when they got to Elsford, but when he wasn't there, either, she began to worry that something was wrong, a feeling that only increased when they arrived at the manor.

For such a well-fortified building, she thought the gatekeeper seemed unusually lackluster and was surprised when he admitted them without fuss or enthusiasm, and that, apart from the odd glance cast by the servants they met in the courtyard, their passage went unchallenged.

There was an undeniable air of disaffection about the place, and although she didn't usually hold with the likes of feelings and atmospheres—much too whimsical and unscientific for a woman of her education—she found it hard to shrug off the feeling that there was, in fact, something very badly wrong here.

A feeling that only increased when she climbed the steps to the front door and, before she'd even had a chance to knock, saw it flung open by Allie, of all people, who immediately collapsed, weeping, into her arms.

They sank down onto the step, Adelia cradling Allie's head in her lap, mouthing silent instructions over the top of it to Lena, who was standing idly in the cold sucking her thumb, apparently happy to freeze to death.

"Oh, my darling," Adelia murmured when Lena got the message at last and ambled inside. "What on earth is going on?"

Her first concern, the one that had nagged at her all the way from the boat, had been that something had happened to Allie, but now that she was obviously safe, her mind had moved on to its next-worst imagining, that something had happened to Gyltha.

"Is it Gyltha?"

Allie shook her head, saying something garbled that Adelia couldn't understand, and continued to sob, unleashing a maelstrom of emotion that was almost as much of a surprise to her as it was to Adelia.

At first Allie had been numbed by the shock of Hawise's disappearance and, in the immediate aftermath, had had too much to do and too many other people to think about to consider her own feelings, but now, in the safety of her mother's arms, her defenses were crumbling.

"Let's go inside," Adelia said, encouraging her gently to her feet. "Tell me all about it in the warm."

As she stood with her arms wrapped around Allie in the entrance hall, Penda came down the staircase toward them, looking equally stricken.

"Mistress," she cried with palpable relief, grabbing Adelia by the shoulders and enveloping her in a hug. "And not a moment too soon. Sorry I weren't there to meet you but somethin' terrible's happened." She released Adelia and glanced anxiously at Allie. "Allie'll explain," she added as she dashed through the door.

AND YOU'RE ABSOLUTELY SURE SHE didn't just run away, the way you used to when you were cross with me?" Adelia asked when Allie told her about the disappearance.

"No." Allie shook her head emphatically. "She wasn't . . . She isn't like me. Oh, Ma, if only you knew her. She was—is—kind and funny and so happy! She would never just run away . . . She simply wouldn't! She . . . has . . . been taken. I know she has."

Adelia, seeing Allie's lip trembling again, put her arms around her until she had composed herself sufficiently to be able to take her to the solar.

GOD BE PRAISED!" GYLTHA BURST into tears when she saw Adelia come in. "Never thought I'd be so pleased to see anyone in me life."

"Likewise," said Adelia, sinking into her embrace and holding on to her as though her life depended on it.

When Gyltha eventually let her go, Adelia sniffed, dabbed her eyes and looked around the room, suddenly ashamed of her tears. Judging by the anguished expressions on all the faces in the room, there had been quite an epidemic of them lately.

THAT EVENING, WHEN THE OTHERS retired after supper, Adelia and Allie huddled around the fire in the hall, transcribing Allie's investigation notes like monks in a scriptorium.

"I'm surprised you haven't done this before," Adelia said testily. "Anything could have happened to them. That slate could have been wiped clean for all you knew, and you would have lost all this vital information . . ." Her earlier concern had transmuted into irritation, an emotion she felt more comfortable with.

Allie sighed.

"Well, I'm just telling you," said Adelia, picking up the piece of vellum they had been working on and backing up to a wall sconce to read in its light. "Now that we've got it all written down properly, let's see where we are, shall we?"

Allie watched her squinting at the page, tilting it this way and that, her mouth moving silently as she absorbed the information and committed it to her formidable memory.

"I'm interested in these wrist marks," she said, looking up again. "You're sure they were postmortem?"

Allie nodded. "Well, pretty sure. I couldn't see any scabbing and the flesh around them had that yellowish tinge to it."

"Hmmm," Adelia muttered as she returned to the page. "DV." She looked up again, this time flapping the parchment against her thigh as though to stimulate her brain. "DV. It means something, must do, but what? The killer's initials, perhaps?"

Allie, still sitting at the table, slumped and buried her head in the crook of her arm. "I have no idea," she said.

"Well, think, woman!" Adelia snapped as she started pacing the room. "It's no good sitting there all maudlin like that. If we're going to find Hawise, we're going to have to come up with something while there's still time."

"But I'm beginning to think there isn't any," Allie said plaintively. "She's gone and she's probably already dead."

"Allie!" Adelia immediately stopped packing and stamped her foot. "You're not to talk like that, you mustn't even think it. Besides, the one thing we do know is that none of these girls were killed immediately. There's a hiatus, for some reason, between when he takes them and when the bodies are found, but, thanks to your investigation, at least we now know that they were alive in between."

She lifted the vellum to the light again and pointed at it.

"Yes, you see. Here. According to these notes there was a period of, what, months between Martha's disappearance and her body being found, and then . . . what . . . several weeks, at least, with the next girl."

"Two," said Allie wearily. "Two weeks with the next one."

"The question is, why?"

Allie decided to get up at last; the fire had gone out, and the cold was almost unbearable. "Perhaps he doesn't start out with the intention of killing them . . . ," she said, starting to pace beside Adelia. "Not at first anyway. Perhaps he takes them for some other reason but then, oh, I don't know, they disappoint him in some way and that's when he kills them!"

"Good girl," Adelia said, linking her arm in Allie's. "Keep thinking and keep walking, it helps."

"Well," said Allie, "this might sound strange, and don't take too much notice of it yet because I'm still working on the theory . . . but perhaps he has some peculiar notion of romance, at least in the beginning anyway, and then . . . Oh I don't know." She broke off with a frown.

Besides, they had reached the other end of the hall and were forced to turn around.

"Keep thinking," said Adelia, giving Allie's arm an encouraging squeeze. "You might be onto something; after all, some complicated notion of romance might help explain why he leaves their bodies in the river. After all, it would be easier simply to dump them in the marsh or a bog or somewhere like that—plenty of those around, and nobody would ever find them there—but there's something about a river, isn't there, when you think about it? Something unsullied about fresh water that might even be construed as romantic, if you were to look at it from the viewpoint of a corrupt mind, that is."

"Shhh!"

An irritable disembodied voice echoed out of one of the corners of the hall and stopped them in their tracks.

"You two goin' to be much longer? Some of us is trying to sleep in 'ere, you know," it said.

"I'm so sorry," Allie called back, peering into the darkness in an attempt to find the complainant. She had forgotten all about the servants who slept there. "I think we've just about finished now anyway," she added, taking Adelia's arm and hastening to the door.

Halfway up the stairs Adelia stopped. "You've done very well, darling," she said, "and I don't want you to think otherwise, but I'm afraid we are going to need more evidence."

Allie felt a chill running up her spine. Adelia was right; it was exactly what they needed. The trouble, and what terrified her, was that they would find it, but only in the form of Hawise's dead body.

CHAPTER 44

FORTUNATELY, THE NEXT BODY TO turn up, wrapped loosely in a grubby shroud and left on the graveyard wall, wasn't Hawise's.

It belonged, or had done, to an elderly man from the hamlet of Long Willow, about two miles from Elsford, who went to bed one night and didn't wake up in the morning because he had succumbed to the ague that had been threatening to kill him all winter.

His neighbors, who discovered the body, went immediately to Father Edward, who refused to return with them, wringing his hands and pointing—futilely, as it turned out, since neither one could read—to a notice that had been pinned to the church gate.

"It's an interdict," Father Edward tried to explain. "From the bishop of Ely."

But the neighbors merely looked blankly at it and scratched their heads. "A what?" they asked. They'd never heard of one.

"An interdict," Father Edward repeated slowly, in case a more careful enunciation would help.

It didn't, as was apparent from their increasingly blank expressions.

Father Edward ran his hands down his face in despair. Ever since the notice had appeared—only the day before yesterday—he had been dreading this moment: how on earth could he explain the principles of an interdict to his parishioners when he didn't really understand them himself?

He took a deep breath.

"It means," he said, speaking in his recently adopted slow and careful manner, which, unbeknownst to him, the neighbors were beginning to find irritating, "that by order of the bishop of Ely"—he broke off and pointed again, this time in the direction of the cathedral—"that, henceforth, I am no longer allowed to celebrate mass or perform the viaticum, or, I fear, offer sepulture in this churchyard . . ."

The neighbors scratched their heads once more.

"Bit late for the viaticum, ain't it, Father?" one said. "Poor old bugger's dead. He just needs buryin'. Can't exactly leave 'im to rot in 'is own bed, now, can we, bor?"

Father Edward groaned. Of course they couldn't, but what else were they going to do?

"But that's just it," he said, a note of hysteria rising at the impasse. "That's what 'sepulture' means, you see; no burial by dint of the bishop of Ely."

He started backing away, inching imperceptibly over the threshold of his cottage, until, once safely inside, he slammed the door.

He leaned against it, breathing hard. He felt wretched, but what else could he do?

"Go away," he begged them through the door and gritted teeth. "I can't help you. I'm very sorry."

Pressing his ear hard to the door, he listened until he heard their sighs of resignation and their footsteps shuffling away.

T HEY CAME BACK THOUGH, AFTER dark, trundling the old man's body in a wheelbarrow to the churchyard, where they laid it carefully on the wall, far away from the predation of foxes but not, they hoped, the eye of God.

CHAPTER 45

"WHAT DO YOU SUPPOSE THAT is?" Adelia asked Allie, stopping abruptly to point at a grubby-looking bundle lying on the churchyard wall.

They were on their way through the village to see Rosa and Ulf in the unlikely event that they could do anything for them.

"And also," Adelia had whispered as they were getting ready to leave that morning, "I want you to show me where the second body was found, just in case—"

"In case I missed something, you mean," Allie had said sharply, interrupting her. "Well I didn't."

"No, of course you didn't, I didn't mean that." Adelia had sighed wearily. Allie was so easily riled these days, especially, it seemed, by her. "It's just that I thought a fresh pair of eyes might see things differently, that's all."

Adelia's response to the prevailing atmosphere of despondency was to meet it with energy. It wasn't that she didn't feel for them all, or sympathize to her very core with their suffering. It was simply that she found crises invigorating; rising and responding to them was what she did best. Besides, if Hawise was to be found alive—God willing—it wouldn't be done mooching about in the solar.

That morning, as she followed Allie down the track to the village, she had been muttering to herself under her breath, ruminating on the little information they had, hoping inspiration might strike as she did so.

"DV . . . ," she had kept repeating. "DV . . ." Allie was beginning to find it unbearably irritating when, to her relief, Adelia had stopped and asked: "Are there any Davids around here that you know of?"

Allie had thought for a moment but shook her head.

"No. No Davids. There's a Daniel . . . Daniel Wadlow . . . but that would be a 'W,' not a 'V,' and those markings were very precise. Besides, I doubt if the person I'm thinking of can read or write."

"Hmm." Adelia had continued chuntering for a few more yards until she was distracted by the bundle on the wall.

"Looks like a body," Allie said, peering at a set of toes poking through one end.

"So it does," said Adelia. "But what's it doing there?" She looked around, scanning the vicinity for clues regarding the mystery, until she spotted the notice pinned to the church gate.

She walked over to it.

"Oh, no!" she said when she had read it, clapping her hand over her mouth. "Oh, Allie." She turned to her, ashen faced.

"What is it?" Allie asked, unable to imagine how such an innocuous-looking piece of parchment could be the cause of such distress.

"Oh, it's dreadful, darling. That bastard Longchamp's only

gone and passed the interdict he's been threatening. It means the diocese will be knee-deep in bodies before the winter's out."

They looked back at the body and saw that a small crowd had already gathered around it and that Father Edward was scurrying out of the church to see what all the fuss was about.

"Do you suppose we ought to do something?" Allie asked.

Adelia shook her head. "Nothing we can do," she said. "But it's a wicked thing. It's a punishment for the innocent to manipulate the guilty, that's what it is! It's just too awful and too unfair for words."

They sidestepped the crowd and continued on their way to the cottage, only this time with Adelia chuntering about the interdict, the injustice of ecclesiastical politics and the folly of male pride, all of which Allie ignored, until they had almost reached the cottage garth, when she decided to put a stop to it.

"We'll discuss it later, Ma," she said firmly. "Ulf and Rosa won't want to hear about that now; I think they've got enough to worry about."

THE COTTAGE WAS BARELY RECOGNIZABLE from her last visit; desolation and despair were manifest almost everywhere she looked, from the unchanged rushes on the floor to the dirty cups and bowls littering a table nobody could be bothered to clear.

"I'll set a fire," said Adelia, closing the window shutters that had been left to flap in the breeze. "You'll freeze to death else."

Ulf didn't seem to care whether he did or not and sat silently, head bowed, forearms on the table, palms down, gazing miserably at his spread fingers, while Rosa stood at the window gazing blindly out over the marsh.

Their desolation was palpable; Allie could hardly bring herself to look at them. But while Adelia busied herself with practical things, she stood around redundantly, struggling to think of anything to say. She was no stranger to grief and had seen the effects of it before—otherwise healthy people physically diminished overnight—but this was the first time she had ever been so keenly and closely touched by it.

When the neglected chores had been seen to and Adelia was satisfied that order had been restored—although nobody seemed to care—she went to Rosa by the window and put her arm around her.

"We will find her, you know," she told her, and Allie, sitting with an arm around Ulf, had to stifle the rejoinder: *Yes, but she might well be dead by the time we do.*

The body was still on the wall when they went past the church on their way home. Only this time Father Edward, arms upraised, was trying to disperse the now-sizeable crowd that had gathered busily and noisily around it.

"Just . . . Just go home, everyone," he pleaded, to no avail. "There's nothing to be done and nothing more to see. An interdict has been passed!"

But the villagers didn't know what an interdict was and cared even less, and simply ignored him, apparently mesmerized and immovable from the scene, until a young girl, in visible distress, came rushing through the graveyard, astonishing everybody when she dived to the ground, prostrating herself at Father Edward's feet.

"What do you suppose the matter is?" Adelia asked, unable to hear what the girl was saying through her convulsive sobs and the disapproving mutterings of the crowd.

"I don't know," Allie said, shrugging off her hood to hear better. "It's . . . something to do with . . ." She craned her neck in concentration, then turned anxiously. "Oh, Ma! She's asking him for the viaticum. She says her mother's dying!"

They watched Father Edward carefully extricate the hem of his robe from the girl's fingers and turn away, just as the onlookers, suddenly mindful of duties elsewhere, began to drift off.

"We have to help her!" Allie said, grabbing Adelia's wrist and pulling her through the dispersing crowd to where the girl was lying motionless on the ground.

"But how, Allie? We can't administer the viaticum!" Adelia said as she was reluctantly dragged through the church gate behind her.

"No, of course we can't," Allie snapped. All the suffering she had witnessed that day had taken its toll on her temper. "But if we're quick we might be able to stop it from becoming necessary."

As they approached, the girl got to her knees, clasping her hands imploringly at Father Edward's retreating back, but when he didn't turn back, she collapsed onto the ground again with a whimper of despair.

She was sobbing so hard by the time Allie knelt beside her that she seemed not to notice her presence. Only when Allie tapped her gently on the shoulder did she respond, rolling onto her back like a submissive puppy, peeling a dank curtain of grubby hair out of her eyes and staring up at her warily.

When Allie had introduced herself and carefully explained that she and Adelia were there to help her if they could, her expression softened, and in an impenetrable Fenland accent, she told them that her name was Epona, that her mother was desperately ill and that they should follow her.

A moment later, she scrambled to her feet and led them back through the village at speed, stopping every few yards to make sure they were keeping up and to chivvy them when she thought they were flagging.

It was a punishing journey, especially for Adelia, who was puffing hard and close to exhaustion by the time, a mile or so beyond Elsford, they arrived on the outskirts of a hamlet, not much more than a straggle of tiny huts built high above the marsh on stilts. Epona stopped at the furthest hut in the row and, with her foot on the bottom rung of a ladder, gestured frantically to them that they should follow her up.

The climb felt like an ascent into hell, only colder, Allie thought, stooping through the doorway at the top into a godforsaken room where Epona's mother, wrapped from head to foot in a bundle of filthy rags, lay motionless in a corner.

At first sight it looked as if they were too late, as if she were already dead, but when Allie knelt down and put her hand to her forehead, she saw a faint flickering of her eyelids. She hurriedly took off her mantle and rolled up her sleeves while Adelia looked around them in despair, wondering how on earth good health could possibly be restored in such an environment.

"First things first, we need to get her fever down," Allie said to nobody in particular, peeling back the filthy layers of swaddling so that Adelia could begin her examination.

It didn't take long.

The moment she opened the woman's mouth, an abscess, so engorged that it was pressing dangerously on her trachea, glistened at the back of her throat like a fleshy ruby.

Now for the tricky bit. Adelia rocked back onto her heels, wiping her brow with the back of her hand, which, despite the cold in the room, was beaded with sweat.

"Quinsy," she mouthed at Allie, then turned to Epona, who was hovering anxiously behind her, and barked: "Don't just stand there, girl! If you want to save your mother's life we need to act quickly and you must do exactly as I say."

Epona gulped and nodded emphatically.

"Good. Well, first things first, you must light a fire," Adelia said, flinging out an arm to point at an untidy mound of ash in the middle of the room. "For what I'm going to have to do here I will need plenty of boiling water." She broke off and wiped her forehead again before adding, "You do have a trivet, I take it?"

The girl nodded again.

"Good," said Adelia. "Well, that's something at least. And when that's done, you're to go to the well and fetch a bucket of water."

She looked around the room, groaning with despair as she was reminded of the dreadful conditions that would make the procedure she was about to perform even more perilous than it needed be. In spite of the cold, the air in the room hung heavy and fetid, and the pervading stench—which she was reluctant to identify—encouraged economy of breath. And yet, there was no doubt about it, she was going to have to do something, and soon. In the short time since they'd been here the woman's breathing had become increasingly labored as the abscess in her throat grew inexorably and threatened to close it.

When the fire was lit and Epona dispatched to the well, Adelia got up and started to ransack the room.

"I need a needle or a knife," Allie heard her muttering as she flung wide the various cupboard doors and turned out all the pots and pans inside, tipping them up and shaking every implement she found. "Where on earth am I going to find something like that in a hellhole like this?"

Allie looked at her blankly for a moment, hoping for inspiration, until she remembered the knife Penda had lent her on the night Hawise went missing and which, in all the confusion, she had forgotten to give back. Snatching up her mantle from the floor, she started rummaging around in the lining.

"Will this do?" she asked when she had found it, holding it up like it was a miniature Excalibur.

"Oh, my darling," Adelia said, "where on earth did you find that? That will do perfectly."

It was a moment of serendipity and she was grateful, but it wasn't sufficient to quell her nerves, because although the procedure itself was moderately straightforward, her lack of practice worried her.

It had been many years since her last operation; in fact, she had not done one since the appendectomy she had performed on the princess Joanna, which seemed a lifetime ago now. Suppose the intervening years had blunted her skill? Or that her ageing fingers had lost their dexterity? And even if they hadn't, what if this unaccustomed bout of nerves got the better of her and her usually steady hand shook at the critical moment? And yet, she had no choice. Without prompt intervention the woman would almost certainly choke to death, and, by the looks of things, quite soon.

"Ma."

She looked up.

Sensing this crisis of confidence, Allie was gazing at her with an expression of such tender reassurance that her nerves melted away in the glow.

AND, AS IT TURNED OUT, she needn't have worried anyway. The woman, by the time Adelia came to open her mouth again, had been rendered almost insentient with the pain and fever and stayed still and mercifully silent throughout, and Allie, the perfect assistant, held her as steady as a rock, one hand holding her body propped in her lap, the other holding her mouth open long enough and wide enough for Adelia to perform her miracle: one deft stab with the tip of the knife and the abscess popped, releasing a satisfying bolus of pus.

"Spit," Adelia told her, and, when she had, gave her a solution of saline to gargle with, then wrapped her in Allie's mantle to keep her warm and laid her gently back on her palliasse to sleep.

She knelt beside her, crippling her knees on the earthen floor, until she was satisfied that she was out of danger and breathing freely again, then got up.

"These will have to be washed," she said, turning to Epona with an armful of grubby rags, only to find that, in the meantime, the hut had filled with a brood of ragged-looking children,

Epona's siblings, by the look of them, all anxiously and silently watching her every move. "Very good," she said, disconcerted by their number and their rapt attention and grateful that she hadn't been aware of it earlier. "Lots and lots . . . and lots of you. Well . . . In that case, it won't take long to get this place cleaned up." She stared at them for a moment, then, fixing each in turn with a stare of pedagogic menace, told them:

"Your mother is suffering from an infection, which may not mean much to you, but it's caused by being dirty and living in dirty conditions. So, my advice, if you don't want her to die and you don't want to catch it yourselves, is that you will have to make damn sure that every inch of this room is scrubbed until it squeaks." She stopped for a moment as another thought occurred to her before adding: "And, actually, that applies to you, too. You should all be scrubbed from head to toe, until you squeak. Do you understand?"

The children nodded.

"Good," said Adelia. "Then our work here is done. From here on in your mother's survival depends on you."

It wasn't strictly true. Inevitably, she would return within a day or two to check up on her—conscience would dictate that she do so—but in the meantime, it wouldn't hurt to encourage them to adopt more sanitary habits.

I T WAS DUSK BY THE time they got back to Elsford, shuffling and shivering under their shared mantle, to find Penda waiting anxiously at the gatehouse, her hands on her hips, staring menacingly into the night.

Allie recognized her stance and its implication and, too tired to be brave, dropped behind Adelia and let her go first.

"Where've you been?" Penda demanded, anxiety giving way to irritation with relief that they were back safely at last. "We've been worried sick, I was expecting you hours ago."

By the time they had explained what had happened, describing Epona and her mother, the sibling brood, the hamlet and the fetid little hut, they were halfway across the courtyard.

"Christ's teeth!" Penda's gimlet eyes opened wider than Allie had ever seen them. "You know who they are, don't you?"

She shook her head.

"The Wadlow family! That's who!"

CHAPTER 46

DURING THE ENDLESS HOURS OF her captivity, Hawise worked hard to make sense of her surroundings to create a picture of them in her mind.

Whether it was an accurate portrait or not didn't matter—she never expected she would see them—but her sanity depended on furnishing this prison with her imagination, to soften the edges of the darkness and make it habitable.

Barring the rope around her ankle, she was physically comfortable. He had provided her with a palliasse to sleep on, warm blankets and a regular supply of clean clothes—sheathlike robes that felt expensive to the touch and smelled of lye and an herb she didn't recognize—and he always brought two buckets: one for her privy and one to wash herself.

Over time she learned the pattern to his visits and realized that he only ever came at night.

When he came she would wake to the sound of approaching footsteps, hear them pause beside the privy bucket; then a stifled breath of disgust, footsteps receding, keys jangling, a door opening—a postern perhaps—water lapping on stone and a sloosh as the bucket emptied into what she assumed was the river . . . But, other than the candle he carried, she never saw any light.

When the postern door closed and the footsteps returned, she would brace herself, closing her eyes when he was close enough that she could feel his breath on her face. And yet, despite the unabating terror, he never touched her; instead, he would kneel beside her, almost worshipfully, addressing her as his "lady," and sometimes, sometimes, he would feed her sweetmeats.

At other times he would reach out to touch the hem of her robe and sing softly to her, and always, when he had finished, would settle down beside her like a child at his mother's knee and ask her for a story.

So far she had been able to rise to the challenge, stifling the panic that threatened to blank her mind and silence her, but always, in the back of her mind, was the nagging feeling that one day either her voice or her imagination or both would fail her and it would prove fatal.

But not, thank God, tonight. Tonight, she felt strangely excited. She had a new story ready for him.

In the darkness a rare smile crept over her face.

"I think you'll enjoy this one," she told him. "I think, perhaps, it's the best of all."

CHAPTER 47

"O H!" SAID ADELIA. "VISITORS?"
     They were on their way to the hall for breakfast when
two unfamiliar male voices rang out from it.

She looked at Allie, surprised and a little irritated to see that
she was blushing.

"Oh. I take it you know them, then," she said.

"Yes," Allie replied, the blush rising as she started straight-
ening her skirts and fussing at the gauze around her wimple,
looking, to Adelia's sharp, maternal eye, uncharacteristically coy.
"I think I do."

So Adelia wasn't entirely surprised to discover that at least
one of the voices belonged to an unusually handsome young man.

Both were around Allie's age, dressed in hunting leathers,
each carrying an exotic-looking falcon and deep in conversation
with Penda.

"Mistress Adelia," Penda said when she saw her come in, "allow me to introduce Lord Peverell of Dunstan and his steward
Sir William."

The men bowed politely.

"Greetings," said Adelia, uncomfortably aware of a frisson in the room and that the scrutiny of all eyes in it was on her.

"Lord Peverell's very kindly come to warn us about the interdict," Penda continued, and—Adelia could have sworn—blushed like a girl as she did so. Something about the friendlier of these two young men seemed to be having a peculiar effect on both Allie and Penda.

"How very kind of him," she said. "But actually quite unnecessary. We learned about it yesterday. We saw the notice on the church gate and the body on the wall."

"Ah," said Penda. "Well, it's not just that, he's offering us the use of 'is icehouse, in case like—"

"At least, I hope it won't be necessary, of course," Lord Peverell interrupted her. "But, as Lady Penda says, just in case . . ."

"That's very generous of you," Adelia said, racking her brain as to why his name seemed familiar, until she remembered the conversation between Rowley and Penda at the Wolvercote feast.

So, it's you, she thought, regarding him with renewed interest.

So that was what all the fuss was about! Well, he was certainly handsome, she'd give him that, with his leonine hair and large, heavily lashed brown eyes; in fact, now she came to think about it, he was reminiscent of Rowley in his youth, although this boy's bones were finer, as the English aristocracy's tended to be. He was also tall and he carried himself with confidence, and just for a moment she wondered if there might be a hint of arrogance or vanity there, too.

Perhaps.

But, on second thought, perhaps not; that scar on his cheek—which, from a beholder's point of view anyway, added something to his looks—mitigated it.

Aware that he was shifting uncomfortably under the forensic gaze she had allowed to linger for longer than was polite, she looked away kindly.

"As you say, Lord Peverell," she continued, smiling with, she hoped, benevolence, if not, perhaps, benediction. "Let us hope that it won't be necessary. In fact I'm hoping that we might be able to nip this damnable business in the bud. I happen to be on good acquaintance with the bishop of St. Albans and shall be writing to him immediately to enlist his help in getting the interdict lifted."

Her last statement was met with a murmur of approval that she barely noticed; her mind had already moved on to other matters, chief among them the information she had so obviously been denied about Allie and everything that had gone on in her absence.

Something was most definitely afoot, and she determined there and then that, before she did anything else, even before writing to Rowley, she would get to the bottom of it.

The problem, though, was: with whom?

The obvious person was Gyltha, but she could hardly pester her about something as comparatively trivial as this in the midst of all her worry about Hawise, which only left Penda, whom she automatically ruled out for being so obviously in league with Rowley.

"Thank you," she said. "But now, if you'll excuse me, I must . . . well, get on, I suppose."

Nodding graciously at them, she swept out of the hall.

S HE RETURNED A LITTLE LATER on, disappointed to find that Lord Peverell had left.

"Bugger!" she said when Allie told her that she had only just missed them. "I wanted to talk to him—" She broke off, irritated by Allie's blushing again. "Oh, really, Allie, darling, you're going to have to stop that, you know," she said. "It could become extremely annoying, it really could."

Allie scowled at her. "You've been talking to Gyltha!" she snapped. "Behind my back!"

"I wouldn't dream of it," Adelia replied. "But you might have spared me a great deal of trouble if you'd had the decency to tell me about this young man of yours in the first place. Why do you want to keep secrets from me all the time?"

When she had left the hall earlier she had rather fortuitously bumped into Jodi and, with a steely guile, persuaded her to divulge enough information to sate her curiosity for the time being.

"God strike me! There's nothing to tell!" Allie said. "And, for your information, he's not 'my young man'!"

"Well that's as may be," Adelia sniffed, "and we'll discuss it later when I've written to your father, but in the meantime, perhaps you would be good enough to tell me where I could find some of that vellum."

"I'll fetch you some." Jodi had been lurking in the shadows. Worried that she had inadvertently betrayed a confidence—

although she had been so ruthlessly pumped for it that she didn't have much choice—she had followed Adelia back into the hall and was now withering under Allie's reproachful gaze. "And you can come, too," Jodi said, turning sharply to Lena, who was slumped on a stool by the fire sucking her thumb. "It'd be useful, so I can show you where everything is."

"I'll come as well, if I may," said Allie, whose enthusiasm to escape Adelia for the moment outweighed her irritation with Jodi.

J ODI LED THEM OUT OF the hall to a doorway Allie hadn't seen before that opened onto a narrow staircase leading to the bowels of the building and an inhospitably dark tunnel where the light from their lanterns cast eerie shadows along the walls. All the way along, Lena mewled like a scalded kitten and only stopped when they came out into an enormous arched cavern that smelled of tuns of wine, spices and the faint aroma of cats' pee.

The size and scale of this subterranean labyrinth was astonishing. If anything, it felt larger even than the house above, and the dark tunnels punctuating the circular wall reminded Allie of sockets in a skull.

"Where do they lead?" she asked. Even in a whisper her voice echoed and reverberated around the walls, making her afraid it would wake things that were best left unwoken.

"Nobody knows," Jodi replied quite matter-of-factly as she picked up some vellum sheaves from a large pile on the floor. "No one in their right mind goes down 'ere 'less they 'ave to."

Allie could see why.

"All I know is that that one," she added, pointing at a tunnel to their right, "the one what looks like a giant nostril, goes all the way under the house and comes out at a secret door on the river."

Allie peered into a darkness as black as death and recoiled, as though from a cliff edge, terrified that some unseen hand might appear to shove her down it.

"Do you mean a postern?" she asked. "How do you know?"

Jodi shrugged. "Lady Penda told me. She's the only one been down that far."

"Did she build it?" Allie asked. After all, she knew Penda's predilection for security.

"Don't think so," Jodi replied. "I think it was already built when Lady Maud give it to 'er. Don't know if she told you 'ow she come by Elsford Manor but Lady Maud give it to her as a reward for saving her stepson's life during the Anarchy."

Allie nodded. The story was familiar; she had heard fragments of it from Gyltha and Hawise, but only fragments, because as usual, when pressed for details about her sister's past, she had become conveniently vague.

"Do you know what happened?" she asked, seizing on any opportunity to learn more. But Jodi shook her head.

"That's all I know," she replied, tucking the vellum sheaves under her arm. "But I think it's time we was getting back, mistress." And once again Allie had the distinct impression that she was being denied information deliberately. On the other hand, standing in this hellhole beside Lena, who was mewling again, she wasn't inclined to pursue it.

They were halfway back when Lena let out a scream.

Instinctively Allie put her arm around her.

"What is it?"

"I . . . I . . . thought I heard something," the girl stammered.

"It's the wind," Jodi called back without breaking stride. "Makes strange noises sometimes, which is why most people's too frit to come down 'ere."

Just then a thought occurred to Allie: Supposing it wasn't the wind? Supposing Lena had heard a voice? Perhaps she was clutching at straws, but in the absence of anything else to clutch at, supposing Hawise had come down here for some reason, tripped and fallen and . . .

"But, Jodi," she called out to her.

Jodi stopped at last and turned around. "No, mistress," she said gently, as if she had read her mind. "Hawise ain't here. Lady Penda searched the place—first thing she did when you got back after the search on the marsh. No, wherever she is, God bless 'er, she ain't 'ere."

T HAT NIGHT ADELIA SAT AT the table in the solar writing to Rowley.

She kept her facts and directive simple:

Hawise was missing, the dreaded interdict had been imposed and, in her opinion, he should drop everything at once and come straight to Elsford.

She knew there wasn't much even he could do about Hawise, but his influence—still considerable, after all—might help to get the interdict lifted, and time was of the essence now because, according to Peter when he came back from the village that afternoon, another body had turned up on the churchyard wall.

Two bodies, in Elsford alone! she wrote. *And the numbers will only increase if you don't do something about it.*

CHAPTER 48

I N THE DARK, HAWISE STARTED to the sound of footsteps and, as he sat beside her, felt the familiar clench of panic in her belly, along with the griping pains of hunger, but she was getting used to those. As time went on he was less assiduous about bringing her food and she was losing weight, developing pressure sores on her haunches.

"How many?" he asked.

She took a breath. "Four," she replied. "Four so far."

Just as she had hoped, the story about the errant knight who killed virgins for pleasure enthralled him, but its success had brought mixed blessings; his hunger for each installment was insatiable and yet her imagination was running dry.

When she had started, she'd intended only to sacrifice one virgin a day, to eke out the telling for as long as she could, but yesterday, for some reason, she had gotten carried away and squandered two in one evening, for which she was now kicking herself.

She had to be more careful.

"Where were we?" she asked, bartering for time, and fancied she could feel him thinking as he cast his mind back to the previous evening.

"Well," he said at last, "the knight was heading to the northlands on his milk-white steed . . ."

"Ah, yes," said Hawise. "So he was . . . or at least, so he will be . . . but first, let's not forget, he has to garland the girl's body with cherry blossom and bury it in the orchard in the light of the moon, and we also mustn't forget that time is running out, because the villagers raised the hue and cry when they found out that the maiden was missing and they are coming for him, getting closer and closer and closer . . ."

She broke off. She sensed him fidgeting beside her and felt an unaccustomed frisson of impatience go through him, which didn't augur well; usually he sat as still as a rock.

"Why does he have to spend so much time on the body?" he asked.

"Because . . ." *Oh, sweet Mary, Mother of God! Why?* She could feel her heart quicken, the panic rising again. It didn't help that, as well as hungry, she was desperately tired.

For the first few days of her incarceration she had slept like a chained dog, but now the interminable darkness had started to play cruel tricks on her body and her mind, depriving her of sleep.

"Because it's God's will, of course!" she said at last, almost crying with relief when the words came.

In the ensuing silence she held her breath, anticipating the moment, the one she dreaded and knew was inevitable, when she would feel his hands around her throat again.

But to her surprise, it didn't come.

"*Deus vult,*" he said brightly.

"Yes," Hawise agreed, although to what, exactly, she didn't know.

CHAPTER 49

THE NEXT DAY ALLIE KEPT her promise and took Adelia to the place on the river where they'd discovered the second body.

By the time they got there, although it was still early, the fishermen had already left for the day, their creels neatly stacked, their boats moored aslant on the shingle so that the area was deserted and Adelia was free to stride up and down thinking aloud with impunity.

Even so, as she watched her, Allie couldn't help the occasional glance over her shoulder . . . just in case.

Perhaps it was the vastness of the overarching sky or the infinite horizons of the Fens, but she always had a strange feeling of conspicuousness out here, as though, wherever she was and whatever she was doing, there were eyes on her. Sometimes it felt pleasantly benign, but at other times, like today, for instance, it didn't.

She looked back across the marsh. The appearance of a weak sun was gradually clearing away the early morning mist and something was emerging from it, towers formulating themselves from the northwest as though out of thin air, giving the impression that Ely Cathedral, as it became manifest through the haar, was floating above the ground.

"Allie." Adelia's voice pulled her attention back. "How far from here was the first body found?"

Holding up the hem of her skirts, which were already damp, Allie picked her way through the marsh and the line of rushes that stretched like sentinels along the bank and made her way down to the water's edge.

"According to Ulf, it was just beyond that bend over there," she said, pointing downstream.

Adelia pursed her lips in thought, quiet for a moment.

"Which means," she said, "that, for convenience, and we assume judging from where they were found anyway, both bodies were dumped in the water at roughly the same point, then the person we are looking for is probably local."

Allie thought for a moment, feeling her breath soak uncomfortably into the wool of her scarf, freezing her nose and mouth.

"Well that's what we think," she said, peeling it away to speak more easily. "But don't forget we've only found two bodies so far."

They stood in thought for a while until the peace of the air above them was rent by a honking, fluting airborne invasion of wildfowl and a thousand beating wings.

Adelia scowled at the sky, raising her voice to be heard above the din of the birds. "And yet they were both washed up round about here."

Allie nodded.

"So, in the absence of anything else to go on—and let's face it, we don't have very much—let us assume that, because the bodies entered the water somewhere upstream from here, then whoever dumped them comes from somewhere in that direction or has some connection with it at least."

Allie looked to the east and the innocent pillars of smoke rising from the cottages in the outlying villages, where, perhaps, a murderer was hiding. The thought made her shiver and pull her mantle tightly around her.

"What I still don't understand," Adelia continued, "and what I think is key to this whole thing, is the hiatus between the abductions and the killings . . . I mean, if he simply intended to rape and murder those girls, why not do it there and then? Why go to all the trouble of abducting them and taking them goodness knows where—and risk being discovered in the process—and then wait to kill them? What we need to think about is why he waits."

Allie stood quietly for a moment, watching the rhythmic drag of the water against the shore.

"Do you remember that theory you told me once?" she said. "That the motive for any murder is almost always love, and that to solve one you first have to work out what the object of that love is? Whether a person, a fortune, power? Do you remember?"

Adelia nodded.

"Well, supposing our murderer convinces himself that he loves these girls, at first anyway. Don't forget that the one thing they have in common is that they are young and beautiful."

Adelia nodded again.

"Well, supposing he sees them, perhaps watches them for a time, and falls in love with them and takes them . . . well, to wherever it is he takes them to . . . only to find that they don't live up to his expectations somehow, and that's when he decides to kill them, so that he can move on in his eternal quest for the ideal woman—" She broke off, suddenly self-conscious, aware that Adelia was staring at her. "What?" she asked.

Adelia smiled and put her arm around her. "Not the fool you look," she said proudly. "But on the other hand, I suppose, you do have rather a good tutor. So, to recap then, what we're looking for is a clever, romantic, idealistic murderer?"

Allie grinned. "And literate. Don't forget the markings on the second body!"

"Yes indeed," said Adelia. "Which might narrow things down a bit."

G EOFFREY SCUTTLED OUT OF THE gatehouse as soon as they appeared on the drawbridge.

"This come for you, Mistress Allie," he said, handing her a scroll.

Allie took it and, having read it, under the watchful gaze of Geoffrey and Adelia, rolled it up and stuffed it into her sleeve.

"Well?" said Adelia. "What does it say? . . . Although, I have to warn you that if it's from a certain person and you start all that blushing nonsense again, I shall have to kick you."

"It's an invitation," said Allie, smiling for the first time in what felt like an age—perhaps for the first time since Hawise's disappearance—and trying desperately hard not to blush. "For you and me and Penda . . . to a banquet at Dunstan."

"Oh." Adelia raised her eyebrows. "He seems to have an

awful lot of banquets, this Lord Peverell. Are they all in your honor?"

"Of course not!" Allie snapped. "Besides, I thought you wanted to meet him again."

"I do! Of course I do. It's just that, oh, banquets!" Adelia grimaced. "All that food, and dressing up . . . it's so unutterably dull."

"And there's visitors," Geoffrey interrupted them.

"Who?" Adelia spun toward him.

He shrugged. "Dunno, bor, two gen'lemen's all I know," he said. "Not expected neither."

The mystery, however, was short-lived. Halfway across the courtyard Adelia spotted a familiar figure leading two horses toward the stable block and started waving frantically.

"It's Walt!" she cried, turning to Allie, beaming with delight. "Oh, darling, your father's here."

CHAPTER 50

"BUT HOW, ROWLEY? HOW DID you get here so quickly?" Adelia asked him over supper, absentmindedly popping yet another piece of chicken from the trencher they were supposed to be sharing into her mouth. "After all, I only just sent the letter."

She had been delighted, quite beside herself with joy, when she saw him, but hadn't told him so. She had always felt it important to maintain an element of mystery, perhaps even opacity, in their relationship, to foster his enthusiasm, which, bless his heart, had never waned. The trouble was that as she got older, she found concealment more difficult as their separations became harder to bear and was reluctant to admit it even to herself.

"Funnily enough," Rowley replied, watching in dismay as his food dwindled before his eyes, "I heard about the interdict from Eleanor and decided to come the moment I got back."

Nor would he admit to her that he probably would have come anyway, because it wouldn't hurt her to believe that she wasn't always his first thought and priority.

"The question is: what are you going to do about it?" Adelia asked.

"There's not much I can do," he replied, slapping the hand reaching for the plate again. "The only person who can influence the Pope is Eleanor herself. All I can do is report to her."

H E WAITED UNTIL AFTER SUPPER, when the others retired for the evening, before broaching the subject of Hawise.

He had noticed how her name had been conspicuously absent from any conversation and that although when he had arrived, Penda and Gyltha had welcomed him with as much enthusiasm as they could muster, even the air around them was so palpably despondent that, while he was anxious to hear news of her, he had been reluctant to raise the subject in case it added to their distress.

"What about Ulf's daughter?" he asked when he was sure they were alone and couldn't be overheard.

"Hawise," Allie said sharply. "Her name's Hawise."

"Hawise," Rowley said, correcting himself. "Well, is there any news?"

Allie shook her head, fighting back the tears that were never far away whenever Hawise was mentioned.

"Everything that can be done has," Adelia said. "They held a search, and a vigil of course . . . but so far . . . nothing . . ."

She glanced at Allie, saw how close to tears she was, and looked away again quickly.

"On the other hand," she said, striving for a chink of brightness in the otherwise impenetrable gloom, "we're hoping that she's still alive, of course, and that—" She broke off, realizing how ridiculous she sounded.

Even if Hawise was still alive, unless they found her soon, which seemed increasingly unlikely, she wouldn't stay that way much longer, and although she dared not say so, all this futile hoping was doing nothing but prolonging what deep down she suspected was an inevitable agony.

Rowley glanced at Allie, too, saw the misery etched in her face and felt his heart melt along with his lifelong resolve that he would never encourage them in their endeavors. He took a deep breath, galvanizing himself for what he was about to do.

"Very well," he said. "What do we know so far?"

Allie's face brightened. She wanted to leap up and fling her arms around his neck; despite their differences there were times when she thought her father was really quite wonderful.

"We've made some notes," she said, seizing on his concession with undisguised delight and, at the same time, squeezing her mother's knee conspiratorially under the table. "I'll fetch them for you, shall I?"

CHAPTER 51

HAWISE'S ERRANT KNIGHT HAD BEEN so busy lately—fording rivers, fighting tournaments, slaying dragons and the like, not to mention traveling the kingdom in search of, well, whatever he was searching for—that if it weren't for the number of dead maidens he left in his wake, she might even have begun to admire him.

But six women were dead, and time was running out, and, crucially, so was her imagination.

In the original story, as far as she remembered it, there hadn't been a single dragon, tournament or battle, but in hers the knight's journey was now so protracted that he could have traveled to the ends of the earth and back in half the time. The strange thing was that, although she knew, without a shadow of a doubt, that her life depended on her ability to eke it out for as long as she could, she couldn't bring herself to kill another girl, and yet . . . there was only one left, and he was impatient for her. She could feel that, too.

During the endless dark days and weeks of her captivity—

what, five weeks? Six now? His visits had become so erratic that she had lost all sense of time or any method of marking it, other than the dreary cycle of hunger and fatigue, times when her stomach burned and tiredness torched her eyes and her mind played tricks on her, making the balm of sleep impossible—she sat, head hanging like an aged dog's, waiting for the draft on her face when the door opened and he came to her again.

AND HE CAME TO A clearing in the old oak wood, where he saw a maiden so dazzlingly beautiful—hair the color of ripened corn, skin as pale as moonlight—that he had to shield his eyes just to look at her."

"Number seven?"

Hawise nodded wearily, irritated by his interruption, realizing that, in a strange way, she was impatient for the end, too.

When he settled down again she continued.

"'Fair maid,' said the knight when he recovered his tongue, 'go at once to your father's house and fetch all the gold you can carry and two of his finest horses and bring them to me.'

"And because the maid was as true as she was fair, she did as he asked, returning a little while later riding a pale white steed, carrying an enormous sack of gold and leading a dapple gray.

"'Ride on, ride on,' said the errant knight, climbing astride the dapple gray. 'Ride on to the deep blue sea, there six pretty maids I have killed and the seventh you will be.'"

"How many more are there then?" he interrupted again.

Under the cover of the darkness Hawise rolled her eyes.

"Wait and see," she said brightly, hiding her irritation. "There's a long way to go yet. You'll have to be patient like the knight, won't you?"

It was a lie, of course, but by the grace of God, she hoped to come up with something before the time came.

CHAPTER 52

T HIS IS WHAT WE DON'T understand, Rowley," said Adelia.
It was very late but they were still poring over Allie's
notes in the hall, only this time remembering to keep their voices
low so as not to disturb the servants snoring softly in its niches.

"This," she repeated, pressing her finger onto the line in the
vellum where the letters "DV" were written. "For some reason
he carved this on the second girl's wrist postmortem, only we
don't know why."

"His initials?" Rowley suggested to a withering look from
Adelia.

"Well it could be," Allie added hastily. Since her father had
always been so disapproving, not to mention squeamish, about
their death investigations, and because she was grateful that, for
once, and for the first time in his life, he was actually willing
to help, she didn't want Adelia discouraging him. Besides, his
contribution might be invaluable; after all, once, on Crusade,
he successfully tracked a murderer all the way across the Holy
Land.

"The trouble though, Pa," she continued, "is that we can't

think of anyone with those initials, and since we have to assume that whoever is doing this is local, we've rather ruled it out."

Rowley shrugged, sat up straight on his stool and yawned. He didn't say so, but actually, he would have been quite happy to be discouraged. He had never approved of what they did and had surprised even himself when he'd agreed to help. He was also terribly tired and finding it hard to think straight—Penda's generous helping of wine at supper was a contributing factor— and longing for peace and quiet. In fact, just then, he was de- bating whether or not he would be able to sneak off to the guest chamber unnoticed, and was slyly easing his buttocks off the stool in order to do so, when a thought struck him.

"*Deus vult!*" he exclaimed, forgetting to lower his voice in his excitement and prompting Adelia to scowl and press a finger to her lips.

"Shhh!" she hissed, about to silence him completely, when curiosity got the better of her. "'*Deus*' what did you say, Row- ley?"

"*Deus vult*," he repeated. "'DV.' The initials or letters or whatever they are."

"Meaning what? . . . At least, I know what they mean, but what's the significance?"

"That, my clever old darling," he said, stifling another yawn, "I do not know. That's your business. It just popped into my head. All I know is that it's the old Crusader's cry, meaning 'God wills it,' which may—or may not—imply that the man you're looking for took the cross . . . You never know, could narrow things down a bit."

Allie and Adelia exchanged glances before Adelia suddenly

leapt to her feet and ran around the table to fling her arms around his neck.

"You're not the fool you look, either," she said, giving him a robust and noisy kiss. "You might even be onto something."

But Rowley shook his head. "Oh no, not me," he said, wagging his finger at her. "You. I've done my bit and now I'm going to bed."

H IS RESPITE, HOWEVER, WAS SHORT-LIVED. Adelia was still chuntering about the initials when she came up to bed a little later on.

"Do you really think the man we're looking for might be a Crusader?" she asked, sitting down heavily on the bed beside him—just in case slamming the door and thinking aloud hadn't been enough to wake him.

Rowley opened his eyes reluctantly. "How would I know?" he said. "We don't even know if that's what it means. It might be something else entirely. It was just a thought, and frankly, one I'm beginning to regret."

But Adelia ignored him. "And yet it makes sense," she continued. "Whoever it is that's going around slaughtering these girls will have some peculiar justification for why he's doing it—however corrupt or perverse it might seem to us—they always do . . ." She paused in thought for a moment. "But if you're right about the initials, then perhaps he kills them because he believes 'God wills it' somehow, which would be reason enough for a woman-hater." She broke off again as another thought occurred to her: "I think I ought to talk to Penda."

"Not now surely?" said Rowley plaintively.

"No, darling," Adelia replied, smiling to herself as she closed the curtains around the bed. "That can wait until the morning."

T HAT MORNING THE GRADUAL APPEARANCE of a weak sun cleared away the mist in time for Rowley and the everfaithful Walt to set off on a tour of the diocese, to see for themselves the devastation the interdict had wrought.

Rowley hadn't been looking forward to it, not just because he expected to find a community cast into darkness, but because he had never been comfortable in the Fens and he never would.

Interdict or no interdict, as far as he was concerned this stretch of the east wasn't a place one could trust. Even the ground was treacherous; one moment's inattention, one false step, and a person could end up in a bog deep enough to suck him into the bowels of hell. Quite what Allie and Adelia found so enchanting here, he would never understand, although he had a sneaking suspicion that it had something to do with the natural anarchy of the place, which, he presumed, amused them.

They were riding warily down a narrow wooded track so beset by thorns that a starving greyhound would have been lucky not to have its flanks ripped off, when the incongruously sweet song of a thrush lifted his spirits. He stood up in his stirrups to look for it, an unexpected bright spot in an otherwise dismal morning, but it was hidden from view, lost somewhere in an impenetrable thicket of trees and bushes where—never mind songbirds—any number of robbers and outlaws might be lying in wait. He sat down again with a nostalgic pang for the gentle countryside of his own diocese in Hertfordshire, where the ground always did what you expected and the prevailing rule that no tree should encroach on a highway by more than a single bow shot was invariably respected.

The rest of the morning was unrelentingly drear as they rode through innumerable villages already scarred by the interdict, where church bells no longer rang to summon the faithful and church doors were barricaded against their worshippers with vicious-looking sheaves of brambles, and where in graveyards makeshift coffins were hung in trees or left to rot on walls.

In the last churchyard they came to, they saw a tiny shrouded bundle tucked into the nexus of a yew tree branch. A newborn baby, judging by the size, unbaptized and unburied but not, apparently, unmourned; beneath it a young woman was keeping vigil in the bitter cold.

Rowley had seen enough and, with a heavy heart, turned his horse around and set off back to Elsford.

T HE FIRST THING ADELIA DID when she woke up to find Rowley had left was to go in search of Penda.

She found her eventually in the buttery, where she was arguing bitterly with an elderly man about a pheasant, which, judging by the way it was dangling limply from her fist, was either dead or pretending to be.

"Your sack!" Penda shouted, shoving a grubby-looking rag into the old man's chest. "My pheasant. Now bugger off and don't let me catch you at it again."

When the old man wandered off clutching the sack and

muttering truculently under his breath, Adelia gave Penda a moment or two to calm down and then announced her presence.

"I thought you hanged poachers around here," she said.

"I do usually," Penda said, lifting the bird onto a hook beside a row of others. "But not that one. Best napper I've ever 'ad. Wait 'til you see my tablecloths. Wouldn't want to lose 'im." She wiped her hands down the front of her kirtle and turned to Adelia. "What can I do for you, then, mistress?"

Adelia told her about the discussion the night before. "So I was wondering if you could think of anyone around here who went on Crusade."

Penda frowned as she thought about it. "Well," she said after a moment, "it's hard to remember 'em all. There was a great mort of 'em went from here after the call from the old bishop."

Before he had died the former bishop of Ely had famously asked every man in the county to take the cross. The call had been widely and enthusiastically received by a variety of men: those looking for lands or fortune, those hoping for excitement and adventure and those simply looking to escape nagging wives, not to mention a host of criminals who, given the choice between taking the cross and having their crimes forgotten, or going to prison, left for the Holy Land without a backward glance.

"Well," Penda said at last, "Lord Peverell went, and so did Sir William. But we can rule them out . . . Oh, I know Allie don't much care for Sir William but 'e's not a murderer, at least I don't think so. And then, from Elsford there was Sir Stephen, but 'e don't 'ave the appetite for wickedness . . . or the energy, come to that."

She broke off as she thought some more and then added

brightly: "Oh, I nearly forgot, there was Peter, too . . . my fal-coner," she explained when she saw Adelia looking at her blankly. "Landed up at Elsford on 'is way back . . . Poor sod didn't make the fortune he'd been hopin' for but didn't fancy goin' into the church, either, so 'e come to me instead." She broke off, discon-certed by Adelia's expression.

"And you think—" Adelia began.

"No." Penda cut her off sharply. "I know what you're think-ing. But 'e's a good lad, that one, and a bloody good falconer. You wanted to know who went and 'e was one of 'em, that's all."

She turned her back and started fussing with one of the dead pheasants, which Adelia took as her cue to leave, thanking her for her time and wondering how unhappy it would make her if she knew that the information she had provided had just cata-pulted her esteemed falconer to the top of the list of suspects.

P ETER!" ALLIE LOOKED SHOCKED WHEN Adelia told her her latest theory. "Well!" she added on a heavy breath. "I knew he was irritating but I didn't think he was a murderer. What does Penda think?"

"Oh, she wouldn't have it," Adelia said. She was staring out of the guest chamber window, the only room where privacy and a view over the mews were guaranteed. "So, we'll have to be a little bit circumspect. And, of course, at this stage, it's only a suspicion."

"An interesting one though," said Allie.

Over the next few days they took turns at the window, care-ful not to arouse the suspicion of the others, who, they felt, were anxious enough already without worrying about a killer in their midst.

Apart from the window vigil they came up with ruses to take them to the mews whenever possible, but on every occasion found Peter behaving quite normally and unmurderously, greeting them cheerfully whenever he saw them.

"I might be wrong, you know," Adelia admitted one day when she had stood at the window watching him do nothing more sinister than train a falcon to the lure. "It has been known to happen. I even suspected your father was a murderer once."

Allie sighed. "I know. I've heard that story a hundred times," she said wearily.

Allie was becoming despondent as it dawned on her increasingly that they were latching on to the idea of Peter as a suspect out of sheer desperation and in the absence of anything or anyone more plausible to go on. And yet, if Peter wasn't the murderer—and it looked increasingly likely that he wasn't—they were no closer to finding the real culprit than they had been when Adelia arrived.

CHAPTER 53

HAWISE RARELY OPENED HER EYES these days, or nights, or whatever they were; there seemed no point. The insuperable darkness was as shocking now as it had been at first, and the thin barrier of flesh she could close against it was the last vestige of her control; otherwise she was as helpless as a mole in a trap, an irony that, in the long, dismal hours, she had had time to consider.

Her only comfort was that it was going to end soon, all of it, her life included; she could feel it, particularly today, in the deep dull ache in her belly, the sign that she was about to start another bleed.

It would be her third since her captivity, and each time it inflamed him, as if she had willfully conjured the blood to make herself dirty and untouchable. He wouldn't tolerate another; besides, she was coming to the end of her story.

But when the door opened and she heard his footsteps, something in the lightness of their tread told her that, for now at least, the trepidation was unwarranted. He was in a good mood.

"Make room," he said brightly, nestling beside her on the

palliasse, rubbing his hands together. "We're getting to the best bit, aren't we?"

"We are indeed," she said, surprising herself because she meant it. In a sense, of course, they were—or she was—and as long as the end wasn't too protracted or painful, she almost welcomed it.

"Now, do you remember where they were?" she asked. "The knight and the maiden?"

"The sea," he replied.

"Good," she said, pulling her knees up to her chest and wrapping her arms around them, ready to begin. "That's right. They'd reached the sea.

"In the rosy twilight they rode their horses over the golden sand to the water's edge, and when they dismounted, the maiden turned to the knight.

"'I have always wanted to swim in the sea,' she said, gazing at it wistfully. 'All my life, but I never have. If this is to be my last day, my last wish, as I believe it is, will you grant it to me?'

"After some considerable thought the knight agreed that he would, but only on the condition that she take off her silken robes, lest the salt water spoil their incomparable beauty.

"But the maiden gave a gasp of horror, clapping her hand over her pretty mouth. She had never been naked in front of a man before.

"'If I must take off all my clothes,' she replied when she had recovered from the shock of the suggestion, 'you must promise to turn your back and not to look at me. After all, it's unseemly for a man to gaze upon a woman when she is naked unless they are married . . .'"

Hawise stopped speaking. She could feel him moving beside her, fidgeting again; another interruption was in the offing.

"But what difference would it make if he saw her naked?" he asked irritably. "He's going to kill her anyway, isn't he?"

"Yes," Hawise replied patiently. "He is. But perhaps she's hoping to persuade him not to. Perhaps," she added, "she's hoping he might fall in love with her instead."

He was quiet for a moment.

"Oh, I doubt that very much," he said at last. "I think he would much prefer to kill her."

CHAPTER 54

ALTHOUGH ADELIA USUALLY DREADED BANQUETS, the dressing up, the scrutiny, the small talk—at which she was exceptionally bad—she was actually looking forward to this one, partly because she was intrigued to find out more about Lord Peverell, but also because the prospect provided a much-needed diversion from the pervading gloom at Elsford.

"You look very beautiful," Rowley said, admiring her from the doorway.

"Now look what you've done," she said. She had just put on her favorite dress, a brocade in the colors of autumn, but, self-conscious under his gaze, had clumsily dabbed a little too much rosewater behind her ears, making the gauze around her wimple unpleasantly damp.

"Anyway, you always say that," she said, closing her eyes, nestling into him as he put his arms around her.

"Because it's true," he said. "Now. Are you ready?"

———

DUNSTAN WAS AS IMPRESSIVE AS Allie had described, and although Adelia was used to the grandeur of the great palaces of Europe, she had never expected to find it in the Fens and was trying very hard to keep her mouth from falling open as she looked around.

The light in the hall was like a celestial aura from the innumerable candles that burned in the silver sconces along its walls; dove-white plumes of smoke had, apparently, been choreographed to drift like angels' wings ever upward to a fan-vaulted ceiling that was so intricately and beautifully carved that it seemed to Adelia to prove the existence of God. Underfoot, and equally heavenly, a sea of lavender rushes was bruised with every footstep, releasing an incense that clung and wafted around rows of tables dressed in embroidered napery.

At the reception of hoods, swords and gloves, she was pleased to see the look of delight on Lord Peverell's face when he saw Allie and how he immediately abandoned all his other guests to go and greet her.

She was less pleased about the fuss he made of Rowley, although it was more Rowley's response to the introduction, the placatory enthusiasm that reminded her of an old dog rolling onto its back, which made her want to kick him.

"Don't get carried away," she hissed. "We don't know if he's good enough yet."

Sensing her reserve, perhaps, Lord Peverell turned to her. "Mistress Adelia," he said with a deep bow. "Welcome to Dunstan."

"Thank you." Adelia gave a curt smile. She refused to be

quite so easily seduced as Rowley; it was going to take more than an elegant castle and untold riches to convince her that any man, even this one, was good enough for Allie.

When the trumpet sounded for supper, Lord Peverell took Allie's hand and, holding it high, led her up onto the dais.

"Where's Sir William?" Adelia whispered behind her hand when she was seated beside her.

Allie leaned forward and looked along the table. "Can't see him," she whispered back. "It looks as if he's not here." She turned to Lord Peverell. "Is Sir William attending this evening?" she asked, and Adelia, who was watching them both like a hawk, noticed that her hand brushed delicately against his as she did so. "Only, my mother would like to speak to him."

Lord Peverell shook his head. "He was supposed to be here. But he's been so elusive lately, I'm afraid. I've no idea where he gets to these days." He looked around in case Sir William had slipped in unnoticed but, seeing that he hadn't, leaned toward Adelia. "Alas, madam! It is Sir William's loss I fear. Another time, perhaps . . ."

"Alas," said Adelia. "Another time indeed."

She spent most of the rest of the evening lamenting her thickening waistline as wave upon wave of servants brought endless plates of food that she couldn't resist, and she was relieved, though feeling a little sick, when the tables were cleared at last and the music began.

As if by magic, the stiff formality of the evening evaporated as a group of musicians struck up from the gallery, four burly, energetic men: a tabor player, two fiddlers and a large, ruddy-faced man who called the steps with a roar loud enough to override the squealing, stamping delight of the dancers. Even Rowley was persuaded to dispense with his usual reserve and danced, throwing himself into the spirit of the evening, whirling Adelia around the hall until she thought she was going to die of laughing.

In the middle of one particular spin she caught sight of Allie and Lord Peverell, who were gazing at one another with such tenderness that somebody of a more sentimental disposition might have been moved by it.

"You're not enjoying yourself by any chance?" Rowley asked, spinning her around once more, sending her into another fit of giggles.

S HE SANG MOST OF THE way home and, as she trotted happily down the track beside Allie, even forgot how much she hated riding.

"Perhaps I'll allow you to marry him after all," she told her.

Allie frowned. "But he hasn't asked me."

"No. But he will," Adelia said, tapping the side of her nose. "Call it a mother's instinct."

A S THEY RODE INTO THE courtyard, Allie's palfrey narrowly avoided a tiny hedgehog that had come too early out of hibernation and was making heavy weather of the cobbles. She kept an eye on it as they dismounted and handed their horses to the grooms, then hung back in the shadows, waiting until Adelia and Rowley—holding on to one another for safe passage and giggling like children—had staggered up the steps into the house.

"Poor little thing," she said, picking up the prickly ball it had become, speaking softly to it as she followed the grooms to the stables, where she planned to leave it for the night.

She knew that they would groan and raise their eyebrows when they saw her, but they were getting used to her by now. In fact, they had only just released an orphaned leveret she had found during one of her archery lessons and insisted they keep in an empty stable until it was big enough to fend for itself. At first they had joked about jugging it or putting it in a nice pie, until her formidable expression had convinced them that levity and leverets were an unhappy combination.

"What do they eat, then, mistress, these hedgepigs?" one of the grooms called after her as she set off back to the house.

"Worms," Allie called back over her shoulder. "I'll bring you some tomorrow."

It was another bitterly cold night. A full moon hung over the house, creating eerie shapes and shadows along the walls, adding to her sense of urgency as she hurried toward the door.

And she had almost made it, with one foot on the bottom step, when someone grabbed her. A hand came out of nowhere, pinning her arm behind her back, another clamping itself over her mouth, as a voice by her ear hissed:

"If you want to see Hawise again you listen up and listen hard and don't make a bloody sound."

For a moment she stood unresisting in his arms, paralyzed by fear and shock, until a powerful confluence of emotion churned into rage, giving her the impetus to launch a backward kick of which a horse might have been proud.

"Bitch!"

The shock of her assault loosened her assailant's grip just long enough for her to spin around and face him.

CHAPTER 55

Danny Wadlow leapt backward, looking almost as shocked as Allie. "Don't scream," he hissed, raising his hands. "Just don't scream."

"Why not?" Allie asked, her heart pounding fit to burst through her rib cage.

"Because I know where Hawise is and I can take you to 'er," he replied, lowering his hands slowly.

"Why would you do that? And why should I trust you?" she asked, emboldened to see him flinch, jutting her chin and taking another step toward him.

"Because I owe you," he said truculently. "For saving my mother's life."

"Oh," said Allie, nonplussed. With all that had happened lately, she had forgotten about the Wadlow woman and was surprised to be reminded of her, and even more surprised that someone like Danny Wadlow could feel anything like indebtedness. She felt an involuntary shift in her attitude toward him but hoped it didn't show.

"Then what are you waiting for?" she demanded. "Take me to her now."

Danny hesitated for a moment.

"I will. But there's conditions," he said, raising a warning finger. "First, you can't never know where I'm taking you . . . and second: no questions. I'll take you to 'er but that's the end of it, d'you hear? You don't go lookin' for no one else afterward. Understand?"

Allie nodded, prepared to agree to anything, to risk anything for Hawise, even, it seemed, disappearing into a cold, dark night with the likes of Danny Wadlow.

"All right," she said. "I agree. But how do you propose we get out of here?"

After all, it wouldn't be easy. They couldn't simply walk out. Elsford was too heavily fortified, Penda had seen to that, so unless they applied for permission to the gatekeeper—who would, most likely, take one look at Danny and have him incarcerated—they were stuck.

Once again she saw the blank look of stupidity cross his face.

Christ's eyes! He hasn't even thought about it.

She took a deep breath.

"Well," she said with labored patience, "how did you get in here in the first place?"

Danny shrugged. "I followed you," he said. "Saw you leavin' Dunstan an' just followed you, slipped in behind the horses afore they pulled the drawbridge."

She stared at him, hostility rising with frustration at his idiocy and the fact that, having raised her hopes, he was dashing them again because his thick, coffin-shaped head was too stupid to formulate a plan . . . And then she remembered Jodi and the postern.

"Come," she said, grabbing him by the wrist and pulling him up the steps behind her into the house.

B ECAUSE IT WAS LATE, THEY got to the door leading to the undercroft without being seen.

Allie took a brand off the wall, lit it with some of the tinder fungus the servants had left on the floor and opened the door.

"Follow me," she said, grabbing Danny's wrist again and dragging him down the stairs into the tunnel.

When they reached the cavern, she stopped and looked around in confusion. She had forgotten how vast it was and, more important, quite how many tunnels there were leading off it.

"Now we go down . . . er . . ." She looked around again hopelessly. It was impossible to remember which of them led to the postern. They all looked the same, so dark, so forbidding, so infinite. She began to stalk the walls like a lost soul, holding up the brand to each entrance in turn, hoping something would spark her memory. Jodi had said something about something that distinguished the postern tunnel from the others, but what? . . . And then, at last, she remembered: it was the one that looked like a set of nostrils, with a thick stalactite hanging down like a septum in an otherwise gaping black hole.

She spun around triumphantly.

"This one," she said, plunging headlong into it.

CHAPTER 56

HIS MOOD WAS DIFFERENT AGAIN this evening, Hawise realized. The atmosphere in the cavern, too, as though he had brought in an extra layer of darkness with him; even behind her tightly closed eyes she could see it, feel the boredom lurking within like a sleeping assassin.

If she had been at her best she might have had a chance, but tonight she was exhausted and desperately hungry—as his interest had waned, so had his desire to feed her—and she was also in pain; yesterday the bleeding had started.

"Well?" His voice sounded different, too. Sharper, increasingly impatient. "What are you waiting for?"

Death, thought Hawise. *To finish my story so that this will be over with.*

For the last time she took a long, deep breath as she steeled herself for the end.

TURN YOUR BACK,' THE MAIDEN told the knight with that sweet smile of hers. 'You must not look at me when I am naked.'

"She could feel the water lapping at her feet and was longing to dive in.

"But the knight hesitated, refusing to turn his back on her quite yet.

"'How do I know that when I turn around you won't just swim away?' he asked suspiciously.

"The maiden smiled that sweet, sweet smile again and shook her head.

"'Because, as everybody knows, I am as true as I am fair,' she said. 'Have I not obeyed your every command? Did I not bring you my father's gold and two of his finest horses when you asked? I could easily have run away then, but I didn't.'

"The knight thought about what she said and realized that it was true, and that although he desperately wanted to see her naked, he would do as she asked . . . Besides, he could always take a peek when she wasn't looking.

"'Very well,' he said at last. 'I will turn my back as you ask and wait for you here on the shore, but on one condition . . . When you have finished swimming you must come back immediately.'

"The maiden nodded and smiled again.

"'Where else would I go?' she asked. 'I cannot swim very far and the sea is deep; besides, we have ridden for so many miles that I am a stranger to these shores; I would be terribly lost without you.'

"This time it was the knight's turn to smile. She really was terribly charming and very beautiful, he thought.

"Then the maiden made a delicate little twisting motion with her hand.

"'Turn around,' she said with a tinkling laugh."

Hawise froze when she heard his sharp intake of breath.

"Why does she keep smiling and laughing all the time like that?" he asked. "Is she going to trick him?"

"No! Of course not," Hawise replied. "She's smiling because, as you know and as she says, she's good and true and kind." She had become increasingly protective of the maiden; they shared the same fate, after all.

"Very well," he said with a heavy sigh. "Continue."

"This time the knight did as the maiden asked and turned his back on the sea and the setting sun—and her naked form—and stood for some time listening to the waves breaking on the shore and the cry of the seagulls, but, curiously, nothing else, certainly not, as he had expected, the soft rustle of clothes being shed.

"'Are you actually taking your clothes off?' the knight asked her impatiently.

"'No,' said the maiden in a small voice. 'I'm too frightened.'

"'Frightened of what?' snapped the knight.

"'I am frightened,' said the maiden, 'because my feet are so tiny and soft and delicate that if I take off my beautiful calfskin boots the stones will cut them to shreds and make them bleed.'

"The knight scratched his head and thought for a while.

"'Well,' he said at last, having come up with a solution, 'why don't you go a little closer to the water's edge so that you won't have so far to walk on your poor delicate little feet?' And then he thought he heard a tiny snort of laughter like the tinkling of a bell.

"'How clever of you,' said the maiden. 'But if I go any closer to the sea I'm afraid a wave will come and spoil my boots and my beautiful clothes, which is exactly what we were trying to avoid in the first place . . .'

"'Hmmm.' The knight scratched his head again and thought some more. 'That would be a shame,' he said.

"'Perhaps,' the maiden said cautiously, breaking a long silence, 'you could clear a path for me.'

"'How long a path?' the knight asked irritably. It had been an awfully long day and he was weary.

"'Oh, not very long, just from here to that little pile of rocks over there,' said the maiden, pointing at a mound of pebbles on the shore.

"'Hmm,' muttered the knight, calculating the distance and the number of stones he would have to move. 'I think I can probably do that. But afterward you will really have to get on with it.'

"'Oh, I will,' said the maiden.

He was walking toward the stones when she called him back.

"'Perhaps,' she said tentatively as he turned around, 'it would be better to start from here. That way you can keep your back to me while you work.'

"'What a good idea,' said the knight, all the while thinking to himself: *She's not only beautiful and true, but she's clever with it. Just the sort of girl who deserves to die.*

"And with renewed enthusiasm he took off his cloak, knelt down by the water's edge and started clearing the sharp pebbles around her feet.

"'You're so kind,' the maiden said.

"She stood watching him for a moment, smiling that sweet, sweet smile of hers, and then raised the hand holding the rock she had hidden behind her back and, still smiling, smashed it onto the back of his head."

Even as she felt the air in the room charging with fury, Hawise continued the story. She was even enjoying herself at last.

"And as the knight pitched forward into the sea, the maiden put her elegant calfskin boot on the back of his head and held it under the waves until he stopped breathing."

It was the strangest feeling, but suddenly, she was imbued with a sense of elation unlike anything she had ever felt before; perhaps it was the thrill of the maiden's triumph—or the proximity to her own death—but, whatever it was, just then she felt more alive than she had thought possible, and she rose to her feet, raucously singing the final verse at the top of her voice.

"'Lie there, lie there, you false-hearted man. / Lie there instead of me, / For six pretty maids thou hast drowned. / But the seventh hath drowned thee.'"

She was helpless with laughter and still singing even when he put his hands around her throat and began to squeeze.

"No trickery . . . ," he hissed, spitting fury, his grip tightening inexorably. "You promised."

"So I did," Hawise said on what she had to assume was her last breath. "But I lied."

CHAPTER 57

THE TUNNEL LEADING TO THE postern was even less navigable than the one before, the cobwebs thicker, the walls narrower, the ceiling low and becoming lower the further they went, so that by the time they could see the faint chink of moonlight in the distance they were almost bent double.

Allie stopped dead, cursing bitterly under her breath.

"What is it?" Danny asked as he narrowly avoided crashing into her.

"It's a bloody door!" she said, tears of frustration pricking her eyes.

She was such a fool! She had been so proud of herself for remembering the postern in the first place that she hadn't thought beyond it, but of course there would be a door. It had been built during the Anarchy as an escape route. There was bound to be a door . . . and a lock!

She was peeling a damp cobweb out of her eyelashes, wondering what on earth to do next, when Danny barged past her and disappeared.

She was about to call him back, take him back to the cavern to think up another plan, when she heard him shouting:

"Come! It's rotten. Look, I can kick it down."

The door gave almost no resistance; a couple of hefty kicks later and they were gratefully sucking down lungfuls of fresh air in a copse by the river.

"Now where?" Allie asked, blinking in the moonlight.

"This way." Danny set off apace, leading her down a towpath for what felt like miles until he stopped at a landing stage where a coracle was moored. "Get in," he said, pushing her toward the boat.

She was reluctant at first; even in the dark it was apparent that the tiny vessel had seen better days. But then she remembered Hawise and climbed in without a fuss.

She was about to sit on a plank that served as a bench in the middle of the coracle when Danny stopped her.

"Not there," he growled, lifting the corner of what looked like an old winnowing sheet that was lying in the bottom and, to her horror, indicating that she should get underneath it. When she hesitated, he glared at her.

"I told you there were rules," he said with an expression of implacable hostility. "From here on in you do as I say. Or I'll throw you in the water." A moment later she found herself lying in a cold, shallow pool of water at the bottom of the boat that smelled strongly of dead fish.

Just before he took up his oars, Danny lifted the sheet and peered at her.

"From here on in you say nothin' and you see nothin'," he said, taking an axe from underneath the bench and waving it in her face. "I see that head o' yours pokin' out o' there even once an' I'll cut it off. Understand?"

Allie nodded, pulling the sheet back over her head.

CHAPTER 58

THE MOMENT OF HER DEATH wasn't turning out quite the way Hawise had expected; on the other hand, ever since her world had turned upside down, all those however many weeks ago it was, nothing had.

What she had expected, or rather, what she had hoped, was that, having confounded him with the climax of her story, she would have a moment to savor her victory—however Pyrrhic it turned out to be—before he killed her quickly. Allie's description of the body she had examined had stayed with her, particularly the fact that, apart from the strangulation marks on the girl's neck, it was otherwise unblemished, with no suggestion of any further violence, so she had rather assumed that her own death would be equally swift and bloodless. What she hadn't bargained for was the power of his rage at the cuckolding, or, indeed, that he would rape her—Allie had spared her that detail—and that instead of strangling her, he would lose control to such an extent that he would try beating her to death instead.

How strange, she thought, as she lay at his feet, convulsing with the blows that rained down on her, how much she resented the pain; not the physical agony of it per se—although it was dreadful—but its constant reminder to her that she wasn't dead yet.

And yet, surely this pulverizing of her flesh and bone couldn't last much longer . . . Any moment now and her body must surely succumb to the inevitable . . .

But she was wrong.

The beating stopped even though her heart hadn't quite.

She lay motionless, for all intents and purposes quite dead, but with the tiny sliver of consciousness left to her, she was aware of him standing over her still patting himself down, rummaging in the sleeves of his cloak, searching for something. When he couldn't find whatever it was, she heard a gasp of frustration and footsteps running away.

She tried calling him back, to beg him to finish what he had started, but the searing pain in her jaw locked her mouth shut.

And so there she lay, not dead but dying, blood oozing from every orifice in great warm gushes, and when, at last, her heart and her breathing began to slow, she felt strangely peaceful, weightless, almost as if she were floating, rising ever upward, except that, when she reached it, heaven wasn't at all what she was expecting.

There were voices, shrill and shocking in the otherwise serene silence, that were almost as painful to bear as the beating.

There was a man's voice. St. Peter's, she presumed—although it was a good deal more raucous than she had imagined it would be—and a woman's voice, the Virgin Mother's, she thought, that was nagging at her, repeating her name and insisting on her attention.

She could feel hands on her, too, touching her, pulling her about, reconnecting her painfully with the body she was so desperate to leave and making her weep with frustration because she knew that if she was hurting, she wasn't dead . . .

And then she heard river sounds—water lapping against wood, the cloop of moorhens, bulrushes crackling in a breeze— and above it all the man's voice again, only this time it was raised against the woman's, who raised hers back.

And then more pain! As a single pair of hands this time picked her up and half dragged, half carried her—muttering with the most uncelestial profanity—only to put her down again on a cold, wet surface that stung her skin and smelled of fish. Then more watery sounds and the woman's voice again, only this time swearing and blaspheming in a way she knew the Virgin Mary never, ever would.

And then . . . Oh, at long last, just when she thought she couldn't take any more, a blissful nothingness.

CHAPTER 59

S HE WOKE EVENTUALLY TO A cocoon of warmth, the scent of lavender and a row of blurred faces peering down at her as though from a distant parapet.

Somebody up there spoke, and she cowered until she realized that it wasn't his voice.

"Her eyes are open!" the voice shouted, making her flinch again and prompting even more faces to appear over her.

She was floating toward them, squinting into the unaccustomed light, and then, as she got closer, the oval halos took form and she recognized her mother's face, then her father's, Gyltha's, Penda's and Allie's all clustered around her like a dazzling ring of light.

She tried to reach out to them but her arm wouldn't move and she whimpered with the pain and the light and the confusion.

"Hush," Rosa whispered softly, stroking her cheek. "That ol' arm's broke but it'll mend, mistress seen to that."

"With Allie's help."

She turned to a voice she didn't recognize and saw a small,

slim, plainly dressed woman standing slightly apart from the others, but although they had never met, she knew her instantly, and for the first time in an awfully long time, she smiled.

Adelia smiled back, taking a step closer to the bed.

"You won't remember very much, I hope," she said. "But you were very badly hurt. You're in good hands now, though," she added, "and you'll make a good recovery. The important thing now is to rest as much as you possibly can."

Hawise nodded and, with that sanction—and perhaps also the help of the poppy-head tea Adelia gave her—closed her eyes and slept peacefully for the first time in a very long time.

CHAPTER 60

THAT AFTERNOON WHILE HAWISE SLEPT, Allie took herself off to her herb garden, the only place she could think of where she would find the necessary peace and quiet to reflect on what had happened and try to make sense of it.

Her relief at finding Hawise alive was surprisingly short-lived, overshadowed by the knowledge that the nightmare still wasn't over; that her abductor and the murderer of at least two other girls was still at large. Even as praise was heaped on her for her part in the rescue, she berated herself, because, although she could describe the bottom of Danny Wadlow's coracle and the underside of that stinking winnowing sheet in minute detail, she remembered nothing of the return journey. All the time she had spent wrestling with the oars on that moonless night she had been too intent, too focused on survival to think about anything else. And now, of course, Danny, the key to the mystery, had vanished completely.

HE HAD STAYED WITH HER long enough to help carry Hawise out of the cavern.

"Elsford's that way," he had said, pointing downriver. "The current'll take you most of the way but you'd best hurry afore 'e comes back." Then he had thrust a set of oars into her chest and run off, leaving her in the middle of God only knew where with a waterlogged boat and a precious cargo who, by the look of her, was as likely as not to bleed to death in the bottom of it . . .

She remembered screaming like a demented fishwife at his retreating back, but after that, the rest of that dreadful night was a blur. She swore a lot, she remembered that: first as a sort of catharsis of her anger with Danny and then, as the habit formed, a rhythmic cue for her oars. In the end, of course, it was a good thing she had; her invective had served as an auditory beacon for the search party long before the coracle bobbed into view in the dawn light.

Rowley, of course, was leading the party.

Something had woken him in the night and his mind, as it did so often these days, had automatically turned to Allie.

Lying in the dark, gazing at the ceiling, with Adelia snoring beside him, he had thought about the banquet and Lord Peverell and how well everything seemed to be auguring, and then, just as he was enjoying a rare moment of complacency, he remembered poor Ulf and his desolation and how dreadful his situation must have been. It was an unconscionable idea, but his mind refused to leave it, which was when, in this chaotic jumble of thoughts, he remembered that he hadn't heard Allie follow them to bed and panicked and got up to look for her.

When, several of the most grueling hours of his life later, he had heard shouting from the river and saw the coracle with Allie, head down, tugging furiously on the oars, he had wept with relief.

———

"ISTRESS!"

M Allie started at a voice from somewhere behind her. She had been so wrapped up in her thoughts that she had lost all track of time, but she noticed that the light had changed; a low sun was dappling the garden with shade, making it hard for her to see the person who was approaching her.

"Mistress," Peter said again.

She stared blankly at him as she recalled an image from the night before, when she had seen him plunge into the river behind Ulf and Rowley, wearing, as he swam toward her, an expression of conspicuous concern . . . perhaps a little bit too conspicuous, she remembered thinking even at the time.

Where do you get to? she wondered, continuing to stare at him. *Stalking the marshes with those birds of yours, a license to vanish for hours on end, accountable to no one.*

"I hope I haven't disturbed you, mistress," he said, frowning, disconcerted by her strange, unflinching gaze. "But I wanted to inquire after Hawise."

"Oh," said Allie. "Thank you. She is . . . as well as can be expected."

"I am glad to hear it," he replied. "Perhaps you would be so kind as to tell her that I was asking after her."

"I will," she replied crisply. "And now, if you'll excuse me . . . I must . . ." But without finishing the sentence—partly because she didn't know quite what she was going to do next and partly because she was beginning to feel uneasy—she turned and walked away.

———

"MISTRESS ALLIE!" JODI AMBUSHED HER on her way back through the courtyard. "Been lookin' all over the place for you!" she said, flapping her apron in excitement. "Hawise just woke up 'n' she's asking for you."

Allie ran up the stairs and burst into the solar to see Hawise, propped up on a cloud of pillows, looking like a fledgling that had fallen too early from its nest.

"Poor darling," she said, climbing onto the bed beside her. "Does it hurt?"

Hawise shook her head. "Not much. It's just a bit hard to see properly, that's all."

Allie took her face in her hands and turned it gently to the light.

"Hmm," she murmured, examining the innumerable welts and bruises covering it. "I'll make a cold compress for those, which'll help with the swelling and make you a bit more comfortable."

She was about to get up when Hawise grabbed her arm.

"Don't go yet," she said so plaintively that Allie felt a lump rise in her throat.

"Of course I won't," she said. "I'll stay for as long as you want me to, of course I will."

Hawise began to cry. "It's just that . . . It's just . . . I can remember everything now and I . . . I wanted to tell you what happened."

Allie froze. It was the moment she had been dreading ever

since she found her, when her relief at finding her alive had faded as she began to realize the extent of her ordeal.

She tried keeping a brave face, for Hawise's sake, but when she heard the details of the rape, she also began to cry, stopping only when the others came back into the room and Hawise went quiet.

As the other women swarmed around the bedside, competing with one another to minister to their patient, Allie noticed that Penda was unusually quiet and distant.

She had behaved strangely all day, barely able to look at Hawise or speak to anyone, or indeed, do anything other than stand at the window reciting passages from the Bible under her breath. In fact Allie was so distracted by her that she missed the opportunity to intervene on Hawise's behalf when Adelia picked that moment to launch her brusque interrogation.

"Hawise, dear," she said before Allie could interrupt, "I realize it's the last thing you want to do at the moment but you must understand that it's very, very important that you think back and tell us as much as you possibly can about the man who took you."

Allie glanced nervously at Hawise, who surprised her by appearing to take it in her stride.

"Of course," she said amiably. "Trouble is there's not much I can tell you. I don't know what he looked like because I never saw his face, it was always so dark and he wore this hood . . ."

"What sort of a hood?" said Adelia, pouncing on the detail like a cat on a mouse.

Hawise thought for a moment, frowning. "Like a monk's," she said. "Pulled low down over his face."

"But not a monk?"

Hawise shook her head. "I don't think so. But then I don't know why I think that."

"So it was a disguise of some sort then?" Adelia asked. "Do you think he wore it because he thought you might recognize him otherwise—?" She broke off for a moment as she thought some more. "But then, if he was planning to kill you anyway, why would it matter whether you recognized him or not?"

Allie blanched and took hold of Hawise's hand for comfort, all too aware that when her mother thought out loud she was capable of saying the unsayable.

"But I didn't recognize him," said Hawise, unperturbed by the robust line of questioning. "He needn't have troubled himself. If I'd known him, I would have recognized his voice, but I didn't."

Adelia, who was pacing up and down, stopped abruptly and turned to the bed.

"Would you recognize it if you heard it again?"

"I don't know . . . ," Hawise replied, frowning. "I might . . . but I'm not sure." The frown deepening, she broke off for a moment and then brightened as another thought occurred to her. "But I would definitely recognize his laugh. *That* was very distinctive."

"Hmm." Adelia made a mental note. "And why do you suppose he didn't just kill you?" she asked, only this time the gasp of shock from the crowd around the bed was audible. After all, it was the question they had all been asking, yet nobody but Adelia dared voice.

Once again, to Allie's enormous relief, Hawise took it in her stride. "God only knows," she said, smiling, actually; she found Adelia's audacity rather refreshing. "But it might have had something to do with the fact that I amused him . . . At first, anyway."

"How?"

"I entertained him, I suppose . . . told him stories," she replied simply.

"What sort of stories?" The question was unanimous, all the bodies in the room bent toward the bed.

"Anything that came into my head," Hawise replied, disconcerted by the rapt attention of the faces peering down at her. "It was a forfeit. He never said anything but somehow I knew that as long as I could entertain him he wouldn't kill me. So I made things up."

CHAPTER 61

THE NEXT DAY ROWLEY, ULF, Penda and Allie set off in a boat to look for the cavern where Hawise had been held, hoping to find clues that might lead them to her captor.

It was a bitter morning. A deep frost coated the boughs of the alders lining the riverbank, pinching Allie's nose and cheeks above her furs. She was sitting in the prow, her head swinging right and left, ready to pounce on any landmark that might prompt her memory, the lack of which weighed heavily on her. After all, it was only by some miracle that she had been able to navigate to the landing stage that morning . . . Beyond that, she couldn't remember a thing. All she knew for certain was that the coracle had traveled upstream; she could remember the drag of the current and, more than once, lying under the winnowing sheet in the bottom of the boat, had had to protect herself against Danny's axe as it slopped toward her in the accumulating bilge.

Other than that, the only other clues were auditory: Danny's groans of exertion as the water became shallow; the bottom of the coracle hissing on the reeds that reached up from the river bed; the distant chanting of monks from an abbey, but which one, she hadn't the faintest idea—the Fens, after all, were littered with them.

Rowley and Ulf took turns at the oars, taking them past acre upon acre of desolate frost-nipped marshland, along stretches of the river dotted with untidy prickles of masts and trees marking the little fishing hamlets along the way. But still Allie could remember nothing of her journey of the night before and, as time wore on, became almost catatonic with self-loathing until an urgent cry from Ulf shook her out of it.

"Mind that!"

Under Rowley's oarsmanship the boat was drifting perilously close to an island in the middle of the river.

"Looks like a bittern's nest," Ulf said.

Allie sat up abruptly. "Did you say 'bittern'?" she asked, brightening suddenly.

"Aye, I did." Ulf nodded. "Tha's a nest on that island! Vicious little bastards, them, worse 'an geese!"

"Then this is the place!" Allie screeched, remembering how, the night before, she had heard Danny curse loudly about "buttleebumps"—the local name for bitterns, who were notoriously protective of their nests and capable of inflicting considerable harm on anyone who threatened them—as he fended one off with an oar.

"The cavern must be very close to here!" she cried. "I'm certain of it."

Shortly after the skirmish with the bittern she remembered stepping out of the boat into bright moonlight and almost immediately into darkness again beneath a thick canopy of trees.

"It's over there!" she said, pointing at a copse in the distance, leaping to her feet in her excitement and rocking the boat dangerously.

Penda pulled her back onto the bench and held her still while Rowley steered the boat to the bank. As soon as they moored she leapt out and ran into the copse.

It was definitely the place; she hadn't been wrong about that. She was looking at the scattered remnants of splintered wood from the trapdoor Danny had demolished to gain entrance to the tunnel, but instead of a tunnel there was only a mound of freshly dug earth where someone had filled it in.

Penda spat on it.

"Didn't waste much time, the bastard," she said bitterly.

They stood staring at it, dumbfounded.

"Well." Rowley broke the silence. "We're not going to be able to get down that in a hurry . . . In which case, does anyone have any idea where it might lead?"

Penda and Ulf shook their heads.

"They built a lot like that in the Anarchy," Penda said. "You're too young to remember—probably weren't even born yet—but they built 'em as escape routes; dug like moles in them days in case of sieges. Some of 'em tunnels stretched a mile or more."

"Pen's right," Ulf said. "But 'less we can get down it we won't know which way it goes. It could be anywhere." He broke off, pointing in all directions. "A mile or so that way you've got Ely, then there's Dunstan to the north, Ramsey east and Elsford west, not to mention all them little hamlets in between. We're in the middle of nowhere and everywhere. That tunnel could've gone to any one o' them places or none. It was worth tryin' but ain't going to help us, I'm afraid."

Penda spat again, then turned on her heel and set off briskly toward the boat. Ulf and Rowley followed her.

Allie stared after them.

"We can't just give up!" she shouted, clenching her fists in fury. "We have to find him."

Rowley stopped walking but didn't turn around. "Do you have any better ideas?" he called back. "Or possibly a shovel or two concealed about your person?"

She stood for a moment, and, realizing that she didn't, followed him reluctantly.

THERE WAS A LETTER WAITING for Rowley when they got back.

"Bugger," he muttered with a weary sigh as he took off his gloves to break its seal with his thumb.

He didn't need to read it. He knew its provenance and exactly what it was going to say.

It was the summons from Walter of Coutances, sending him to Portsmouth to meet the queen, who would be arriving from France any day now, to dissuade John from invading Normandy with the French king.

"Idiot boy," Rowley muttered, scrunching it up in his fist.

"Does that mean you're leaving again?" Allie asked.

He nodded. "I'm afraid so. Go and fetch your mother, would you?" Then, turning to the messenger, he told him, "Wait here, if you'd be so good. We'll ride with you."

A little while later the three of them were standing in the courtyard waiting for Walt to bring the horses.

Adelia was trying hard not to show how sad she felt at the prospect of yet another separation, but she was suffering. In fact, she didn't know how many more she could bear. After almost a lifetime of these great yawning absences, she ought to have been getting used to them, but actually, she was finding them increasingly difficult. In the old days, when she was working for Henry, it had been different, and although Rowley's leaving had never been a prospect she relished exactly, at least being busy had tempered the pain. Nowadays it was harder to fill all the days and weeks and months without him. And yet it was a private sorrow that she couldn't share with Rowley or anyone else, because it was largely self-inflicted, the price she had to pay for refusing to marry him when he asked her all those years ago. The fact that she had grown old and weak and more in need in the meantime was nobody's burden but her own.

"Now, Rowley," she said brusquely, brushing a piece of fluff off his shoulder, "don't forget to tell Eleanor everything about the interdict. Don't spare a single dreadful detail."

The situation was even worse, the diocese now littered with unburied bodies. Only the other day Bertha, the pregnant laundress, had nearly gone into premature labor when a fox, carrying a dismembered hand in its jaws, ran across her path in the drying court.

"I won't, my love," Rowley said. "Of course I won't. But I can't promise she'll do very much in a hurry. I rather suspect she has other priorities at the moment."

"Oh you do, do you?" Adelia sniffed, and was about to offer her wisdom, for him to hand on to the queen, about the prioritizing of priorities, when a bank of ominous black clouds drifted overhead and distracted her. "Oh! It's going to snow," she said, looking up at the sky anxiously.

Rowley looked up, too. "Ah well," he said with a shrug. "Even you must agree that there isn't very much Eleanor can do about that."

They were interrupted from their concern about the weather by the sound of hooves on the cobbles behind them.

"Ready, my lord?" Walt asked, leading the horses toward them.

"Ready, Walt," Rowley replied, then kissed his women, climbed into the saddle and set off into the glowering light of the snow-threatened afternoon.

Just before she went into the house, Adelia paused on the step and glanced back at the sky again.

Emma would consider that an omen, she thought with a shiver, and hurried through the door.

CHAPTER 62

FORTUNATELY THE SNOW DIDN'T FALL until the early hours of the next morning, smothering the Fens in white and freezing the land as hard as iron so that even by midday, it took two strong men with heavy staves to break the ice on the manor well.

By the time Allie woke up, the air in the solar was already thick with peat smoke—Jodi had set one of her special fires—but the room was still so cold that even when she got dressed, she had to rush back to bed, teeth chattering, to snuggle under the blankets with Hawise.

She was also exhausted.

During her waking hours Hawise was unstintingly brave, but her nightmares were taking their toll, and last night her cries had even outlasted the ten-hour candle Rosa insisted they burn lest she wake to the darkness that terrified her.

Nobody had slept, and in the middle of the night, in desperation, Gyltha had braved both the cold and Adelia's wrath by staggering across the room, swaddled in all her bedclothes, to beg her for a draft of poppy-head tea. She was swiftly and irritably dispatched back to her own bed, with Adelia's admonishment ringing in her ears that it was only to be dispensed in cases of dire emergency.

THE IRONY WAS THAT HAWISE slept longer than any of the others that morning, and by the time she woke up Allie was the only one left in the solar.

"Bit bright, isn't it?" Hawise said, shielding her eyes in the crook of her elbow.

"It's been snowing," said Allie, patting down the rumpled sheets around her. "Came down hard last night . . . There." She leaned across the bed to her. "How are you feeling this morning?"

The cuts and bruises were still painful to look at but at least there was a little more color in her cheeks.

"Better, I think," Hawise said. "Less tired, anyway."

"All right for some, then," said a voice. They looked up to see Penda coming into the room. "There's summat I want to tell you," she said, fixing on Hawise as she perched on the edge of the bed. "Because I think it might help you to hear it."

She looked different again this morning, Allie thought, even more preoccupied, if that was possible, than she had yesterday, and she could see her hands fretting nervously in her lap. Whatever she was about to say was obviously serious, and she seemed hesitant about saying it.

In the heavy silence as they waited for Penda to speak, a peculiar tension filled the air, causing Allie to wonder whether perhaps whatever it was she was about to say wasn't for her ears and it might be easier if she absented herself from the room for the moment.

She got up. "Perhaps I should go . . . ," she said, surprised when Penda shook her head and motioned for her to sit down again.

"I ain't good at this," Penda said on a heavy breath. "Ain't a talker like you, Hawise, or clever like you, Allie, but, the thing is—" She broke off, tension straining the sinews of her jaw as she steeled herself to carry on.

"Well, the thing is . . . I was raped, too, see, just like you, and left for dead . . ." Despite her earlier hesitancy, she delivered the information so fluently and matter-of-factly that it took Allie a while to absorb it. When she had, she put her arm instinctively around Hawise.

"It happened during the Anarchy," Penda continued. "The time when, like they say, God and his saints slept . . . I was just a girl, mebbe nine, ten years old at most . . . Christ's eyes!" She grinned, flapping her hand at all the vanished years. "It's so bloody long ago now I don't rightly remember . . . But, well, Father was taken from us, forced to fight for some local baron, as lots were in them days, leaving me, Gyltha and Ma to fend for ourselves . . .

"Anyhow, one day . . . middle o' winter, we ran out of fuel . . . So Ma took us into the marsh to fetch some more . . . and that's when we heard 'em . . . The riders . . ."

She broke off again, her chest heaving as she took another galvanizing breath.

"Well . . . we knew, first off, they was up to no good because they was going so fast. Ma dragged me and Gylth into a ditch to hide but it was too late . . . They'd already seen us . . ."

Allie heard the catch in her voice even before she stopped again, gazing bleakly into the distance as though at the sleeping giant of her memory.

"So there we was, crouched in that ditch . . . hearts beatin' nineteen to the dozen, and then, I dunno . . . being headstrong and fearless and a bit of a fool in them days, I decided to make a decoy of myself . . . lead 'em away from Gylth and Ma if I could, and next thing I knew I was running across that marsh like the devil was behind me, which, in a way, I suppose, he was . . . But my little ol' legs weren't no match for a horse and he soon caught me . . . and that's when it happened."

She stopped for the last time, and Allie wondered whether anyone would ever dare break the ensuing silence, in which it felt as if even God was holding his breath, until Hawise said simply:

"Thank you."

Penda nodded and stood up.

"Better be goin'," she said, as though they had only been discussing the weather.

They watched her walk to the door, turning back when she reached it.

"Tell you what though, bor," she said, grinning. "It felt wonderful when I killed 'im eventually."

WHEN THE DOOR CLOSED ALLIE and Hawise sat silently for some time digesting what they had just heard.

"Did you know?" Allie asked.

"No," said Hawise. "Not that. Sometimes she talks about

when she disappeared but never that. She likes to talk about the man who rescued her, Gwil, I think his name was, some Flemish mercenary or something. It was him who brought her up after that and taught her to be an archer."

It was an extraordinary tale, more complex and more traumatic than anything Allie could have imagined, and although part of her wished she had never heard it, another part felt privileged to have been entrusted with it.

"Do you think Gyltha knows?"

Hawise shook her head. "No. Not the rape. Somehow I don't think she would have told anyone else, not even Gylth. Maybe you won't understand but it's not something you'd ever talk about, not unless you had to."

CHAPTER 63

THE SNOW FELL FOR DAYS, smothering the meres and the marsh in white, and all the bodies on the churchyard wall.

"I hope it isn't like this in Portsmouth."

Adelia was watching a group of servants from the solar window struggling to clear a path in the courtyard.

"If it carries on like this your father will never get through."

"Course he will," Allie said, although she was only half listening; otherwise she was concentrating on the game of chess she was playing with Hawise, whom she was bitterly regretting having taught in the first place, because at that very moment, Hawise was threatening her queen.

"Are you quite sure you want to do that?" Allie asked her. "Quite, quite sure that's the move you want to make? Is it?"

Hawise frowned at the board, deep in thought for a moment, and then, with a dexterous flourish and broad grin, plucked up the ivory figure and tossed it onto the bed beside her.

"Yes I am," she said, clapping her hands in delight. "Checkmate. Hurrah!"

"Oops!" As if by accident, Allie's knee suddenly spasmed,

tipping the board off the tray in her lap and spilling the pieces over the bed. "Oh dear, oh dear," she said. "What a dreadful thing to happen! Clumsy old me."

Hawise glared at her. "That was horrid. How am I supposed to pick them all up with only one hand?"

Distracted by the bickering behind her, Adelia spun around to the room.

"Oh, Allie!" she said, confirming Allie's long-held suspicion that she did indeed have eyes in the back of her head. "What has gotten into you lately?"

Boredom, Allie thought but didn't say. On the list of sins her mother found intolerable, boredom was fairly near the top.

It was true though. She was bored, almost to her bones. In the aftermath of the recent events—terrible, shocking and traumatic although they had been—she had been beset by a stultifying sense of anticlimax.

Life at Elsford was irrevocably changed; a new chapter had been promised but had not yet begun, and the hiatus seemed interminable. Not only that, but everything was still so untidy. So many loose ends left hanging, and dangerous ends at that.

She had expected to feel eternal satisfaction and gratitude at Hawise's return, but, it turned out, even that miracle wasn't enough. She wanted more. She wanted resolution and justice, too; and yet they were still no closer to finding the person responsible for these crimes than they had been when she arrived.

"Come." Reading the signs, Adelia acted quickly. In this mood Allie had to be kept busy, so, taking her firmly by the arm, she ushered her out of the solar.

"I need your help with some comfrey infusions, my stocks

are getting low," she explained when Allie was surprised to find herself in the kitchen. "Take these," she added, sliding a pestle and mortar and a bushel of herbs along the counter toward her. "Make yourself useful."

She affected reluctance, tutting and sighing and pretending she would rather have been anywhere else, but secretly she was pleased to have something to do other than to lose at chess to Hawise.

"Now," Adelia said when they had finished, wiping her hands down the front of her apron, "perhaps you'd like to tell me what the matter is."

Allie rolled her eyes. "It's nothing."

"I see," Adelia replied crisply. "And that nothing wouldn't have anything to do with a certain young gentleman that we know of, I suppose?"

Allie thought for a while.

Perhaps.

There was certainly something of him mixed in with all the other malaise, but it wasn't everything . . .

"You do realize that your father is getting very excited about him," Adelia said. "As a marriage prospect, that is . . ." She was looking at her quizzically. "Just so long as you're happy, of course. That's the main thing."

"I am . . . ," Allie began, and then corrected herself. "At least I would be . . . It's just that . . ."

"Just that what?"

"I don't know whether marriage will make me happy. I mean, for the first time I'm beginning to think it might, but how do I know? . . . For certain, that is?"

She looked so lost all of a sudden that Adelia felt herself battling both an impulse to throw her arms around her, hold her close and never let her go . . . and a rare pang of self-doubt.

For the first time ever Allie was asking her for a comfort she couldn't give, and yet even as she withheld it, she was questioning her right to do so. Since she had been at Elsford, she had seen how independent Allie had become and had even begun to accept how divergent their lives would be: Allie would probably choose to marry, as everybody seemed to think she should, and in time, Adelia would come to terms with it. What troubled her was whether her own antipathy toward the institution was based on instinct or prejudice. Or, worse than that, perhaps, an instinct based on prejudice. After all, although she had always been secure in the knowledge it wasn't right for her, could she really be so certain that it wouldn't be for Allie?

"That's the trouble, darling," she said, once again resisting the impulse to grab her up like a baby and clutch her to her bosom. "Nobody does . . . I mean, of course, I did, without a shadow of a doubt. I didn't even want to marry your father, who, as you know, is the best of men, but, as he's always at such pains to point out, things were very different for me. In many ways mine was an easier decision to make."

Allie nodded, looking so young and vulnerable that Adelia felt her heart wrench all over again.

"I'm just so confused . . . ," Allie began, looking on the verge of tears, when Jodi interrupted, bursting into the room red faced and breathing hard.

"Come, mistress, quick if you please!" she cried, beckoning frantically to Adelia. "Lady Pen needs you. Says it's urgent."

Allie and Adelia exchanged glances, then trotted after her into the hall to find Penda waiting for them with a face like thunder.

She was sitting beside Sir Stephen on the dais and, as soon as she saw them, picked up a scroll and shook it at them.

"Just got this from your Rowley!" she shrieked. "Tells me 'e's coming back—with the bloody queen!"

Adelia swallowed. "Oh dear!" was all she could think to say. "I'm so sorry."

She wasn't, of course. She was delighted. It was exactly what she had wanted. Only Eleanor had influence enough to settle the rift between the warring bishops and to persuade the Pope to lift the interdict. And yet, she couldn't help feeling sorry for Penda, too. Royal visits, however brief, were a terrible affliction, capable of bankrupting even the most affluent household: wells would be drunk dry; land destroyed; most, if not all, livestock slaughtered just to feed and water a vast and greedy retinue.

"Perhaps she won't stay long," she offered weakly.

"It's the cesspits, you see," said Sir Stephen, barely audibly above the awful growling sound Penda was making in the back of her throat. "They can't take it, you know," he added mournfully.

"Never mind the bloody cesspits." Penda turned on him, bashing the table with the sides of her fists, making him jump. "That's the least o' my worries. They can shit in their pants for all I care. What I want to know is 'ow I'm going to feed the buggers . . . in this weather!"

"Do you know how many she's bringing with her?" Adelia asked.

Penda put her head in her hands. "Sixty," she mumbled through her fingers. "Sixty of the bastards! Where am I going to put 'em?"

Adelia shrugged. She didn't know. Nobody did.

"Oh, go!" Penda flapped her hand irritably at them. "Ain't your fault, I suppose. I'll just 'ave to think o' something."

"YOU WON'T TELL HER, WILL you?" Adelia asked when they were out of earshot.

"Tell her what?"

"That it was my idea to send for Eleanor."

"I didn't know it was," said Allie. "But I must say, although I'm sorry for Penda, it would be nice to see her again. Why do you want her here though?"

"To get this bloody interdict lifted, of course. Unfortunately she is the only one who can do it."

She had mixed feelings about the queen. Apart from the fact that they were as different from one another as land is from water, she could never forgive her for the suffering she had caused Henry when she encouraged their sons to rebel against him.

And yet, however bitterly she felt about that, she wasn't able to indulge in the luxury of loathing her entirely, either.

Like Rowley's relationship with her, theirs had also been long and complicated, and even Adelia couldn't ignore the woman's considerable charm, or her courage, or, indeed, the strange affection that had been engendered in Adelia when she had saved Eleanor's life.

"But was it really her life you intended to save?" Rowley had asked many years later, when, in a rare moment of hubris, Adelia had brought it up. "Wasn't it more the security of the realm you were saving?"

The truth was that it was probably a little bit of both.

When she responded to the call to prove Eleanor innocent of the murder of the fair Rosamund—Henry's beloved whore—it had been out of concern for national security, not the queen's neck.

The prevailing fear was that if Eleanor was found guilty, Henry, mired in grief and full of hatred, might, in an unguarded moment, shout for her death—just as he had for Thomas à Becket's. And if, under those circumstances, Eleanor was executed, as was likely, the princes would rise up against their father, prompting a civil war that would make the Anarchy look civilized in comparison.

So in a sense, Rowley had been right, and yet it didn't explain why, during the course of the investigation, Adelia had thrown herself instinctively and bodily between the queen and Rosamund's grief-stricken, knife-wielding maid when she tried to kill her. Nor did it explain the peculiar bond that had developed between them when each had fostered the other's daughter for a time, Adelia when she reluctantly agreed to accompany the princess Joanna to Italy for her wedding, Eleanor when she accepted Allie as her ward during Adelia's absence. The fact that the care they had both extended to the girls went above and beyond the call of duty created an unspoken mutual debt of gratitude.

. . . And jealousy, Adelia admitted reluctantly.

Like the good mother she was and always strove to be, she hadn't wanted Allie to suffer while she was away. Nevertheless, when she returned to discover that she had not only flourished in the meantime but grown deeply fond of Eleanor, too, she found it a little galling.

She couldn't help it, any more than she could help despising herself for feeling it, but for that alone she would never truly like her.

CHAPTER 64

THE IMMINENT ARRIVAL OF THE royal guest sent Elsford into a spin.

Penda set about transforming the fallow lands of the demesne into a canvas village, clearing acres of snow to erect a forest of tents for all the royal servants, dogs and horses who might not otherwise find accommodation in the village rooms that Ulf and Sir Stephen had commandeered for them.

The kitchen courtyard was turned into a low-level labyrinth of makeshift pens full of fodder for the interlopers: wildfowl, geese, swans, ducks and hundreds of larks in cages singing away cheerfully, oblivious to the fact that they were soon to be divested of their precious tongues.

"If it carries on like this, there won't be any animals left," Allie lamented one morning when, once again, she was flattened against the wall to make way for yet another carcass as it was hauled into the kitchen. "Are you sure they're going to eat all this?"

Gyltha, who was directing the operations and enjoying herself immensely, nodded.

"Don't forget, me ol' lover," she said, "there'll be a banquet an' all. Pen sent the invitations this mornin'. Likes a bit o' entertainment, does Eleanor."

To make room for the queen and all the ladies-in-waiting, Hawise—who was still not strong enough to go home yet but reluctant to miss the excitement—was moved to the guest chamber.

"Now, missy," Gyltha said as she and Jodi set out a palliasse for her in the corner of the room. "Prepare yourself, it's going to be crowded in 'ere for a while and a good deal noisier than you're used to—carousing buggers, them lot, if I remember right—and you won't be spared much."

The guest chamber was directly above the hall, its floor-boards notoriously flimsy. But Hawise told her that she didn't care and, in fact, could hardly contain her excitement at the prospect of meeting the queen.

"Don't get your hopes up," said Gyltha, tucking the blankets around her. "You might not clap eyes on 'er at all for all I know, not 'less she comes lookin' for you, which I doubt. An' anyway, with your face the way it is at the moment, I don't want you wanderin' around the place frightenin' the royal 'orses."

Hawise laughed. "Allie says I look much better now, and anyway, she's promised to introduce me to her . . . Says she'll bring her up the first chance she gets."

"Oh she did, did she!" said Gyltha. "Well don't hold

your breath. I think the queen might be a bit busy with other things."

But Hawise wasn't listening. "When do you think she'll arrive?"

Gyltha shrugged. "God knows. You'll just 'ave to wait and see like the rest of us."

T HEY DIDN'T HAVE TO WAIT long.

At around noon the next day Ulf struggled through the snow with the news that the royal cavalcade had been spotted near Ely that very morning.

"Blessed Mary, Mother of God!" Penda shrieked, flinging on her cape and wimple in her rush to get to the gatehouse, where she found Geoffrey already peering through the squint.

"Any sign?" she asked, elbowing him aside to have a look herself. Seeing nothing, she turned to him. "Did you remember to oil them bloody winches like I asked?"

His slumped shoulders and diffident expression confirmed her suspicion that he had not.

"Ah well. Too bloody late now," she said, brightening suddenly as a thought occurred to her: "Perhaps it's a good job you didn't, because, now I come to think about it, if it can't come down they can't get in, can they?"

But a moment later a herald's trumpet sounded, announcing the arrival of the royal party, and when Geoffrey put his shoulder to the wheel, although it ground and screeched like the mills of hell, the drawbridge lowered.

"Ah well, never mind," Penda sighed as she stepped out onto it to meet the queen.

E VER SINCE NEWS OF THE royal visit had broken, speculation had been rife—especially among the Elsford women—about how the encounter between their chatelaine and the queen might go. On the whole most people assumed that their very different sartorial styles would set them against one another from the start.

"Be a bit like the Romans meetin' the Gauls," Gyltha said, to the amusement of the others.

Less amused by the prospect herself, and to minimize the embarrassment she assumed would be inevitable, she spent most of that morning searching for Penda's wolf pelts, which she was planning to confiscate. When she couldn't find them, she decided, if only for the sake of her nerves, that she wouldn't attend the reception, would stay away from the windows and, as a small courtesy to Penda, who, after all, couldn't help looking the way she did, try her best to keep her mouth shut.

O N THE DRAWBRIDGE PENDA LOOKED up from her curtsy to a smile she hadn't expected.

She knew all about royal personages, or thought she did, having spent a considerable amount of time in the company of the empress Matilda, Eleanor's mother-in-law, when they were besieged together during the Anarchy. Therefore her abiding memory was that, on the whole, they were a rather haughty breed, especially the women.

Strangely enough, though, not this one, by the looks of things.

This one, although as ethereally beautiful as the empress, despite her considerable age, was, unlike her, redeemed from chilly loftiness by an earthy sparkle in her wide green eyes that expressed a beguiling combination of humor and curiosity. The moment she saw it, Penda relaxed.

"Lady Penda," Eleanor said, her smile broadening as she watched her rise from her curtsy, recognizing, no doubt, a fellow independent spirit. "That, if I may say so, is a remarkably splendid cloak. How wise of you to choose such a robust garment in this weather."

Penda grinned and, to the astonishment of the onlookers, who were watching with trepidation, proceeded to take it off.

"Got another one just like it, lady," she said, draping it carefully around the otherwise elegantly ermine-clad royal shoulders. "This one's yours, if you'd care for it; be a good deal warmer than that ol' thing."

At the solar window, Gyltha, who had found herself drawn to the window by some strange compulsion, gasped and grabbed hold of Jodi.

"Did you see that?" she said in a tone of pride combined with horror. "She's only gone and given the queen her bloody cloak! And, look! She's wearing it! Oh, God's teeth, I'll never hear the end."

They continued to watch in openmouthed amazement—and

Jodi only through her fingers sometimes—as the royal procession, led by Eleanor, still wearing Penda's wolf pelt, progressed through the gatehouse into the courtyard.

Just before they disappeared from view Penda looked up at the window and waved.

CHAPTER 65

ELEANOR'S ARRIVAL TURNED ELSFORD UPSIDE down with immediate effect.

A procession of elegant ladies-in-waiting dismounted from equally elegant liveried horses and wafted into the hall, trailing clouds of silk and exotic scents like a caste of beautiful, bejeweled bees. Behind them, an army of servants bearing elaborately woven rugs, cushions, chairs and divans caused umbrage among the resident wolfhounds and bratchets, who found themselves unceremoniously ousted from their positions around the fire.

Although the Elsford servants complained bitterly about the chaos the royal party brought, secretly they welcomed it, if only as a distraction from the terror still lurking in the marsh beyond.

Over the last few days since Hawise's return, they had grudgingly come to accept that the killer would probably never be found because no one with the resources to do so had any incentive to look for him now. The dreary pattern of their lives was set forever; no woman would ever feel safe alone again and the prevailing atmosphere of mistrust contaminating their community would remain unchanged.

———

A
S THE ROYAL PARTY MADE itself at home, Adelia stood in a corner of the hall feeling, as she so often did in the queen's presence, dowdy and rather dull.

Hoping not to catch anybody's eye or to be noticed in any way, she was staring fixedly at the toe of her boot, ruing the appearance of a grubby ring-shaped stain on the top of it. Eleanor wouldn't have had boots like that; in Eleanor's world boots would barely be boots at all, but dainty little slippers of golden cloth, rather like—well, not unlike the ones that, at that very moment, had stepped into her field of vision . . .

She looked up, horrified to discover that, in fact, they belonged to Eleanor, who happened to be standing in front of her.

"Mistress Amelia!" she said, extending her hand from an exquisitely embroidered filigree sleeve that trailed almost to the top of Adelia's grubby boot. "We are delighted to see you."

Oh, that smile, Adelia thought as her knees buckled into a curtsy, that warm golden glow that insisted you bask in it like a rapture and that was almost as off-putting as her inability to get her name right.

Nevertheless, she took the hand and kissed it.

"And Almeison?" Eleanor asked, looking around hopefully. "Rowley told me she would be here."

"She is, lady," said Adelia, rising stiffly. "And if you'll excuse me, I'll . . . well, I'll just go and fetch her for you."

As she scuttled to the door she bumped into Rowley coming the other way, wearing full bishop's regalia and in the company of Jean-Luc, who was otherwise known as "the queen's man"—

although nobody quite knew what he did—and another man Adelia assumed was her chamberlain, all wearing the somber, satisfied expressions of men who had just concluded important business.

She raised an eyebrow as she hurried past.

"I'll tell you later," he mouthed over his shoulder.

S HE FOUND ALLIE IN THE guest chamber, where she was keeping Hawise company, and, with apologies to Hawise, chivvied her off to the hall, where they spent the rest of the day trailing around in Eleanor's wake, eating and drinking far too much and fending off the amorous advances of the various young men in her entourage.

"I'm too old for this," Adelia hissed as one of them grabbed her hand and started to serenade her with a love song that, he told her, had been inspired only that very moment by her incomparable beauty. "It's ridiculous!"

Allie laughed. "It's the fashion, Ma," she whispered behind her hand. "Bear with it, they won't be here much longer." And then, disconcerted by the uncharacteristically wistful look in Adelia's eye, she asked: "What are you looking at me like that for?"

Adelia shook her head, reluctant to confess, even to herself, that she felt suddenly overcome by seeing her for the first time in Eleanor's company, noting how easily she moved among just the sort of people who had always made her feel so awkward, and although she was hardly a stranger to royal company herself, somehow it had been different in Henry's day, more fluid . . .

more down-to-earth . . . more her. Allie's assimilation among these people invoked a sense of pride but also regret; it was another reminder that one day, and before too long, her farouche, fierce, clever little girl would tear herself free of the cocoon of maternal love and spread her wings. In all probability she would marry this Lord Peverell, or someone of his ilk, become a lady of the manor with all the trappings of wealth, comfort and privilege that came with it and be, therefore, a whole world away from Adelia.

And the alternative? Despite the many years she had had to think about it and to persuade Rowley of its existence, she was coming close to admitting defeat. Now that Mansur and Henry were dead, she could no longer hold up her own life—which, after all, hadn't been so bad—as an example because Rowley would dismiss it, and with some justification, as a dangerous anachronism.

Perhaps, with the caution of age, as she felt herself hurtling toward the grave, she was becoming increasingly conscious of the fact that neither she nor Rowley would be around much longer to keep Allie safe and that an arranged marriage might indeed be preferable to her falling into Richard's clutches as his ward.

She looked up to see Allie awaiting her response.

"It's nothing," she said. "It's just that . . . well, you look so beautiful and grown-up, and I suppose I can't help feeling a bit nostalgic . . . But it's nothing, really, so go, go on. Go and enjoy yourself." She wafted her away with a smile and stood watching as she floated off into the crowd.

"Ah well," she sighed, reaching for comfort for the bowl of

sweetmeats on the table beside her. "I suppose Rowley will be pleased."

"Pleased about what?"

His voice beside her made her jump. She hadn't seen him approaching, nor had she realized she was thinking aloud.

"That," she said, pointing at Allie. "Our daughter becoming courtly."

"Oh yes." Rowley tilted his head back and folded his arms proudly across his chest. "Magnificent, isn't she?"

"And soon to be married off, I suppose?" Adelia snapped.

Rowley looked at her. "I hope so. Don't you?" he asked.

Just for a moment she was teetering on the brink of resurrecting their age-old argument, until something about the set of his jaw decided her against it. Besides, she was tired of fighting and also knew that, whatever she said or did now, nothing would prevent him from starting the negotiations necessary to secure Allie's match with Lord Peverell at tomorrow's banquet.

"I don't want to talk about it," she said. "I'll just get cross . . . So tell me your news. I want to know what happened with the count. I presume he won't be invading Normandy now?"

Rowley nodded. "Lengthy business though," he said. "There were endless bloody councils: we had to go to Oxford, London, Winchester, Windsor, all over the place, actually—Eleanor's still indefatigable, you know, even worse than you . . . but you're right, there won't be an invasion, not for the time being at least and not while she's regent. In the end she had to threaten to confiscate his estates and now he's off sulking in Wallingford."

"Good," said Adelia. "Let's hope he stays there . . . But what about the interdict? What's the news on that?"

He stared at her incredulously. She was as ruthless as Eleanor in her way; perhaps all women were, he thought, when you spent enough time with them.

"Do you mind if I sit down?" he asked. "I'm exhausted."

Adelia found him a stool and hurriedly shoved it into the back of his knees. "There," she said. "Sit down on that and tell me, tell me, tell me."

"Well," he said, "you'll be pleased to hear that I think it'll be over pretty soon. On our way here we traveled through quite a bit of the diocese, the boarded-up churches and the bodies in the snow, not to mention all the pitiable wretches who came shuffling out of their cottages to tell the queen about their suffering . . . Anyway I think it was enough to convince her to see Walter of Coutances on her way back to France and persuade him to return Longchamp's estates if he'll agree to lift the interdict."

Adelia gave a squeal of delight and clasped her hands together. "Thank you, oh, thank you," she said. "I knew you could do it."

"Don't mention it," said Rowley, closing his eyes, wondering whether he would have the energy to open them again. *One more day,* he thought while Adelia chattered away beside him. *One more day until everything is resolved and we can go home and live peacefully. One more day . . .*

CHAPTER 66

THE NEXT DAY ALLIE KEPT her promise and took Eleanor to the guest chamber to meet Hawise.

"I imagine you're quite pretty under all those bruises," the queen said, smiling at her benevolently. "Nasty accident, though, by the looks of things . . . Riding, did you say?" she asked, turning to Allie, who nodded quickly and decided that the conversation had gone as far as it ought and it was time to leave.

"I'll come back later," she mouthed to Hawise from the door.

When it closed, Hawise flopped back onto her pillows in a state of euphoria.

Allie needn't have worried; Hawise hadn't heard a word of what the queen had said. She had been too excited and too mesmerized by her resplendence, the dazzling clothes and exotic scents that wafted into the room with her, to notice anything else at all.

But, as the day wore on, the memory faded and the room became drab once more, making her wistful for a little more of the magic, wondering how much longer she would have to lie here alone.

Now that she wasn't in quite so much pain—apart from the occasional twinge in her arm, although even that was improving—the imposed bed rest had started to feel less like a cure than a curse. Far from feeling better, she now had too much time to think and dwell on things . . . And "things" were getting worse, the nightmares especially, prompting her memory, which in turn resurrected details of the ordeal she had happily forgotten, along, of course, with the inexorable fear that her captor was still at large and might yet come for her again.

Sometimes she felt it so intensely that she wanted to scream, only she dared not for fear of disturbing the ladies-in-waiting who had been garrisoned with her and who treated her with disdain as it was, as if she were a disease they might catch.

She settled back on her pillows and closed her eyes. Despite the nightmares, sleep was the only respite she had from this incipient boredom, and she was just drifting off when the door opened and Lena, holding a lighted taper, came into the room.

"Come to do your candles," she told her, amused by the look of alarm on Hawise's face. "Sorry. I didn't mean to frit you. But it's gettin' dimpsy, ain't it? . . . Quiet, too," she added, looking around with a frown as if she disapproved of the fact that there was nobody there to disturb the peace. "Never mind, the banquet'll be startin' soon."

As she went about her business, lighting the candles and ineffectually tidying, Hawise found her inane chatter—usually so irritating—strangely comforting and was surprised at how much she missed it when Lena left eventually and the room went quiet again.

———

A T SOME POINT SHE MUST have dozed off again, because she woke with a start to the sound of footfalls and the burble of conversation drifting up through the floorboards as the guests arrived for the banquet in the hall below.

She lay staring at the ceiling, listening to the rising cacophony of people enjoying themselves, fighting pangs of envy that she wasn't there to see it for herself, imagining the lords and ladies, resplendent in their finery, their mouths watering, like hers, in eager anticipation of the great feast Gyltha had so lovingly described. And then she thought about Allie, no doubt reunited by now with her Lord Peverell, and wondered whether—as everybody seemed to assume—an arrangement would, indeed, be made this evening to secure her future happiness . . . She hoped so, the future happiness at least, even if, deep down—however wonderful Lord Peverell turned out to be, and he did sound wonderful—she worried about it.

During her confinement she had given Allie's marriage prospects a great deal of thought and had come to the conclusion that it was an aspect of her life she didn't envy. In fact, it made her increasingly grateful for her lower status, which exempted her from the social and economic politics of the more exalted. At least she had the freedom to choose a husband—within reason, of course—and, best of all, Penda on her side, who was so antipathetic to the idea of marriage, whether arranged or not, that she had promised her, very early on, that in the unlikely event her parents came up with an unsuitable match, she would veto it. And because Ulf and Rosa were her tenants and, therefore, subject to merchet, she could.

Whether she married or not, Hawise knew that her future

would be governed by hard work, but at least she would have a certain dominion over it and she wouldn't die of boredom in a gilded cage.

D
OWNSTAIRS THE NOISE LEVEL WAS rising dramatically. Such was their enthusiasm to meet the queen that in spite of the weather, all the guests had made herculean efforts to get there, arriving in their droves, stomping through the court-yard like cattle to the trough, the men barely breaking stride as they divested themselves of their swords, the women flinging their cloaks at the servants as though they were human pegs.

Allie was standing in the middle of the hall trying to make conversation with one of Eleanor's ladies-in-waiting but, with one eye and half a mind on the door, found it hard to concentrate.

The trouble was that the Dunstan party hadn't arrived yet and she was increasingly anxious that Lord Peverell's attendance might be the sole casualty of the weather.

"You'd 'ave thought some o' them buggers might've 'ad the decency to get snowed in," Penda grumbled as she went past her. "Even that miserable old bastard the abbot of Elsford's got 'ere!"

Allie stiffened when she saw her lips purse—the precursor to the spitting that invariably accompanied any mention of the abbot—but was relieved when she saw her shake her head rue-fully and wander off.

"Stop it!" a voice beside her hissed.

"Stop what?" she hissed back.

"Worrying, twitching like that," said Adelia. "You can stop it right now because he's here. Look!"

Allie looked up, heart pounding, to see Lord Peverell, gazing at her from the other side of the room as though she were the only person in it.

"My apologies for the late arrival," he whispered when he took her hand and kissed it. "Only it seems that Matilda has developed an aversion to the snow . . ."

Allie grinned, in sympathy with both the capriciousness of horses and the forbearance necessary to deal with them, and was about to inquire after her further when Sir William interrupted them.

"Unpredictable like all women, my lord," he said. "But perhaps before we leave Mistress Almeison will perform some of her magic and cure her of it."

He was smiling as he said it but Allie felt the sting of his barb nonetheless . . . and the threat . . . "Magic" was a dangerous word to bandy around, especially around her, and the fact that it had fallen from his lips was alarming.

"It isn't magic!" she snapped, ready to deliver a robust homily about the science of horse medicine, when a loud trumpet blast ended the conversation and the guests rushed to take their places at the tables.

*F*OOD, HAWISE THOUGHT WISTFULLY, CORRECTLY interpreting the hush downstairs. Her mouth watered as she envisaged the sumptuous dishes Gyltha had described to her: plates of crane and venison, boar and pheasant, larks' tongues and . . . beeves—she still wasn't quite sure what they were, but Gyltha had made them sound delicious. Then she remembered

Allie's promise to smuggle a plate of food up to her and, despite being desperately hungry, resolved not to get cross if she forgot, because tonight Allie could be forgiven for having more important things on her mind.

A little while later the drone in the hall began again, low-level at first, like the rumble of distant thunder, until—fueled, no doubt, by the copious quantities of wine and ale Penda served—it became a roar.

Hawise half leaned out of bed, pressing her ear to the floor, hoping to catch a thread or two of the conversation, perhaps pick out the queen's voice or Allie's even, but it proved impossible, not to mention uncomfortable, and eventually she eased herself back onto her mattress and fell asleep.

F ROM HER VANTAGE POINT ON the dais, Penda was enjoying another moment of self-congratulation.

Despite her earlier misgivings, or perhaps because of them—she was a great believer in giving hostages to fortune, after all—the evening had been a success; everyone appeared to be enjoying themselves, even the queen, who, she had been delighted to hear, would be leaving tomorrow. Although mercifully brief, the royal visit had been an expensive interlude, but, God be praised, not ruinously so, and worth every penny if, as she promised, Eleanor managed to get the interdict lifted on her way back to France.

Looking along the row of diners, she was inspired to a belch of contentment by the sight of Rowley chatting happily to Lord Peverell and, no doubt, securing Allie's match.

Ah well, good for him, she thought. She liked James Peverell and thought he would make as good a husband as any, but, never having married herself, or ever wanted to, was profoundly grateful for the means that enabled her to pay the annual amercement to the king so that she need not have a husband foisted on her.

Whether or not marriage would agree with Allie, she didn't know and had almost deliberately avoided thinking about until now, first because she couldn't help feeling guilty for her part in the conspiracy with Rowley, and second because now that she had gotten to know her, she had a sneaking suspicion that Allie's natural independence and strength of personality might make the confines of matrimony difficult. She hoped she was wrong about that, Christ's blood she did, but if not, at least if Allie did marry James Peverell, she would remain close enough for Penda to keep an eye on her.

A wheelbarrow trundled noisily over the dais to take the last of the leftovers, and while the tables were being cleared, she signaled to the musicians in the gallery to strike up. As soon as they had done so, she pushed her stool back into the shadows from which she would enjoy the rest of the evening vicariously.

H AWISE WOKE TO LOUD MUSIC and the rhythmic thumping of feet in the hall below.

Dancing; people dancing and having fun with their bellies full, the lucky things. It felt like torture to be missing out, but having resigned herself to the fact that with all the renewed vigor of the activity in the hall, she was unlikely to get back to sleep, she decided she might as well join in. And before long, the fingers of her good hand tapping, her feet jiggling, she even forgot to feel hungry and was enjoying herself when the chanting began.

"Penda! Penda! Penda!" It was a lone voice at first, but gradually others joined in, rising in volume and drowning out the music.

Hawise pressed her hands together in delight. She knew what was happening and imagined Gyltha standing proudly in the hall leading the campaign to persuade Penda to perform. She could almost see Penda's expression of shy reluctance, too, as a firm hand—most likely Ulf's—propelled her to the door to fetch her bow.

She leaned out of bed again, staring at the floorboards, holding her breath, and listened intently.

WHEN PENDA REAPPEARED WITH HER bow and quarrel, a hush fell on the hall as the guests gathered, forming a circle around her.

"You," she said, pointing at a man in the middle of it. "Yes, you, sir," she repeated when the man hesitated. "Step over here, if you please, and put this on, if you'd be so kind."

Up in the guest chamber, Hawise giggled. She could almost see the look of trepidation on the poor man's face when, anxious not to disappoint the audience, he reluctantly put on the ridiculous-looking hat Penda had given him.

"Thank you, sir," Penda said.

By now he would be red faced, grinning with embarrassment— they usually were—wondering what on earth he had let himself in for.

"Step back please, sir . . . Further, further if'n you don't mind . . . further . . . and a little bit further please." Penda would blindfold him now, leading him to the other side of the room, where she would position him with his back to the wall.

"Don't be nervous, now, sir," she told him. "I ain't never missed."

The next sequence was Hawise's favorite; the burst of raucous laughter as Penda—warming to her role—turned to the crowd and mouthed "often"; then a collective gasp and nervous squeals when she squinted, pretending that her eyesight was failing. Then there was more giggling followed by a sepulchral hush as, at long last, she raised her bow, loosed her arrow and sent it ripping through the hall into the very tip of the conical, comical hat.

Hawise held her breath, anticipating the gasp of wonder as the astonished man turned to the wall in which the hat was now firmly pinned and, with an expression of awe and gratitude, acknowledged how very narrowly he had just avoided death.

The applause that evening was rapturous. Hawise lay back on her palliasse soaking it up as though it were hers. It seemed to last forever and she was even beginning to feel sleepy again when at last it began to die down and she heard the voice . . .

. . . A man's voice, rising above the others, familiar with that faint but unmistakable inflection of laughter in it.

"Bravo, Lady Penda! Bravo!"

Hawise froze, and from then on was deaf to everything but the blood pulsing in her ears as terror swelled her veins.

Her first instinct was to hide, to pretend that she had been mistaken, that she hadn't heard him . . . But that was the old

Hawise, the one who had been destroyed in the cavern that dreadful night and yet, by some miracle, been reborn and cast in strength. So instead of cowering in her bed, she got up, got dressed and made her way down to the hall.

ALLIE SPOTTED HER IMMEDIATELY, AMUSED at first by her peculiar appearance, her disheveled hair, the inside-out, badly laced bliaut, and assumed she must be sleepwalking and that, if she could only get to her in time, she might be able to save her blushes and send her back to the guest chamber before anybody else noticed.

With that in mind, she slipped quietly off the dais and made her way through the crowd toward her. It was only when she was close enough to see the expression on her face that she realized something was wrong—very badly wrong.

"Hawise," she said, forcing herself into her line of vision, which was otherwise fixed on a point somewhere behind her. "Hawise, it's me," she said, glancing back over her shoulder, trying to see whatever or whoever it was she was so transfixed by.

When Hawise still didn't respond, she took her by the shoulders and shook her gently. "In God's name, what is it, Hawise? Tell me!"

She saw her blink, the spell, whatever it was, broken for a moment, but her gaze, when it turned on her, was so cold that she recoiled.

"He's here, Allie," she said, pushing her to one side. "Here in this room. I heard him."

For a moment Allie stood rooted to the spot, helpless to do

anything but watch as Hawise made her way toward the dais, turning every head she passed, forcing unsuspecting congregations of people to part skittishly as though a wild animal had been let loose among them.

When she reached the foot of the dais, she stopped, craning her neck, listening with renewed intensity for something; only this time, when she heard it again, Allie was beside her, standing close enough to feel a sharp spasm course through her body.

"Which one?" she whispered, starting to tremble herself.

Hawise didn't reply but, instead, raised her arm, pointing into the small crowd gathered around Penda, among whom was Sir William.

CHAPTER 67

HE TURNED WHEN ALLIE CALLED him, his expression of mild surprise changing the moment he saw the smelting fury of hers . . . but not the way she had expected . . . Instead of looking guilty, he looked . . . confused.

In her own confusion, she turned to Hawise.

"It's not him, Allie," she said quietly, raising her arm again, only this time to point at the man beside him.

"Him," she said.

Lord Peverell's expression also changed when he turned and saw Hawise.

Allie watched his smile fade, his eyes widening in alarm, and for a moment wondered whether the shock of it might bring her to her knees, or even stop her heart. When it didn't, an extraordinary sense of calm washed over her, as though time itself were standing still, recalibrating the enormity of the revelation within her.

The room went quiet around them as the other guests sensed the peculiar charge in the atmosphere: those who were already aware of Hawise fixed on her; those who weren't yet cast around for the focus of this new, invisible dynamic.

The ripple of alarm spread quickly but hadn't yet reached the dais, where they were still chatting happily, oblivious to Hawise, until she suddenly launched herself onto the platform, but because their first instinct was to rush to defend their queen, nobody noticed Lord Peverell slipping out of the hall.

Or almost nobody . . . Allie noticed him, as did Penda, who, having tired of the fuss and hearty congratulation heaped on her, had, only moments before, taken up her vantage point at the back of the stage, where she had observed everything.

When the pandemonium broke out, she quietly picked up her bow and quarrel and followed him out.

F OR AN ELDERLY WOMAN SHE moved fast but was no match for a young man's pace, so that by the time she reached the courtyard, with Allie at her heels, he was already halfway across it, heading for the gatehouse.

"It's hopeless, Pen," Allie gasped, grabbing hold of her sleeve to pull her back to the safety of the house. "We'll never catch him . . . We can't . . . Let's go back, please, we'll tell the others and let the hue and cry take him."

But Penda shrugged her off and carried on running. "You go back if you want to," she called over her shoulder. "But I wouldn't trust them buggers to catch a three-legged dog."

With no choice but to follow her, Allie did, haring behind her through the gatehouse, catching her up on the drawbridge to run beside her. When they got to the snow-hummocked rushes marking the outskirts of the marsh, Penda slowed down briefly and motioned for her to get behind.

"I know the paths through here," she told her breathlessly. "Don't want to lose you in one o' them bogs."

By the time they were running along the cambered lip of the causeway, Lord Peverell was nowhere to be seen, only his footprints in the freshly fallen snow, but still they ran, the wind-whipped snow scouring Allie's face and Penda's increasingly ragged breath whistling in her ears like a lament.

"It's hopeless, Pen," she called out, terrified that, at any moment now, she would see her drop to the ground as her heart gave out. "He can't escape . . . He can't, not now that we know." But Penda either hadn't heard her or was ignoring her, and she plowed on into the night.

As Allie ran her mind raced as fast as her legs, churning over the recent past in a chaotic sequence of memory and emotion, great waves of horror and revulsion breaking against the shores of her heart, battering her conscience with the same unanswerable questions: How could she have been so blind? How could she not have known? How could she not have seen him for the monster that he was? And then, halfway along the causeway, confusion and incredulity gave way to anger, refreshing her legs and spurring her on so that she was running effortlessly and painlessly when, from somewhere up ahead, she heard a muffled thud, a curse and a peal of bitter laughter.

Penda glanced back at her and stepped up the pace, driving them on faster and faster through the deepening snow until they could just make out a dark shape crouched by the side of the track and she stopped.

"Stay where you are, there's a good lad," she said, clouds of warm breath etched in the frigid air like a veil around her face. "I think that's probably enough now, ain't it?"

Allie watched as he struggled to stand up and limp away, shrugging when he realized he couldn't, before turning around to them, arms raised in mock surrender.

"That bloody ankle of mine again," he said, small white teeth glistening in the moonlight. "Or perhaps I should say my Achilles' heel."

"Sounds about right," Penda said, grinning. "Although, on the other hand, mebbe not; some might say perhaps it's the wages of sin."

When they started to laugh Allie was incredulous, looking from one to the other thinking they were both insane; under the circumstances the levity seemed to her grotesque, a diabolical inversion of the innocent day when they had gone to his rescue.

They were still grinning at one another like conspirators in a private joke when, from the corner of her eye, she saw Penda's right arm reach up and back, bringing her bow over her head and down in the same motion.

Lord Peverell saw it, too.

"Come now, Lady Penda," he said, his grin broadening as he cupped his hands to his chest. "You wouldn't shoot me in the heart, now, would you?"

The glint of the vicious little teeth again as he started walking toward them sent a shiver down her spine. Now that she knew him for what he was, he was no longer human but a contagion that, unless somebody did something soon, would be upon them. She turned anxiously to Penda, horrified to see that she was faltering, staring at him like a bird mesmerized by a gyrating weasel, oblivious to the treachery in every step that diminished the range of her bow; any moment now and it would be useless.

"Stay where you are," Allie screamed, panic rising, preparing to hurl herself into the no-man's-land between them, to tear him apart with her bare hands if necessary, but just as she was about to do so a flicker of movement beside her, the sharp flap of a cloak's edge, alerted her to Penda placing her foot into the stirrup of her bow . . .

"Nah," Penda said, an almost imperceptible movement of her head signaling for Allie to get out of her way. "You don't need to worry about that, my lord, course I ain't going to shoot you in the heart."

She was still grinning at him when she loaded her arrow on the bow.

"The trouble with shootin' you in the heart is . . . ," she said, closing her left eye, "between you an' me, I don't reckon as you've got one." Then she changed trajectory, loosed her arrow and sent it straight through the middle of his forehead instead.

LATER, WHEN IT WAS ALL over, Allie remembered looking at his body on the ground, mesmerized by the beautiful crimson halo that formed around his head as his blood seeped into the snow.

"Ain't goin' to cry, are you, bor?" Penda had asked her. "Ain't worth a single one of your tears . . . not the likes of 'im."

Funnily enough, she didn't think she would. In fact, she felt strangely peaceful.

"I don't know what I'm going to do," she said absently, staring at the perfectly fletched arrow poking out of his forehead.

How long they were standing there, she didn't know, but at some point, from somewhere down the causeway, she became vaguely aware of the belling of hounds, snow-muffled hooves pounding the ground and anxious voices calling her name and felt, at that moment, that it would be rather nice if she could just unscrew her head for a little while . . .

After that, all she remembered was Penda's arm around her and everything becoming terribly quiet and still, as though she had just woken up or fallen asleep, although she couldn't decide which.

EPILOGUE

ELEANOR WAS AS GOOD AS her word. Only days after her return to France she sent word to Penda informing her that the interdict had been lifted and thanking her for her hospitality and, of course, her wolf-skin mantle. At the same time she wrote to Allie, inviting her to France, where a more suitable match might be found for her—if, that is, Allie was still interested in suitable matches, but, if not, where she would always be welcome.

"Over my dead body," Adelia said when Allie read it out to her. "You're not considering it, are you?"

Allie glanced at Rowley, who looked away sheepishly.

"Probably not," she said.

They were in the solar, packing their things preparatory to leaving Elsford.

Allie had been reluctant at first, but when Hawise had agreed to go with her and Adelia had agreed that it would only be temporary, she consented, and in fact, when the time came, was rather looking forward to the peace and routine of Wolvercote, if only for the time being, to clear her head and contemplate her future.

It had been two weeks since Lord Peverell's murder, and although his assailant had never been found, rumors abounded, chief among them that a highway robber—who was also quite obviously a very fine arbalist—had seen him leave Elsford on foot and followed him. It was simply unfortunate and most unlike his lordship that he had forgotten his horse that night, but, on the other hand, he had been at Lady Penda's; she was a renowned and indulgent host, and he did like his wine, and, well, strange things happened in the Fens.

There was one small mercy though: at least his body was spared the predation of the foxes, if not the thief, because, by some miracle, Sir William found it that very night, even though it was half-buried in the snow.

In the glut of funerals that followed the revoking of the interdict, Lord Peverell's was to be the last, although by quite some distance the most elaborate, but, by another strange quirk of fate, he was even deprived of that.

The night before his burial was due, a fire razed Dunstan Castle to the ground, destroying every last vestige of his lordship and his line but, by the grace of God, no one else. It was also strange, in this extraordinary glut of peculiar events, that, around that time, the Wadlow boy had been seen in the area again.

On the night of the fire, a disturbance in the inner bailey roused the Dunstan servants from their beds, and lucky for them that it did, but when they went outside to investigate, they saw only a young man, who looked very much like Danny Wadlow, running away.

And there was something else: when Allie woke up the next

morning, although news of the fire hadn't reached Elsford yet, she was surprised by a summons to the stables. During the night somebody had abandoned at the entrance to the drawbridge, carefully tethering her to a post beside a bale of hay, and because abandoned animals were known to be Allie's forte, the grooms were wondering what she thought they ought to do with her.

"Fine-looking animal, Mistress Allie," one of them remarked as he led her to the stall where they were keeping her for the time being. "She's got a beautiful coat, look, a very unusual color for round here, too. Where do you suppose it come from?"

Allie shook her head and by some act of mercy was able to suppress her squeal of delight.

"I have no idea," she said gravely. "But leave the matter with me, if you don't mind. I'll make inquiries, of course, but I think we will probably have to keep her."

ACKNOWLEDGMENTS

The dedication is short. This is for my mum.

The acknowledgements, however, are infinite:

First, a big thank you to Rachel Kahan, my editor, whose phenomenal talent and gentle persuasion have enabled me to turn some ragged early drafts into a manuscript I'm proud of.

Ditto Helen Heller, my agent, whose tough love and no-nonsense approach to the writing process, over several tortuous years, have bashed me—almost literally at times—into shape. Then there's Emma, my sister, without whom I don't know where I'd be and, of course, all my friends, particularly Caroline and Geraldine, whose tireless support and encouragement have sustained me more than they'll ever know. A special mention too, to my sons, Harry and Charlie, who make life so joyful; and lastly, Spider, without whom this book would have been finished much, much earlier, but who is forgiven, for making me laugh even when I haven't felt like it.